Strange
Embrace

CW00632059

Strange Embrace

GAIL LEVY

QUARTET

First published in 2012 by
Quartet Books Limited
A member of the Namara Group
27 Goodge Street, London W1T 2LD

A catalogue record for this book
is available from the British Library

ISBN 978 0 7043 7258 0

Typeset by Antony Gray
Printed and bound in Great Britain by
T J International Ltd, Padstow, Cornwall

PROLOGUE

THREE – ALEX

Strange Embrace

PROLOGUE

Regent's Park, London. 22 October 1946. 7.35 p.m.

His shoes made a loud squeaking on the parquet floor so he didn't hear her approach. She must have been hiding somewhere and her bare feet had made no sound. The first sign was something whizzing past his head, roughly grazing his ear. He stared down at the long silver blade of the kitchen knife skidding across the Aubusson rug in front of him.

It spun to a halt by his feet, the sharp tip submerging about a quarter of an inch into one of the sideboard's slim wooden legs.

On the top, next to the decanter of whisky and a soda siphon, was a bowl of overblown roses. A few golden petals had fallen onto the gleaming wood. Thoughtfully, he gathered the petals up, crushing them between finger and thumb. Then he bent down, eased the knife out of the wood and placed it carefully besides the bowl.

When he turned, she was standing in the doorway. His voice was flat with shock.

'You could have killed me,' he said.

She was wearing a small diamond brooch in the shape of a half moon on a red woollen dress. Barefoot, hands hanging loosely at her sides, dark hair tied back. She didn't speak, just staring at him, blank faced. He felt quite clear-headed, though he was breathing strangely. They looked at each other across the frozen space. He felt his anger rise.

'You could have bloody well killed me!'

She turned and made a dash across the hall, then up the stairs, taking them two, three at a time. He caught her by the ankle when she was almost half way up and yanked her back. Her hand slid down the banisters. Before her foot had even touched the floor, she aimed a vicious kick at his face. He dodged it easily and grabbed the waist of her dress. The belt broke off in his hand. She landed a blow on his head with something she'd grabbed from the table – it sounded like the crack of an axe on wood. He stood where he was, stunned.

She dropped the object – a heavy glass ornament in the shape of a bird, he now saw – twisted round and dashed up the stairs on all fours, only straightening to run across the landing. The bedroom door slammed.

Got you, he thought grimly. He waited for a moment but couldn't hear the sound of a key turning in the lock.

The door opened noiselessly.

She was crouched in the corner, her face pressed into her knees, arms wrapped round, slowly rocking herself backwards and forwards.

'I said – you almost killed me, you bitch!' he yelled.

She spoke for the first time. 'Good!' she hissed, lifting her face. 'I'm glad!

Then he struck her across the cheek, he had meant to only clip her ear but missed and the swing gave his blow more weight than he intended. She almost fell but, steadying herself, looked up at him with dark hating eyes, a wide, stupid smile on her face. He felt the rage flaring up in him at the sight of that deliberately blank, meaningless grin. His head had started to throb quite badly where she'd struck him. For a moment, he lost control. He didn't know what he was doing. He just felt a blinding hot rage flooding though him, eliminating everything else.

He dragged her out of the corner by the neck of her red dress, ripping the front seam in the process, and flung her bodily on the floor in front of him. She didn't resist, only hanging limply so that she was a dead weight.

'You're mad!' he snarled. 'Quite mad. You know it, don't you?'

But still she smiled although he knew she hated to be called mad more than anything, opening her lips wide and baring white, even teeth.

He shook that heavy body again and again, thumping hard, shouting, 'Stop it! Stop it!' or something. And her dress was tearing, it was torn right to the waist, her hair was loose, her right breast exposed, and he held the nipple in hard fingers as he unbuttoned himself, his face pressed close to hers, her breath on his cheek, and suddenly, in that strange embrace, he didn't know whether he was trying to hurt her or make love to her, he didn't know. He was thrusting into her again and again and, when it was all over, she looked up at him with such empty eyes that for a moment he imagined she really was mad and lost to him forever.

Her long hair was spread out around her and her face was pale, very pale. He could see the blue veins beneath the translucent skin of her throat.

When he lifted himself off her, the life returned to her dark eyes, and with it the viciousness, too. 'I hate you,' she said clearly.

She drew the torn material around her and began crawling backwards, away from him. An angry pink weal had come out on her cheekbone where he'd hit her. Her breathing was hard and uneven but she kept her gaze steadily on him. She didn't move it off him for a second, not until she reached the bathroom door. Then she reached for the handle and used it to pull herself to her feet.

Opening the door just enough to step through, she closed it, very quietly, behind her.

For the first time he realised he was hurt. There was blood on his forehead and his ear was burning. He felt sick. There was a foul taste in his mouth, really foul. It tasted like he had bitten into raw meat.

He buttoned his trousers and walked slowly down the stairs, staggering a little at first but soon regaining his composure. Across the white stone floor of the hall and out the house. Open the door and then close it. Using all three keys, he turned the locks carefully behind him.

He took the half dozen stone steps from the front door to the street. He did not carry his raincoat. He left it hanging on the peg in the hallway next to his hat although it was now drizzling gently.

ONE

ANGEL

'It's too late, my darling, too late,' he said. 'We've lost our little chance of happiness.'

'No, Maxim. No,' I said.

'Yes,' he said. 'It's all over now. The thing has happened.'

'What thing?' I said.

'The thing I've always foreseen. The thing I've dreamt about, day after day, night after night. We're not meant for happiness, you and I.' He sat down on the window-seat, and I knelt in front of him, my hands on his shoulders.

'What are you trying to tell me?' I said.

He put his hands over mine and looked into my face. 'Rebecca has won,' he said.

DAPHNE DU MAURIER, *Rebecca*

ANGEL

1

Court 1, The Old Bailey. September 1952

ANGEL WANTED to place her hands over her ears and shut out the fanfare of trumpets that screamed out as the Judge, in ermine and crimson robes, took his seat in the courtroom. Instead, she glued her eyes onto the counsel straight ahead of her, bowing vigorously at the rostrum, and tried to stop her gaze from straying towards the solid wood dock where the prisoner would soon stand.

It felt like every pair of eyes in the public gallery were locked onto the back of her head. Behind her – a sea of watchful faces. To her left – almost as bad – Laura's sympathetic gaze, Uncle Francis and Aunt Margaret ready to smile reassuringly the second their eyes met hers. And, seated at the crush at the back, Brioney Parsons, in a cheap fur tie and shapeless black felt hat, who had shaken her hand and murmured kindly before taking her seat, 'You mustn't blame yourself. It's really not your fault.'

Angel had smiled and nodded and ducked away as soon as she could, glad of the low brim of her hat. Because if it wasn't her fault, who the hell's was it?

Over to one side, before the witness box, rose the old wood-panelled seats of the jury. Twelve ordinary men and women who would weigh up the evidence put before them and decide the prisoner's fate. There was nowhere she could look that didn't make the butterflies do an ice-cold dance in her stomach and her hands grow clammy and damp. She stared down, feeling the familiar tightness in her scalp and tension at the back of her neck. *Not now*, she thought. *Please, not now. Not a migraine – that's all I need.*

She must have risen to her feet with everyone else at the Judge's entry because now she was sitting down again. Even tugging her skirt over her knees as if modesty still mattered to her. A warder was bringing the prisoner up the steps into the dock. Angel felt the blood drain from her face. For a moment she thought she might faint. She felt light-headed, dizzy. She could hear the Clerk of the Court speaking but couldn't make any sense of his words.

' . . . All manner of persons having anything to do before my Lords the King's Justices . . . draw near and give you attendance . . . George the Sixth, by the Grace of God . . . '

She seemed to only make out part of what the Clerk was saying as if the volume of a wireless set were being twiddled on and off. Just when she most needed clarity, she found she couldn't hear properly, let alone think straight. Now he'd turned and was addressing the prisoner in the dock:

'You stand accused upon this indictment that you, on the 17th day of April 1952, feloniously, wilfully and of your malice afore-thought did kill and murder . . . '

Did kill and murder . . .

She must have let out her breath too sharply at these words, or slumped a little on the hard bench, because Laura turned to her and squeezed her hand, looking concerned. Angel gave her a tight nod and smiled grimly. Sat up straight.

The Clerk's voice rang out clearly. 'How say you – are you guilty or not guilty?'

There was a silence. Quite a long silence. Her mouth was bone dry. The journalists on the bench in front of her leant forward, lips parted a little, eyes eager. The court stirred slightly. Through her own anxiety, Angel could feel the embarrassed hush of the crowd all around her as they waited for the response.

The Clerk asked again: 'Are you guilty or not guilty?'

'I am – '

Angel caught her breath. Was the plea going to be guilty after all? Oh, God, it is, she thought, it's going to be guilty . . .

She heard, 'I am not guilty.'

She closed her eyes for a moment and the images seemed to have been waiting for her in the darkness. Two years worth of memories called up in the blink of an eyelid –

– Laura in a pale blue dress, long skirt brushing the floor: 'Smile, Angel, for heaven's sake – it's a *party*, not a bloody funeral . . . '

– Richard, gazing down at her, blue eyes warm and admiring,

shouting above the noise on the dance floor: 'Frightfully hot in here, isn't it? Though I don't expect you feel it so badly in that dress . . . '

– Alex, stroking her cheek, whispering: 'I never thought I'd be happy again . . . '

The engagement party – God, she hadn't thought about that night in years. Now she remembered each moment vividly. How odd to think that if she had gone into any other room but the library that night she wouldn't be here now. *None* of us – she corrected herself, feeling mildly sick – would be here, now.

'The medical evidence' – a man's voice, a barrister's clear, confident voice – 'can definitely establish the direction in which the knife was held when it entered the victim's body . . . '

Angel opened her eyes and forced herself to concentrate as the prosecution began outlining the case for the Crown.

*   *   *

It must have been – what? – the end of May? Early June? Two years ago, anyway. Laura had knocked on the bedroom door and walked in without waiting for an answer.

'What *are* you doing?' she asked.

Angel had been lying face down on the floor at the time, poking an arm under the wardrobe. She sat up, blinking, her face flushed. 'Hunting for my other shoe.'

'It's over there.'

Angel looked in the direction Laura was pointing. 'Oh, yes,' she said, brushing her skirt. 'So it is.'

'Let me have a look at you,' Laura said, once she'd hopped across the room and eased her foot into the silver satin slipper. 'Mmm, nice, Angel. Very nice. But why do you look all sort of *hunched*?'

'I don't seem to know what to do with my arms.'

'What do you normally do with them?'

'That's the trouble. When I think about it they just seem to hang.'

'For God's sake. Just *relax*.'

'I feel I'm plonking down my feet like a cart horse.'

'Well, you are a bit. Can't you smile? It's my engagement party, you know, not a blinking funeral.'

'I can't dance in these shoes. I can't even balance properly.'

Laura looked at her as if she was stupid. 'Of course you can.'

'No, really. I don't think I'll be able to. All those steps.'

Laura took her by the elbow and pulled her over to the long cheval mirror. 'Look at yourself – just *look*,' she said impatiently. 'That dress really suits you.'

Angel gazed uncertainly at herself. A tall girl with grey eyes and fair hair in a white satin ball gown stared back at her. 'You don't think it makes me look a bit – '

'What?'

'Well, thin.'

Laura yawned, stretched. 'You idiot. You look very glamorous.'

'No, I don't.' She looked young and thin and nervous, Angel thought, making a face at her own reflection. The single dangling white silk rose sewn onto the shoulder of her dress was definitely a mistake, she decided, trying to press the rose flat. Her gaze shifted to the older girl standing beside her in pale blue. 'You really *do* look glamorous, Laura,' she said shyly. 'Like Greta Garbo in *Camille*.'

'Thanks very much – I suppose you're going to say in the death-bed scene?'

'Of course I'm not. I mean it – you look lovely.'

Laura smiled at her sweetly. 'All *you* need is the final touch.' She opened her little blue quilted evening bag, drew out a small cylindrical gilt case and screwed the base round. A narrow pink column rose into the air.

'Lipstick? Oh, no – no, I really don't think it's quite my – '

'Oh, do shut up. Don't move or it will go everywhere.' Laura stepped back after a moment to admire her work. 'Now, how does that look?'

They both gazed into the mirror.

'Terrible,' Angel grimaced. 'Actually beyond terrible. It makes terrible seem like a compliment.'

'Yes . . . Perhaps not *exactly* the effect I was hoping for . . . '

Grimly, Angel scrubbed her mouth with the back of her hand.

'Well, now you've smeared Coral Kiss everywhere,' Laura said dispassionately. 'Have you got a hankie?'

'In this dress?'

Laura searched in her bag and produced a tiny scrap of lace. 'Here. Now let's get downstairs before you do anything else to yourself.'

'Me? It was you who – '

'Oh, come on.'

Laura took one more look in the mirror, gave her embroidered bead belt a final tweak and was out of the door before she'd finished her sentence. 'Anyway – ' she said softly, as they stood on the landing, peering over the top of the carved wooden staircase – 'I have a feeling that something special's going to happen to you tonight.'

'What kind of feeling?'

Laura shook her head. 'My lips are sealed.'

'That's just the lipstick.'

'Don't be snippy because it doesn't suit you. But just to show you how certain I am, I'm going to bet you half a crown – '

'Make it five bob.'

'A half-crown,' Laura repeated firmly, 'that in the morning you'll tell me something really wonderful happened. Oh, look, there's Richard – ' In the hall below, amongst a crowd of people, they could make out the top of her brother's head. She gave a little giggle. 'Come on, let's go. I'll be right behind you.'

'Laura – you beast! Don't *push* . . . '

And of course something special *had* happened that night, though not what Laura had expected. Not quite what Angel had expected either, she thought later. Moving through the crowd, she could feel the excitement of a party all around her. She had to admit it was fun seeing the reaction of people she had known for years as she crossed the room – the flash of interest in their eyes when they saw her in a long white dress with her hair swept up. Quite ridiculous really, she thought, feeling the pulse in her wrists start to thump.

The great stone hall had been transformed into a glittering sea of diaphanous dresses and white waistcoats. In the ballroom, a platform had been built for the string quartet and later for the jazz band. Laura was swept instantly from her side but everything seemed possible after the first glass of champagne, even dancing in heels, and on the parquet floor she'd helped wax a few days before, under the blaze of chandeliers, Angel soon found herself being twirled and squeezed by a succession of polite young men.

'Hot in here, isn't it?' Richard said, smiling down at her flushed face and shining eyes.

'Yes, isn't it.'

'Though I don't expect you feel it so badly in that dress. You look very cool.'

'Do I? I'm sweltering actually – ouch!'

'Oh, sorry – oh, my fault.' Shuffling his feet, he recovered his step. 'You've grown up,' he said seriously, once they were circling smoothly again. 'I noticed it as soon as I got back from Cambridge. Angel looks jolly nice nowadays, I thought to myself. I say, the next one's a quick-step. Shall we sit it out?'

'Good idea,' Angel said, gratefully.

'Better still, let's get out of this crowd. Grab a breath of air. We could go out into the garden and cool down. Be by ourselves for a bit.' When she didn't respond he stopped dancing and smiled at her. 'Well?'

Oh, no. 'Oh, yes, let's – ' she said lamely. 'That would be – ' She took a half step back. But, moving too quickly, her heel turned.

He grabbed her elbow. 'Here, steady on. You'll do yourself a mischief in those shoes. You all right?'

'Yes – I just . . . Thanks.'

When she looked up, his eyes, smiling down at her, were warm and friendly. Too friendly. Her heart missed a beat. She could feel his hand, hot and slightly damp, on her skin. She wished he'd take his sweaty hand off her because, looking at her like that, he was really giving her the creeps. Was *this* what Laura had meant by something special? Being made love to, in the garden, by Richard? Odd comments she'd had made over the last couple of weeks suddenly fell horribly into place. Angel looked at his familiar tall frame and thick fair hair combed back and shiny with what seemed to be several tons of brilliantine and her stomach tightened. He wasn't unattractive – just lanky and red-cheeked and slightly tipsy. Actually he was very like his father. It would be like Uncle Francis kissing her, she thought, appalled, trying not to let the disgust show on her face.

'Thanks,' she said again, detaching herself politely from his hand. 'Look, I really must . . . I must just powder my nose . . . shan't be a sec . . . ' Throwing him a quick smile, she pushed her way through the flushed, excited crowd clustered round the dance-floor and hurried from the room.

At the end of the hall she hesitated, then turned sharp left and emerged cautiously into a stone-flagged passage. She'd take the French windows from the library and skirt round to the front of the house that way. With a bit of luck she could avoid Richard for the rest of the evening. On Sunday, first thing, he was catching the train back to Cambridge to continue the second year of a medical degree. It would be at least seven weeks before term ended and she'd see him again. Anything might have happened by then, she thought optimistically.

The passage was empty. She walked swiftly along it enjoying the sudden quiet. The wide doors to the library were slightly ajar. She threw a quick look over her shoulder and stepped inside.

It was dark in the library. The heavy velvet drapes were closed. Angel stood for a moment with her back against the door, breathing in the room's pleasant slightly musty odour. Pushing her hair back from her forehead with hot fingers, she slipped off the satin slippers, then, after a second's thought, unfastened her stockings and peeled them off too. It felt wonderful in bare feet without the pinch of heels. Dangling the shoes from a finger by their strap, she crossed softly to the French windows.

The keys were kept in a red Chinese lacquered box on top of her uncle's desk. Shifting the curtains a foot from the window, she jiggled the key in the lock. To be opened, the door had to be first pulled towards you, then pushed hard away and at the same time lifted slightly. She was beginning to push when a man's voice, quiet and deep, said: 'I'm afraid you may have closed it again. I think it's already unlocked.'

She jumped around, startled. There was a dark form she hadn't noticed sitting in one of the high-backed armchairs by the window.

'I hate these damn affairs, don't you?' the man said pleasantly.

She thought she was going to choke. 'Excuse me?'

'I find all this,' he gestured with one hand in the general direction of the party, 'a little boring. I rather supposed,' she caught a gleam of teeth, 'that you did too.'

'It wasn't that exactly – though I suppose I did want to – '

'Escape?' he supplied.

'Well, yes. Just for a moment.'

Another flash of teeth. 'Me too.'

She was standing in the soft light that fell into the room through the window but the man was sitting in shadow. She could only see his hand clearly, long fingers outspread on the arm of the chair, and the orange tip of the cheroot he was smoking. 'Don't you like parties?' she asked curiously, staring at the glowing tip.

The man pulled on the cheroot so that his expression was briefly visible and she could see that he frowned. 'I used to once. Not now.'

'Then why did you come?'

He shrugged. 'Bit of a mistake really. I'm staying nearby with friends for a few days. They suggested I join them – so I did.'

'What a pity.'

'That I came?'

'That you don't like parties any more.'

He didn't answer but sat and smoked his cheroot. She looked longingly at the unlocked French window, wondering when she could politely step through the door. For a moment the only sound was the faint music of the jazz band drifting across from the ballroom.

'And with whom did you come to this festive occasion?' he asked. 'Your boyfriend?'

'My – ? Oh, no. Actually I live here. Laura Merlowe is my cousin.'

'Laura Merlowe?'

'This is her engagement party.'

'Ah,' the man said. 'Then I'm sorry if I was rude about it.'

'That's all right.'

The orange tip glowed. 'And what's your name?'

'Angel. Well, Angelica, really, but everyone calls me Angel. The name's sort of stuck from childhood.'

'Mm. Angel. Rather nice. Suits you. I can see why it stuck.' From the shadows she could feel him considering her. A forehead and watchful eyes showed in the next couple of puffs. 'And you live here with – what was it? The Merlowes?'

'Yes, that's right.'

'So Angelica, whom everyone calls Angel, are you a Merlowe too?'

'I am, yes. Uncle Francis was my father's first cousin, you see.'

'Was?'

'He's dead, I'm afraid.'

'Your uncle?'

'Oh no – my father.'

'Where's your mother?'

'She died too,' she said apologetically.

He took another drag of the cheroot and stared thoughtfully at the red burn of its tip. 'Pretty tough, I should think. Becoming an orphan so young.'

'Yes. But . . . well, the Merlowes are awfully nice.'

'Not the same as one's own parents though, is it?'

'That's true,' she admitted. 'I suppose I did mind a bit when I was a child.'

He laughed at that. 'Aren't you one still? How old are you?'

She felt the colour rushing into her face. 'Eighteen.'

'Good God, really?'

'Hardly a child.'

'Almost though. Not exactly ancient, is it?'

She felt a spasm of irritation. 'It's old enough for most things,' she said coolly.

There was a cigarette box and a lighter on the table. She leant forward and took a cigarette from the box. 'How old are *you*,' she asked defensively, blowing out a cloud of smoke.

'I don't think you should ask a gentleman his age,' he said lightly. Then, 'Far too bloody old,' he muttered, any lightness disappearing.

His cheroot was almost out. Scowling moodily into the half-darkness he chewed on it for a moment, then shifted his weight towards the open window next to him and flicked the slim stub out.

Poor Aunt Margaret's irises, she thought. Some light fell on his face and she saw that he was dark, with what looked like black hair, and that he had heavy-lidded eyes beneath dark, winged brows and a strong, well-shaped nose. Only as he leant forwards to re-fill his glass from the decanter on the table did she see his face fully. Instinctively, she averted her eyes. But even a quick glance showed he was quite tall and, even in his dress-suit, clearly well-built.

Damn, she thought, feeling suddenly ridiculous standing there in bare feet, silk stockings strung round her neck, clutching a high satin slipper in each fist. Balancing on one leg, she reached down and worked a foot into a shoe, then, wobbling slightly, eased on the other. 'Well – ' she said, taking the cigarette from her lips – 'I suppose I really should be getting back . . . '

'Have some whisky before you go,' he suggested, nodding to the decanter. 'I'm sure your uncle won't mind.'

She wasn't so sure, especially after all the wine, but something in his tone decided her. Faintly challenging, provocative. Amused. 'Thank you, I will,' she said, taking a glass from him, aware that her hand trembled. She tossed the whisky down, feeling her eyes and throat firing up – opened her mouth wide and exhaled, the almost neat spirit nearly choking her, desperately hoping she wasn't about to show herself up and cough – 'Well – good evening . . . ' she said after a moment, breathing out slowly.

She supposed he'd say a polite good-night now, too, and she'd scuttle through the French windows back to the party, but he hesitated. He drained his glass of whisky and frowned into the empty glass. 'Would you like to go for a drive, Angel Merlowe?' he asked.

She stared. 'With you?'

'Well, yes.'

'When?'

'Right now. Tonight.'

'That's not possible.'

He put his glass down on the table and got to his feet – *very* tall, she thought. 'Why not?' he asked.

She stared back at him, feeling her heart beating rapidly again and wondering when it had begun to do so. 'Well – ' she said – 'it's late and everyone will be wondering where I've – And besides, I don't know you. I don't even know your name.'

'It's Alexander Sorel. And you're right – it *is* rather late. Perhaps tomorrow instead? No, damn, I can't tomorrow. Sunday then. I'm not going back to London for a few days yet. Are you free on Sunday?'

Suddenly, alarmingly, she was conscious of a constriction in her chest. She could feel her pulse still running far too fast. *Dark brown eyes, a deep voice, hair almost black, the trace of a moustache along his top lip.* When in doubt, she told herself, be casual. Pretend this sort of thing happens to you every day. Just as well she'd had the whisky – Dutch courage, she thought. She heard herself say: 'Well, yes – yes, actually I am . . . '

'Good. I'll collect you at twelve. Wear a headscarf. The car has an open top.'

And that was the beginning, Angel thought, looking back later from the confines of a stuffy courtroom, listening to a case for murder being made out by the Crown. She closed her eyes. Oh, yes, that was exactly when it had all begun.

2

Two Years Earlier: Haywards Heath, West Sussex. May 1950

I'm doing this for myself, Angel told herself feeling the wild beating of her own heart. I'm doing it because Laura will be married soon and be off before you know it. I'm doing it because I do *not* want to go out into the garden with Richard with all that involves. I'm doing it because I am my *own* person with my *own* path and I will not do something simply because it's expected of me. I'm doing it because it will be *fun*, she told herself, hearing her own strained, breathless voice undercutting her attempt to appear unfazed – '*Sunday? Actually I am free, yes . . .*'

She stared up into Alexander Sorel's disconcertingly dark brown eyes that didn't move off her for a second and felt not just her face but her whole body grow hot. It *will* be fun, she repeated to herself with a slightly different emphasis. It isn't just the whisky talking – as long as I remember that I won't lose my nerve.

*   *   *

There were two immediate problems. The first was that Angel knew her aunt and uncle would never in a million years let her to go for a drive with a strange man so easily. At the very least they'd expect an introduction – more likely, a full family background, names, dates, locations, references, the whole works. Of Alexander Sorel, darkly attractive, so much older, she had the unhappy certainty they wouldn't approve. And if pressed too hard, if checked and counterchecked, why should he bother with her any further? It was all so simple for him; a careless request, offered easily to fill a spare hour, thrown out at a dull party without much thought. She must appear to accept just as casually as he'd asked in the first place. And she knew she had to see him again. Which was problem number two.

She stood for a while after he left, gazing unseeingly out of the window at the dark garden, one palm against the glass, trying to think.

One solitary white lie. A single, harmless little fib. That's all it would take.

So on Sunday after church, as the congregation was filing out dutifully after Morning Service, she found herself leaning across and muttering an excuse in Laura's ear. A migraine – she said she had a migraine. Ironic really, she thought afterwards. That pretending she had one *then* meant she'd be sitting in a packed courtroom two years later warding of the real thing.

'It's been threatening to come on all morning . . . I'm afraid I shan't be able to come to Edward's with you, after all . . . '

'Oh, you poor thing!' Laura turned, her eyes full of sympathy. 'You haven't had a headache in months.'

'Sorry.' Angel couldn't hold her gaze. 'Missing the luncheon and everything . . . '

'Oh, well, it can't be helped. I'm sure they'll be another one soon. I'll take you back then.'

'There's really no need . . . '

'Of course I will.'

'No, really no. I'd rather you didn't . . . I mean, I'd rather be alone . . . when I'm feeling as rotten as this, I'm better off, quite honestly . . . on my own . . . '

'Will you be alright?'

Angel hesitated for a second, cupping one hand over her eyes as if the light really was hurting her. But she couldn't tell Laura what she was planning, not without telling her aunt and uncle, too. And that would mean – 'Absolutely,' she replied a little shakily, which of course Laura only put down to the effects of a blindingly bad headache.

'Take an aspirin,' she suggested. 'There's a tube of tablets in the bathroom cupboard. We won't stay late. But I don't expect we'll be back much before eight.'

'Oh, please don't hurry! I shall probably be asleep for *hours*. Will you apologise to Lady Roundel for me? Tell her – tell her I'm awfully sorry . . . '

The shaky feeling subsided slightly once she was sitting on the white quilt cover of her bed with the curtains drawn. But there was a strange, tremulous feeling in the area of her stomach, a heady cocktail of nerves and guilt and excitement. She forced herself to wait half an hour before cracking open the door and peering out. Everything was quiet. None of the servants appeared to be about. She tiptoed to the end of the passage. When she came to the great staircase, she peered over at the hall below. Still no sound at all.

Quickly, she ran down the wide flight of stairs, her feet echoing horribly loudly on the flags as she passed the huge open fireplace and crossed the stone hall. Somewhere above a board creaked. She didn't turn her head, just forced herself on. *Good morning, Norah*, she would call to the housemaid cheerily. *Feeling a bit ropey, just thought I'd get a breath of fresh air.* But her heart was pounding and the blood drummed hard in her ears as the heavy oak door swung shut behind her.

The sunlight was dazzling after the cool of the hall. Black spots danced momentarily in the air in front of her eyes.

Out of sight of the house, she struck into the back meadow and ran swiftly past the grove of crab-apple trees, through lush, deep green undergrowth into the woods. It was very quiet, only the sound of the wood pigeons in the topmost branches. After the glare of the sun, it was wonderfully cool and peaceful. She stumbled once over the twisted roots of an old oak. When she reached the path that zig-zagged down to the stone wall marking the boundary of their land, she vaulted over.

Ahead of her, a low green sports car was parked on the bend in the road. A man was leaning against it with his back to her, smoking. She stood still for a moment, waiting for her pulse to return to normal. For the first time, she began to feel uneasy. He turned slightly and saw her. There was no choice but to walk forward. Her breath was coming absurdly fast. 'Good afternoon, Mr Sorel . . . '

'Alexander,' he corrected her. He threw his cigarette to the ground and squashed it with a twist of the foot. 'But you can call me Alex.'

The car was a two-seater with a let-down hood that was pulled right back. He walked round to the passenger side, a tall man with broad shoulders in a grey suit, plain white shirt and dark blue tie.

He was bareheaded – she could see a black soft hat lying in the back seat where he'd chucked it.

'It's such a beautiful day – I thought we might drive to the coast,' he said, holding the door open for her. 'There's a place I know where we can lunch. You don't have to be back at any particular time, do you?'

'Oh no . . . ' she replied. 'Not particularly . . . ' She had trouble finishing the sentence. In daylight he seemed different, the gap between them more pronounced. The man from the shadows had disappeared. In his place, in a gleaming new Lagonda, she sat next to a stranger. A dark, sophisticated stranger in a light grey suit. What on earth could she find to say to this man for the course of a whole meal? She should have said she had to be home by one and could they please just go for a drive as agreed?

Her sense of unease returned in full force. When he stretched out his arm to the handbrake she could see a few silky black hairs on his wrist below starched white cuffs. She felt suddenly like she'd swallowed a small rather sharp lump of glass.

No one has the faintest idea where I am, she thought, knotting a yellow silk scarf under her chin. Everyone thinks I'm at home in bed, nursing a migraine. She must have been mad to have agreed to this, quite mad. Finding something to say over the course of a lunch might be the least of her problems.

She clutched the leather seat with damp hands, her heart pounding like crazy, staring blindly at the highly varnished walnut dashboard.

'I hope you like fish?' he said, reaching for the ignition.

'You mean to eat?' she said stupidly.

He flashed her a look. 'That's the usual idea.'

'Oh yes . . . lovely . . . yes, I do.' She hoped she didn't sound as panicky as she felt. Her thudding heart made her voice come out strangely. Her words seemed to come from a long way off as if someone else had spoken them for her.

They shot along familiar winding lanes. The wind whipped against her, filling her eyes and nose. Fine strands of hair escaped from the scarf and danced madly round her face. She kept her mouth shut, her eyes fixed on billows of dusty cow-parsley growing in the high hedgerows at the sides of the road, bitterly regretting the whole impulsive escapade, wishing with all her heart that she were sitting next to her Uncle Francis in his rattling old jalopy, travelling at a legal 30 miles an hour, instead of zooming smoothly along at more than double the speed in this flashy green sports car with a stranger.

She felt a sudden hysterical desire to laugh out loud. Biting her bottom lip, she stared out the window, her eyes blurred with tears from the wind. *Serves me bloody well right,* she thought.

'Too fast for you?' he yelled over the sound of the engine.

She gritted her teeth, shooting a sideways look at him, then, shaking her head, looked away quickly.

After about fifteen breathtaking minutes he swung sharply into a narrow, bumpy lane and slowed almost to a stop. On their right, fields sloped down to a crooked stream and a church and a few houses clustered round the base of a little rise. To their left, set back from the road between tall pines, a low brick building.

He pulled over and switched off the engine. In the sudden silence, she could hear the distant bleating of sheep. She breathed in the smell of freshly turned over earth mingled with the stench of manure from a field nearby. *When in doubt fake it . . . pretend you do this kind of thing every day . . .* She dragged off the scarf and stuffed it, still knotted, inside her handbag next to a creased pair of gloves. Found her comb and ran it through her hair, wondering whether she should get out her compact and dab some powder on her nose. But her hand was trembling slightly. She was sweating too. Better not risk it. 'Where – where exactly – where are we exactly?' she asked, trying to sound casual.

'Clee St. Margaret.' He pushed open the car door. 'About four miles from Brighton. Been here before?'

'No – no, I don't think I have . . . '

He considered her for a moment before getting out. There was something about him in that measured gaze that made her feel a little more confident. A familiar disheartened look. A strong face marred slightly by the dusty, withdrawn lines of depression. Not so different from her own father's face. His features were very different, and he was dark not fair, but Alexander Sorel had a similar lost, unhappy bearing. His shoulders were hunched against life in the same way.

She felt a sudden comforting pull of recognition. She was being ridiculous – nerves were getting the better of her. *Just bloody well relax*, she told herself fiercely. 'Have you?' she asked more easily as he handed her out.

'You mean – been here before?' He snatched his hat from the back seat before slamming shut the car door. 'Once,' he said, pulling the hat on.

'Did you come with the friends you're staying with?'

'I did, yes. The St Clare's?'

That brought her up with a jolt. He glanced at her. 'Friends of yours?'

'Oh, yes – yes, rather,' she answered breathlessly, staring fixedly ahead. 'We see Charles and Jenna all the time.'

'The children?'

She nodded unhappily. 'Yes.'

'I don't know the family all that well,' he said, as they began walking towards the restaurant, 'but they own a painting I'm interested in. A Frederic Bazille. Very good example of, actually. I'm a collector. Of paintings,' he added.

'Is that your job?'

'No, my hobby. I'm nothing that exciting. I'm just a businessman.'

'Will you buy it?'

'The Bazille?' He'd pulled the hat forward over his eyes. He smiled, setting his teeth together, but his eyes were deep in the shadows. 'Yes, perhaps.'

La Sirène she read over the restaurant door. She walked through, feeling horribly self-conscious. However much she tucked in her arms, her elbows seemed to stick out too far and her feet felt clumsy and enormous. The restaurant was small and almost empty. The flagstones on the floor were uneven; dark beams lowered the ceiling. It was still early. Only two tables on the far side of the room were filled. She checked quickly. No one she knew. She let out her breath.

A waiter approached with a welcoming smile, yanking down a

striped waistcoat. Alexander took off his hat. 'Where do you want to sit?' he asked, gesturing round the room with it. 'It seems you can choose pretty much anywhere you like.'

'You decide.'

'Over there?'

They sat by an open window. The day was warm and sultry and the faint cool tang of the sea reached them every now and again. Alex ordered for them both in rapid French without even asking what she wanted or looking at the menu. The food came quickly, large, curved wooden platters of seafood, delicious things in knobbly black or coral shells, all draped artistically with dull greeny-brown strands of seaweed and piled high on a bed of ice. Also dishes of Scottish salmon and caviar and a small pale blue bowl of gull's eggs. All the fish and seafood had arrived on the boat that morning, the waiter assured them, misinterpreting Angel's amazed expression at the sheer quantity of food. As if rationing had never existed, she thought.

Her stomach was too tight to be able to eat much. She managed a few mouthfuls then toyed with the rest.

What did they talk about that first time together? Angel found it hard to remember precisely even later that night. She recalled the darkness of his eyes and hair without any difficulty, the shape of his hands, the tender almost trembling look of his top lip beneath the line of his moustache and the frown lines etched so deeply between his eyes, but everything else seemed a little blurred. Her family? Yes, they spoke about her life with the Merlowes. Alexander Sorel seemed genuinely interested, why she couldn't imagine. Because there was really nothing much to tell, ever since she'd come to live at Longlands she'd led a perfectly ordinary, mundane life. But over the main course he wanted to hear all the dull, uneventful details of her time at boarding-school and the six months in Paris at a finishing school for young ladies, seemed almost to relish them the more prosaic and everyday they sounded.

He sat with his head tilted to one side, listening carefully, brows lifted, an enigmatic smile on his lips. 'A perfect example of an upper-class English upbringing, in fact,' he concluded, as the waiter was removing her plate.

32

'Yes,' she said, but her look was troubled. 'I suppose it was.'

'It's a very fine house.'

'Longlands? Oh, *yes.*'

'Tell me about your father,' he said, his dark eyes never leaving her face.

She thought for moment. 'He was tall and lean and fair. I remember him in the garden nailing up a fence that was always falling down. He would sing as he hammered the planks back up.'

'What did he sing?'

'Oh, popular songs and his version of arias mostly. He travelled a lot. He'd be away for two or three nights and when he came home he always brought me something. A bracelet or necklace, once a child-size sewing machine that really worked. Of course I would have preferred another doll. I think he guessed and was rather disappointed.'

'Why was he away so often?'

'He was a travelling salesman.'

He looked surprised. 'A salesman?'

'Not a very good one. He sold vacuum cleaners. Actually the vacuum cleaners were the last in a long line of unsuccessful ventures. The family disinherited him when he married my mother so he had to work and wasn't trained for anything, you see. My mother was a dancer. Only *corps de ballet.* From a perfectly respectable family but – '

Alex smiled thinly. 'Not good enough?'

'They were both terribly young. When the family banned the match they ran away together. She gave up dancing once they were married.' Angel didn't speak for a moment, then said with a jerk: 'She was ill. It was very sudden. I was almost ten.'

'And your father?'

'Two years earlier.'

'What rotten luck. In the war, I suppose?'

'Yes.'

'A lot of good people died,' he said grimly. 'On both sides.'

'My mother said later she thought he'd always felt ashamed. She didn't mean for fighting or anything – she meant for never being able to make a go of it and look after us properly. She said – she

33

said he thought that he'd failed us.' Angel looked down at her plate, a slow, deep frown gathering between her eyebrows. 'I once asked her if he had.'

'What did she reply?'

'Just sighed and said no, not really.'

Suddenly, alarmingly, she found her eyes were filled with tears. She didn't usually talk about her parents. Everyone acted as if she'd been an orphan all her life. As if the Merlowes were all the family she'd ever had. And she didn't mention her parents either, just took it for granted that, in the circumstances, it was normal enough. She wondered why she'd blurted it out now, of all times. The glass of wine? She shouldn't have gulped it back so quickly on virtually an empty stomach. Stupid of her. She kept her eyes fixed firmly on the heavy linen tablecloth hoping she wasn't about to make a complete idiot of herself. 'I'm sorry,' she said formally. 'I've got a bit of a cold.'

And was relieved when Alex only replied seriously, 'Summer colds can be very nasty.'

She heard the click of his lighter. The smell of smoke drifted into the air. He smoked for a moment in silence. It gave her enough time to recover. 'And then you went to live with your cousins?' he asked.

'Yes.'

'Where you've been very happy?'

'I haven't thought much about it.'

When she lifted her gaze and met his, he had a strange, speculative look in his eyes. A sort of far away, dreamy look. He tapped some ash from his cigarette into a glass ashtray and smiled. 'Then you must be.'

A waiter was hovering near their table. Alexander said something to him in French. The waiter bowed and disappeared in the direction of the kitchens.

'Your French is very good,' she said, crumbling her bread.

'It should be. My mother is French.'

'Is she really? You don't seem at all foreign.'

'Don't I?'

'No.'

It wasn't really true. There was something she couldn't quite put her finger on, something different about him. She looked him full in the face for the first time, examining the dark hair, not quite black, swept back from the high forehead, the high-bridged nose and black eyebrows over a dark, generally sombre, heavy-lidded gaze. He was older than she'd thought, maybe fifty, forty-five at least. She sat for a moment, slowly sizing him up. 'I mean, you don't *sound* like a foreigner.'

'Well, I'm bilingual. French mother, English father. Mother's still hale and hearty although, sadly, my father is no longer alive.'

'I am sorry.'

'That's all right. It happened years ago. I was older then you are now. Come to think of it, you wouldn't even have been born at the time.'

She looked at him thoughtfully. Twenty-six, twenty-seven years difference, maybe more. 'Now I suppose you're going to say how very young I am.'

'Actually I was going to say that being eighteen seems both very mature and very young at the same time. And really rather – ' he hesitated, examining her skinny young body arched against the table – 'rather a desirable age to be.'

He smiled suddenly. She smiled back at him, then, feeling the colour rush into her cheeks, looked into her coffee cup.

'Does your mother live with you in London?' she asked, forcing herself to raise her eyes to his.

'Lord, no! She lives in Italy. She was born in France but considers the French too provincial – Paris is awfully grey and shabby nowadays, you know. And the English too – Well, I can't tell you what she says about the English.'

'Even your father?'

He laughed. '*Especially* my father. My parents weren't very well suited, I'm afraid. They'd been separated for years before my mother was widowed. Never divorced, well, one didn't then, simply parted amicably when I was in my teens. My father always detested Italy but it suits Mother very well. She lives in Venice at a palazzo near the Grand Canal – a most civilised existence, she informs me.'

She nodded and smiled as Alex talked about Italy and what it was like for his mother living abroad. People had been sitting down as they were eating. Most of the tables were now filled. Laughter and chatter filled the smoky air around them. A few people were waiting by the bar to be seated, though none that Angel recognised. She checked nervously.

'Well, I suppose we'd better make a move,' he sighed, after they'd finished a second cup of coffee. 'Want anything else? Some cheese and biscuits, perhaps?'

'No cheese. No, thank you. Actually I don't seem to have eaten very much at all. I'm sorry – it seems an awful waste.'

'Oh, I don't expect it will be thrown away. They'll probably eat it in kitchen, or give it to the cat.'

'That's exactly what I mean. There's hardly anything most of the time and then – well, the cat.' She pulled a face. 'You think I'm silly.'

Alex was looking at her. 'Quite the opposite,' he said quietly. 'I was thinking – how very nice you are.'

They gazed at each other for a moment in silence. There was the intent expression in his eyes again, as if the restaurant and every-thing in it had melted away and there was nothing he was aware of except for her. She could feel herself blushing again – *damn it*. But she suddenly knew exactly why she'd been so determined to see him again. *He's gorgeous*, she thought. *He's the most gorgeous man I've ever met.*

The trick he had of lifting and dropping his eyelids lazily as he asked the waiter for the bill . . . the pronounced, sensitive curve of his top lip as he paid it . . . He must think me a perfect idiot, she thought, feeling the hot flush spreading over her, her neck, her forehead, her cheeks, I'm certainly behaving like one. She fixed her eyes on the white tablecloth, cursing herself in silence, wondering if he had any idea how she felt. She kept her eyes down, hoping not.

When they got back to the curve in the road where he'd parked the car earlier, the shadows cast by the roadside trees were beginning to lengthen. He switched off the engine. She unknotted the yellow silk square from under her chin. 'Thanks for an awfully nice time,' she said. 'It was – well, awfully nice.'

'For me too.'

'Was it really?' Her words came out with a husky catch that she found embarrassing. 'Oh – good.' She fumbled with the handle. Opening the door, she stretched out a leg and, resting one foot on the grass, turned slightly. 'Goodbye, Alex,' she said, sounding faintly desperate.

Then he did something so unexpected that for a moment she couldn't even breathe. He reached out his hand and ran one gentle finger down the curve of her cheek. 'You have a face from a painting. A Whistler, perhaps. Do you know his portrait, 'The White Girl'?'

'I'm afraid I – no – no, I don't . . . '

'It's of a young girl in a long off-white dress, standing straight, rather serious, her brown hair tangled loose. You remind me of her. You know, in your party dress the other night? You had exactly that look.' He dropped his hand and smiled, a sad, dreamy smile. 'Except, of course, your hair's fair, isn't it, not dark like hers . . . '

Something he'd said or thought had made the frown lines return to his face. He shifted his eyes without moving his head and said brusquely: 'Now you'd better get off home. Or the Merlowes will think their favourite niece has been sold into white slavery and let out the dogs.'

The abrupt words were a dismissal. She sat for a second, feeling crushed and rather confused. His touch was still burning her skin. *So that's that*, she thought. Grabbing her handbag and jacket, she scrambled out the car. But as she began walking across the grass, he called out to her: 'Angel?'

She turned quickly. 'Yes?'

'Look, we could meet up tomorrow. If you'd like to.'

Yes, yes, yes! 'Yes, I would. Very much so.'

'I won't have long,' he warned her. 'I have to back at the St Clares by lunchtime.'

'That's OK.'

'Ten thirty suit you?'

She took a deep breath. 'Yes. That would suit me.'

He gave a sudden quick smile that lit up his whole face. 'Good. Shall we say – here?'

She nodded happily. As she passed through the open gates and began running under the poplars that lined the length of the drive, she heard the engine start. She looked back. The sports car shot off along the road. She cut across the lawn and ran through the woods. The house loomed suddenly in the glaring sunlight.

She stopped for a moment, leaning one hip and shoulder against the broad trunk of an old oak and stood in its cool shade, trying to collect herself. She felt a mixture of guilt and exhilaration as she looked over at the old house, hearing her own rapid breathing and, in the distance, the faint drone of a car engine.

Long shadows cast by the trees lay on the lovely rich stone. Flowerpots stood on the terrace; the terrace sloped down to the lawn. The Merlowes weren't back yet. The tall windows in the drawing room were still shuttered.

She suddenly realised she was smiling. A wide, foolish grin was plastered across her face. Her breathing slowed down. Angel came out of the cold earthy shade and moved slowly towards the light, across the purpling shadows on the grass, through the perfect, shining present.

3

Isola di San Pietro, Italy. 8 July 1939. 9.05 p.m.

The dining room was brilliantly lit. Candles everywhere – on the dining table, along the mantelpiece, in the iron candelabra which swayed above their heads. And white flowers, large exotic blooms he didn't recognise. Their heady aroma filled the air.

Before dinner they drank champagne. He'd drained most of it when he noticed the sediment at the bottom of the glass.

'What's this?' he asked, holding it up with a smile.

'What?'

'The powder at the bottom.'

She shrugged disinterestedly. 'It happens sometimes. Shall I pour you another?'

She took a clean glass and poured in some more of the light fizzing liquid. Behind one ear she'd stuck a flower and her black hair was loose, falling in rippling waves down her back. She wore a long plain white dress made of some sort of silky fabric which left her shoulders bare. Her skin gleamed in the flickering candlelight.

'You look beautiful tonight,' he said, as she handed him the glass.

She smiled, her eyes watchful. 'Do I?'

'And you smell quite delicious.' He bent to kiss the nape of her neck. 'Mmm – what is it?

'This scent? Oh, I've worn it before. Quite often. It's called – "Irresistible Impulse".' She laughed suddenly.

Her laughter sounded strangely thin and drawn out to him as if it were resting on the air for too long, or coming from too far away. He frowned, lifting his hand to his forehead. There was sweat on his brow. His limbs felt heavy. The room had shifted slightly. The ground was slanting away. He felt like he might fall. At any moment, thump, helpless, to the floor, incapable of the slightest movement.

He shook his head, trying to steady himself. He was smiling he distantly registered. He could feel his lips bared over his teeth in a grimace. Quickly, he caught hold of a straight-backed chair, the smile frozen on his face. His knees sagged, though for only a split second. Then the world came back again. The room righted itself. Fingertips tingling, he drew himself straight. But still the weird feeling in his head.

He didn't wait until they had finished eating to make love to her. He took her hand and pulled her, laughing, to the sofa. The diamonds round her wrist and on her fingers glittered. He wondered why he hadn't realised before quite how desirable she was. How very, very lovely. He could barely move his eyes, or lips, from her skin.

He knelt on the floor in front of her and placed both hands round her waist. Holding her, he felt like a giant, like someone from another, clumsier, planet, enormously strong and powerful. 'Your waist is so tiny,' he said wonderingly. 'I could easily crush you. Like this, with my hands.'

'Just you try,' she smiled.

He kissed her full lips.

Then he buried his face in that heavy, dark, sweet-smelling hair, pressing his mouth to the cool of her throat, the lobe of her ear, the curve of her shoulder, dragging the white dress down so that her breasts were bare. The nipples were long and hard in his hand.

Head flung back against the seat, she whispered: 'It's too light. Someone will see.'

He blew out the candles so that only two were left burning, one on the table, the other on the mantelpiece. The room was full of shadows. Untying the sash, unfastening each tiny button at the back of her dress, slipping off the silk underclothes with great care, he undressed her slowly till she was wearing only the wide diamond bracelet and the pale low-heeled shoes. That other black hair was thick and curling. He sat down on the sofa, pulling her with him. Drawing her onto his lap, he put his arms round her and rocked her like a child, his hand tangled in that damp, short curling hair. He kept it there until she gave a long, low moan.

'What do you want?' he asked fiercely, holding her face between his hands. He stared intently into her eyes. Her eyes were dark, the lashes thick and long; he could smell her on his fingers. 'Tell me,' he demanded. 'What is it you want me to do? There's something you'd like – something special – yes, in your eyes, I can see it.'

But she would only shake her head.

Her dress, with its wide silk sash, lay crumpled on the floor. She rested back languorously on the sofa, her pale limbs relaxed, silently following him with her eyes as he took off his own clothes and bundled them onto a chair. From the loops of his linen trousers he drew a slim leather belt. Stooping to slide the sash from her dress, he walked over to where she lay.

Lifting her arms over her head he fastened the belt around her wrists. Ignoring her 'ah' of surprise, he pulled it so tightly that it bit into the smooth flesh.

Round her throat he wound the silk sash, running it loosely through his fingers, enjoying the sudden feeling of power that surged through him. She tried to sit up, struggling slightly, her eyes no longer so languid. It wasn't difficult to hold her back, even with one hand.

Then he kissed her mouth for the last time before laying the sash over her face, covering the long, dark eyes, the too full mouth, the small attractively curved nose between high cheekbones, slipping the ends around her neck and knotting it loosely at the back. The material rose and fell slightly with her breath.

Slowly, he traced the shape of her lips through it with a finger. He could feel her trembling: he couldn't see her expression. All he could see of her were her full breasts, her belly, the leather belt cutting into her wrists and the tender, pale skin on the insides of her thighs. It was strangely arousing – having her so exposed and yet her face completely hooded.

He stared at that moist, secret place between her legs surrounded with curling black hair. He felt the fire welling up in him.

Then he entered her, thrusting with long, hard strokes, pushing roughly into her body as if he wanted to take it all from her, as if he could possess all of it in one violent movement, as if he could, if only he could thrust hard enough. Till his body arched and he groaned against that silky white mask, once, for a long, long time, at the height of the act that is called love.

*   *   *

41

He woke in the early hours after dreaming someone was turning a knife in his stomach and even awake the twisting feeling continued. He lay for a moment, eyes shut, hoping the unpleasant sensation would soon disappear.

She was still asleep, one arm curved up on the pillow, her long black hair spread over her like a shroud. He could see the steady rise and fall of the sheet on her body, inhale the sweet, heavy perfume that clung to her hair and pervaded the whole room.

On the dresser were some wide-open lilies in a silver vase. Orange pollen had dropped from them and powdered the scarred wood. The stink of the flowers mingled with her cloying perfume made him feel nauseous.

Remembering the night before, a sense of dirtiness, of self-disgust, swept over him. He felt first hot, then cold with shame. He turned to the heavy sleeping body next to him. What only two hours before had filled him with savage desire now repelled him. On the pale skin of her throat were two raw-looking love-bites and, where her arm had thrown free of the sheet, a large ugly blue bruise circled the wrist. He didn't want to think about what other marks there might be on her body beneath the sheet.

It was her fault, he thought, staring at her, sickened. She put something in my drink: she poisoned me. I wouldn't have done any of it if she hadn't encouraged me, any of it.

He passed a moist, trembling hand over his forehead promising himself that he would never again spend a night like this. What drug had she given him to make him behave like that? What witches' brew was hers?

The intoxication had worn off leaving him only with the memory of the long night before and the after-effects of the drugged wine. And the sick, turning feeling in his belly.

A sudden wave of heat ran over him. He wiped the cold sweat off his forehead with the corner of the sheet and concentrated on breathing. In. Out. In again. Then he threw off the sheet.

Clenching his jaw against a rush of acid saliva into his mouth, he walked urgently to the bathroom. For a second, he stared at his grey face in the mirror. Then, feeling his mouth filling, he leant forward and vomited into the lavatory pan. Everything he'd eaten, all chewed up and partly digested – meat, lettuce, tomatoes, the Pecorino cheese, the tiny salty biscuits, all swilled down with the fizzy yellow bubbles of champagne. The attack of vomiting that followed almost brought him to his knees. He heaved with such violence that his stomach hurt, spasm after spasm that kept him there for some time, head down, hands gripping the cool edge of the basin. He was very quiet, he didn't make a sound other than the pressure of his chest and stomach as the burning liquid rushed up his throat and out his mouth, and the clean water whirling round as he flushed the mess down the lavatory. She didn't wake.

When it was over, he sat on the cork mat with the cool tiles of the wall against his back, his throat burning, too weak to move.

She didn't have to do it, he thought weakly. She didn't have to.

Then he retched again and again till there was nothing and, when he was able, staggered back to bed.

4

ANGEL

Haywards Heath, Sussex. May 1950

Angel lay on her single bed, thinking of a tall man in a pale grey suit.

I'd like to make him really happy, she thought dreamily. I'd like to wipe all the frown lines from his face and replace them with laughter lines.

She pressed her face against the crook of her elbow and inhaled the familiar warm scent of her own skin, thinking of her last sight of Alexander in the fish restaurant – across a table, long fingers caressing his silver cigarette case.

When she'd returned from school, she'd imagined she was in love with Charles St Clare. Now she wondered how she could have thought so, even for a moment. A change had happened inside of her and only she knew of it. In the past few hours, the world had been subtly but definitely transformed.

I'm in love, she groaned. I'm in love and I can't breathe a word about it to anyone.

She pictured Laura's fiancé, Edward, square, lean and solid. Surely Laura didn't feel about him like *this*? This sort of shivery feeling on the surface of her skin and in the pit of the stomach; this lurching, lunging, empty sensation, almost like panic; the dizzy, breathtaking joy. She'd never felt so sharply alive before. Or so vulnerable.

He was worth lying for, she thought defiantly.

The window was open. The air was still and warm. Stiffening, she heard the rattle of her uncle's old black Humber saloon as it crunched gently forward on the gravel, swept round the circular drive before the front door and stopped. Footsteps scrunched across the pebbles. Raised voices sounded on the terrace below. Angel lay very still, listening to the shuffling echo of footsteps heading up the stairs. Somewhere in the house a door slammed.

Across the bedroom, she caught sight of her face reflected in the mirror, pale, stricken, guilty. She closed her eyes, trying to shut out the image, but she could still see Alex's dark, unhappy face as plainly as if it were photographed on the inside of her eyelids. Her breath caught in her throat. What was he doing now? Perhaps smoking a cigarette as he scrutinised a painting? Sipping whisky? Chatting to St Clare? Almost certainly not thinking of her. She must try not to think about him any more, either.

At least there was tomorrow. Her aunt and Laura were unlikely to notice her absence. They were driving into Brighton to choose the fabric for Laura's going-away suit. They would be far too busy with preparations for the wedding to consider her. After which, everything would be different anyway. Alexander Sorel would be long gone for one thing.

She opened her eyes and stared at the ceiling for a bit, missing him already.

* * *

But she must have finally fallen asleep because, when she woke next morning, he was her first thought. All she could hear for a second was the thud of her heart pounding in her ears. Then she threw back the sheets and jumped out of bed.

Pouring cold water into the china basin on the washstand, she splashed her face and dressed quickly.

Laura was in the hall downstairs, squashing on a rust-coloured straw hat. 'Oh hullo, Angel. Feeling better?'

'Yes, much.'

'You still look a little washed out.'

'Oh, God, do I? How was the luncheon?'

'Very enjoyable.'

'Oh, good, good. And you're feeling well?'

'What do you mean – feeling well?' Laura lifted her brows in an exaggeratedly surprised expression. 'Of course I am. *You* had the migraine headache, not me.' She pulled a pair of gloves out of her pocket. 'We're driving into town today. Shopping for material for the going-away dress.'

'That's right. You said.'

'We're off in a moment. Mummy's bringing the car round.'

'Is she?' Angel could hear her own voice, tense and defensive. 'Well, carry on.'

'I am carrying on.' Her head tilted slightly, Laura looked at Angel through narrowed eyes. Angel stood there, pale and out of breath and guilty. Would Laura see the new heat in her body, or that her heart was pounding to a different beat? But she didn't seem to notice anything different.

'Oh, dear,' Laura frowned. 'You really *are* looking peaky this morning. Was it very bad?'

'What?'

'The migraine.'

'Oh – no, not really, it wasn't too bad at all – ' Angel said with a terrible light-heartedness. She shifted from one foot to the other and smiled weakly, feeling as if the word 'liar' was plastered across her forehead. *Now I'll tell her*, she thought, *now. Actually I didn't have a headache yesterday, I was feeling exceptionally well. I was off careering about the countryside with the most gorgeous man I've ever . . .* 'You were right about the party, Laura . . . ' she said with an effort. 'What you said about it being special . . . you know.'

'No, I don't. I haven't the faintest what you're talking about. Come on, Angel. Cough it up – oh, hell!'

From outside came the sound of a car horn.

'There's Mummy now.' Laura made a final adjustment to her hat. 'I'd better dash. We'll speak later . . . Toodeloo!'

The front door slammed behind her.

There was a dish of scrambled eggs on the hot plate on the sideboard and glass pots of marmalade and honey on the dining room table but Angel felt too unsettled to eat. She hated lying to Laura but it had seemed somehow impossible to tell her what she'd been doing yesterday. Could she say something tonight? Throw it into the conversation quite casually – oh, did I ever mention the jolly odd time I had at your engagement party? No, it was too late. After she'd met Alex Sorel secretly for the *third time*? She'd missed her chance. It would take a lot more than a throwaway comment now. Besides, was there really any point? He'd be gone soon, anyway. Her stomach lurched at the thought.

And it executed exactly the same backwards flip in Merton's tea-rooms two hours later, watching him pull out a chair for her from a table in the window, a tall figure in a lightweight linen suit and a white panama hat. Not that he was wearing the hat by then – he'd hung it on the stand by the door. She'd squashed hers onto her lap and was gazing admiringly at him over the grey marble table top.

'What's that pink thing with wafers called?' he asked, examining the menu.

'An Ice Sundae?'

'Would you like one?'

'Yes, please.'

'Anything else? Tea? Coffee?'

'No, thank you.'

'An Ice Sundae for my friend,' he told the waitress. 'And a coffee for me.'

Dull mirrors covered the length of one wall. Over the pastries on the counter flies circled, settling briefly on the muslin covering them. It was warm in the window. Sunlight poured through a half-pulled down blind. A fan revolved slowly and ineffectually above their heads. The waitress placed a glass bowl in front of her, the ice cream already beginning to melt.

'Are you liking it at the St Clare's?' Angel asked politely, slipping soft, pink ice cream into her mouth.

'Yes, I am quite.'

'They have an awful lot of paintings, don't they? Think you'll get to see them all?'

'I expect so. I'm working my way round, room by room. Yesterday morning I found a Hubert Robertson in the room next to mine. He isn't my favourite painter by a long chalk but it's a very good example.'

'Are there many more?'

'Paintings?'

'Well, rooms.'

'Only two.'

'I suppose you'll be returning to London once you've seen them all?'

'I'm not sure. It depends.'

47

On what? When she looked up his eyes were on her contemplatively. Did she have ice cream on her chin? It would be just like her if she did. But it was hard to look sophisticated scooping up strawberry ice. Why hadn't she had the sense to ask for a cup of tea? There was a pause that grew longer. She racked her brains trying to think of something else to say. Desire seemed to clog up her throat. She felt hot and stupid with it. How broad his shoulders are, she thought breathlessly. She felt limp and hopeless with longing. He was staring into his cup. How boring he must think her. She simply couldn't think of anything. Her mind was blank. 'I suppose you miss your life in London awfully,' she said at last.

He looked up with an abstracted frown. 'Miss it? No, I don't miss it.' He stared bleakly across at the striped sunblind. 'Not at all really.'

Silence again. Angel became very aware of the steady murmur of conversation at the other tables, the chink of crockery being set discreetly down. 'I hope it wasn't a nuisance picking me up today,' she ventured, after a moment.

He was still frowning across the room. He didn't seem to hear her at first, then looked up. 'What?'

'I hope it wasn't a bother having to – '

'Oh, not at all. I was out already, hours before.'

'Oh, were you? Oh, good.'

Under the table, she wiped a sticky palm on her skirt. How gauche she was, how stiff and stupid. And how loud and English her voice sounded with its clipped upper-class accent. His sounded so colourless and flat that she looked at him curiously. He didn't look simply drawn today, he was haggard. *Well here he is* – she thought savagely – *stuck attempting small talk with me.*

He took a sip of coffee and pulled a sour face, then slipped his silver cigarette case out of his pocket. 'Mind if I smoke? Want one?'

When she shook her head, he divided the case with his thumbnail, took out a cigarette and lit it. He sat at a slight angle to the table, one leg crossed over the other, chin tilted slightly, taking long thoughtful drags of the cigarette.

'So what do you do in the long summer months,' he asked, 'in that beautiful country house?'

48

She looked at him, trying to understand his tone. He sounded almost mocking. 'Oh, ride, or go to tennis parties with Laura, visit friends – you know, nothing much. I suppose that will change once Laura's married though. I hate change, don't you?'

'Well, I rather like it. But only if it's change for the better, of course.'

'You never know at the time, do you? You only find out later.'

'You've probably had enough changes already.'

'Mmm. Probably.' She couldn't mistake the sardonic note in his voice this time.

She concentrated on the ice. He tapped his fingernails on the marble table top in a sharp, impatient rhythm. *He's wishing he'd never asked me out today*, she thought. *He's wondering why he didn't squash down whatever kind and careless impulse made him suggest it.* 'And you?' she asked, half angry. 'What do *you* do in summer?'

'Also nothing much.' He looked at the tip of his cigarette. 'Visit my mother usually.'

'That doesn't *sound* like nothing much. I mean – Venice. What do you do when you're there?'

'Oh, sit on her veranda, staring down at the canal, or play cards, or go out to dinner.'

She frowned, trying to imagine it. 'In a boat?'

'In a gondola, yes. Occasionally there's a masked ball.'

'Well, it sounds rather thrilling.'

'One would think so. I suppose I did once. One gets a little tired of the same old things. Even in Venice.' He gestured to the bowl. 'How's the ice-cream?'

'Oh, delicious!'

'Yes?'

'It's rather fun eating one *before* lunch instead of, you know, *after*.'

'I suppose it must be.'

She looked down, flushing uncomfortably and angry with herself for doing so. 'Yes. It is.'

He smoked for a while without speaking. She tried desperately to think of something interesting to say. Not thinking of anything, she slowly finished the last spoonfuls.

'What would you say to a picnic?' he asked, very unexpectedly.

'A picnic?'

'I realise it's not exactly an invitation to a masked ball,' he said dryly. 'But would you like to go on one?'

'Oh yes! Yes, I would.'

'Free on Thursday?'

Laura and her aunt would be busy unpacking wedding presents, or arranging them in the ballroom, or deciding on a final seating plan, Angel supposed. She'd be free all right. Her heart suddenly beating hard, she nodded.

'Anywhere particular you'd recommend? Since you know this neck of the woods so much better than me.'

'Scaynes Hill is rather nice. I go there sometimes with Bruce.'

'Bruce? Who the devil's that?' He grinned sarcastically. 'Another cousin?'

'Actually a retriever. Do you like dogs, Alex?'

'I prefer cats.'

She pulled a face. 'Why is it whenever you ask if someone likes dogs they always reply they like cats better? One doesn't have to choose between them, you know.'

'It's just that – well, I prefer cats. But, look, just to prove I'm not completely prejudiced against the canine species, why don't you bring the dog along?'

'Can I really? He'd love to!'

'You provide the dog, I'll provide the packed lunch,' he said almost lightly, and his face suddenly looked less lined and grave. He was tied up with the St Clares for the next few evenings, he explained, but his afternoons were generally free. 'Alright with your family, is it, you're going off with me like this?'

Her voice came out strangled. 'Oh, they're awfully busy – with Laura's wedding and everything . . . '

'Yes, I see.'

He stubbed out the cigarette and got to his feet. She must have stood, too, though she wasn't aware of doing so. Picking up her straw hat from the table, he held it out to her. They stood for a second in the window, each holding one side of the hat's shallow brim. Angel could almost imagine that the rapid throbbing of her pulse was passing from her wrist to his through the straw.

'Shall we say eleven thirty?' he said, letting go. 'Same place?'

She gave a nervous, idiotic smile. The handbag dangled from the crook of her elbow as she squashed on the hat. 'Oh, yes, rather.'

He tweaked the curved brim. 'Scaynes Hill it is, then. I'll look forward to it. Until Thursday.'

'Until Thursday.'

Nothing in life is ever quite as one expects, she told herself later, hearing again her own high, breathy voice responding, *nothing*.

*   *   *

No one at home noticed anything different about her. Amazingly and rather dreadfully, no one sensed the new heat in her body, or recognised the small, dreamy smile she found constantly trembling on her lips. She thought Laura would notice and try to prise her secret from her. And then her Aunt and Uncle would have to be told, and then –

But no one seemed to realise there was anything at all unusual. Everyone was too busy with the arrangements for Laura's wedding to pay much attention to her.

And thank God for that, she thought.

*   *   *

Angel didn't recall much of the picnic itself, she just had a general impression – the sun baking down; the scent of grass and hot earth; Alex laughing as he doled out food. She remembered the snatch of conversation they'd made in response to his toast at the beginning and, of course, the really astounding request he'd come out with at the end.

They sat at on a tartan rug looking over the Downs with Bruce, at last tired of chasing sticks, panting at their feet.

'I may have seemed a bit out of sorts the other day,' Alex said straightaway. 'If so, I'm sorry. Business,' he explained. 'A little bit stressful. But today I feel much better. Like a great weight has been lifted from my shoulders.' He smiled at her. 'I've come to a decision.'

'Important?'

'I should say so, yes.' His smile grew thoughtful. 'None more so really.'

51

He didn't say anything more about it, just slopped some water from a thermos into a bowl for the dog and filled two monogrammed champagne flutes from an icy cold bottle of Dom Pérignon for them. 'Well.' He raised a glass. 'A toast. To us and chance meetings!'

'Yes – chance meetings!'

They clinked glasses.

'Do you think it was?' Angel asked, after she'd taken a sip. 'Just chance? Our meeting at the party?'

'Yes, I do. The war showed me just how a random an affair life is. There's damn all purpose in it. People die, they're maimed or wounded, the stupid and talented alike. It's all quite indiscriminate. Look at London in the blitz.'

'Were you – '

'No, I was fortunate. Though, god knows, I've certainly had my fair share of bad luck. Things one can't possibly know would turn out badly,' he said, more to himself than to her. 'And then, years later, when you least expect it, back they come and give you a good wallop, straight between the shoulder blades.'

He looked up and smiled but his eyes were still clouded as if he were thinking of something else. Not something very nice, Angel thought, judging by his expression. Was he about to grown cool and distant now, she wondered with a sinking heart. And if so, how should she handle him? What should she do? What *could* she do? Not much, if the other day was anything to go by.

'I've always believed,' she said, forcing a smile, 'that there's a *bit* more to things than that.'

'What? Destiny? Fate?'

'From your tone, you obviously don't.'

'I think it's all tommyrot, if you really want to know. No, if there hadn't been a sudden downpour on the Avenue des Champs Elysées one warm July afternoon and my mother hadn't agreed to wait under my father's umbrella while he hailed her a cab – '

'Is that how they met? How romantic.'

'How *lucky*. She was only in Paris for one day.'

'And if she hadn't been?'

His frown deepened for a moment, and then, as quickly as they'd arrived, the clouds lifted. 'Then you'd be sitting on your own, I expect,' he grinned. 'With an awful lot of food.'

She grinned back, feeling an enormous rush of relief. The frown between his brows had gone, he sounded almost light-hearted. *It's going to be all right*, she thought. *He isn't going to sink into a black mood again*. Smiling, she parried, 'So if your mother hadn't gone – what was it, shopping?'

'Yes. For a huge cartwheel hat.'

'If your mother hadn't wanted a new hat – then we wouldn't be sitting together on a blanket sipping champagne?'

'Almost certainly not.'

'Strange to think, isn't it?'

'Almost intolerable,' he said tranquilly.

'I wonder what we *would* be doing.'

'Well, she did, and we are, and so on.' He took out a cigarette and watched her as he lit it. 'So when good luck comes our way we must seize it in both hands. Seize it and hang on tight and never let it go. Chance is everything. You have to work bloody hard to make your luck.'

Far below, a tractor was crossing a field. It looked so tiny and far away it seemed just like a toy. They could barely hear the sound of its engine above the humming of insects and the shushing of the grass. It was a hot, clear day with only a gentle breeze. A few sheep grazed, an empty road twisted like a white ribbon stretched tight between the fields. The sky was very blue.

'You're enjoying today, Angel?' he asked.

'Oh, yes! Aren't you?'

He smiled and said: 'I am. Immensely. It's a marvellous day. Hungry yet?'

'Practically starving.'

'There's some quails stuffed with oysters – you quite liked those the other day, didn't you? Also lobsters with mayonnaise and a coleslaw and – oh, Dauphenoise potatoes.' He'd opened the wicker hamper and was unwrapping brown paper and lifting off silver lids as he spoke. 'Or if you prefer – ' he looked up – 'smoked salmon sandwiches?'

'Um, the lobster, I think – And some of the potatoes, please. And could I have a slice of lemon? I'm not sure if I've ever seen a whole fruit up close before. They're still terribly expensive. Mmm,' she held it to her nose and inhaled, 'what a wonderful scent. Better then perfume.'

'Cut it in half and put a squirt of juice behind your ear if you like the smell so much.'

'I think I might.'

'A lemony scent would rather suit you.'

She giggled. 'Think so?'

'Mmhm. Just the ticket. Blondes should always smell of lemon.'

'Should they? What should redheads smell of?'

'Ginger, of course.'

'And brunettes?'

He frowned and said: 'I really have no idea.' He took a moment getting a silver salt cellar out of the wicker basket. 'Salt?' he offered.

'Just a little, please.'

'I'm beginning to understand what you mean by a little.' He poured a thin stream onto her plate. 'There's a knife and fork somewhere. Ah, here they are.'

'Perfect.'

She took the white china plate he was holding out to her, balancing it in her lap. She had a tight feeling in her chest as she ate. I'll just enjoy the present, she told herself. I won't think about the time when he's gone. She thought: Because I'm happy – happy – happy . . . She didn't know when she'd ever felt so much. Perhaps when she was a child, before her father had died, when she still had the strong childish certainty that everything would always remain just the same forever: no hurt, no changes, no loss.

Later, there were strawberries. 'Cream?' he asked, pouring it on liberally without waiting for her reply. 'You look like you need fattening up.' He sprinkled some sugar onto her plate and sat for a second, sipping bitter black coffee from a thermos, studying her as she bit into the sweetened fruit. When she'd finished and was wiping juice from her mouth with a napkin, he gave himself a little shake, yawned, stretched, and glanced at his watch.

'Oh, Lord! Is it half past five already? I must go. I've got to be back at the St Clares for cocktails. Tonight's my last night and it would be rude not to be on time for the party especially since the damn thing's being held in my honour.' He yawned again. 'We'd better start packing away.'

She stared at him. 'Tonight's your last night?'

'Yes,' he said casually. 'I'm returning to London tomorrow.'

She'd always known it was coming, she'd been expecting it all week, hadn't she? Even so, she felt disappointment tightening her bowels. So this was the decision he'd made, the one that had lifted a great weight from his shoulders. He was glad to be going back home. She sat and looked down at her bowl. Picked up the spoon, put it down, reached for her glass, pushed it away again. *Well, it was fun while it lasted*, she thought gloomily.

Gazing into the bowl, she felt an overwhelming sense of loss. *How ridiculous*, she thought. *I barely know him. You can't lose something you've never even had.* She ate a strawberry without thinking with her eyes fixed on nothing. 'When?' she asked in a small voice.

'First thing. I'm afraid it had to come some time. I have a horrible feeling I've rather outstayed my welcome as it is. I suppose I'll have to buy the Bazille now simply for the sake of good manners.'

'The painting? Yes, you probably will,' she said unnaturally cheerfully, trying not to look at the shape his long limbs made as he stretched or the way his shirt strained across his chest. That was it then. She hated goodbyes, especially this one. 'It's been a lovely day,' she said brightly, but unable to stop the wobble in her voice. 'I shall never forget it, never. Thank you ever so much.'

'Oh, not at all,' he said meaninglessly, sounding distracted.

'I suppose we'd better start sorting this lot out. Cocktails at the St Clares generally begin at 7.30 sharp.' She jumped up and began frenziedly piling plates into the wicker basket.

'Angel, wait a moment. There's something I'd like to speak to you about before we go.' He squinted up at her and patted the tartan rug next to him. 'Sit down for a moment, will you?'

Slowly she sat down again, hoping her face didn't show too clearly what she was feeling. 'What did you want to talk about?' she asked, playing with the buckle of her sandal.

'This is difficult for me,' he said. 'I'm not quite sure how to begin.' He cleared his throat. 'So I'm not going to beat around the bush. There's something I want to ask you.'

'Well, here's your chance.'

'Yes.' But he hesitated for a little longer.

She tried to make her expression more encouraging. But he wasn't looking at her anyway. His attention seemed to be held by the weave of the rug. He said, looking at it, not her: 'What I wanted to ask is – will you marry me?'

She sucked in her breath. 'Is this a joke? Because frankly, it's not much of one.'

He looked up quickly. 'God, no – not at all. I couldn't be more serious. Just now. When I was speaking about good luck and all that? You know – hanging on for dear life if it happens to come your way? Actually I was thinking of how we met.' He gave a small half-ashamed smile. 'Only I couldn't bring myself to come right out and say it. Well, you're my bit of good luck, Angel, and I'm asking if I can be yours.'

Very gently he took her hand. He held it as if it was a piece of the most fragile porcelain. His own was warm and dry to the touch. 'I realise there's an awful lot we don't know about each other yet – I know you like both dogs *and* cats but I don't know your favourite colour, or whether you prefer tea or coffee for breakfast. But sometimes it doesn't take any time to know what you want – it happens in a flash. I think I knew everything I needed to about you from the moment we first met – in the shadows at your cousin's dreadful party.' He smiled shyly. 'Love is an excellent conductor of another's soul.'

She stared at him. 'Love?'

'I could reach out my hand and touch it.' He made a grasping gesture with his free hand. 'Can't you feel it too?'

Feel it? Feel that he loved her? She felt giddy, hardly able to breathe. She couldn't think clearly . . . couldn't reply . . . He wanted to marry her . . . Marry *her*?

'Look, I apologise if I've got it wrong,' he said in a different voice when she still didn't answer. 'I thought – I'm sorry. I've made rather a fool of myself, haven't I?' He tried to smile but his face didn't seem to be working properly. 'After all, you're so very young and I – well, I must seem like an old man to you.'

His face had taken on all the lines of tension. She wanted to reach out her hand and wipe the weary lines away. She wanted to say he didn't seem old to her at all – he seemed quite perfect. That she loved all the little laughter lines at the corners of his eyes and the odd flash of silver at his temples. She thought them distinguished and strangely desirable. Very desirable actually. But all she seemed able to do was sit there with her jaw dropped open, one arm stretched limply in front of her, her hand clasped in his, gaping like an idiot.

'We've only known each other a week,' she brought out at last.

'I know, I know,' he groaned. 'Not long enough for you to care about me.'

She shook her head unhappily. 'It's not that. It's just that – well, I can't see how you could possibly – '

'Possibly know what I want in such a short time?' He gave a grim twist of a smile. 'Well, I can. I do. One of the few advantages of age, I expect.'

He let go of her hand and ran his fingers through his hair. 'Oh, this must all seem terribly rushed to you. As if I haven't properly thought it through. But actually I've considered it a lot over the last few days. I really can't impose on St Clare any longer. Which means I'll have to return to town. And after that – well, there's no reason to carry on seeing you unless – Christ!' he said harshly when she simply carried on staring at him, 'do you really have so very much to lose?'

'No, I haven't,' she said miserably. 'I know that.'

'I didn't mean it like that,' he said hastily. 'It's only that I'm sure we could be happy together.'

'It's not that – you feel sorry for me?'

'God, no.'

'Because I think I do love you,' she said, staring at him with big, lost eyes. 'I mean – I do. What I can't understand is what *you* can see in *me*.'

He gave an odd little smile. 'You are silly, Angel.'

Their bodies at an angle, fingers almost touching, her right, his left, they sat for a moment in silence. Angel tried to absorb the full meaning of what was happening. It was all so unbelievable. He was asking her to be his wife. *Alex* was asking her to be his wife. Her throat contracted. She'd live in London and see Alex every single day. She'd be Mrs Sorel. She'd be his *wife*!

She wasn't used to drinking wine at lunchtime. Her head was beginning to throb. Her face felt hot and red and flushed from the sun. *Oh God, I'll never be able to do it*, she thought. *I'll never make him happy.* It didn't cross her mind for a moment to wonder if he could make *her* happy. There was no question in her mind that he could. 'I wish I were more – oh, you know – more sophisticated or something . . . ' she mumbled.

He put a finger beneath her chin and tipped her face up to him. 'I wouldn't love you half as much if you were.'

'I would do anything to be different.'

'Well, please don't,' he frowned. 'I've had enough of sophistic-ation to last a lifetime. I'm sick to the back teeth of it. You're very young and you're very pretty and – ' this next said rather stiltedly – 'it would make me very happy if you'd agree to become my wife.'

'I would like – ' she said, her voice tight to disguise her tears, 'I would *like* to make you happy . . . '

'You will.'

'Will I?' she asked, a catch in her voice.

'Yes. I'm sure of it. Do you know what *I* would like?'

She shook her head.

He gave his sudden smile. 'For you to look at me just as you are right now every single day of my life.'

'How am I looking?'

'Adoring, loving. Like you think I'm absolutely bloody marvellous.'

'I suppose I do.'

'Don't ever stop thinking that,' he said, suddenly serious. 'Don't ever.'

'I won't,' she whispered.

For a moment, he gazed at the curves under her downcast lids. 'I never thought I'd be happy again. I never thought I would be. It's a miracle but after all this time – beyond all my hopes or expectations – at last I've found you. I really have been, you know – ' he said softly – 'Waiting.'

'*Have* you?'

'Oh, yes. I just didn't realise.'

He reached out his arm and held his palm to her flushed face. Keeping it there, he leant forward and rested his mouth on hers. It wasn't so much a kiss as an act of possession, a promise. His mouth was hard and unyielding; she could feel the teeth behind his lips. She felt her nose graze his cheek. When she opened her eyes, her hands were still clasped in her lap and he was looking at her with an unbearably tender expression.

'So that's settled, then? You will marry me?'

She gave a long shiver.

'Yes, please,' she said, her voice still shaky.

*   *   *

Yes, please.

Had she really said that? Yes, *please*? *That* was how she responded to a proposal of marriage? Like he was offering her mashed potatoes rather than boiled? I'd really prefer boiled, if you don't mind, Mr Sorel, oh, yes, yes please. *Don't look now but your desperation's showing* . . .

She couldn't think straight. She was full to the brim with joy, and fear. She hadn't said a word about Alex to anyone. She'd kept him totally and absolutely hidden. She hadn't intended to, but somehow that was the way it had turned out. She'd thought it wouldn't much matter – that he'd soon be leaving Sussex for good. Thought she'd have to nurse a broken heart in secret as she once had her love. Was this how she repaid her aunt and uncle who'd always been so kind? A secret love affair with a much older man?

She felt, like a punch in the stomach, how beastly her conduct had been. She'd lied, shamefully and repeatedly, to her Aunt and Uncle and to Laura. And it was worse. Much worse. She wasn't just hopelessly in love now – it wasn't simply her chance of a few reckless days of heady, unrequited romance. She was *engaged* to him. To Mr Alexander Sorel, yes, that tall, dark man who was her fiancé. You know, the interesting looking one over there in the corner, glowering into his glass, with the impossible charm and intense eyes and the black lock of hair he's always brushing impatiently off his brow? Dark moustache following the line of his mouth – elegantly silvering sideburns? Yes, to him!

It's like the impossible has happened, she thought, something completely and utterly amazing – as if her father had turned up one day after all these years and offered to take her out for lunch. They'd go to a Lyons Corner House and sit at their favourite table on the first floor and she'd tell him that Alex had just proposed to her and she'd said yes – yes please!

Francis and Aunt Edwina won't understand, she thought desperately. Words like 'love' and 'romance' and 'miracle' would mean nothing to them: they'd think them an absurd reason to marry. Honour and duty and sensible, lasting devotion were more the kind of thing they spoke of in that respect. They might even forbid the match altogether like her father's parents had done. Probably will, she thought grimly, given half a chance. They'll think Alex too old, too middle-class – too damned foreign altogether . . .

So she'd kept up the deception. After the first falsehood, the second followed naturally, then the third, and then it was hopeless anyway, the pattern impossible to break without admitting all the original lies. Oh, what a web we weave, she thought miserably. And in between, life carried on as normal. Tennis parties, luncheon parties, teas, suppers, fittings for the bridesmaid's dress, all the paraphernalia of a long country summer. It was easy enough to slip away and meet Alex with the turmoil of Laura's approaching marriage. The whole house was upside down. Even the servants were in a tizz. Angel had only to murmur that she had another fitting or was walking the dog.

What was it that allowed her to so easily break the rules? Their rules, she reminded herself, not mine, not ours. Love, she supposed. First love with all its burning force and intensity that made its own laws. She loved him so much she'd do anything that seemed necessary. His intense, dark eyes filled her mind in everything she did. There was a shivery feeling in the small of her back, a sort of fluttery sensation in the pit of her stomach turning easily to nausea, especially before meals and in the half minute upon waking as reality, in all it's acute, aching meaning, rushed back with a jolt – the glorious, chill thought of Alex.

Alex made her feel whole again; loving him made her feel properly *herself.*

A hundred times she opened her mouth to speak and a hundred times she closed it again. Her spirits lurched between shame and irrational optimism. Guilt settled on Angel like a steady, constant ache in her gut. She'd built her house of cards up high and it might tumble down around her ears at any moment.

Secrets and lies seem to be my forté, she told herself accusingly – or was that only later when the tapestry of her whole life was already beginning to unravel with only the first and tightest knot of deceit remaining intact? Because just then, if she were honest, she was more or less filled to the brim with a strange wild happiness. She felt deliriously happy and sick with guilt.

It was inexcusable. She was behaving like a mad woman she knew.

5

Regent's Park, London. 17 November 1946. 1:05 a.m.

It was all wrong. He'd known it as soon as he opened the front door. The house was too quiet. He pulled his key out of the lock and called, 'Hel–lo? Anyone home?' But he already knew there'd be no answer.

He set his leather overnight bag on the white stone floor and stood for a moment in the hall, puzzled, listening to silence.

As silent as the bloody tomb, he thought, trudging up the stairs.

The bedroom was empty. No clothes in the wardrobe, all the surfaces stripped bare. In the other room, the bed had been made in a hurry – the silk quilt hung lopsidedly over the edge. Sea-green, her favourite colour. Pale green tinted walls, parquet floor, a silvery-green silk armchair on a cream rug near the fireplace. The only thing on the mantelpiece was an enormous piece of marble curved like a shell. The white lilies on the table were long dead.

He picked the flowers out of the vase and looked around for a wastepaper bin while stinking green water dripped onto the rug. She hadn't slept here for several nights, he was sure of it. Even the air had the cold remote feel of absence. He'd started off angry, now he began to feel frightened. She was gone. Where? She had nowhere to go.

Christ, he thought anxiously – what's she up to this time?

He chucked the flowers into the bin and began searching methodically, starting at one side of the room and moving across to the other. In the fitted closet, dresses. Mostly black of course – a chinchilla wrap, a couple of ankle length fur coats, one fox, one sable, and a pair of black velvet boots lined with sable to match. Rows of shoes, some never worn. He ran a hand lightly along the top shelf. A pair of long black suede gloves, a tiny fur hat, a red beret, no, two – what on earth did she want two for? Sheets and sheets of fine blue tissue paper – nothing else.

Her perfume caught in his throat as he slid the doors shut – Shalimar. His heart gave a slow throb at the familiar musky scent.

On top of the dressing-table were small cut-glass bottles, gold initialled brushes and combs all sprinkled with powder, and the same clutter inside the drawers. He rummaged though trinkets, endless perfumed rubbish, then turned to the bedside table. Address book, unfilled pen, a cardboard box of sleeping powders. On the label: 'One powder to be taken at bedtime.' He shook it – empty.

Cigarette butts in the ashtray, three smeared with lipstick, two without. That stopped him in his tracks for a moment. He picked up the ashtray and stared with distaste at the half-smoked stubs twisted together in it. A sudden flash – her lying flat, breast rising and falling with the regular breathing of sleep, long dark hair tangled on the pillow. Perhaps she was in another bed screwing someone else right now . . . perhaps beneath rumpled silken sheets passionately kissing him . . .

He closed his eyes, trying to escape the sudden image.

If only it were that simple, he thought.

Lying face down by the ashtray was a silver-framed photograph of them both, taken on the island just a few months after they'd met. She was laughing, one arm hooked around his neck, dark curls tied back. Her smile was dazzling; his, caught unawares, was almost savage in its intensity. His mouth smiled while his eyes remained distant. Guarded. Things had been better then, he thought, hadn't they? Now, examining the image, he wondered if that were true.

He stood looking down at the photograph. Then, pushing the wooden strut back with one finger, set it back on the table, upright this time.

By the door was a tall cherrywood chest of drawers. He hesitated, but only for a moment. Black stockings, black lacey suspenders and lacey lingerie, a whole drawer of silk pyjamas, another full of softest cashmere. There was a certain grim pleasure in tipping the whole lot onto the floor in a tangled heap.

In the fourth drawer down he found what he was searching for. The photographs. Ten glossy A4 prints all of the same subject – a man and a woman in a restaurant, recorded in shiny black and white. His hand on the small of her back as they cross the smoky room; touching her elbow before pulling out a chair for her; her head bent close to his over the table. The way they were looking at one another, like they could eat each other up. It didn't take much to imagine the rest, he thought grimly.

He sat down heavily on the bed, feeling slightly sick, averting his eyes from the photos on his knee. Although he'd been expecting the images, they still gave him a shock. What the hell was going on? An empty house but she'd left the bloody photographs. It didn't make sense. At least the sense it was beginning to make was too enormous to consider yet.

He walked downstairs, unfastened the leather bag he'd left on the mat and packed the black-and-white prints on top of his carefully folded clothes – they fitted smoothly if he left the zip half open – then hoisted the long strap onto his shoulder. He had switched off the lights, locked the front door and was settling the bag on the seat of the car when it occurred to him to try Rachel. He looked at his watch. It was still early. Not even properly light yet. Yes, she'd be home.

He slammed the car door shut and walked back up the stone steps into the house.

The overhead light in the drawing room wasn't working. The bulb must have gone. He tried it twice then clicked on the tall alabaster lamp instead. The telephone was on the table next to it. When she answered, Rachel's voice sounded tired, the accent more pronounced. Her tone changed when she heard it was him. 'Oh, it's you. She's dead.'

His mouth went dry. 'When?' he asked, sitting down suddenly on the sofa.

'Monday night. Well, Tuesday morning to be precise. At twenty past twelve. That's when they called me anyway.'

'Suicide?'

She didn't speak for a moment. Then, 'Yes, suicide,' she said.

'How? How did she – '

'Ask the doctor,' she said wearily. Then, suddenly angry, 'Like the last time. An overdose. Brandy and sleeping pills. Just for old times' sake, she threw in half a bottle of aspirins. And this time – '

He held his breath. 'Yes?'

'This time she almost succeeded.'

'Almost?' A croak not a word.

'Almost but not quite. She's not dead yet.'

'So why the hell say – '

'She's just hanging by a thread, that's why.'

'Did she mean it?'

'Barbiturates? Oh yes, she meant it. Apparently on the slim chance she pulls through she'll have severely damaged her liver. Likelihood is that barbiturates will do that to you if you try to overdose on them and fail. The moral is – don't fail.' She gave a short mirthless laugh.

'You mean – they'll prosecute this time if she lives?'

'Actually no, that's not what I meant. That isn't what I meant at all. I've been with her all night at the hospital since you weren't. This is all your fault,' she said, suddenly bitter. 'You do realise that, don't you?'

His throat locked. He couldn't breathe. He put the phone down without saying goodbye. He sat there, slowly drawing in air, staring down at his hands clasped loosely between his legs, his mind blank.

I am free, he thought dully after a moment. *If she is dead, then I am free.*

*   *   *

There was an unopened bottle of whisky in the drawing room cabinet. He was amazed to find it. The others, as he expected, were all empties. He examined the label. Cheap and nasty. Gut rot. Why? She had enough money to buy something decent, didn't she? He took a long gulp straight from the bottle, then wiped his mouth with the back of his hand and screwed the top back on.

Bottle pressed against his chest, he took the stairs steadily, pulling his knotted tie over his head, ripping apart the buttons of his shirt with his free hand. By the time he reached the bathroom he was stripped down to his shorts, leaving a trail of clothes strewn behind him. He set the bottle down carefully on the tiles just inside the door and, naked, turned the handle of the shower hard. Without testing the water he stepped underneath.

Dead.

He stood beneath the tap, too-hot water pumping down on his upturned face, flattening the hairs on his chest, streaming down his belly, his groin, his thighs, raining down on his large ungainly feet.

Safe, he was safe.

It was some time before he swished aside the oil-silk curtain and stepped out. Still dripping, he took the door through to the bedroom and lay down on the bed. The skin of his fingertips and toes were wrinkled like prunes.

He closed his eyes, the lids flickering.

Once, when he was a child on holiday at his mother's house in the south, he'd seen a dead cat. Bella. Her body had been found at the side of the road by sheer chance. He'd watched as they'd put Bella's stiff body into a sack and buried her under the vine trees. In life, she'd always sat in the same spot, drowsing in the heat under the green louvred windows. For three nights after she'd been buried, her son, black Enzo, took her place. There he crouched, very still, tail curled, paws tucked, green eyes half shut, before taking to his old haunts again. He'd often wondered later – was it grief that had drawn Enzo irresistibly to his dead mother's place? Or triumph?

There was a dirty glass on the bedside table. Round the bottom, a circle of dried white scum. He didn't bother to rinse it out but poured neat whisky straight on top. He lay in the empty house, propped up on the pale green pillows, arms by his sides, palms up, legs straight, prick limp, chilled by the water drying on his skin. Except to pour another drink he kept his eyes closed. Next to him, spread out on the bed, were the glossy black-and-white photos. He didn't look at them, he kept his eyes shut, but by his side he kept that other picture – the framed likeness of them both taken on the island six years earlier, laughing, still happy.

Now that was a year, he thought, smiling crookedly, already a little drunk. 'That was a fucking year,' he said aloud, the smile twisting. 'If you'll excuse the pun.'

And the memories when they came were as scalding hot as boiling water, as rough as the liquid gold in his glass. The alcohol didn't blur his thoughts, not even slightly. Image after burning image. It was like having someone else's memories, not his own –

like watching a movie in which he, a stranger to himself, played the lead role. Even now, he didn't want to admit there had been nothing like it for him, before or since. Nothing that came even close to those days on the island, with her.

There had been no boundaries, no limits to their love. He had shocked himself by the savagery of his desire, hated her for her acquiescence, her abandon. Fucking, sucking, pissing, loving, those dark eyes looking up at him, beautiful, willing. Eyes you could drown in. And he had. Oh, yes, he'd drowned. Gone right down to the very depths. *And* survived. Every night a sweet ferocious heat, a wild longing that nothing but her body could satiate, nothing but her supple, eager body. Every morning, disgust. There was nothing like it in all the world, nothing.

He set the glass down on the floor a little crookedly so that it overbalanced. Cheap whisky spilled onto the cream rug, he didn't notice. He raised a hand to his cheek, feeling the wetness on his stubble. He was weeping he realised. Hot tears were squeezing out from beneath his closed lids and running down his cheek. He was back on the island, he was drowning in memories, oh, drowned.

*   *   *

Red-eyed and bleary, he locked the front door behind him. It made no difference – outside he still heard her song. *I'm your dream, I am your destruction, I'm every fantasy you ever had.* Heard her wild laughter – *I am your hope and your despair* . . . Her voice echoed through the silent streets. *Set you free? You'll be lucky.*

In death she has triumphed, he thought, driving too fast up the road. Oh, yes, the snake-haired woman is dead. She is dead and I am free. He was almost persuaded, almost blinded by his tears. He had to wait through two sets of lights before he could see properly.

'Let her be dead,' he prayed as he sat there. 'Please. Let her be dead. It would be better for everyone.'

The hospital was in St. John's Wood. As he let out the clutch he realised he'd forgotten the photographs. He'd left all ten prints behind on the crumpled sea-green silk quilt.

He went through on amber, not caring.

6

ANGEL

Haywards Heath, West Sussex. June 1950

Alex had been married before but hadn't seen his ex-wife in years. He'd told Angel shortly after they'd become engaged. He thought it only right, he'd said with a smile, that she should know exactly what she was getting into. It meant their own wedding would be small, probably only a registrar's office – did she mind? No, of course she didn't, of *course* not.

'I haven't exactly been a saint,' he admitted, 'there have been other women.' He grimaced. 'Rather a lot, I suppose. Though marriage was never on the cards,' he added quickly, seeing her expression. 'Until now.'

She hadn't liked to question him about his first marriage too closely, especially since he'd said quite categorically that there was no reason to talk much about it. He'd been young and foolish, he'd made a mistake. That was the beginning and end of it: a mistake.

It had been shortly before the outbreak of war when fighting was beginning to seem inevitable. It had seemed hard to die without leaving anyone behind to mourn you except for your mother. So, quickly and thoughtlessly, he'd married. 'A common enough tale,' he said, with a movement of bitter carelessness.

But he'd survived – here he'd smiled – he'd lived to fight another day. The marriage, unfortunately, hadn't. They'd barely lived together, just a few weeks in total. After the divorce, he'd never seen her again. They'd gone their separate ways. He had no idea where she was now or what she was doing, none whatsoever. He didn't know if he'd even recognise her if he passed her in the street.

'Oh, but surely, Alex – ' Angel admonished him, siding for a moment with all the lost women in the world, all the estranged and rejected women – 'surely you *would*. It seems so terrible not to. You were once married to her, after all, however briefly.'

'Well, I'm not so sure. By now she might be enormously fat – or scraggy and thin – '

Angel giggled. 'Or have dyed her hair.'

'Well, she might.'

'Bright red,' she suggested. 'Blue!'

'Why not? A pale blue rinse? *Very* nice. You see, she'll be middle-aged by now, perhaps – ' here a slight smile – 'with a brood of grown-up children. She may have gone back to Germany, for all I know. Probably has.'

'Is that where you met? In Germany?'

'Yes.' His dark eyes flickered. 'Berlin.'

'It must have been tough for her,' Angel acknowledged, 'once war broke out. She wouldn't have been able to contact any of her family or friends. Her loyalties must have been torn. She must have sometimes wished she hadn't been forced to leave everything behind so completely when she left her own country to marry you.'

'Actually, no,' he said shortly. 'She was very glad to leave. She's Jewish. Things were hard for her even before war was declared.'

'Getting a Jewess out of Nazi Germany? *That* couldn't have been easy.'

'It wasn't.'

She looked at him in admiration. 'It's not an exaggeration to say that you saved her.'

He laughed. 'From a fate worse than death? Some might say I brought that on her. Smoke?' He offered her a cigarette and, when she nodded, lit it for her.

They were sheltering from the sun in the little bar-parlour of the Red Lion Hotel that hot afternoon. There was only one other person there, an old man in a flat tweed cap, his pint glass on the scarred dark wood counter in front of him. From behind a frosted glass screen which divided the bar from the hotel a radio was playing very quietly.

'How did you meet in the first place?' she asked, while Alex was lighting a cigarette for himself.

'I was introduced to her.'

69

'Who by?'

'Do you know, I can't remember. One of her schoolfriends, I think. Might have been Antoinette Meyer . . . ' He considered for a second, frowning. 'Yes, I remember now. It was. Antoinette Meyer – God, *that's* a name from the past.' He looked amused. 'I wonder what she's doing now?'

Angel felt a sudden fierce stab of jealousy. Unreasonable she knew, since she'd have only been about four or five at the time. But she couldn't help sounding thoughtful as she said: 'You must have once loved her very much – I mean, to go through all that for her.'

His face tightened. 'I suppose I briefly thought so. But only *very* briefly. I did try to make it work. And to be fair to her, I suppose she did too. It's no use blaming anyone. She was a perfectly nice woman, just not the right one for me.'

One more question. Angel couldn't resist asking just one before dutifully dropping the subject forever. 'What's her name, Alex?'

'Zara,' he answered, after an almost imperceptible pause. 'Maiden name – Hoffman. Of course I don't know what she calls herself these days. Now, if you *don't* mind, that's quite enough on that subject. It all happened a very long time ago but the memory's still raw. I find it quite painful to speak about.' He gave a wise and melancholy smile. 'Failure always is, isn't it?'

Angel nodded, sympathetic. It must have been awful for him to have been tied to someone he didn't love. But he didn't blame or criticise Zara Hoffman, even for a moment. She reached across and silently took his hand.

'You needn't worry about my ex-wife,' he said, smiling a little sadly into sympathetic grey eyes. 'She doesn't exist for me any more.'

'In what way – not exist?'

'Not in any way whatsoever,' he answered firmly, thus ending the conversation.

But, sitting in the same stuffy low-ceilinged bar almost two weeks later, the subject of marriage cropped up again.

'Look, I don't know how to put this nicely but I'm getting a little tired of all this – ' Alex announced, removing his hat while he watched himself in the mottled mirror advertising Gilbey's Gin next to them and she admired his profile – 'Not to put too fine a point on it, I'm really rather bored.'

Alarmed, Angel swung her gaze back to him. '*Are* you?'

' 'Fraid so.'

'Of – of what exactly?'

'Well, all of it.'

'Of *me*?'

'No, of course not. Of lukewarm beer and endless cups of tea. Of all of this – ' he gestured round the cheerless room – 'I'm too old for it. Too old and out of practice. As it happens, my mother telephoned yesterday. Asked if I was intending to visit this summer. I said, yes, I was. But the whole thing became suddenly clear. We should get married sooner rather than later and travel to Italy on our honeymoon. Take in Venice whilst we're there.'

She took a gulp of beer. Swallowed. 'When?'

'Well, I thought – August?'

'In a month?'

'More like six weeks. Seven nearly. Shouldn't take much longer to organise, should it?'

She put the glass down carefully. Then, even more carefully, lined it up with the edge of the table. 'No, I shouldn't think it would,' she said slowly. 'And Venice in August – ' she gazed down bleakly at her knuckles – 'will be awfully nice.' But despite her attempt to conceal it, she could hear the wobble of fear in her voice.

'Well, I don't know about that,' he said, apparently not hearing it, too. 'Uncomfortably hot and sticky in late summer I always find. But that aside, I see no reason to hang about. On the contrary, I see every reason *not* to. Do you?'

'No – absolutely none at all.'

'Think it over.'

*   *   *

An imaginary scenario that had Angel sweating between the sheets that night:

Alex, white-faced and furious, demanding: 'Were they that easy to deceive? I did *wonder* why Francis Merlowe hadn't asked to meet me. Well, now I know. The man knows sod all about me.'

Or worse – 'Are you ashamed of me? Is that it? Am I too old or something? Am I not quite *your sort*?'

'No, Alex . . . no, no, no . . .'

'Then why haven't you told your family about us yet?'

Yes, why hadn't she? Angel kicked off the blanket and climbed out of bed. Once relief had subsided, anger and self-disgust quickly took its place. She was being cowardly and deceitful and, without really meaning to, downright cruel.

He doesn't deserve this, she thought. He doesn't deserve any more bad luck or disappointment in his life. He's had enough already. What he needs is to be loved and looked after till the hurt look has gone from his eyes.

He was going to France on business for a few days, he'd told her later that same afternoon. Not for long, three days at most. She'd talk to the Merlowes while he was away. At least Laura would understand and be happy for her. Angel felt her chest lighten at the thought.

*　　*　　*

But of course Laura wasn't the slightest bit happy when she told her about Alex; not happy at all. Angel hadn't expected her to be quite so totally and unrelentingly angry. Stupidly, she realised now, staring into Laura's wide, shocked eyes.

'You're pulling my leg,' she said, staring at Angel in stunned disbelief.

Who were this man's people? Exactly where were they from? No, she bloody well didn't believe in love at first sight, but she did believe in *lust* at first sight, especially amongst foreigners who were cut out for that kind of thing and, frankly, she found it vulgar and disgusting. She hadn't expected this from Angel. She was behaving like – like an alley cat.

'You know what really sticks in my throat? To live so closely to you and never even *notice*. I thought you were taking the dog for long walks and all the time – this. Lucky old dog, I thought. Kind, thoughtful Angel.' She gave hard unfriendly laugh. 'I feel rather a fool actually.'

'Look, I know this isn't the way you do things. I know that you and Edward – '

'Edward and I have known each other since childhood. Don't even *think* of bringing him into this. Don't bloody *dare*.'

'I believe that two people can meet and realise straight away that they're made for one another. Don't you believe in soul mates? You said you did the other day.'

'That was in a book,' Laura said sharply. 'It was fiction. Not real life. Because love's not like that. Not really. You can't simply *invent* what someone's like. You have to discover it. Which takes a hell of a lot longer than five or six weeks. Oh, look, go out with him if he's so frightfully dishy,' she reasoned at the end of a long and desperate few hours. They were in her bedroom by now, sitting stiffly opposite each other on dusky pink wicker chairs in the window. 'Meet his family and his friends, get to know him better. But for God's sake don't go rushing headlong into marriage. Wait a few months – find out a bit more,' she almost begged. 'If he's halfway decent, he'll understand.'

Angel's lips were trembling so much she could barely bring out the words. 'But I don't need to find out any more. I just know in my heart this is right. I just know.'

'You can't just *know*.'

Angel thought of how she'd felt in Alex's arms – the roughness of his stubble against her cheek, the smell of his skin and texture of his hair, the taste of his mouth and lips. *Yes, you can*, she thought. Looking at Laura, she thought how long ago it seemed since they'd stood together at the top of the staircase gazing down at the party below and Laura had made a bet with her that 'something wonderful's going to happen to you tonight.' She was tempted to say – 'I owe you half a crown.'

Instead, she said: 'This is it for me, Laura. I love him. The extraordinary thing is – he feels the same way. He doesn't want to wait any longer. And I don't either. You see – he needs me.'

'What a very strange reason to marry.'

Angel shrugged.

Laura searched her face for a moment. 'You really mean it, don't you? You really intend to jump straight in and go ahead with this.'

'Yes,' Angel said coldly. 'I do.' She looked back at Laura's white stiff face and her stomach contracted. *Listen to me*, she thought. *What a bitch I sound.* She said helplessly: 'I'm sorry.'

'Sorry? For God's sake, Angel.'

And the whole horrible scene had ended with Laura springing up from the chair with a swish of her skirt and saying: 'Here. This is yours. I think you're bloody well going to need it.' Dropping the handkerchief still damp from her tears into Angel's lap, she added spitefully: 'You barely know this man. This will end in *disaster.*'

A view fortunately not shared by her father. 'May I have a word, Angel? About a long distance call I received this morning from Mr Sorel? I'll be in the garden after luncheon. That all right?'

Found by Angel, her mouth dry and feeling sick, sitting in a striped deckchair under the shady branches of a spreading chestnut tree in a battered straw hat, reading an old, scarred copy of the *Field*.

For a few minutes – Angel had no idea how many, it could have been two or twenty – neither of them spoke. The whole experience with Laura had been so harrowing she wasn't even sure how to start. Sitting in the cool grass at his feet, she struggled to find the right words. How could she explain that she'd never intended to hurt anyone, how desperately sorry she was that she had and, at the same time, admit she would have done anything to see Alex, whatever the consequences? She felt incredibly guilty and looked, as a result, stubborn and defiant.

'I'm sorry but . . . well, I didn't see I had much choice . . . '

'Oh, there are always choices, Angel,' Francis said grimly.

But thrashing round that night between tangled sheets, she grinned to herself remembering their parting conversation.

He'd taken a pipe from his jacket pocket and pressed some tobacco into the bowl. 'I remember your father very well at the age you are now,' he'd begun, breaking a long silence. 'He was a bit older than me and always seemed terribly grown up and dashing and brave. There were four years between us that seemed a great deal then and so very little now. I was always trying to catch him up.' He sighed. 'I was very fond of Evelyn.'

He'd put the pipe in his mouth and began patting his pockets for the matches. She'd made a muted gesture. 'They're on the ground by your feet.'

'Oh, yes, so they are. Thank you, my dear.'

He sucked on the pipe once or twice, then struck a match to light it. Brown smoke drifted up in the air under the trees. The dark post-war tobacco had a rank, rather musty smell. 'I've always thought that your grandparents had a great deal to answer for,' he said thoughtfully, puffing on the pipe. 'I'd hate to wake up one day and find I'd done the same thing.'

'What do you mean?'

'Refused to let you marry the man you'd chosen.'

Her eyes widened. 'You mean – '

'I can't promise anything more till I meet Mr Sorel and hear what this man of yours has to say,' he warned. 'But I received rather a decent letter this morning from his legal firm detailing his financial circumstances in full. Obviously of some concern since you have a little money yourself. Or will when you're twenty-one. However, they tell me – and I quote – Mr Sorel is amply provided for. Apparently, his father's family was rather well off. Of course, this will have to be looked into further – ' He pulled at his ear lobe – 'But it all seems quite satisfactory so far.'

'Oh, thank you! Thank you, thank you!'

'I hope you really have something to thank me for one day,' Francis had replied gravely. 'If you change your mind, tell me,' he'd said, still serious, watching her as she stood up. 'No one would in the least bit mind.'

'Oh, I won't because I really do – ' But her throat closed up and she couldn't say any more.

She'd dropped a kiss on his forehead and walked across the grass towards Longlands. Walking, she remembered, rather unsteadily, as if she were a little bit drunk.

*   *   *

Angel didn't remember much about her actual wedding day. It was as though she'd become briefly short sighted, everything happening in a blur. It had rained, she recalled later. The heatwave that had begun so brilliantly on the morning of Laura's engagement party had broken finally and it wasn't just rainy, it was cold. Her wedding dress had clung damply to her legs.

They had gone back to Longlands after the registry office, a rather solemn party of thirteen – Uncle Francis and Aunt Margaret, Laura and Edward, Richard, the St Clares. Alex had insisted on providing glasses of pale gold champagne. There was an air, if not of happiness exactly, then of restrained celebration. Angel must have downed a glass or two of wine because she could remember the woozy way she'd felt in the car, her head lolling back against the smooth cream leather seat.

She recalled getting in with Alex and driving off. She was so happy she hadn't even turned to wave goodbye. Not even a backwards glance at the house or the Merlowes. They must have been drenched, she thought afterwards. Or, more likely, dashed inside before the rain began in earnest.

Further down the drive, Alex had jumped out to fix up the car's hood. As he climbed back in, it had started bucketing down. They stared out the windscreen at the wind blowing white sheets across the lawn.

'Look at that,' he commented. 'A typical English summer. Just as well we're leaving it a long way behind.' He reached out his arm to put the car into gear. He'd had raindrops on his face, she remembered later, large sparkling drops, like tears.

7

ANGEL

Venice, Italy. August 1950

Post-war Italy was full of beautiful but destroyed cities, a garden of
ruined buildings and little shattered squares. Angel was used to
bomb damage in England but this seemed quite different, both
better and worse – the damage had been mostly caused by American
rather than German bombs.

They'd spent a few days sightseeing in Rome, then driven
through Tuscany, stopping to sleep in the little villages set in the
hills amongst olive groves, or eat delicious prosciutto and pepper
sandwiches on Italian white bread for lunch. Through the car's
open windows Angel could feel the sun baking down. The land was
parched and hazy with heat, the valleys scorched brown. When the
sun went down it was still hot, hotter even at night than at midday
on a summer's day in England.

They saw women in black, shawls covering their heads and
skinny dark, bare-foot children who stopped and stared in sudden
silence as the wheels of the car stirred up sprays of brown dust.
Foreigners were rare outside the cities, cars even rarer. A hundred
times a day Angel would stop and look at Alex. He'd be twisting
and turning along the dusty roads, eyes narrowed against the
glaring light, or lighting a cigarette after dinner, or stepping onto
the balcony of their room to linger in the balmy evening breeze.
She loved him so completely it made her almost feel sick. She felt
like she had loved him all her life without knowing it.

'I'm not dreaming am I?' she asked, as they sat in the shade of a
fig tree one afternoon, protected from the fierce sun. Because it did
seem a bit like a dream. But when she looked across the white-
clothed table, there was Alex stretched out in a chair, drinking the
sour local *vino*, looking relaxed and happy.

'No,' he said, suddenly serious. 'You couldn't be more awake.'

When she looked in the mirror she saw an unfamiliar face – the same thin oval but tanned by the sun, surrounded by long blonde slightly bleached hair, grey eyes brilliant.

She lost track of the days. 'Funny that there's no one around,' she commented as they stepped out of the car one morning into a little cobbled square. An hour before noon the heat was already fierce. The sun burned down, white and hot on the stones. Ahead of them was an improvised café with two wobbly tables covered in dusty white cloths but it was empty. 'Where is everyone? Having an early siesta?'

'They're at church, my darling.'

'Church? On a Saturday?'

'It's Sunday.'

'Oh, is it? Is it really?'

'Uh huh. We should get to Venice tomorrow.'

Angel's heart sank. They'd been enclosed in their own space for three wonderful weeks – now they were entering the real world again. She said too brightly, too forced: 'Will we?'

'I'll telephone this evening to let my mother know when we'll be arriving,' he said, not noticing her change of mood.

He telephoned from Seronto, a small village high in the hills surrounded by crumbling golden brick walls. The hotel was the only complete building in the little shattered square. They ate outside on the veranda next to a mountain of rubble, the sunlight hazed with dust. But Venice was perfect, a city untouched, as if the war had never happened. It was dark by the time they arrived, wandering over a maze of bridges and alleys through the crowds down to the waterfront and hired a gondola. As they rounded a bend in the boat, the many twinkling lights of the Grand Canal disappeared, the water rippled blackly against the sides. From her seat, Angel stared up at a marble palazzo. Pink marble, she saw next morning.

'It's wonderful, Alex. Did you come here for school holidays?'

'Oh no – this was given her by a friend many years afterwards.'

'Some friend.'

He shrugged. 'A lover, I expect.'

She tried for a moment to imagine what his mother would look like, be like. 'Was she *very* beautiful?'

'Very.'

'Dark like you?'

'Once. Very long black hair. More a silvery-grey now. You'll see.'

The narrow boat was tied to a post at the bottom of high stone steps. The moon had gone behind a cloud and a high wall bent forward so that Angel couldn't see anything much above them except a sheer rise of dark brick, weeds sprouting from between the cracks, and the spikey branch of a small tree jutting out from the top. Little waves of black water splashed over the stone.

Alex climbed out first and said something to the boatman before reaching out his hand to help Angel. The steps were ill lit and slippery. He gripped her hand tightly. 'Be careful,' he warned. 'Watch your footing.'

Behind them, she could hear the light, sure tread of the gondolier following them up with their bags. Alex pressed a lira note into his hand. '*Grazie, signor, grazie, grazie,*' the boatman called. Soon Angel could hear only the rhythmic splash of his pole as he ferried the boat away and the lapping of the water against the wall. Below her feet, she could see the dark water slipping by.

Alex stooped to brush moss from his trousers. 'Our stuff will be collected later – we needn't lug it with us now. Come along. It's damp out here.'

She followed him across a small shadowed courtyard. Oil lamps cast a flickering light, making strange, jumping shadows over the stone-flagged ground. Alex stood before an immense black door studded with brass nails and yanked an iron bell hanging at the side. In the distance, they heard it jangle out.

Angel hung back a little. She could feel a growing weight like a stone in her stomach. The eerie light, the palazzo surrounded by dank, dark water, mixed with fears of her soon to be met mother-in-law unnerved her completely.

The heavy door creaked as it opened. A slight, middle-aged man in tight black trousers and an embroidered waistcoat stood before them. He gave a wide smile of recognition when he saw Alex. '*Buona sera, signore,*' he said with a little, formal bow.

'*Buona sera*, Fabrizio.'

The man stepped back and gestured inside.

The hall was vast even by Italian standards and dimly lit by candles in iron sconces on the walls. A great staircase of polished stone rose up into darkness. Worn smooth by the centuries, the stairs dipped towards the middle, then slanted gently up again. They followed Fabrizio into the *salone*, a large, high-ceilinged room plastered in what appeared to be palest blue with unshuttered windows overlooking the water. The moon had come out from behind the clouds and the rippling water of the canal shone silver in the moonlight.

A huge wrought iron chandelier hanging from the ceiling had been wired to hold electric bulbs. Fabrizio clicked a switch by the door and the room was suddenly flooded with harsh yellow light. He made a remark in Italian.

'*Si, si, grazie,*' Alex replied.

Fabrizio gave a dignified bow from the hips and left the room.

Along one window stretched a sofa covered in pale blue silk. They sat on it and Alex lit a cigarette. He had half smoked it when Fabrizio returned carrying an espresso coffee pot on an engraved silver tray. Setting a starched white doily on a wooden table he poured about an inch of coffee into two little brown glazed cups. Straightening, he said something in Italian.

'My mother won't be long,' Alex translated.

Angel's stomach lurched. 'Oh – good,' she said distantly.

As she leant forward to pick up the cup, she caught a glimpse of herself in a huge, ornately framed mirror on the far wall – hair lank and uncombed, face sunburnt and tight with nerves. She drank a mouthful of bitter coffee.

A slight sound made her glance towards the opposite end of the room. A tall, beautifully dressed woman was walking towards them. She wore a silver grey chintz evening dress with an enormous skirt which rustled as she walked, diamond earrings and a wide bracelet of diamonds encircling one wrist. Her silvery-white hair was scraped back into a chignon, she had large, heavy-lidded eyes, a small, perfectly straight nose and her cheekbones were prominent over attractive hollows. As she drew nearer, Angel could see she was older than she'd first appeared. There was a fine network of lines on the lovely face.

Stubbing out his cigarette, Alex rose to his feet. Getting up too, Angel returned her cup and saucer to the tray. Unsure what to do with her hands, she clasped them behind her back. Alex walked towards his mother.

She said: '*Mon fils . . .* '

He lent towards her. Her lips passed a fraction of an inch from both of his cheeks in turn. 'Hello, Mother,' he said.

'*Laisse-moi te regarder un moment.*' His mother drew back and examined him. Then, in English, with a rueful accusing look and only the faintest of accents: 'It is gratifying to see you looking so well, Alexander.'

Angel's heart was thumping. Behind her back, she could feel her palms beginning to sweat. She forced her lips into a stiff smile. Madame Sorel was talking rapidly in French, gesticulating and laughing at something Alex had said. Her laugh rang out, a musical sound, clear and confident. Angel stood in the magnificent room in front of the powder blue sofa, smiling foolishly, listening to them speaking in a language she couldn't follow very well, feeling completely out of place. They looked so right together, so tall, so straight, so *different.* Now they were almost on top of her, Alex looking straight at her. But not at her exactly – he seemed to be looking *through* her, and his eyes were dark, opaque, foreign. Eyes she didn't recognise and which didn't recognise her. She felt a sudden panic. He didn't see her, not really. He was looking at, but not seeing, her. In that moment, she had the strange dizzying feeling that *she did not exist.*

They stopped in front of her. Close-up his mother was still incredibly beautiful. 'So – ' she said, smiling graciously – 'this is Angel.'

'It's awfully nice to meet you, Mrs – Signora – ' Angel faltered – 'Madame Sorel.'

His mother scrutinised her closely for what seemed a very long time. Her pale blue eyes had lightened round the edges of the iris to a paler, lighter blue. Her welcoming smile did not seem to reach them. Angel felt herself burning dull red beneath the sunburn of her cheeks under that critical gaze. Her heart was thudding against her ribs and her jaw ached from the unnatural, protracted smile. She wasn't sure what to do. She had to resist the desire to curtsey.

'Angel . . . ' his mother murmured. 'But that is a shortening for something I am sure.' She smiled encouragingly. 'For – ?'

'For Angelica,' Alex supplied quickly.

'Angelica? But that is so pretty. Why spoil it?'

She took Angel's hand and held it high in the air between them. Her own felt so delicate it could have been made of fine, white paper. Angel desperately hoped hers weren't too obviously sweaty. She was sure beads of perspiration had broken out on her brow.

'Charming,' his mother said. 'Quite charming.' She turned to Alex. 'I congratulate you. The girl is lovely – *Une Belle Anglaise.*' Still smiling, she withdrew her hand. 'Dinner has already begun, of course. I hope you will join us. Or perhaps you have dined already?'

'No, we haven't eaten. We're starving, aren't we, darling?'

'Oh yes – yes, we are.'

Alex's mother nodded. 'I will inform the cook. Fabrizio will show you to your room. You can wash the dust off there. *Quand tu es prêt descends à la salle à manger*, Alexander.'

The bedroom Fabrizio showed them to was enormous. It had a huge black four-poster carved with nymphs and cherubs with an embroidered canopy, several brocaded armchairs, a pear wood escritoire and the heavy tapestry curtains were pulled across high arched windows. Their bags had already been unpacked.

Alex yawned, throwing his jacket onto an armchair. 'We dress for dinner here, I'm afraid.'

'What do you think I should wear?' Angel asked anxiously.

'Oh, a little black frock will be fine.'

'But, Alex, I don't *have* a little black frock.'

'No? Then you must get one. It will come in very handy.'

'That's all very well,' Angel said, nervousness making her irritable, 'but what should I wear *now*?'

'Oh, I don't know . . . anything will do,' Alex said carelessly, pulling a white tie from a drawer.

Opening the magnificent wardrobe, Angel examined a turquoise moiré frock swaying on a hanger besides three others dresses. They all seemed wrong. She decided on the chiffon. The creases didn't show too badly and it looked the most appropriate. If not suitable exactly, then, at least, not completely *un*suitable. It was white and very faintly patterned with roses and green leaves; shorter than the others, just above the knee, the skirt was fuller. At home, she'd thought it perfect but examining it now, it seemed almost dowdy. Perhaps if she flounced it out a bit . . .

'Here, let me do that,' Alex said, glancing over at her as she fumbled with the back buttons. 'This is a bloody bore, I know. But there's really no avoiding it. Mother expects it of us.'

'Oh, but I *like* it, darling, honestly.'

'Do you?' He offered her his arm. 'We'll get you a decent evening dress as soon as we're back in London, I promise.'

Her arm linked through his, they walked down the polished stone staircase and through a number of high, echoing rooms, finally halting at one where a long oak table had been set for dinner. A huge display of fruit piled high in a bowl stood in the centre and two great silver candelabra were placed at either end. The tall windows were open and, though the night was still, a sudden breeze coming into the room with them made the flames on the candles grow long and flickering. They shed soft, flattering light onto nine or ten people. Angel had a general impression of bare shoulders and expensive dresses, waistcoats, white ties and hair piled high. They all fell silent and turned disconcertingly to stare as she and Alex entered.

'*J'ai le plaisir de vous présenter mon fils et son épouse* – Angelica,' Madame Sorel swiftly informed the table. Everyone murmured, flashing smiles.

The chiffon was definitely wrong, Angel decided, looking around at the other guests – frumpy and creased. She'd forgotten to ask Alex what she should call his mother. Signora Sorel? Madame? How unbelievable stupid of her. She wrapped her arms round herself feeling horribly self-conscious. She wished –

'Angelica – you are to sit besides me,' Diane Sorel ordered, gesturing to the empty chair next to her. 'Alexander – there is a place for you besides your old friend, Simonetta.' She waved her hand towards a voluptuous dark-haired woman with bright red lipstick and scarlet fingernails in a green satin sheath. Angel watched Alex wander along the table, touching shoulders lightly in hello. She heard murmurs of, '*Ciao*, Alix!' as she slid into her seat.

His mother said: 'May I introduce Baron von Henkel?'

Angel murmured, 'How do you do?' to the stout man with a bald head sitting opposite. His neck bulged over the stiff collar of his white shirt and, tucked into his waistcoat, was a monocle on a narrow black ribbon which he stuck into his right eye to greet her. The single eye, greatly magnified, flashed ferociously in the candlelight. He smiled, revealing two shiny rows of large, white, impossibly even teeth.

'My daughter-in-law: Angelica.' Alex's mother raked Angel from head to foot with expert appraisal as she made this introduction, just once, a quick up and down, noting the slender, pliant figure and the unpressed chiffon frock. The quick upwards and down-wards glance was intimidating.

'What a charming dress you are wearing,' she drawled.

Angel flushed. 'Oh, is it? I wasn't quite sure . . . I thought it might seem a bit . . . '

'But of course it is . . . ' Madame Sorel murmured, eyebrows raised politely. A black lace scarf was draped around her shoulders held in place by a diamond pin in the shape of a crescent moon. Drawing the delicate scarf up to her throat with one hand, diamonds glittering, she leant towards the Baron and confided to him – '*So* much better than the other one . . . a really great improvement . . . ' before starting a lively conversation with him in German.

Angel's heart did a little flip. She chose a knife and fork at random from the dazzling display round her plate. The other what? Englishwoman? Surely not daughter-in-law?

The *prima* had been served already. The next course, Diane Sorel informed her, was a traditional Venetian dish – *bavette al nero di seppia*; the *secondo*, *fritto misto di mare* – fish and seafood in a spicy sauce, Angel translated silently to herself, tasting it. There was a knot just below her ribs making it hard to eat and her hands fumbled annoyingly. Nerves always affected her appetite and her stomach was tight. Her digestion was always the first thing to go.

Sometimes it was only the ache in her bowels that told her she was upset. Aromatic steam rose from the plate. She toyed with the food, looking round the table.

There were eight other guests for dinner. Two women, their hair arranged formally, their gowns expensive, and two dark slim men with little toothbrush moustaches, presumably their husbands since they all seemed to be speaking Italian. Then Alex and the elegant Simonetta, almond-shaped eyes glittering, black glossy hair piled high. On her left, a middle-aged man, very fair and fit-looking if rather overweight, cracking nuts. A big, blonde woman in a purple satin off-the-shoulder dress sat opposite him, talking to one of the Italian husbands.

Smooth, dark skinned servants waited on the table. Angel's plate was changed, once, twice. She felt she should say something to Alex's mother, something light and witty, but didn't know what. She cut a piece of fish and speared it with her fork.

Breaking off her discussion with the Baron, Diane Sorel turned to her. 'Alexander informs me that your family is part of the English aristocracy,' she said in her attractively accented English. 'A very great improvement on his last connection. Did he tell you his first wife was a Jewess?'

Angel felt herself grow hot. There was no doubt now who she'd been talking about before. 'Well, yes . . . actually he did . . . although he doesn't like to talk about it much . . . ' she mumbled.

'Oh, she was neurotic, that one, quite unbalanced, I could see that straight away. I tried to warn Alex but – ' a shrug of thin, elegant shoulders, 'my words were to no avail. Ill-health is quite common amongst that race, especially mental sickness – although of course they don't speak about it *before* the wedding, only after-wards when it is too late.' Diane Sorel sat, her lips pushed forwards slightly, remembering. 'My poor, poor boy,' she said musingly. 'What a marriage *that* was . . . '

Angel's appetite had disappeared completely now to be replaced by a cold knot in her stomach. She stared fixedly down at her plate, memorising its border pattern.

'Of course we're not allowed to say there's anything wrong with the Jews nowadays,' Madame Sorel continued, misinterpreting the expression on Angel's face. 'What ought we to say?' she called down to Alex, 'about the *Ebreo* now? Nothing considered too unpleasant, I suppose? Some of our best friends are Jews, after all.' She gave a little laugh. 'Or Americans, at any rate.'

If Alex heard her, he didn't show it. He was talking to the beautiful Simonetta in emerald satin and smiling at something she'd just said.

'I was just saying to the Baron – ' Diane Sorel went on, making a graceful backhand gesture with her wrist, 'that they make such a fuss since the war about one's heritage.' She pronounced it the French way – 'heritage'. 'All talk of good breeding has gone *quite* out of fashion. They call it "anti-semitism".' She drawled out the elongated syllables in her charming accent. 'We may have to talk nicely about the Jews nowadays but no one has to pretend they want them in the family. Luckily, there was nothing to worry about on *that* score. There were no children from the marriage. Can you imagine? Little Jewish boys getting ready for their bar mitzvah?' She laughed, quite genuinely. 'But good aristocratic English stock? A little dull perhaps, a little lacking in *je ne sais quoi*, yet mixed with a brilliant dash of *l'esprit français*?' She shrugged. 'The results might be charming.' The lids of her eyes dropped lazily then widened again, as Alex's did so attractively.

Worse and worse. Angel felt a prickling heat spreading over her from her scalp down to her thighs. Under her tan she knew she'd gone scarlet. She'd have liked to have said quite sharply to Diane Sorel that she had no right to speak like that about the English, or her first daughter-in-law, whatever she thought in private. But she was eating at this woman's table, she'd just married her only son. How awful for Alex if she offended his mother on their very first night. She wished she could think of something clever to say without seeming openly rude. Instead, she simply gritted her teeth and stared at her mother-in-law, hoping her outrage didn't show too clearly in her eyes.

Apparently not. 'I assume there is no Israelite blood flowing in *your* veins, Angelica?' Diane Sorel said pleasantly. 'Only good, pure Anglo-Saxon blood?'

She and the Baron both looked at Angel, waiting for her answer.

He was smiling encouragingly, his big white teeth gleaming. It was hard to think of a way of responding even reasonably politely. 'That sounds rather like – ' Angel began, intending to answer quite lightly, make a joke of it, not actually *offend* anyone, but when she tried to swallow her tongue got stuck to the roof of her mouth. 'Like – ' she tried again, but her voice didn't sound light at all, it seemed simply weak and high and silly.

They were still smiling at her. Across the table, the Baron's dentures gleamed a perfect, improbable white. His magnified eye met hers. She had to speak. Their eyes were on her expectantly. She had to say *something*. Sweat broke out in the pits of her arms. She could feel beads of perspiration dropping heavily down her body.

'Like – what?' Diane Sorel prompted sweetly.

Angel choked a little, then rattled out: 'Oh, you know, the sort of thing the Nazis were always going on about. Asking if one has the right sort of blood and that kind of thing . . . only pure Aryan, of course . . . ' *Quite* the wrong thing to say, as it turned out, judging by their expressions. She tried to smile but it came out more like a grimace.

'It seems a perfectly good question – ' Diane Sorel said coldly – 'to me.' She glanced at the Baron. 'But I forgot – the English do not talk openly about such things. It is like money – one simply assumes one has it, *if* one is of the right class. It must never be actually mentioned. And now it seems we must all become hypocrites, too. Germany lost the war, so naturally the theories of National Socialism must be wrong. And since the Allies are the ones that have the power, it follows *their* views must be right. Is that it? It is great pity, Angelica – ' she went on with really breathtaking friendliness – 'that the British did not understand what National Socialist Germany hoped to achieve. Because there are a great many people – English people, too, I assure you – who believe their Government chose entirely the wrong side in the war.'

Around her, Angel could see people's mouths moving but for a second she couldn't hear anything over the pounding of blood in her ears. *Oh, my God, she's a Nazi*, she thought. *Alex's mother is a bloody Nazi* . . .

She looked around wildly, seeing everyone suddenly with awful sharpness and clarity. The big blond man and his Germanic wife . . . the vain little close clipped military moustaches of the Italians . . . Holding glasses, cutting pieces of fruit or cheese with silver round-edged knives, smiling, it seemed to her, with ferocious calculation into each other's faces . . .

She folded her arms to stop her hands shaking. She knew that if Alex glanced across now it would look like they were simply having a pleasant conversation. 'And you?' she said quietly. 'What do you think?'

'What do I think? *I* think that the war was a dreadful mistake. England and Germany trying to annihilate one another? Europe a ruin? Of course Italy understood the political situation perfectly well, as France did, at least soon enough. But the British? Their leader's aggression and obstinacy caused a great deal of suffering and harm.'

'The Germans started it – when they marched into Poland,' Angel said doggedly, sounding just like a child, she thought, so very young and stupid. And a little afraid, something she hadn't realised she was until that moment. 'We *had* to fight back. We had no choice.'

'But the British *did* have a choice,' Diane Sorel said quickly. 'And were quite ruthless in their choice of victim. Germany had already lost the war and still they picked the weakest and most toothless on which to vent their spleen. Churchill did not select military targets or Nazi headquarters in Berlin when he dropped his bombs. He didn't decide to fight against soldiers – no, he chose ordinary Germans and ordinary German cities. Have you seen Cologne or Hamburg? Nearly totally destroyed by Churchill's terror bombing. Beautiful old medieval cities completely engulfed by a sea of flames. Thousands of people killed in the firestorms, innocent people, civilians . . . If you're looking for wrongdoing, *ma cherie*, there is the war crime . . . '

Angel stared into her mother-in-law's beautiful blue eyes feeling the hair on the back of her scalp prickle. What could she say that would wipe the smile off that perfect face even for a second? She hadn't even *heard* of the German cities Diane Sorel referred to so easily.

'I hope you will have babies soon, Angelica,' Madame Sorel said as they rose from the table later, and really there was no reply to that either. 'Alexander is not getting any younger. And, after all, I suppose that is what he had in mind when he married you. Charming but her clothes are quite ghastly,' she said to Alex in what was supposed to be a whisper when she kissed him good-night. 'Get her something chic, will you? I cannot bear to even *look* upon that terrible frock. The other one might have been a scheming, hysterical bitch but at least she knew what to wear,' she was saying clearly in English, as she walked slowly up the magnificent white stone staircase.

*   *   *

Six days is a very long time, Angel realised by the end of the second. Breakfast, lunch and dinner with a group of people all jabbering away in a foreign language you can't understand very well is humbling, infuriating and, finally, very, very boring. Even when they did break off to address her in halting English, they found she had nothing of interest to say and conversation soon flagged. She'd seen too little, read too little; she was too young, too dull, too disinterested in clothes and fashion. Too shocked by their sort of politics: in their eyes, too English.

She was reduced to sitting next to Alex and nodding occasionally, smiling vacantly into space, praying she didn't look as foolish as she felt. By the fourth day, she felt so crushed by the whole experience she decided she honestly had nothing of interest to say to anyone, neither trivial, nor important, not even Alex.

'What do you think of my mother?' he asked, as they stood in the Church of Frari among the other tourists a few days later. 'Pretty good for her age, isn't she?'

Angel hesitated, thinking of the beautiful bones and elegant clothes, the exquisite shoes and dresses, the fabulous jewellery. She tried to concentrate on the painting in front of her. They were in the sacristy, standing before Bellini's painting of the Madonna and child. At the mother's feet, little cherubic angels strummed musical instruments; two tall saints stood protectively on a panel at either side. Examining the central panel, Angel thought how very much she had disliked Diane Sorel. Disliking his mother, rather than the other way round, had been the last thing she'd expected, the very last. How fortunate their wedding had been too small and far away to be worth travelling to. She couldn't imagine what Francis and Edwina Merlowe would have made of her.

'Oh, yes, very beautiful. I admire her kind of looks very much,' she replied with forced enthusiasm. She *is* beautiful, Angel thought, but her eyes have a hard, empty quality. Trying to sound more convincing, she repeated, '*very* much,' but her voice still sounded strained to her ears.

Clearly it didn't sound as false to Alex as it did to her. He said with satisfaction: 'She adored *you*. She thought, quite perfect. *La belle Anglaise*, she said.'

Angel examined the painting for a bit longer, then said, her tone determinedly casual: 'You don't agree with her politics, do you, Alex?'

'Oh, Christ, no.' He glanced quickly at her. 'Did she talk to you about them?'

Angel nodded gloomily. 'A little,' she admitted.

'Oh, don't mind her. She's always doing it. I do wish she wouldn't. Bloody annoying, really.' He hesitated, looking slightly oppressed and fingered his moustache. 'I suppose she made it clear that she sided with the Fascists in the war?'

Angel looked at him, her face scarlet, her grey eyes embarrassed. 'Yes, I gathered.'

'She wasn't offensive, surely?'

'What? After I told her I didn't feel the same way? Oh, no, just a little more – charming.'

'Oh, dear. How very ominous that sounds.'

'She didn't say anything about it to you, then?'

'No. Didn't mention it. Just said how very young and pretty you are. I'm to get you lots of smart new clothes when we get home to show you off.' He resettled a guiding thumb inside her elbow. 'Quite frankly, I should keep off the subject of politics, if I were you. You'll find she's perfectly sweet if you ignore all of that.'

Angel said a little too loudly, a little too soon: 'Oh, yes! Yes, I'm sure.'

He's nothing like her, she thought. Any resemblance is purely physical, and there's not even much of that. My poor Alex. A mother who's a Nazi and an early marriage that failed? No wonder he sometimes looks so sad and drawn.

She felt a surge of love and loyalty. Slipping a hand through his arm, she squeezed sympathetically.

How vulnerable love makes one, she reflected. Another person's happiness becomes as important as one's own. Perhaps even more important.

They walked past steps leading down to a dim chapel into the main body of the church and stopped at Titian's great painting of the Virgin, then moved off towards the North exit. Standing in the austere gloom of the basilica, just before they passed into the blinding sun of the Campo, Angel had a sudden overwhelming longing for cool autumn evenings in England. As they stepped out, she was immediately hit in the face by the heat and glare. She would have given a great deal just then to feel the soft breezes off the Sussex downs instead.

Turning, she asked only: 'Alex – you love me?'

'Yes, of course. Why?'

'Then nothing matters,' she said, almost believing it herself in that moment.

8

ANGEL

Regent's Park, London. September 1951

Later, she realised she should have spoken then, asked a few searching questions, probed a bit more, but by that time it was too late of course. Writhing on a hard wooden bench in a packed and stuffy courtroom, trying to piece together that first year of marriage, Angel's memories of those days had no ordered sequence. The tall white house they returned to from honeymoon – the cream stucco pillars on either side of the front door – the high beeches edging the garden – the park across the road – Alex's face across the candlelight – his sudden smile – the gleam in his dark eyes . . . But all that was before the telephone call. All that was a hundred years ago. Because from that moment on it all became quite startlingly clear and distinct in her memory. So, yes, it was the phone call that had fixed that Saturday night so firmly in her mind.

They were holding a dinner party. Everyone was due to arrive at eight. By seven thirty, Angel found herself standing before the double doors of the dining room. Pushing them open, she switched on the chandeliers and surveyed the long walnut dining table laid for sixteen. Dazzling white cloth, brilliant glasses, silver candelabras, shallow bowls of pale gold roses . . .

The ice, she thought suddenly. My God, the ice. '*Has* the ice been delivered from the fishmongers yet, Maisie?' she called anxiously, catching sight of the parlour-maid coming up the stairs.

'Yes, ma'am. It's just come.'

'Thank goodness for that. What about the oysters and canapés?'

'All done.'

'Who's going to take the coats?'

'Well, it was a toss up between John and me but we decided I should.'

Angel looked puzzled. 'John?'

'Mr Laskell. The manservant that's been hired for the evening?'

'Oh, yes, I see. And the baby – '

'Fast asleep. Nannie Hillyard's with her.'

'That's it then, isn't it? Everything appears to be taken care of.'

'Looks like it,' Maisie agreed. 'Shall I ask Mr Laskell to chill the champagne flutes before bringing them into the drawing room, Madam?

'Oh, Maisie – I'd forgotten. Would you?'

And the myriad of other things that might have slipped her mind too must still have cast their shadow one floor up in the bedroom, even after Alex had clasped the double string of pearls around her neck, his breath hot on her bare shoulders, and finished knotting his own tie, because he'd taken one look at her face and told her not to *worry* so much.

'Just relax and enjoy it, will you?'

'Laura always used to tell me that.'

'Well, for once she was right. I'm sure it will go off perfectly. So the champagne's warm? Or the meat burns? So what?'

But Angel was too nervous even to return his smile and, watching him fitting gold cufflinks into a dazzling white shirt, she had a moment of stinging impatience with him. It was all very well saying it, she thought, but if it *did* . . . Alex expected perfection, whatever he said.

'This evening will be a resounding success,' he assured her, shrugging on his jacket. 'Look, you'll have pearls all over the place if you carry on doing that – '

She dropped her hand. 'God, yes – sorry.'

But seated at the head of the long dining-table a little later, gazing across the heads of their guests to Alex at the far end, Angel had to admit that he'd been right and everything *was* going spectacularly well. The candles shed soft light over the womens' dècolletages, the men looked distinguished, especially Alex, she thought fondly, watching him bend his head to the woman on his right, Olivia Westbury – married to the balding man with pale, clever eyes sitting next to her, Julian, eldest daughter Claudia, if she remembered correctly. The wine and the warmth of the room induced in her a pleasant state of haziness. The whole poached salmon in aspic brought in by John Laskell on a silver tray had been perfect. Now she *could* relax.

'How's Claudia doing?' she asked Julian Westbury.

'Very nicely indeed, thank you very much.'

'I gather she's just gone away to school. How's she finding it?'

'Oh, she's liking it very much.'

'I'm so glad.'

She took another mouthful of wine, feeling a warm glow spreading through her, and looked across the candles, willing Alex to look up and notice how well she was managing. Not at all shy or tongue-tied. Not hunched over a bit. He was talking to Olivia Westbury. She pressed a deep cleavage towards him, laughing loudly at something he'd said. 'Oh, that is so *amusing*!' she was saying, flirting outrageously. 'Oh, you funny, funny man!'

'To be perfectly honest, I think our darling Claudia's a tad homesick,' Julian Westbury admitted. 'Still, I expect it will pass.' He sighed heavily before sipping. 'It usually does.'

Angel murmured agreement. She lifted her gaze to the far end of the table. The rest of the party, on the whole, appeared to be enjoying themselves, she thought, as she listened to a description of the educational difficulties of the Westbury daughters from birth through to teens. Olivia Westbury was still flirting with Alex, diamond necklace twinkling somewhere deep between her breasts. Alex was flirting back of course, not too much, just the right amount so as not to appear unfriendly. Angel hoped she hadn't been too ratty with him earlier. He was right – she worried too much. Well, at least, thanks to him, she looked the part. No more ill-fitting sweaters and comfortable Harris tweed skirts for her, no more baggy brown Balbriggan stockings. As soon as they were back from honeymoon he'd swept her off to Paris where they'd attended the autumn *ensembles* and he'd chosen for her little black frocks for the daytime, vibrant yellows, blues and greens with full, stiff satin skirts for the afternoon, off-the-shoulder gowns exquisitely cut for the evening.

And here she was, Angel thought, looking down the candlelight – chic, elegant, well-turned out, ready. But ready for what? Because of course there hadn't been time to wear any of the latest frocks.

When she'd got back to London she'd realised almost straight away that the slight little thickening round her belly hadn't been caused by too much foreign food after all – she was pregnant. They certainly hadn't wasted any time everyone said with – was it suspicion she could hear in their voices? The ticking of their brains working out of the exact number of months and days that had passed – So *that's* why they were in such a hurry to get married? Of course it wasn't helped by Georgina arriving in the world almost three weeks earlier than planned, but she didn't care, they could believe what they jolly well liked, for now, Angel thought with a great and secret gratitude, now she wouldn't be lonely ever again because she'd have the baby to keep her company. Even walking in the streets had a purpose when she was pushing a pram. Strangers stopped to peer beneath the hood and turn fond smiles on her . . .

Which was exactly how Julian Westbury was smiling at her at this very moment, Angel realised, in precisely such an openly affectionate way. And oh, God, was that his *knee* pressing deliberately against hers? 'Of course, one can feel a little homesick at first,' she murmured as intelligently as possible, shifting both legs to one side, just in case. 'And the two younger girls? I expect they're finding it strange with their sister away?' she asked, not missing a beat.

And it was then, listening to his answer, a bright, attentive smile on her face, that the telephone began ringing in the hall. Maisie will get it, she'd thought. Or the housekeeper, Mrs Minity. She'd heard six or seven rings and was just beginning to feel a little edgy when the ringing stopped. Glancing down the table a few minutes later, there was Maisie, neatly attired in black and white with an immaculate starched white cap on her dark head, murmuring something in Alex's ear. He was apologising, he threw down his napkin with a smile and stood up. He was still smiling as he turned to the door but he'd gone white.

Angel's smile became fixed. She felt suddenly sober. She realised she was gripping her wine glass too hard. She loosened her fingers and set the glass down carefully. There were four faint, smeared fingerprints, she saw, near the rim.

'Still, I shouldn't imagine they'll mind for very long,' Julian Westbury was saying, 'since they'll be joining Claudia shortly . . . '

What was he talking about? Boarding school? She tried to respond as enthusiastically as she could, the smile nailed to her mouth. 'Oh, *will* they? How very nice for her. So it really won't matter, will it, if at first she's a little . . . '

He talked on. The difficulty of finding acceptable accommodation in London nowadays, living standards had dropped in every way since the war, you couldn't find a decent loaf anywhere for love or money, food didn't taste of anything nowadays, though of course the dinner tonight was excellent, excellent . . .

Smile, she told herself, *keep smiling*.

Down the table, Alex had returned and was talking to his neighbours again. And he, too, was smiling brilliantly, almost too brilliantly. Behind the dazzling smile he looked worried. His laughter was loud but an anxious frown had settled on his brow.

He's got that look on his face, Angel thought unhappily. That hunted look. The brave, rather browbeaten look she recognised from her father's face – the look of a decent man bowed down by the misfortunes of life. A clamp closed over her chest. She picked up her glass but, this time, the wine didn't help at all. *Oh, dear God,* she thought. *Who was it on the telephone?*

'No one,' Alex said swiftly when she asked him quietly later. They were in the drawing room by then. Coffee had been brought in and delicate hand-painted cups of amethyst porcelain placed in saucers on the tray.

'But it must have been *someone*, Alex.'

'Actually the accountants.' He smiled but he looked guarded, like a barrier had come down over his eyes. 'I meant no one in particular.'

'Oh, I see.'

'Only business, my dear.'

She thought of the look on his face when Maisie had bent her dark head and spoken in his ear and the way he'd grown pale and hurried from the room. 'Is business going badly?' she asked worriedly.

'A little irritating, nothing more. They must hang a large sign on the door. Having a dinner party, please telephone with any problems at once. The more trivial, the better. The timing is spot on.' He gave a humourless bark of laughter. 'Really, it wasn't anything.'

But whatever he said, however casual he sounded, the worried expression didn't clear from his eyes and he'd never called her 'my dear' in that distant way before, like he wanted her and all the world to go to hell and leave him in peace.

'Just some decisions to be made in a hurry,' he added, in an offhand voice. And, when she continued to look at him anxiously, a sharp, 'Please don't go on about it, Angel,' though she *wasn't*, and then just as impatiently: 'Help Maisie out with the coffee, will you, darling? It looks like she needs it rather badly.'

He was silent and preoccupied for the rest of the evening. He seemed far away, thinking his own thoughts. Fortunately no one seemed to notice except for her. To all outward appearances, the evening ended as brilliantly as it had begun with the Sorels braving the night air to stand on the doorstep and wave their guests good-night. They came in linking hands.

'There are some papers I must examine before bed,' Alex muttered, dropping her hand as soon as they were inside. 'I shouldn't wait up – it could take a while.'

'Surely you don't have to do it *now* . . . '

'Unfortunately, yes.'

'Oh, but Alex – '

'Look, is this something important, Angel, because if it's *not* – '

'It's not important,' she said in a low voice.

'Then good-night, my dear.'

Something about the tone of his voice made her look up sharply. Her eyes followed him as he crossed the hall and opened the study door. She caught a flash of a dark, panelled wall. The door closed behind him.

*   *   *

Angel stood for a moment, staring blankly at the door.

She was feeling a little sick of Alex and his sudden moods that always shut her out so completely, sick of everything, herself included, and of being so exhaustingly charming throughout the evening. Instead of taking the flight of stairs up to the bedrooms, she swung round and headed back towards the drawing room. Ignoring dirty cups and full ashtrays, she pushed open the long windows and stepped out onto the balcony.

The moon was almost full. Hands resting lightly on the ironwork bar, she inhaled the cool scents from the garden, before taking the spiral staircase down. The grass felt springy underfoot, an earthy smell rose up to her nostrils. The electric light from inside fell away till only the garden surrounded her, dark and cool and mysterious.

She strolled across the damp shadows of the lawn, feeling instantly better. It was a relief to escape from the stifling atmosphere inside into the silent night. A sudden breeze made the pale flowers under the trees stir in the shadows and the leaves rustle on the branches. She moved towards the dark outline of the rockery, then, by the sunken rose garden, swung round and looked back at the house. From here, the drawing room was hidden by trees. She could only make out a narrow chink of light escaping through the nursery curtains. The rest of the upstairs windows were curtained into darkness.

She wandered further up the garden. The grass was damp when she stooped to touch it. Cupping a white rose in her hand, she inhaled its delicate scent and stood for a moment, enjoying the mingled smells of the flower border. Head slightly bent, she gazed at the damp grass beneath her feet, then straightened and carried on walking. But after only a few steps she halted, feeling suddenly uneasy. Around her, the garden was quiet. Just the whispering of the breeze in the tree-tops. All just as you'd expect really. Except she found herself looking around, overcome by the sensation that something wasn't quite right.

She glanced behind her, feeling her stomach growing tight. It wasn't something she could see, she realised suddenly. It was something she could *hear*. She could hear breathing. The faint sound of someone breathing seemed to mingle with the breeze and the perfume of the roses.

Angel stood stock still, her skin creeping, holding her breath for as long as she was able, trying to sort out sound from silence. There was nothing unusual. Just the gloom of the lawn all around her and the damp, cool feel of the night.

She swallowed and started walking again. But she couldn't shake off the sense of being watched. The weight of someone's gaze seemed to follow her as she began walking, rather more rapidly now, across the grass. God, she was getting ridiculously nervy. She didn't think of herself as given to silly imaginings but she suddenly knew she didn't want to be in the garden for one moment longer, vulnerable to anything prowling about in the darkness – she wanted to be back inside, behind brick walls . . . which suddenly didn't seem so oppressive to her, after all . . .

There it was again. Every hair lifted on her body. She wheeled round and stood with her back to the house, her heart suddenly beating hard, eyes wide and peering, ears alert to the slightest shift in sound. A crack of wood under foot as someone adjusted their position, the hiss of indrawn breath. She hadn't imagined *that* surely? Yes, there was someone in the bushes, someone crouched and hidden from view . . . something sinister in the gloom of the foliage which had been making a sound just before and was now holding its breath . . .

Over there, she reckoned. Amongst the dark tangle of bushes on her immediate left. Her throat contracted into the menacing darkness.

Something flew up with a startled cry. From amongst the leaves, there was a scrabbling sound. Angel let out her breath, feeling a little weak-kneed. Probably a bird, that was all. An owl rustling amongst dry, fallen leaves. Yes, that was it. Some small nocturnal animal sensing her presence, scurrying back to its hole. Reason told her that was all she had heard. But she took the iron stairs up to the balcony two at a time anyway and, cursing herself for her foolishness, barred the wooden shutters doubly firmly against the troubling night.

*　　*　　*

Alex was back to his old self next morning, Angel saw with relief, only more so, very much more so – quite like the earliest days of our romance, she thought, bewitched all over again. Lunch was a lively affair with a walk in Regent's Park suggested after the baby's afternoon sleep. In a brown Homberg hat and overcoat, Alex was humming a little careless tune as he pushed the pram serenely over the zebra crossing.

It was a beautiful autumn day. Golden leaves floated down from the trees and fell in soft heaps by the paths. As they turned into the park, he pointed to a small poster behind glass. 'Look – there's a Viennese orchestra playing at six. Must be the final outdoor concert of the year.' He checked his watch. 'Ten past. Let's drop in on it, shall we?'

They strolled across the bridge towards the open-air theatre. 'Did Zara Hoffman like music?' Angel asked impulsively.

He stopped wheeling the pram and stared. 'Why do you ask that?'

'I don't know – ' she faltered – 'I just – Alex – ' she said with a nervous smile – 'you look like you've just seen a ghost.'

'Because it's really none of your damned business,' he said pleasantly. So pleasantly, in fact, that she was not quite sure she'd heard him correctly for a moment.

They crossed to the Inner Circle in silence. The music, muffled by the hedge and the hollow of grass, barely reached them until they walked through St Mary's gate when faint but vigorous strains of a march could be heard. Rows of chairs set out on the grass slope faced the band. They sat near the back, the pram with the sleeping baby inside parked beside them at an angle. Angel looked anxiously at his profile, seeing the way his mouth pulled down at the sides.

'I'm sorry, Alex,' she murmured. 'That was horribly insensitive of me. I should have thought a bit before blurting it out like that.'

'Yes? Only I don't understand why it occurred to you now.' He fixed his eyes on her. 'Why do you think it did?'

She looked back uneasily. 'No reason.'

'Isn't there?' he said, peering hard at her.

'No, of course not. What reason could there be?'

He considered her for a second longer, then sighed and shook his head. 'Forget it.'

'I should never have said that.'

'It doesn't matter.'

'Yes, it does.'

And Alex, with a face so haunted by his past that it twisted her heart right in two, only smiled rather sadly and said: 'Shall we stay till the end? It's not cold.'

She nodded quickly and smiled back. When she checked inside the pram, the baby was fast asleep, tucked between layers of thick blankets. Angel could make out only the tip of a nose and the curve of her head inside a pink knitted hat. In the distance, the St Marylebone clock began striking. 'Yes,' she murmured on the first stroke. 'Yes, let's stay.'

'So why do you think it *did* enter your head at that precise moment?' Laura asked curiously when, some time later, Angel described this conversation to her.

'I'm not really sure. Maybe I wanted to hurt him a bit. Said the first thing that popped into my head that might. I knew how much he disliked talking about his first marriage. I feel rather ashamed of it actually.'

'And you really had no idea?'

'None.'

'Seems pretty hard to imagine how you couldn't, quite frankly.'

'Well, it's easy to be wise after the event,' Angel said irritably.

'Yes, but three things happening like that one after the other?'

'Actually, it wasn't three. Not yet.' *Not yet.*

'And then Monday dawned and – '

'Yes. Monday.'

Actually, Angel had felt quite happy that morning – not wildly, madly, exuberantly happy or anything like that, simply calmly and pleasantly contented. Just tickety-boo, as she put it to herself later. Somewhere in her consciousness, she'd heard the early morning sounds of the household stirring. She was subliminally aware of the heavy front door bolt being shot back and the wooden shutters in the drawing room below being opened. She heard the shuffle of the housemaid with the dustpan and brush on the stairs and the scrape of the curtain rings as the curtains were drawn back.

About fifteen minutes later, still more asleep than awake, there were measured footsteps along the passage and the subdued clink of teacups as the tray was set down on the table outside. Then the creak of floorboards, a soft knock on the bedroom door. Rubbing her eyes, she slid upright as Maisie entered with the early morning tea and opened the curtains.

She ate downstairs with Alex in the breakfast room. Toast and coffee for Angel, eggs and bacon for Alex. Then he left for Old Bond Street and Maisie brought the baby in to her.

Most of the early afternoon was spent in the park feeding the ducks with Nina. Returning home, she found Maisie in the hall and asked if she'd mind holding the baby for a moment while she took off her coat.

'It's really quite warm in the sun,' Angel said, tugging off brown leather gloves. 'Nippy, of course, when you're not. Certainly pleasant enough for Georgina of have her sleep outside today, I think. Well wrapped up, of course.'

'Of course.' Maisie bounced the baby up and down on her hip. 'Who's a lovely girl, then? Shall I take her up to the nursery?'

'Oh, would you? I have a couple of calls to make and a letter to write. I've parked the pram just inside the gate.'

'Would you like me to bring you a cup of tea once I've settled her?'

'Oh, Maisie, thank you. Yes. Yes, I would.'

'Dear Aunt Edwina – ' she wrote a little later, taking a gulp of lukewarm tea – 'I'm sorry not to have written before to thank you for the lovely present for the baby – it was so kind of you. The pink angora matinée coat and hat fit her perfectly and she looks terribly sweet in them. Georgina is adorable, and very good and putting on weight well. I do hope – '

Angel stopped. She thought she heard a cry. Georgina? She listened, head cocked to one side, sucking the top of the fountain pen. It was far more likely to have been a child in the street outside, she decided after a moment, licking her top lip thoughtfully. She could taste ink in her mouth. The pen must have leaked. She examined it. Finding nothing wrong, she sat with it poised, ready to write. What did she hope?

Another cry. Very faint but definite. Surely that was Nina? She smiled fondly. A single, short wail, another, then nothing. Glancing at the small porcelain clock on the writing-table, she saw it was almost twenty to five. She'd been writing letters for almost an hour. Soon time to wake the baby, anyway, and get those chubby legs kicking in the air. Fifteen minutes? But wondering about Nina, she couldn't concentrate any longer. Screwing on the top of the pen, she pressed a sheet of blotting paper over the page. She took the short cut from the balcony down the spiral steps into the garden. Breathing in the smell of freshly-mown grass, she strolled across the lawn.

The pram was under the mulberry tree. 'Ni–na,' she half sang as she approached. 'Time to wake u–up . . . '

The fine netting to keep off cats was hooked to one side. A string of coloured beads swayed from the arch of the pram's hood, a small wooden parrot dangled. No sound came from inside. For the first time, a sense of disquiet brushed her.

'Nina?' she said, reaching inside.

She stood, the smile frozen on her face. Her stretched out arms held their position stiffly.

The pram was empty.

'Nina?' she repeated stupidly, fumbling around in the still warm space inside the pram. Her heart was banging suddenly. She felt it rising in her throat to choke her. The mattress still bore the imprint of a small body. The pastel sheets were hollowed into the shape of Georgina's baby warmth.

Angel picked up a yellow blanket that had been kicked to one side and stared at the white silk rabbit appliquéd on it.

Nannie has taken her in, she told herself, trying to stay calm. Or Maisie. It must having been Nina I heard crying, after all. One of them decided she's had long enough in the garden without company and has carried her inside.

The blanket dropped from her trembling hands to the ground. She trampled over it as she raced towards the house. She was behaving stupidly she knew, it was just an empty pram, but she felt quite panicky. To come looking for her baby and find only absence – there was an immediate physical reaction in her gut, a twisted, hollow feeling beyond the reach of any rational argument.

'Mrs Minity? Mrs Minity! Have you seen Georgina?'

'She's in the garden, Madam. Having her sleep outside today.'

'No, she's not! The pram's empty!' Anxiety had drained

the colour from Angel's face. She turned, distraught. 'Where's Maisie?'

'Hanging the laundry upstairs. Now please don't upset yourself – I'm sure there's a perfectly simple explanation – '

'But what?' Angel said in exasperation.

Not waiting to hear the housekeeper's reply, Angel took the basement stairs two at a time, pushed open the green baize door at the top and dashed across the hall, calling 'Maisie! Maisie!' before she'd even reached the stairs.

'Here I am,' Maisie said, appearing at the top. 'What's up?'

'Have you got her?'

'Who?'

'The *baby*! Have you got Nina?'

'No, I haven't. I'm folding sheets for the airing cupboard. But I know where she *is*.'

Angel's face cleared. 'You do? Oh, thank goodness! I was beginning to imagine all sorts of – Where?'

'Why, she's in her pram in the garden, of course,' Maisie replied comfortably.

Angel felt like she was choking. 'Oh, *no*! – No, she's not! She's *not*!' She took the first three stairs in one go. 'Perhaps Nannie has her,' she said, suddenly wildly hopeful. 'Is she in her room?'

But – 'Have you forgotten Nannie Hillyard's away on her holidays, ma'am?' Maisie stated, looking down at her curiously from the top of the stairs. 'It's her annual fortnight in Hastings at her sister's. She went off in a taxi cab this morning first thing.'

Angel stopped half way up. 'Oh, yes! Yes, of course! For a moment I *had* forgotten.'

She turned and walked blindly down to the bottom, Maisie following a few steps behind.

'The pram is still there,' Angel said clearly. She could hear herself, quite calm and clear. She leant against the banister, suddenly needing support. 'But Nina's not. She isn't in her pram!' she said, hearing the nervy ring entering her voice.

'Isn't she? The little minx. She's probably – ' Maisie broke off, unsure exactly what a baby of five months could be doing.

'Oh, come *on*!' Angel said, dashing across the hall.

She ran down the basement stairs and out of the side door, Maisie close behind her. Coming to a stop by the tree, Maisie exchanged a glance with Mrs Minity. The upper classes, her whole body clearly said – too much time on their hands, whatever will they think up next? 'Now who's going to want a baby?' she cooed, peering into the pram, an indulgent smile on her face. 'Tell me that.'

When she straightened the smile had disappeared. 'Well, you're right, she isn't here,' she said, looking frightened.

No one moved for half a second. They stood, frozen, round the empty pram. Angel felt waves of panic surging up her chest, black and hot, threatening to choke her. For a moment she thought she might be physically sick. Fighting the nausea down, she cried out: 'Mrs Minity – look round the house! Maisie – follow me!' and dashed through the tall wrought iron gate at the side.

In the street they split up. Angel, already running up the road, shouted over her shoulder to start checking in the other direction. When she glanced back, she could see Maisie was still standing outside the house.

'Oh, Madam, shouldn't we telephone for a policeman?' she called uncertainly.

'We've wasted enough time as it is!' Angel yelled back, cursing herself for listening to Maisie in the first place. 'She can't be long gone. I heard her cry out a few minutes ago – I *heard* her!' And when Maisie still didn't move, more fiercely: '*Look* first, damn you!'

She ran quickly along the high hedge edging the park. There were a few people in either direction but no one holding anything even remotely like a baby. Not even a bundle or brown paper bag. Five minutes is long enough to vanish, she thought desperately. But how far could they be? A little further to her left, a curved bridge spanned the water. A couple were standing on it, both hands on the wide stone, peering over the edge. 'Did you see someone go by carrying a baby?' Angel called desperately. They stared at her. '*Did* you?' she asked again insistently.

Silently, they shook their heads. Bareheaded, without a coat, her eyes huge and panic-stricken, Angel saw from their faces how strange she must look and sound. Not waiting for any further reply, she started running again. Her heart was slamming in her chest, she had a sharp pain in her side. She pounded down Gloucester Avenue. No – no, nothing there . . . She quickened speed, looking round wildly as she ran, but there was nothing on the next road either. Gulping back tears, she and plunged on. Maisie had been right – they should have notified a policeman straight away. It was madness to run around randomly searching, she realised.

She stopped for a moment at the T-junction, her hands braced on her knees, her breath coming in short, painful gasps.

Hastings, she thought suddenly. Perhaps Nannie Hillyard has taken her to her sister in Hastings. Perhaps she hadn't really set off in a taxi for the station this morning as they'd all assumed. Seeing her drive away with her luggage they'd believed she had, but what if they were wrong? What if she'd been waiting round the corner, clock ticking? What if she'd returned unannounced a few hours later, stolen Nina and *then* continued the cab ride to the station? What if she wasn't really a nanny at all but a fraud only pretending to be, the black rustling silk, pull-down hat and flat, sensible shoes just a very clever disguise?

But recalling her dour face and respectable clothing, her impeccable references (which could *not* have been forgeries, Angel now recalled), she knew this was too far-fetched to be credible.

But it was *all* so incredible. It all had a desperate air of unreality about it. She could barely believe it herself, even as she stumbled up to the front door, limping slightly, she must have stubbed her foot on the kerb without realising. It seemed like she'd been searching for hours but there was only Mrs Minity standing on the front step, a muddy yellow blanket draped over her arm, her plump face creased into lines of worry.

'I think you should call the police, Madam, I do really,' she said, as soon as she saw Angel.

'Maisie might have found her,' Angel gasped, pressing her hand to the stitch in her side, disbelief and fear making her slow and stubborn and just plain *stupid*. 'She *must* have.'

But when Maisie appeared round the corner, looking pale and shocked, her arms were empty.

'A six month old baby,' Mrs Minity said faintly. 'How can she just have disappeared into thin air?'

Angel sat on the bottom step and put her head in her hands. Rage, fear and grief made a knot in her chest. 'She couldn't. She hasn't. Someone's kidnapped her. Oh, God – ' she sobbed as the truth finally sunk in – '*Who's got Georgina?*'

*　　*　　*

'The baby is missing,' she said tonelessly, without preamble, when she heard Alex's voice on the other end of the line. 'Her pram is outside but she isn't. Oh, *please!*' Her voice broke suddenly. 'Please come home and find her!'

Angel had said this, or something like it, on the telephone and Alex was standing in front of her now, handing her another large brandy and soda. At Mrs Minity's insistence she'd had one already but she felt more sober than she ever had and the shaking had not stopped. His reaction was strange, when she considered it. Not then. She was too numb to think about anything then, she was just *feeling*. An anxiety so deep it hurt physically: stunned disbelief, fear, horror.

She'd said on the phone in response to his first, actually his only, question: 'No, I haven't called the police. Not yet. I intend to as soon as I get off the telephone to you.' To which he'd responded straightaway – no police, is that clear? Which she didn't think odd until later, when she thought it very, very odd. Also the immediate, indisputable sound of relief in his voice at her answer. He seemed to be expecting this, or something like it, she thought, from the distance at which she was surveying things. But how could he be? Expecting *this*?

He was pale but determined. Ashen faced. And surprisingly calm. He must have been pretty good in wartime, Angel thought. He doesn't fall to pieces, not like me. Her whole body ached with tension. Her head felt empty, her face actually hurt. *Oh, God, oh, God, where is she?* She sat on the sofa in the drawing room, arms crossed and clutching her sides, as if she had to physically hold herself together or otherwise she would, she'd fall apart, actually crumble into tiny little pieces, too numb to do anything but follow him with big, frightened eyes.

'There was someone in the garden the other night,' she whispered, staring up at him as he took the empty glass from her unresisting hand. 'It was late, about midnight. I'd just – I just stepped out for a breath of fresh air. I didn't see anything – I *heard* him. Breathing, I thought. Then a sort of scrabbling sound from the bushes. Nothing really. It's only an owl or rabbit, I told myself. Only my imagination playing tricks. Telling me something sinister was about when really there wasn't. I – I simply ignored it. Alex – this is all my fault. I left our baby outside in her pram, alone, unguarded. Oh, God – you must really hate me . . . '

But he only said, sounding distracted: 'Hate you? No, of course I don't.'

He didn't seem shocked by what she'd just told him, he didn't even seem interested. He'd just gone into operational mode. He reassured Maisie and Mrs Minity: 'Everything's taken care of – no need to worry any further. Thank you *so* much for all your help,' handed them both a stiff drink, then shut the door firmly in their faces and poured more brandy down her throat. He disappeared into his study and made a call. From the drawing room, she heard the click. Five minutes later he handed her the brandy and when she swallowed it *(that's it, Angel, down the hatch, yes, all of it, there you are, good girl)* and, the warmth spreading through her, began to cry, her face all contorted, said, a grimace of pain passing fleetingly across his features. 'Don't. Please. It doesn't help.'

She nodded, closing her eyes for a second, tears squeezing out from beneath her lids, her chin wobbling with the effort to stop. He was right – being emotional didn't help anyone. She had to pull herself together. When she'd finally managed to, he held out her warmest coat, the tweed one with the mink lining he'd chosen for her in Paris. He hadn't taken off his own, just opened it so that he could move about more freely.

'Come on,' he said, tight lipped. 'I think I know where she is.'

'You *know* – where? Where is she? *Alex?*' she said more sharply when he didn't respond.

He sidestepped the question. 'It's about a three hour drive,' he said grimly. 'If we drive fast.'

She stared at him. She didn't care how long it took if Nina was at the end of it. Did he really think she did? He mouthed, 'not now' so that she understood that she wasn't to ask any more questions for the time being. Because Maisie and Mrs Minity might be listening? But it didn't matter, did it, because the main thing, the really huge relief, was that he knew where the baby was.

'Wait on the steps outside,' he said. 'And I'll bring the Bentley round.'

He didn't say much more once they were in the car. Just, 'Warm enough for you? There's a rug on the back seat if you need it and a pair of chamois leather gloves in the dashboard locker. They'll be a bit big but better than nothing.' And when they stopped at a garage on the way so he could fill up: 'They'll make a cup of tea here if you ask nicely. It's quite a bit further.'

She shook her head. 'I couldn't.'

She wrapped her arms round her body, hunching over herself as he paid for the petrol and got back in the car. She felt frozen into place – the moment she moved, she became real again and panic flooded through her. He knew where Nina was, he'd said so. She wanted to scream at him: *Where? How?* And most urgently, *Who?* But when she'd asked, he'd just said: Later. I'll explain everything later. So they were driving in silence. She couldn't utter a word. What else was there to say apart from that?

He showed no inclination to speak either. He was concentrating on driving, going very fast. They were racing through the night, in another land, a rocky place, a desert, a hard, black terrain, a place that was, most of all, *without Nina*. Angel's whole existence seemed to be in his hands on the wheel and his foot on the accelerator.

Over the miles she studied his profile. Except for the rapid movement of his pupils fixed on the road ahead he might have been carved out of white stone. Black eyebrows at a slant, his face was overbearingly blank. A familiar face, the man she'd married but, at the same time, the pale, frowning face of a stranger. Someone she had nothing to say to. Except: when will we be there? When will I hold my baby again? When? In the car, they sat in estranged silence next to one another.

They sped smoothly on. Bright lights flashed behind Alex's face. She had meant to look at the signs out of London to see where they were heading but, when the time had come, she'd forgotten. She saw signposts racing past without being able to form from them the words the letters made. Then the lights were gone. Behind his set profile the glass was black. They were off the main road, still driving very fast, weaving along dark, winding roads under a blue-black sky. The road widened and straightened between low stone walls. Hedges, cottages and tree trunks riding swiftly past. The moon showed itself every now and then, a thumbprint of dull yellow light. Then hedgerows cast crooked shadows onto the road in front of them, blacker still beneath.

On and on and on. The world took sudden shape. A signpost showed briefly in the sweep of the headlights. She recognised one of the villages they shot through. It was on the other side of the county to Haywards Heath but she'd been there several times with Laura.

'We're in Sussex,' she said in surprise.

'Yes.'

'Is it near here? Where we're going?'

'Not far now. Light me a cigarette, would you?'

He was still smoking it when they turned off the road, bumping upwards over a rough track. 'A short cut,' he explained briefly.

After a moment, the path sloped down and joined the road again. They drove a little further along, swung left suddenly, slowing down over cobbles, then abruptly he stopped the car.

To their left, a house. Nothing else. Just fields all around and the outline of a large, rambling house that had been built on them. Stone walls and dark foliage rising up, a glimpse beyond of lights spilling onto a high porch. A stretch of road in front of them and, parked right ahead of the Bentley, bumper to boot, an old non-descript four-seater Morris Twelve.

He switched off the engine. 'This is it,' he said in a voice that seemed to echo across the wide empty spaces.

She made a move to open the door. He stilled her with a swift gesture. 'No. Wait here.'

'I'm coming with you,' she said firmly, pushing open the door.

'No.'

She stared at him. She could feel the anger mounting in her. 'Is this where Nina is?'

'Yes. I believe so.'

'Then I'm coming with.'

'Better if you stay here.' And, when she hesitated, 'Really. You'll do more harm than good.'

After one more look into his haggard face, she didn't argue any further. He had more than the fatigue of several hours driving there. And if sitting docilely in the car is what it takes to get Nina safely back again, she decided grimly, then that is what I'll do. She nodded stiffly. 'Hurry then,' she said, her bottom lip trembling. 'She'll be very hungry by now.'

'I'll be as quick as I can,' he promised, jumping out. He walked round the car, pausing for a moment on the kerb beside the open window. 'Don't worry,' he said to her. 'I'll get her back if it's the last thing I do.'

The sudden hardness in his voice surprised her but, when she looked up, his face was just as blank and unreadable as before.

She watched him stump out his cigarette and walk quickly through heavy iron gates with mossy pillars on either side, past a massed bank of shrubs and up a steep incline. At the top, on a high porch, he took a key from his greatcoat pocket and inserted it in the front door. The door closed behind him.

*   *   *

The sense of isolation was overwhelming. Angel opened the car door as soon as he'd disappeared and jumped out, suddenly alive to the possibility that Nina might soon be in her arms again, that she was in all likelihood only a few hundred yards away at this very moment, and stood by the gate, staring through the wrought iron bars at the moonlight lying in strips on the path in between them, willing Alex to appear on the front steps with the baby.

It seemed a perfectly ordinary house from the outside. Quite large, with fields behind and to one side, bordered along the road by shrubs and a low flint wall. Grey flint and red brick with tall double gables, she saw when the moon came out. Six windows across the first floor, five windows below, and a dark green doorway. A stone flowerpot stood at the foot of a few deep steps and there was a wrought-iron shoe-scraper fixed to the stone. Even in this light it all seemed somehow dilapidated. The front door looked like it was in desperate need of a fresh coat of paint and the shoe-scraper was thick with moss as if no one had used it in a long time.

The gate had swung to behind Alex. Pushing it open, Angel walked uncertainly up the path. Her legs felt weakened by the strain of the day and from sitting stiffly in the car for so long without moving. A tangle of thick, untended shrubbery grew along the edge. By the crumbling stone steps she halted. A cry came from inside. Not a baby's cry but a woman's voice, a single shout of complaint as if she were in sudden, unexpected physical pain, then another, just as dismayed but less surprised. Then loud, unrestrained weeping.

Angel's first instinct was to move towards to the sound. She took a couple of steps forwards then, remembering Alex's warning, stopped sharply. Took a deep breath. *Better no*, she thought. *Better wait for a bit longer.* She forced herself to turn round and walk back down the path and out the tall gates. Unable to sit still, she began pacing up and down the road outside, weaving between the two cars.

The weeping grew suddenly louder. Angel swung round. The front door opened and Alex appeared on the doorstep, grim faced, holding Nina in his arms.

Angel gave a sharp cry and ran towards him. The baby was swaddled in a faded pink crocheted blanket Angel didn't recognise. She held out her arms, suddenly steady, and he placed the baby in them.

'For God's sake, let's get out of here,' he said edgily.

She could barely reply, she felt so relieved. The reassuringly warm weight of Georgina was against her chest.

'Come on. Let's go.'

She nodded and followed him down the path. As she climbed into the car, a scream rang out. A single, long animal wail. Even with the car door closed and concerned mainly with getting the baby safely settled in her lap, Angel started at the note of pure desperation in it. Distracted, she looked up through the bars of the gates at the house.

In the open doorway, she caught a glimpse of a woman being dragged out of sight. A skirt and two arms in grey flannel were pulling her back. Or perhaps pushing her forwards? Either way she was resisting. Before Angel could tell which, the front door slammed. The screaming didn't stop but grew muted.

Nina's little fist reached out, grabbed a strand of her mother's blonde hair and yanked hard. Angel bent over her, the aching fatigue in her body immediately forgotten. 'Oh, Nina!' she smiled, letting her hair fall over the baby's upturned face, inexpressibly relieved to be holding her. 'Are you hungry?' she cooed.

Alex started the car. 'She's eaten,' he said shortly.

Angel looked up, startled. 'But how – ?'

'They gave her a bottle.'

'A *bottle*! But she isn't weaned yet!'

He shrugged. 'Apparently she loved it.'

'But who? Whose house *is* this?' she demanded. 'I don't understand. Why do you have a key?'

'I'll explain everything when we get home,' he said wearily.

'*Who* gave her milk?' A thought occurred to her. 'Why didn't you want to involve the police in this? Alex – tell me!'

He threw her a look that could have been apology or mistrust. She saw the muscles in his jaw clenching. He twisted the steering wheel and pulled out smoothly past the parked brown Morris. 'You have the baby back, don't you?' he said evenly.

'That's hardly an answer! That's – '

'For God's sake don't argue!' he hissed, suddenly fierce. 'Not you too! There's been enough to deal with without that! Enough angry, disappointed women to last a lifetime!'

'What do you mean?' she whispered.

He drew a deep breath, clearly making an overwhelming effort to remain calm, and said through gritted teeth: 'Leave it for now. Please. We're both tired. Let's just get back to London. Once we're there . . . once we're home . . . I'll explain everything.'

It was true, Angel realised – she *was* exhausted. Shock had turned her limbs to jelly. Now relief wasted her too. Nina was a warm weight in her lap.

He glanced at the baby. 'Will she sleep in your arms on the way?'

Not looking at him, Angel kissed the top of the Nina's head. Wrapped in the blanket, she was half asleep already. 'I should think so, yes.'

'When we get home,' he promised. 'Right now, I want to concentrate on getting you both back to Portman Terrace safe and sound.'

'But once there, you'll explain?'

'I promise,' he said grimly.

* * *

As they started slowly up the road, the moon came out and Angel caught a glimpse of someone standing at the side of the house, watching the car. A woman. The one who was being pulled out of sight or the one who was pulling? Or perhaps someone else altogether? She looked like she was breathing heavily – she must have dashed across the grass to catch them speeding away. The light from the open door spilled out into the garden and, in the dull moonlight, Angel could see, in that short moment before they all disappeared from each other's view, that she was short and stocky, heavily built, with a tangle of thick, grey-streaked hair loose to her shoulders. Her eyebrows were bushy and dark, her complexion showing greenish and ghostly in the moonlight. She wore a dark shapeless jumper pulled over a pleated tartan skirt, flat leather sandals and, ridiculously, over thick, bulging calves, the white ribbed socks of a schoolgirl pulled up to the knee to meet the skirt.

Angel frowned, swivelling back in her seat. 'Alex – who *is* that?'

He kept his eyes on the road. 'Where?'

'There in the garden. The old woman watching the car. Just standing, watching us.'

His head moved casually in the direction of the house. They had picked up speed and were rounding the corner. Dark trees blocked out the view. They couldn't see the house at all now. 'I didn't see anyone,' he said.

'Didn't you?' Angel felt too dazed, too completely washed out with relief to even care very much.

She hunched down, inhaling the familiar, delicious smell of her baby's scalp. He knew where you were all the time, she realised, drinking the sensation in. There wasn't a moment's doubt in his mind. *The instant I told him you'd gone, he knew. Even before* he'd made a telephone call. And he lied about the creepy old woman outside the house. He'd seen her alright.

Well, he could lie till he was blue in the face, she decided grimly, tightening her hold on the sleeping baby in her arms. She didn't care. And when they got back to the house, he could lie a little bit more if that's what he wanted. She didn't *care*. Because he'd been right about one thing – she had Nina back. She hugged the baby tightly. And when you got right down to it, when you got right down to rock bottom basics, Angel thought, suddenly hating him, that was the only thing, the *only* thing, that really mattered.

*   *   *

But once they were home, he didn't tell any more lies. Nina was asleep on the sofa, the crocheted blanket tucked around her, cushions piled protectively high. Alex sat on the armchair, grey-faced. Angel, sitting opposite, wondered what her own face looked like.

'A few days ago she telephoned,' he began, his words coming out stiffly as if they were reluctant to move passed his lips and find themselves in the cold, unforgiving light of day. 'She said she was going to steal the baby. She didn't say exactly how or when. Just said that was her intention. She gave it a month. A warning – one month, she said. I didn't believe her.' He looked down at his hands, clenched in his lap. 'I didn't see how she could. I didn't see *how*. All the same, I contacted Mary Peto straightaway –

Pale with stupidity, Angel asked: 'Mary Peto? Is that who – ?'

He shook his head. 'No, just the housekeeper. I merely warned her to look out for anything unusual. Any unusual behaviour conducive to snatching a child. And apparently over the next fortnight she swore she saw nothing out of the ordinary. Everything was normal. Everything. I was reassured.' He grimaced. 'Sounds stupid now, doesn't it?'

'And this telephone call,' Angel said, trying to absorb his words, trying desperately to find a place for what he was saying in her tired and puzzled brain, 'it was the night we held the dinner party, wasn't it?'

'Yes,' he confirmed. 'That night. At the time, I was angry, unsettled – '

'I remember,' she said, with an attempt at irony.

'I didn't know what to think.'

'You didn't think of telling me?'

'I didn't want to worry you.'

'Not *worry* me?'

He looked at her broodingly. 'It was my problem, not yours.'

All around them was silence but the blood drummed hard in her ears. She could feel the anger building inside her. The sense of helplessness and isolation growing thicker every second, like a tangle of brambles rising higher and higher between them. *My problem not yours.* 'So what did you do?' she asked after a moment, rubbing her temple with trembling fingers.

'Nothing. I mean, apart from contacting Mary Peto. I didn't think she meant it. Not really. I thought she just wanted to frighten me. She was always phoning up with some excuse or other, it wasn't the first time she'd called with some god-awful threat – '

'To kidnap a *baby*?'

'Well, not usually as serious as *that* . . . '

'But sometimes?'

He paused for a moment, then said: 'Yes. Sometimes.'

She could barely bring out: 'Ours?'

'She was always trying to attract my attention. Whatever it took. And this time – ' He laughed, or something roughly like it. 'This time she succeeded.'

'So who is this, Alex? This *she* you keep referring to?'

But Angel already knew who it was. Something about his expression – or lack of it – told her. How incredibly stupid of her not to have realised straightaway. Too stunned by everything that had happened, if she wanted to be kind to herself. Too bloody foolish, if she didn't. 'Your first wife?' she said, her eyes narrowing. '*That's* who we're talking about, isn't it?'

He got up suddenly from the armchair. 'I need a drink,' he said. 'Want one?'

'No.'

He shrugged. Unscrewing the cap from the bottle, he located a glass. Looking down at a vase of bronze and gold chrysanthemums on the sideboard, he muttered something under his breath.

'What?' she asked sharply.

He touched the crinkled petals gently. 'These are rather pretty, aren't they?'

'Oh, for God's sake, Alex! Don't treat me like a child! I'm not one!'

His arm dropped. 'I don't think one you as one,' he said wearily. 'Well, was it?'

'Yes,' he said listlessly. 'It was her.'

'You mean *Zara* took our baby?' she demanded, white with tension and rage. 'Zara – whatever she calls herself nowadays – ' She glued her eyes on his and didn't move them off him – 'Hoffman?'

He hesitated for a split second, then, 'Yes,' he admitted, his mouth a little pinched as if it were hard to get the name out: 'Zara Hoffman.'

'But you told me you'd had nothing to do with her for years! You said that you hadn't even *seen* her since the divorce! That you wouldn't recognise her if you did! You said – But *why*?'

She meant, why did you lie to me? But he took her question to have a different meaning. He turned, still holding the opened bottle.

'She's crazy,' he replied wearily. 'Quite crazy. She always was.' He put the bottle down carefully. 'A nasty, deranged, crazy bitch. At first I didn't notice. But then – I did. Then I did,' he said, speaking like a man who realises the complete and utter futility of words to capture what he wants to say even as he utters them. 'Everything she touches becomes unspeakable,' he said, his lips twisting as if he'd bitten into something devoid of any sweetness like a lemon. 'I didn't want you contaminated in any way. I knew the two things must always be kept apart.' He held two clenched fists in the air. 'You on the one side.' He illustrated, moving one hand. '*Her* on the other.' He moved the other.

'But that's insane!' she cried. 'That's insane, Alex! You can't control things like that!'

He filled his glass. 'Apparently,' he said wearily.

He walked back across the room, sat down in the armchair and drank without speaking. She'd been too angry for tears. Now, in place of the anger, she was beginning to feel pain. She felt consumed with tiredness and misery. She could see the same desperate fatigue in him. A weariness which seemed to envelop his whole being, smothering his body like a fine sprinkling of dust: despair, defeat and bitterness, all rolled into one.

Closing his eyes as if he couldn't bear to see her pale, bewildered face any longer, he said: 'I needed you so badly, Angel. I *needed* you. In part, of course, as an antidote to *her*. But only in part. That wasn't everything, not by a long chalk. Meeting you was like a miracle – my chance to start again. I tried not to hope – I tried not to. But I knew straight away. The first moment I saw you, I knew. In that ghastly stiff ball-dress – ' He smiled sadly. 'My very own White Girl. I fell completely and utterly in love.'

With a dream, she thought, staring at him in dismay. You fell for a dream, not a real woman. For a painting, an unframed life. She wondered if her expression revealed any of the confusion and misery that had taken root somewhere behind her ribs.

'I can't explain it really.' He gave his slow, sad smile. 'You weren't truly beautiful, at least not in any obvious way. All half tones, not crude splashes of colour like her – yet so much more *alive* . . . And the way you looked at me! With such adoration! Looking into your eyes made me feel – well, I felt looking at you that perhaps I could start again . . . that loving you I could find what I'd lost . . . It was a very appealing idea . . . '

He stopped and took a swig of straight whisky, a long, long swig till all the whisky was gone. 'I suppose she couldn't bear that,' he said, examining the empty glass, his voice suddenly flat. 'The thought of my being happy with someone else. The possibility that I could find real love. Not like with her.' His lips thinned. 'That was all muck from start to finish. When I look back I see myself as smeared all over with the filth of her. The filth,' he repeated, staring into his empty glass.

'You should have told me . . . I could have helped . . . '

He made an eloquent gesture. 'But how?'

'At least I could have *tried*. Instead I discover that you have an ex-wife who so hates you so much she'd do this to you! And rather than mentioning anything to me, rather than breaking it to me gently or *warning* me, you take a unilateral decision to spare me all the nasty details! You've had this locked inside of you for all this time and I had absolutely no idea. I didn't realise . . . '

But even as she said it, she knew she *had* realised. There had always been something between them – something she couldn't quite articulate. Hadn't wanted to really.

'Have you *ever* been happy with me?' she asked wonderingly. 'You can't have been, not really. *This* must have always been in the background, spoiling everything. The house you're paying for her to live in is in Sussex. You have a key to her door. That part of the county is not so very far from Haywards Heath. What, thirty miles? Maybe less. Very likely, after you had taken me on one of those magical picnics – after we'd packed it all away and you'd dropped me safely back at Longlands – you stopped off there. You thought – I'll just pop in on the way back to London and check on her, why not? Or perhaps, oh, God – ' she caught her breath, struck by a sudden thought – 'perhaps you were only staying with the St Clares so you could more easily visit her?'

She recalled the unpredictable moods, the return, every now and then, of the bitter, dissatisfied lines on his face . . . in a tea shop in Haywards Heath . . . in the Red Lion hotel . . . the sudden, pressing desire to marry and rush her off to Italy, the sheer madness of it . . . '*I hope it wasn't a bother picking me up today?*' she'd innocently inquired. And his curt reply – '*No, I was out already, hours ago . . .* '

What had he been doing all those hours before? Was that why he'd looked so furtively and ashamedly unhappy? '*I suppose you'll be returning to London soon?*' – '*I'm not sure. It depends.*' On what? On what did it depend, Alex? Not on me, she thought – on *her*.

Her heart was suddenly hammering. She felt a kind of fury and despair. And a terrible, heart-stopping jealousy. 'And this past year – ' she said, still trying to cope with the realisation that Alex had deliberately and with forethought lied to her throughout their marriage – 'I suppose you were still seeing her.' She gave a strangled laugh. 'Over these so-called *perfect* first two years of marriage, you were driving down to Sussex and seeing her, weren't you? *Weren't* you?'

'The marriage was a mistake,' he said tonelessly.

'What – *ours?*'

'No, no – mine! To Zarah! I was *tricked* into marrying her! I didn't know what she was really like! Two people can ruin one another's lives if they try hard enough. Mine looked briefly like it had been. But then everything changed. I met you and – There's nothing more to say. What do you want me to *say*?'

She didn't speak for a moment. The rational world seemed to have swung completely out of kilter. Everything she'd believed was turned on its head. One moment she felt furious and wanted to hurt him back, the next utterly miserable. She said at last, not sure which emotion was uppermost: 'God knows.'

'I had to keep this from you – I *had* to.'

'Why didn't you just tell me the truth?'

'The truth? My God. You can have it if you want it.'

At the sound of their raised voices, Nina stirred. Quickly, Angel half stood in front of the sofa and placed a trembling hand on the baby's tummy. Never really waking, she settled immediately and went straight back to sleep. As Angel sank down in the armchair, she suddenly remembered the woman she'd seen as they were driving away from the house. Her head jerked up. She'd assumed it was Mary Peto but – It couldn't be . . . it couldn't . . . *Her*?

The room swam for a moment. She had to clutch hold of both arms of the chair tightly to steady herself against the beating of her heart.

'Was *that* her?' she whispered. 'As we were leaving? The woman in the garden?'

He said in a low voice: 'It was a long time ago. I was young and naïve. I tied myself to her without knowing the first thing about life.'

'But she seems so much older than you. Years older surely. And so – so – ' Angel pressed her hand to her mouth and stared at him over it, eyes wide and shocked. The pain in her side had become so pressing she could barely breathe. 'You *are* divorced?'

'Yes, of course I am. I'm not a bigamist for Christ's sake.'

'Who knows what you are?' she said dully.

'Well, I'm not. Even *she* can't add that to my list of sins. You and I were properly married. You're my legal wife.'

For a moment it almost sounded to her like a threat.

'Your second wife . . . ' she muttered.

'Yes. You always knew that.'

'But not that you were still in such close and constant contact with your first!'

'I didn't want to be!' he said loudly and wildly. 'How I wished that I weren't! But she wouldn't let go of me! Even the divorce made no difference – it didn't count, she said, and I'd never be free. Or I would only in law, not in the ways that really mattered. She'd sunk her claws deeply into me and she wouldn't let go. She actually put it like that! Those are the words she actually used! I didn't believe her about that either. I thought – what in the end can she do? I felt so ashamed of her. So ashamed. I didn't want anyone to know. I mean, that she was still skulking in the background. It was – well, it was humiliating, if you want to know the truth . . . '

His voice broke. He didn't speak for a moment. Raking his fingers though his hair, he stared down miserably.

'The marriage was hell,' he began again, in a slightly steadier tone. 'She'd began drinking heavily right from the word go. My first wife was a lush, pissed from morning to night. She complained she was unhappy. She probably was. Her excuse – loneliness. Living so far from her family and friends. Oh, I don't pretend I was blameless. I expect I wasn't the best of husbands to her. I never really *loved* her, you see. Just briefly thought that I did. I tried to, God knows I tried, but perhaps it never was really possible? You can't *make* yourself fall in love with someone, can you, however hard you try?'

He looked at Angel pleadingly. She didn't reply. She didn't think she could have spoken just then even if she'd wanted to.

'She'd always flirted with the other husbands,' he went on, addressing his shoe. 'Especially when she was drunk. Which, in the end, was pretty much always. She was grotesque with exaggerated movements and blurred speech. Her foolish drunken gestures. It was horribly embarrassing. And later – disgusting. All our friends, one by one, disappeared . . . ' He took a deep breath. 'What no one else knew – what nobody had any idea about – were the scars all over her body. She used to deliberately hurt herself, you see. Then show me and laugh. She has a very – a very wild laugh. She tried to poison me once . . . '

'*Poison* you?'

'She put some powder in my wine. Some drug or other. God, I was sick that night.' He smiled shakily. 'After that, she seemed better. Or so I thought. Mistakenly, as it turned out. Because one day, out of the blue, she threw a knife at me *from behind*. It shot past my ear only missing by a fraction of an inch. She had some idea, a fixation, really, that I'd been unfaithful to her. That I was sleeping with another woman. Actually – ' the smile twisted – 'with quite a number of other women.'

He paused, remembering. 'It was her of course. *She* was the promiscuous one. She'd turned it all round in her mind, then tried to murder me – her unfaithful lover.

'That's when I realised I had to get out,' he said, making a sharp movement of the hand as if he could brush all the ugly memories away. 'That's when I realised. I couldn't fool myself any more. She intended to kill me. She'd already attempted suicide once. They'd found her just in the nick of time. Now she'd decided to kill me first. First me – then herself.' His lips were a thin bloodless line. 'That was her plan. If the word can be used for something quite so crazy and illogical. She became obsessed with the thought of my death . . . '

Angel became aware her legs were trembling. She tried to conceal it by clenching her hands on her thighs and pressing her fists down hard. What she was feeling now was worse than any jealousy had been.

'You wanted the truth?' he said roughly. 'Not very pretty, is it?' He was practically bent over his knees, his eyes fixed on his shoes again. '*Now* you can see why I never intended telling you. I didn't *enjoy* hiding it from you. I did what I could to protect you from these horrors. After we split up, I had to pay someone to keep her safe.'

'Mary Peto.'

'Yes.'

'Thank God we got her back unharmed,' she said in a low voice, glancing at the sleeping baby.

In silence, they both gazed at Nina. Angel thought of the strange, wild-eyed creature she'd glimpsed from the front seat as they were driving away from the house. Alex's mad, murderous first wife. Even hearing him admit it aloud, she could barely credit it. She recalled the triumphant grin revealing yellow, crooked teeth, the clever black eyes and thick, knotted grey hair round a puffy, sweating face and couldn't imagine Alex close, let alone married, to her. His hands on her body, his tongue inside those cracked, twisted lips. She'd held their baby in her arms: perhaps, to comfort her, rocked her, crooning sweet lullabies in her ear . . . Somehow this idea made the danger seem greater, not less.

Yet whatever his first wife's madness, Alex had deceived her from the start, *that* was what Angel couldn't stop herself thinking about. Two years of evasions and blinding omissions, the full-blown deception. He had deceived her and she had allowed herself to be deceived . . .

She said past the dull ache in her throat: 'I wanted to make you happy. That's all I ever wanted – for you to be happy. Silly of me really. As if one can.'

'But you did. I am.'

'Are you? Could you ever be?'

'I never should have married you,' he said sadly. 'I know that now.'

She looked across at his grey, haggard face, at the strong well-drawn features scored deeply with lines of worry, the broad shoulders hunched against life as her father's had once been, and felt a kind of desperate sympathy.

What does it really matter, she asked herself helplessly, that he lied to me from the start if he did it believing it was for the best? He hadn't meant to push us apart – he intended to keep us together. He was just *wrong*.

After a moment, she said: 'Tell me honestly, are we still in any danger? Am I? Is Georgina?' Her voice dropped. 'Are *you*?'

He said quickly: 'All I can say is – she's very well guarded.'

'She was before.'

'Better than before. I've made sure of it. I will – make – sure of – it. Because if I thought,' he said, his voice still flat, 'if I thought that she'd ever try something like this again I'd – ' He shook his head, unable to find words to continue. 'I know I don't deserve any

assurances from you after this . . . and . . . I'm in no position to
make conditions, I realise that . . . but promise me one thing . . . '
His dark eyes were suddenly intense. 'Please don't ever make any
contact with her . . . And if she ever tries to get in touch with you *by
any means whatsoever* . . . which she might because she's crazy
enough . . . God knows, she's crazy and dangerous enough to try
anything once . . . '

He stopped and took a deep breath. Letting it out very slowly
with a strange sort of wheezing sound, he said: 'Promise you won't.
Swear to me you will remain safe from her and her craziness always.'

Angel looked into his dark, unhappy face. He seemed older than
this morning by years. Old and beaten. Almost as old as –

'Promise,' he said urgently.

'I promise,' she said, after a moment.

If he'd told me before we married, she thought wretchedly, I
wouldn't have minded. I'd have done anything for him without
question, even set a guard over my own child. Didn't he realise?

'So that's agreed then, is it?' he said, attempting a smile.

She nodded. At the overwhelming look of relief on his face, a
wave of pity swept over her. She thought of the hideous creature
she'd seen on the lawn, imagined her clinging, with claws sunk
deep, desperately clutching Alex tight, her face, distorted and
grimacing, her heart thumping against his, and said only: 'I'm so
sorry, Alex. I'm so very sorry . . . '

Tears began to course down her cheeks on the last word. She
tried to cover her eyes but they fell through her fingers. Weeping
bitterly, she just managed to say: 'For you as well as me,' before
beginning to sob too hard to be able talk any more.

He stared down at his clenched hands on his knees. Above the
sound of her own relentless sobbing she heard him say: 'She always
said she'd ruin my life. She always said it.'

She looked up, her face wet. He was looking over her shoulder at
the room beyond her. Through streaming tears she could see his
heavy-lidded eyes, dark and, as ever, unfathomable.

'And this time she has,' he said. 'Hasn't she?'

*   *   *

They sat in armchairs a few yards apart like actors on a stage who have been given directions not to move, or touch, or cross the space between them under any circumstances. Outside the window was the sad, pale light of dawn. The only sounds in the room were Nina's soft, regular breathing and the stop and start of the milk-float as it creaked slowly down the street. Angel heard the heavy stump of boots coming up the front steps and the chink as glass bottles were set on the porch, then footsteps tramping down again.

Beyond this house cars will soon begin circling the park, she thought numbly. Only a few hundred yards from here is the normal world.

It felt like an enormous effort to reach out her hand and say: 'Alex – I understand,' even though she didn't, not everything, not really. Then, despite everything, despite the lies and falsehoods, despite the evasions, the prevarication's, all done with the best of intentions but right from the start, from the very first moment they'd met, still trying even then to make him feel better, she whispered: 'I think I can see why you didn't want to tell me, Alex . . . '

He looked at her, at the pale, rigidity of her face, at her stiff, extended arm. 'Can you?' he asked gruffly, the frown not clearing from his face, if anything deepening, but taking her outstretched hand.

'Yes,' she said sadly. 'I can.'

'Still?' he asked stiffly, giving her arm a little tug. 'Even after all – this?'

After a moment she said: 'Yes. Still.'

Then his face seemed to splinter, it broke up. For the first time in this whole thing, despite her on-and-off tears, her shock and sorrow, her damned English *niceness* about it all, his mask slipped. It disintegrated suddenly, shattering into pieces before her eyes. He gripped her hand hard but she wasn't sure that he was aware of doing so. Held tightly within the iron bands of self-control, within the demands of elegance and perfection under which he had striven to lead his life, the sounds that came from his lips seemed all the more awful when at last this restraint snapped.

Still holding her hand, he dropped his head forward. Ugly, driven noises escaped him, each begging for release. But his chest was too tight to allow any fluidity, his features too used to order to let anything more normal be emitted. He rested his head on his arms, his chest heaving from the force of years of unexpressed tears, of years and years and years of them, crying in harsh, grating sobs as if, once started, he was unable to ever stop.

'Oh Angel – Angel!' he keened, repeating her name over and over again, over and over. She heard it later, echoing horribly in her mind when she finally managed to fall asleep – 'Oh Angel, Angel . . . Oh Angel, Angel . . . Oh Angel, Angel, Angel, Angel, Angel . . .'

9

They made an unspoken pact. After that one terrible scene they wouldn't discuss Alex's first marriage again. Wouldn't talk about that first disastrous relationship and endanger their own. It wasn't exactly a decision or anything quite so deliberate on Angel's part. She just found, almost by default, that silence became the accepted way of life.

What is it about me that's so accepting of the unspoken, she asked herself despairingly. It felt so ugly, so prying when she pressed him: somehow so lacking in respect. That? Don't let's speak about it. Let's have a cup of tea, let's go for a walk or to the pictures. Even love carried with it a sort of stiffness, a terrifying reserve. They lived alongside each other in a silence she chose to call companionable. She didn't dare rock the boat – their life went along smoothly and he looked so unhappy when she tried, so fierce and lost and devastated.

A part of her was always hoping he would show more vulnerability now. But, aside from that time when he'd broken down in her arms, he'd never again revealed any weakness. It was like he'd hardened up, closed off from her once more – and maybe from himself too. As if he'd returned to being the stranger she'd met so unexpectedly at Laura's engagement party – on a warm summer's evening when everything was still absolutely fine and neither ex-wives nor secrets were even a glint in his dark mysterious eyes. Or loneliness a constant shadow in her own.

She wondered uneasily if all married people were like this. Did everyone have dark areas of their soul they didn't share, even with those they were supposed to be closest to? She'd have liked to ask Laura but they saw each other on their own so rarely nowadays. And somehow, when they were alone, she could never seem to find the right words. She had a horrible feeling Laura would say – I told you so. Or perhaps not – which was worse.

It was strange, she thought, how everything could alter so subtly yet so significantly. Because after the shock of Nina's disappearance when Alex was forced to admit the truth about his first marriage, ever since then her feelings *had* changed. She still loved him, of course she did, just not quite in the way she had before. Not quite so desperately, so painfully. Her feelings were more real now, she told herself. She'd outgrown that first foolish, childish adoration. Her love had gained another dimension. Nowadays she felt even more fiercely protective. Even if he didn't ever let it show, underneath her husband's dark troubled face was a little boy who had wept and called her name.

A promise on his side, too – he'd change, he swore it, he had the strength and power to change, and if, for some reason, he was ever forced to visit his ex-wife again he'd tell Angel first. They understood each other better now, didn't they? Knew the other's defining bounds. All lies, all deceptions were firmly in the past.

In the long ago, distant, very silent past.

*　　*　　*

Until Georgina's birthday.

When everything started up again in earnest.

A few months respite, Angel reflected later – just long enough to breathe a little easier once more; just long enough to ignore all the warning signs and fool oneself for perhaps a *bit* too long that things had settled back to normal again. Certainly long enough, she thought bitterly, to behave like a perfect idiot and endanger everyone and everything one held dear.

Georgina's birthday was the thirteenth of April. They'd had a small tea-party, some balloons, a banner with 'Happy First Birthday Georgina' painted on in bold curling red letters; Alex helped blow out the candle on the cake. A few days later, returning from France after an overnight business trip, he'd suggested a walk in Regent's Park.

'Just us,' he'd said, on that cold mid April afternoon. 'I need a bit of air. Let's get some while it's still light, shall we?'

Angel had opened her mouth to say but it's nearly bath-time and I always play with Nina in her bath, but something in his set expression stopped her and she'd just got into her fur-lined boots and coat, squashed on her Cossack style hat and followed him out into the late afternoon chill.

The park was almost empty. Only a few bundled up figures remained, heads down, hurrying home out of the raw air. At a fast pace they crossed the Inner Circle, did a sharp circuit of the rose garden, now just bare earth and clipped branches of thorns, then swung back in the direction of Portman Terrace, and she wondered why, since he was always two steps ahead of her, he'd been so insistent that she come.

But on the iron bridge, he'd stopped and frowned down into the muddy brown water. His face was partly hidden from her by the high, turned up collar of his overcoat, hands deep in his pockets, shoulders squared against the cold. And Angel had suddenly realised that beneath the deceptive casualness of his stance there was an iron tension in his body, an unnaturally fierce control. When he turned to her, his face was jagged with it.

Something's up, she thought apprehensively. *Something's happened.* She was sure she'd glimpsed in his eyes a strange, urgent appeal. She wanted to ask him straight out what the matter was but the words seemed to choke in her throat even before the impression had disappeared.

He's often like this, she told herself, trying to ignore the quickened beating of her heart. Often silent and preoccupied. He's frequently remote and impenetrable. It's not unusual. It's how we are. He's withdrawn, I don't like to ask why. It's not so different to any other day. Yet he *did* seem different this afternoon – she sensed he was on the verge of telling her something and if he didn't, it wasn't because he didn't care to, but because he *couldn't*.

It's like someone's cast a spell on him, she thought fancifully and a little wildly, a magic spell that only she could break. She stood there helplessly next to him in the gathering gloom, cursing herself for her ineptness. I'm hopeless, she thought. I must say something. Ask. Why the walk? Why today? What the hell's *happened*?

'Cold, isn't it?' she ventured at last, to combat the fear that was beginning to grip her.

He turned to look at her fully and she marvelled that, after all this time, she still could not read his expression.

'Cold?' he said and his smile was so natural and at ease, his words of such studied unconcern that she wondered how on earth she could have imagined anything was wrong. 'Yes, it is rather, isn't it?'

Yet, despite the convincingly careless words and manner, somehow all the months of unspoken doubts rose suddenly to the surface, mingling with all her unacknowledged fears. 'Is everything all right, Alex?' she brought out harshly.

His eyes rested on her blankly as if he had heard but not understood her question. For a second he continued looking at her in this chillingly abstracted way. Then awareness flickered over their surface. He seemed about to say something, then changed his mind. She watched the sudden emptying of his eyes again.

'All right? Oh, yes,' he replied with a flawless smile. 'Couldn't be more so, really.'

But his eyes if not his expression said exactly the opposite, revealing something of the turbulence within, like dark, shifting water beneath ice.

'Were you about to say something?' she asked doggedly. 'You looked as if you were.'

'Did I?' His face impassive, he stared over at the far bank. 'No, I don't think so. Nice here, isn't it, if cold. I think I was about to say that.'

Angel smiled dutifully. 'Yes, it is.' No, I don't notice anything at all wrong, she thought irritably. You don't seem at all tired and nervy. Everything is just as usual. It's all so damn familiar. Here we are, just the two of us, having a pleasant walk in Regent's Park. Bit chilly, otherwise fine. 'You should have worn a hat,' she said abruptly.

'What?'

'A hat. You should have worn one. You do usually.'

'Oh, yes. Yes, I suppose I should.' He smiled distantly and ran his hand over his hair in a controlled movement. 'I forgot.' After a moment he dropped his hand. 'Don't worry,' he said abstractedly. 'It will be all right.'

'What shouldn't I worry about?' she asked more sharply than she intended. 'If you mean the hat, I'm really not.'

'Oh, no! I didn't mean *that*.'

'Then what on earth are you talking about?'

But he didn't really reply, not in any meaningful way, just clammed right up at her words. She could see the straight, trembling line of his mouth as he placed his hand over her leather gloved one on the chill iron rail.

Angel had turned to him, prepared to be angry at last, but she saw he wasn't even aware of her. The deadly stillness had returned to his body and he was staring fixedly across the dark water, his vague words of reassurance, forgotten already, fading into the damp evening air. He looked so lonely as he stood there, on the bridge beside her, one hand on the rail, over hers. Despite the hand, every inch of him seemed cut off from her.

Oh, Alex, she thought helplessly, any anger fading fast. What is it, my darling? What's so wrong that I shouldn't worry because it will be all right? What *it*?

She stared down in dull despair at her hand lying passively under his, assailed by a sudden vision: their walking into a little fish restaurant near Brighton on their very first date. He'd taken off his hat and was gesturing round the room with it. 'Where do you want to sit?' he had asked. 'It seems you can choose anywhere you like.' And her own stupid, stupid reply: 'You choose.'

She suddenly felt an overwhelming desire to turn away from him – from that over-controlled smile, those dark, remote eyes fixed on some point in the middle distance and that unyielding silence which she couldn't ever seem to budge – move away from her own desolate feelings of sadness and helplessness. She wanted more than anything to sit Nina on her lap, bouncing her up and down, burbling meaningless happy talk to her; wished so desperately to pour tea from the ornate silver teapot into delicate cups and lay thin slices of crumbling Madeira cake onto fine china plates that her hand shook beneath his. Was this was getting your heart's desire really meant? The taste of guilt always between your teeth? All just dust and ashes?

So it was her who moved away from him, God forgive her, and who said decidedly, mustering a forced smile: 'Shall we go in? It must be time by now for tea.'

'Yes, indeed,' he said with chilling ease. 'Good idea. Let's.'

And when she breathed out, fine vapour hung in the darkening air between them for a second, like the end of patience.

*   *   *

But that everything was *not* all right, very much not, disproving all his paper thin assurances and confirming all her own unspoken fears, was shown next morning when she woke to find a note in Alex's small, neat handwriting on the dressing-table. Seeing the creamy envelope, Angel went cold. A creeping sense of foreboding that brought the goosebumps out on her body as she tore it open. Inside, only six brief scribbled lines addressed to her.

'I didn't want to wake you since you looked so peaceful asleep – ' she read – 'but I've had to leave immediately. Business matters have arisen which are too complicated to explain here. Suffice to say, a difficulty has come to light that needs urgently sorting out. There is no need to worry or attempt to contact me. All will be explained on my return.' No signature at the end. Just – 'A'.

Angel looked up dazed. Don't worry? After everything that's happened? Of all the bloody stupid phrases in the world, she thought, irritability covering anxiety, perhaps the single most meaningless. For a moment she couldn't move, couldn't speak. She sat in front of the mirror looking at her own sombre eyes in reflection and thought how bleak a consolation it was knowing that her intuition yesterday had been right after all. Then she got up from the dressing-table and walked towards the door. She seemed to move on automatic.

For the rest of the day she'd gone through the motions. She'd kept Nina close at all times – taken her to feed the ducks in the park, eaten meals by her side without tasting a morsel, mooned round the house, distracted, examining the note in every spare second as if it would give her a clue as to where he'd gone and why. Hoping there'd be a telephone call or that the door would burst suddenly open and in he'd stride, something. *Oh, Alex, darling, please come home, I'll never even ask what happened, or who it's been happening with. I won't ask where you've been or anything, I swear I won't* . . . She watched herself from outside, behaving as usual. But the ordinary times seemed to have melted away and there was just this crisis now and the other when, Georgina found and safely returned, Alex had told her the grim, frightening truth of his first marriage. The rest of her life in between seemed to have disappeared. Only the chill feeling of fear and worry deep inside her was familiar. And the false, superficial calm.

When Alex still hadn't returned the next morning, Angel covered up for him with the servants, telephoned as many friends as she could without raising the alarm, which had been difficult, near impossible, sometimes. 'Oh, I just wondered if he was, you know, with you, or if you'd seen him at all? . . . No?' A careless little laugh – 'No, of course not . . . Yes, he *is* a naughty boy, isn't he? *So* sorry to have troubled you . . . '

They can think what they bloody well like, she thought furiously. Nothing they imagine can be worse than this. Lying in bed in the dark, a desperate panic rose in her, a compulsion to *do* something. Don't, her better judgement told her. Take one day at a time. He'll probably be home tomorrow.

But another day passed without any contact – three long days and nights merging into one single leaden day, all a miserable feverish blur, punctuated only by times of troubled sleep. Angel didn't know how she lived through it. For now fear had really woken in her. A cold clutch of suspicion deep inside that became ice-cold certainty the more she examined his letter.

This has the stench of Zarah Hoffman all over it, she thought, her panic growing. She's cooked up some story to get him to race down to her – got him to swear he'll say nothing to me – maybe said she'll harm someone he loves if he does – just like the last time . . .

Lying in bed, sleepless and alone, fears went round and round her mind. Chilling images kept breaking through however much she tried to quell them. Alex lying in a ditch somewhere bleeding to death, desperate and alone, unable even to crawl for help . . . Alex in a pool of rank-smelling blood, fatally stabbed . . . Alex poisoned, Alex by himself, horribly wounded . . . While here she lay in her soft bed, beneath warm blankets, calmly wondering.

He might be regretting with every fibre of his being telling her not to try and seek him out, hoping against hope that she'd ignore the instructions in his note and somehow find him – desperately wishing she'd follow him to his ex-wife's house. But she couldn't even remember where it *was*. Somewhere in Sussex was all she knew for sure. At the end of a short rather bumpy path, surrounded by a wide stretch of overgrown land. She'd been in such a state of confusion and upset at the time Nina was kidnapped, she had absolutely no clear idea where.

Oh, why had she been so impatient with him on the bridge the other day? Why so bloody unsympathetic? There must have been *something* she could have said that would unlock that cold forbidding exterior. If he was still alive and in any danger now, it was *all her fault* . . .

She had a bad feeling about this, very bad.

There was nothing she could do except blame herself, and worry. And wait.

*   *   *

But with so many fears for Alex firing through her brain, there was no point in staying in bed. She'd simply carry on tossing and turning all night, tortured with anxiety. Angel got up about three and dressed. Dragged on a short tweed jacket, a matching skirt and lace-up brogues.

If only she could remember where Zarah Hoffman lived, she thought, her fingers fumbling over the buttons. There had to be *something* she could dredge up. After all, she could picture the house easily enough – she knew the name of its inhabitants. All she had to do was just work out roughly where it *was*.

She sat down in the deep armchair by the fireplace and took a breath.

Sussex, obviously. East Sussex, she knew that, too. That narrowed it down slightly. OK – what else? *How* had she known they were in East Sussex? She'd seen a road sign. That's how. Looking out the car window – a sign for a village. Somewhere she'd visited once with Laura. What the hell was it called? *Think, think.* A sign for – Oh, for God's sake, why hadn't she paid more attention at the time? Why did you not *look*, she asked herself furiously. Frustrated, she massaged her temples. Locked somewhere in her brain was the answer. If only she could get to it.

A walk – she'd go for a walk. A quick turn round the park might help her dig up the name. She jumped up. Yes, walking always helped.

A crack of light spilled onto the landing as she opened the bedroom door. She ran lightly down two flights of stairs and pulled her Burberry from the coat rack. Quietly closing the front door behind her, she shivered as the early morning air struck her. Inside the pockets were her brown doeskin gloves. She pulled them on. She'd warm up soon.

It was still dark, the wide streets empty. Turning left, she crossed the road, raincoat flapping, and walked briskly along the tall hedges outlining the park, trying not to concentrate on anything other than the momentum of marching and the sound of her feet striking the pavement. Further up the street, she began looking around. Tall houses opposite showed in the light of the street lamps. Chipped cream stucco pillars by a red front door – a blue door – dark green. A gap where a house had once been, smashed by a bomb and never rebuilt, only a shell remaining. Boarded up windows next door, scaffolding and a tarpaulin enclosing one corner, ladders and paint-splattered planks –

Angel stopped and stared across the road at the scaffolding criss-crossing the building. *Nothing.* Leave it alone, she told herself. Think of something else. It will come if you let it. She pressed on.

But by the time she'd circled the park and stomped up her own front steps, the name still hadn't come to her. Her mind was depressingly empty. Standing dispiritedly in the hall, she realised that there might be something she could do meanwhile. She took the stairs two at a time to the drawing room and threw the burberry in a heap onto the sofa.

Crossing to the writing-table, she took out a crumpled letter out of the drawer.

It had arrived the day before, brought in to her by Maisie with the rest of the morning post. Attempting the appearance of normality, she'd slit open the lilac envelope and read it slowly through. Or tried to look as if that was what she was doing – the words kept blurring before her tired eyes. The handwriting was small and neat, slanting slightly to the right with lots of flourishes and curls, the lilac notepaper cheap and thin. The spelling is appalling, she'd thought on one level, her eyes moving listlessly over the lines. She's spelt offended with two d's and tragic with a j.

But she had noticed, before blindly thrusting it into a drawer, that the letter was about someone called Antoinette and was signed by a Miss B Parsons. At the time, she'd been too desperately worried about Alex to care in the slightest about a women she'd never even heard of before. But now she examined the letter more carefully, an idea forming in her mind.

It was a strange letter, really quite strange, even under ordinary circumstances.

Wells Cottage, Keyes Cross, Suffolk.
Telephone: Keyes Cross 300.
Thursday, 19th April, 1952.

Dear Mrs Sorel – I hope you will not be ofendded at receiving a letter from a total stranger or think my writing it to great an imposstion, but the circumstenses in which I am sending this are somewhat peculier.

The lady who was in my care for some years uttered your name a few months before she was carried off this earthly vale and asked that I inform you of her passing.

She left in my possesion a parcel, adressed to you, which I am to keep until the arrival of such sad time as this. I should emphasise that it was my poor lady's desire that <u>no one</u> else be allowed to peruse its contents <u>apart from you,</u> or, I should add, even be told of its existense.

In writing to you under such trajic circumstences, I am attempting to fullfill my duty as best I can. Strange as my actions may appeer, all may become clear when I say that my lady's name was Antoinette . . .

Antoinette. Angel stared down at the lilac paper. *Antoinette.* Wasn't that the name of the friend who once had introduced Alex to Zara Hoffman? She frowned, thinking back to a long ago conversation in a pleasant country pub. Yes, surely it was. Antoinette Meller or Mower or Moyat or something.

She began to feel excited. There was a tear in the page when she'd stuffed the letter too hastily into the drawer so she couldn't make out the last name properly. An M surely, then something indecipherable. But Antoinette wasn't such a common first name, after all. And if it were the same girl, then it wasn't completely impossible that there might be something inside the package containing a clue to where Alex was right now. A note, a scrap of paper, an address even – anything that might tell her *why* . . .

She glanced at the clock on the mantel. Twenty to seven. Too early to phone Miss Parson yet. She couldn't call before eight – seven thirty at a pinch. She had at least an hour to kill. Frustrated, she paced the room backwards and forwards.

When it came, it came suddenly and with enough force to stop her cold. She stood by the mantelpiece with her eyes closed, recalling a conversation between herself and Alex, like a recording played back at too slow a speed. Heard his deep voice echoing distortedly over the months – *'Promise me you'll never get in touch with her in any shape or form* . . . ' And her own voice, solemnly replying – *'I promise, Alex.'*

The 'her' in question being his first wife, Zara, and the promise she'd given so promptly, so easily, just a perfectly straightforward response on her part, because why the hell would she want to get in touch with his ex-wife, anyway? Leaving her with the nagging question *now* as to how she could have forgotten *that* promise, even in all this mess?

Her chest was tight, she felt hot, almost feverish as the dilemma became clear. What should she do? Ignore the letter? Do the right thing and keep her promise? But what was the 'right thing' anyway? Alex had been missing now for seventy-six hours – wasn't doing *something* better than doing absolutely nothing at all?

She sat down heavily on the sofa and fixed her eyes on the ivory telephone. Right or wrong, the misspelled letter was the only real clue she had. There was just a vague, woolly memory . . . and a feeling she had in her bones . . .

And suddenly the feeling became a certainty, that there was something inside the parcel that would help her find – and save – Alex. A whir from the clock on the mantelpiece – it was just going to strike the half hour. She picked up the telephone.

'Oh, I didn't see you sitting there,' Maisie said, coming into the room. 'You gave me quite a start.'

'Well, you rather startled me too.'

'You feeling alright?' Maisie threw her a quick glance. 'You've seemed a bit odd over the last few days, if you don't mind me saying. And now – sitting on your own in the dark . . . With only that small lamp on in the far corner . . . ' She clicked on the light switch. 'There. That's better. You can see what you're doing now.'

Politely declining a cup of tea – a stiff brandy would be more like it, Angel was tempted to say – she waited for Maisie to swish back the curtains and leave before picking up the phone again. She sat for a second, holding the receiver in her hand, until the address at the top of the letter had straightened into words and numbers. Then she dialled and waited for the Exchange to answer.

'A trunk call, please.' Her voice was calm but her heart was pounding. 'Keyes Cross three double o.'

'Hold on, please.' After a moment, she heard the operator's voice again. 'Speak up London, you're through.'

*   *   *

'Miss Parsons?'

'Yes?'

'Good morning – this is Angel Sorel. I'm sorry for calling so early. I hope I haven't dragged you out of bed or anything?'

A pause. 'Oh, no – I've been up for some time. I was just listening to the weather report on the wireless.'

'Only I thought I'd better call early just in case you intended going out this morning. I received a letter from you. You say you have a package for me from an old patient of yours – ' Angel cleared her throat, her mouth suddenly dry – 'Antoinette Meller?'

'Do you mean Antoinette *Meyer?*' Miss Parsons said, after another interminable pause.

The phone felt suddenly slippery in Angel's hand. She wiped her palm on her skirt before swapping it over. *Meyer.* That was it. 'Yes, that's right. I'd very much like – ' she tried to sound casual but she could hear the tension in her own voice – 'to come down to Keyes Cross and collect it.'

'Yes, of course, Mrs Sorel. When were you thinking of coming?'

She had a high, slightly quavery voice, an old person's voice. In those first few seconds Angel could imagine the woman on the other end of the line very well – faded grey hair dragged back into a tight bun, a thin, upright frame, a black dress. She took a deep breath.

'Well, I wondered – if it isn't inconvenient – would later today be at all possible?'

'Today?'

'I could come any time that suits you,' Angel said hopefully.

There was a long silence on the line. Then Miss Parsons said doubtfully: 'Well, you *could*, I suppose. The 11:38 from Liverpool Street is a very good train. It doesn't stop much and has a restaurant car. It would get you into Keyes Cross at about half past three . . . '

'It's good of you, Miss Parsons. That would be perfect.'

Angel was dimly aware of scribbling directions for Wells Cottage on the back of the torn lilac envelope and saying a polite goodbye before replacing the receiver. She sat for a moment, staring at its high cradle.

'Maiden Newton,' she said out loud, remembering suddenly. The village they'd driven through on the way to collecting Nina was Maiden Newton. *That* was the road sign she'd passed in East Sussex. Of course.

She could feel fear and panic rising up in her. Travelling to Keyes Cross and back wouldn't take less than about seven or eight hours, even in the unlikely event that she simply grabbed the package from Miss Parsons and caught the very next express train to London. Which meant she couldn't even begin looking around Maiden Newton before tomorrow. Even knowing the general area, searching for an isolated house would take time. And time was one thing she didn't have . . .

She picked up the phone and asked trunks for a Haywards Heath number. She'd decided what she'd do before she caught the train to Keyes Cross. She was surprised by how certain she felt. At last things were moving. She just had to pray it was quickly enough.

Laura still lived in Haywards Heath now she was married, only

139

about eight or nine miles from Longlands. When she'd answered, Angel hadn't been able to speak for the first few minutes. She'd had to wait, knuckles pressed to her mouth, before she could talk. Pulling herself together, she croaked out – 'Laura – it's Angel.'

'Angel? What are you playing at? I was just about to put the phone down again. Thought it must be a practical joke. It's a bit early for a call, isn't it? I'm still in my dressing-gown and slippers. Is anything wrong?'

'Actually I wanted to ask for your help.'

'Oh yes?' Laura sounded surprised.

'It's Alex. He's – ' Angel took a deep breath, throwing caution to the winds. 'He's disappeared.'

'What do you mean – disappeared? As in a magic trick?'

'I'm not joking, Laura, he really is missing.' Angel could hear the sudden thickness in her own voice. 'Hang on a minute, will you?' She didn't want Maisie returning unexpectedly and overhearing this conversation. She went over to the door and checked it was shut. Crossing back again, she picked up the phone and, keeping her voice low, outlined the situation.

'Obviously you must ring the police straight away,' Laura said, when she'd finished, sounding serious now.

'Absolutely not! He made me promise never to tell anyone about his first wife. What she's like – what she's like with him. I haven't told anyone but you.'

'Well, I don't know . . . I still think you ought to telephone the police.'

'I *promised* him, Laura,' Angel said, starting to get desperate. 'I'll be breaking my word as it is. Besides, I may be completely wrong – this may just be a wild goose chase. This is – well, just in case it isn't.'

'Hm. So what do you want me to do? Apart from not calling the proper authorities.'

'I need you to find the house.'

'Of the crazy first wife? You really *must* be joking.'

'You don't have to approach her or anything – just get an idea of where the house is. Actually, it's quite near where you and Edward live now. Somewhere round Maiden Newton.'

'A jolly large area.'

'But not *impossibly* large. You could comb it all in less than two days.'

'Can't you do this yourself?'

'I wish I could, I really do, but I've made another arrangement – look, I'll be down first thing tomorrow and – oh, Laura! Until then, I badly need your help!'

'Oh, all right.' Laura must have heard the desperation in her voice. 'I'll make some excuse and take a drive in the direction of Maiden Newton. Though it all sounds pretty dicey to me. Tell me again – exactly what am I supposed to be looking for?'

Angel described the house to her. 'And look, you'd better write this bit down. The names of the women who live there are Mary Peto and Zara Hoffman. Got it?'

'Well, I'll have a go. Can't promise anything, of course.'

'Your three minutes are up,' broke in the operator.

'Oh, yes – thank you. Laura?' There was such a complete silence on the line that Angel thought she'd already gone. 'Laura? Are you there?'

'Yes, I'm still here. Can I get dressed now?'

'Thanks, Laura, really thanks.'

*   *   *

And here she was, Angel thought, several hours and a long train journey later, gazing at a thatch cottage painted a soft reddish-pink standing alone in a neat garden edged by a border of dying daffodils – almost inside Wells Cottage and no more certain than she'd been earlier that she was doing the right thing. *Well, too late now*, she thought. *Too bloody late.*

Drizzle was coming down fairly heavily as she unlatched the gate and walked up the path to the front door. A chilly wind blew cold drops onto her cheeks and forehead. Apart from her footsteps crunching on the gravel the only sound was the steady falling rain. She stood for a second, her stomach tense and knotted, before ringing the bell.

Miss Parsons opened the door.

'Mrs Sorel? Please come in.'

She wore an olive green dress with a brooch carved from bog oak in the shape of a harp that dragged the neck down slightly, flat lace up shoes and thick black stockings. Her hair, drawn back in a loose bun, was the kind of sandy grey that might once have been red. In her early sixties, Angel guessed, with the soft, powdery, unlined cheeks some freckled skins get around then.

'I hope you don't object to sitting in the kitchen?' Miss Parsons said as she led Angel down a brown oil-clothed passage into the front room.

'Oh, no, not at *all*. Jolly good idea actually . . . '

'I use this as a sort of sitting-room nowadays as well as a kitchen, you see. It's so much more convenient. I'll just put the kettle on – ' Miss Parsons smiled pleasantly – 'I'm sure you'd like a cup of tea.'

The room they entered was so small and crowded with furniture that Angel had to squeeze between a table and a dresser to reach the chair being held out to her. 'It's very kind of you. That would be lovely.'

Miss Parsons filled a kettle with water and stooped to light the gas-ring underneath. 'There's an iced cake and some scones freshly baked this morning, although not, I'm ashamed to say, by me. There seems no need nowadays, does there, when one can buy such nice things in the shops? I think the ABC's *very* good, don't you?'

Angel murmured agreement, looking round the small, neat kitchen. A coal fire burned in the grate beside her. Cups and a few different sized jugs hung from hooks on a single shelf over the sink. On the floor were polished red tiles. A bakelite wireless set stood on a table by an easy chair with a creased cretonne cover and there was some beige-coloured knitting on the seat, needles stuck firmly into a ball of wool. Whatever she had imagined on the phone this morning it wasn't this – not tea and freshly baked scones with a nice old duck in black knitted stockings.

'You mustn't bother for me, Miss Parsons,' she said a little desperately, thinking that perhaps a sour-faced spinster all in black with thin, disapproving lips pressed tight might have been a better bet, under the circumstances. Her eyes felt bloodshot, her head pounded. She was empty but she couldn't imagine eating. 'I mean, it all looks delicious but – '

'Oh, I always have something myself about this time. Habit I suppose, from the old days on the wards. We'd always have a cup of tea around four. Then what I call *proper* tea at half past five. I always think habit is such a powerful and underestimated force, don't you? And it's nice to have the company.' Miss Parsons looked at Angel with her rather protuberant blue eyes. 'Oh, how very rude of me. I haven't even taken your jacket. Not too wet, I hope.'

'Only very slightly.'

'April is such a treacherous month.'

Angel glanced at her quickly but she seemed to mean nothing else by her words than a comment on the weather. *I'm getting too jumpy*, she thought. *I'm reading meanings into everything.* She shrugged her arms out of the tweed jacket.

'Your hat, Mrs Sorel?'

Angel shook her hair from her hat, a little grey felt thing with a blue jay's feather stuck in the band she saw with surprise, she had no recollection of putting it on, and passed it to the outstretched hand. Miss Parsons took it with an air of fussy concern – 'Oh, dear, it *is* damp, isn't it?' – and left the room briefly to hang them on a peg in the hall. When she returned she was carrying a mid-blue tablecloth with a wide crochet border that she unfolded before spreading on the table.

'Did you know Antoinette well?' she asked, smoothing the material out.

Angel hesitated. 'Not very well, no.'

'It's funny then, I mean her being so keen for you to have her things.'

'Yes, it is rather.'

'I thought perhaps you'd grown up together or were related. One sets great store by those sort of ties as one gets older, doesn't one?'

'Yes, one probably does.'

There was a pause while Miss Parsons opened a tin marked 'Tea' and spooned four heaped spoonfuls into an earthenware teapot, then set two china cups and saucers with large roses on the table. Angel shifted uneasily in her seat. She couldn't carry on giving short, cagey answers like this right through tea. Nor could she pretend to know more about Antoinette than she really did, especially to her old nurse. She'd soon be found out. She pulled the chair closer to the table. 'It's all rather distant really,' she admitted, with what she hoped was a natural smile.

'Indeed? A slice of cake, Mrs Sorel? Or would you prefer a – ?'

'Oh, a scone please.'

Miss Parsons looked at her curiously as she handed her the plate of scones. 'So what exactly *is* the connection between you and Antoinette?'

'She was a friend of my husband's first wife.' Angel looked down, choosing a scone. 'Zara Hoffman, as she was called at that time. Did Antoinette ever speak of her?'

'No – no, I can't say she did.'

'They were at school in Germany together.'

'Schoolfriends – well, well. That *is* rather distant, isn't it?'

'To be quite honest, we never even met. I only ever heard about her through my husband. And he only mentioned her very generally. Almost in passing. I really can't imagine why she'd want to give me anything,' Angel said, with a nervous laugh.

'Can't you?'

'Can *you*?'

Miss Parsons looked surprised. 'Me? Oh no. But Antoinette was so often mysterious, even about the silliest things. I really didn't take much notice. One has to humour patients sometimes, I'm afraid.' She gave a little trilling laugh. 'Rather more frequently than one likes to admit.' Pouring thick, dark tea through a silver strainer into the cups, she added a good dash of milk. 'I hope you like it strong.'

'This is fine. Lovely actually. Thanks.' Angel accepted a cup of tea and moved the saucer closer to her elbow.

'Sugar, Mrs Sorel?'

'No, thank you.'

'I like it strong and sweet myself.'

Angel watched her drop three sugar lumps into her cup with small silver-plate tongs to demonstrate. She sat for a moment holding her teacup and staring over it consideringly. 'I suppose you have no idea what's *in* this package?' she asked after a moment.

'I fear not. Antoinette was terribly secretive about the whole thing. Just asked me to send you a letter and gave me your address. I was to post it to you immediately I heard that she'd passed away. Then I was to hand the parcel to you *in person*. No one else was to be told. She was very insistent about it. You won't forget will you, Brioney? she'd say. I agreed to do as she asked and send a letter but I'm afraid I didn't take any of it very *seriously*. I believe I explained that I was her nurse for several years – ?'

Angel screwed her face into a thoughtful grimace and nodded.

'Alas no longer, I'm now retired. We'd kept in touch, of course.'

'Had Antoinette been ill for some time?'

'Yes, I believe so. Though Ellen Haines, my predecessor, wasn't one to answer questions. *Very* discreet. I suppose that was why she was engaged. Although one might be forgiven for thinking her a little *unfriendly*. I'm not one for idle chat on the wards but one does have to say *something* over a cup of tea, doesn't one?'

Again, the jarring high-pitched laugh. Angel smiled politely but the smile was rather strained. Miss Parsons sighed heavily:

'I'm afraid once Antoinette's health had gone, she bothered less and less. You see, there's no one to bother *for* Brioney, she would say to me quite sadly. And I suppose that, at least, was true. Really there wasn't. Stuck down there we often didn't see anyone from one month to the next. No, it was a job in the end to get her to brush her hair,' she spooned some jam onto the side of her plate, 'or even wash. She would just sit looking out of the window for hours. Just sit and look,' she said again, daintily separating a damson stone from the jam with a small bone handled knife. 'It was as if she were waiting for someone. I can't imagine who.'

Hesitating, she looked at Angel inquiringly. Angel just shook her head. Miss Parsons smeared a scone with jam and took a small bite.

'Well, this won't buy the baby a new pair of shoes, I used to say, you know, quite brisk, hoping to cheer her up,' she went on, after she'd swallowed it. 'But, in the end, nothing would, really. Goodness, she'd cry like a baby if I so much as went down the road for a pint of milk. I had to get quite cross with her sometimes or else I'd have been chained to the house. As it was, I had to watch her like a hawk. She really could be extremely trying when she – '

She broke off, just failing to utter that maddening little laugh.

'Well, we mustn't speak ill of her now, must we? And she was very generous to me as it turned out, I must say.'

Rain fell down the chimney and made the fire hiss. Angel put her hand to her forehead, feeling suddenly claustrophobic. The small kitchen crammed with so much furniture, the warmth from the coal fire, she felt she could barely breathe . . . the heat was suffocating . . . stifling . . . She could feel damp patches on her blouse under her armpits. She took a gulp of the cold dregs of her tea. Had she really believed she could help Alex with any of this? It had been stupid of her to come in the first place. Stupid? It had been crazy.

What the hell do I think I am doing? she wondered. My husband is missing, feared harmed, and where am I? Having afternoon tea and engaging in polite chit chat with the retired nurse of a woman I've barely even heard of, who, for reasons known only to herself, decides to send a mystery package to the *present* wife of the *ex*-husband of an *old* schoolfriend . . . Talk of a wild goose chase.

Angel dug her nails into her palms and tried to concentrate on the crocheted pattern of the tablecloth.

Miss Parsons talked on, what she'd done, how she'd done it. When she finally stopped for breath, Angel broke in hurriedly: 'I wonder – the package – could you possibly . . . ?' and could hear Miss Parsons distantly saying: 'It's upstairs on the dresser in the spare room ready for – Oh dear, Mrs Sorel. You're looking rather pale. Are you feeling quite well?'

'Yes, yes, I'm fine. I'm a bit worried about the train to London though. I'll have to be pushing off soon.'

'You'll have time for another cup of tea?'

'I don't think I'd better.' Angel stood up, her chair scraping on the tiled floor. 'I've trespassed on you enough. But before I go – may I use the lavatory?'

'Yes, of course. It's at the end of the passage.'

The tiny loo had wallpaper with knots of blue ribbon and wreaths. Angel ran cold water into the sink and splashed it on her face and down her neck. Pushing open the stiff metal-framed window, she stood for a moment, gulping damp air. On the ledge was a tin of talcum powder. Sweet geranium, she saw. As she washed her hands with a cracked cake of plain carbolic soap she could hear the old nurse's footsteps clumping up the stairs, then come slowly down again. She just wanted to get out of here as quickly as possible now without seeming too horribly rude. She'd been tired, she'd made the wrong decision. She only hoped Laura was having more luck.

When she returned to the kitchen, Miss Parsons had cleared the table. She'd poured hot water from the kettle into a papier-mâche washing-up bowl, tied an apron round her waist and was stacking gold rimmed cups upside down on the draining-board. The table-cloth had been folded and placed on the side. She pointed with her free hand.

'I've put it on the table.'

A flat parcel wrapped in strong brown paper lay where the tea things had been. It was fairly heavy, about the same weight as a large book. There was no stamp, just Angel's name and address in bold flowing letters and a red wax seal on the flap. The writing was large and round, a childish hand.

'She was most eager for you to have it. She said it was important.'

Angel frowned down at the package in her hands. She wondered if there was something fraudulent about taking a parcel like this. But there, unmistakeably, was her own name and address on the front, so there couldn't be. 'I hope so,' she said soberly.

'I don't suppose you'd have travelled all this way if you didn't. Oh, dear. I'm afraid I put it down to one of Antoinette's whims.'

'Thank you for writing to me, Miss Parsons,' Angel said, without looking up. 'And for the delicious tea. It was ever so kind of you to go to the trouble.'

'At least it's stopped raining. I'll fetch your hat and coat, shall I?'

Brioney Parsons untied her apron and left the room, returning with Angel's jacket over her arm. Angel could smell damp wool as she struggled into it. She stuck her hat back on, she hoped not too crookedly, but the feather seemed to jut over one eye however much she tilted it. She was closing the garden gate when Miss Parsons came puffing up the path after her and thrust something into her free hand.

'Her photographs,' she explained, still breathless. 'She'd have wanted you to have them, I know.'

Angel looked down at a fat manila envelope stuck at the edges with Scotch tape.

'There's no one else,' the old nurse said sadly, seeing her hesitation.

Angel shoved the envelope inside her handbag. She'd think about it later. 'Well – thank you again. For everything,' she added, suddenly meaning it.

She must have dozed off on the train, clutching the parcel in her lap, lulled by the rhythmic motion as they rushed through the darkness, exhausted by the tension and sleepless nights and frighteningly long days, because sitting in the taxi at Liverpool Street, her neck felt stiff.

Open the parcel, she told herself irritably, staring down at it beside her on shabby black leather. You've made the journey, you've collected the damn thing, now examine what's inside.

It was hard to rip off the brown paper it had been taped up so well. Angel tugged off her gloves for a better grip. She tore off a layer, then another. Underneath, a hard dark-blue cloth corner – an A4 size notebook – no, two. She flicked quickly through. Pages of handwritten lines in the same large, round hand. Day, month and year at the top of each entry. Inside the package were two diaries. Antoinette's diaries.

Angel shut the notebooks, wrenched her head back, stared upwards and breathed. *If Alex isn't home when I get back*, she thought, *then I'll read them. But if he is . . .*

But Alex wasn't home. Angel's hand trembled slightly as she let herself in with a latchkey under the glow of the porch lamp and saw that the hall-stand was still bare of his Burberry and brown Homburg hat. She tried Laura's number from the telephone extension in the hall but there was no answer. She'd try again later.

And I'll begin the diaries, she thought wearily. *You never know.*

Keeping the notebooks jammed under her armpit, she tramped up two flights of stairs. Outside the nursery door she paused to brace herself. Then pushed the door open and poked round her head.

The overhead lamp glowed softly: Nina was still awake. 'Hello, darling! Mummy's back!' she cried too brightly, still running on automatic, stepping into the room.

* * *

148

The photographs were held together by a strong india-rubber band. Angel peeled the band off carefully and let the wad of photos fan out into an untidy heap on the writing-table.

The first photograph had 1934 written on the back in faint blue ink. It was the picture of a slender young girl of about fourteen in an old-fashioned cream calf-length dress, dark hair scooped loosely away from her face and tied with a wide black velvet ribbon. She was wearing pale stockings, a little wrinkled over the ankles, and a delicate necklace of stones that matched her dark eyes. The metal was silver, very ornate. Her face was so pale, her eyes so dark and sombre. But even the uncertain smile and questioning eyes didn't hide the firm set of her jaw.

She's stubborn, Angel thought. You couldn't easily push her around. How much she probably doesn't even know herself yet.

Shuffling quickly through, she saw that the dark-haired girl appeared in nearly all the photographs. Sometimes alone, sometimes with others, but always the same girl.

She's *lovely*, Angel thought. So delicate, so vulnerable-looking, even the spotted sepia print couldn't hide that creamy skin and mass of ravishing dark hair, staring at the camera with those big solemn brown eyes.

The portrait reminded her of something but she couldn't for the life of her think what. Narrowing her eyes, she examined it more closely. Was it something about the girl? The set of the jaw . . . the mouth . . . Or perhaps simply the sight of an old spotted photograph? Angel frowned, puzzled. No, that wasn't it. It was more than just a faded image. There was something . . . something she couldn't put her finger on . . . something familiar enough to have stirred up a connection in her mind . . .

An idea hovering tantalisingly just beyond the edges of her consciousness.

After a moment, she shook her head. It had gone. Whatever had been triggered by the photograph, whatever lingering impression had been jogged loose, had disappeared. She replaced the photographs on top of the manila envelope, shuffling them into a neat pile, taking longer than was strictly necessary to line them up. She felt a little shaken. Antoinette wasn't simply a name any more. She was a slender girl with long, dark hair and a determined mouth and a wide, generous brow. Nothing Brioney Parsons had described had prepared her for that.

It had begun raining quite heavily again. Angel could hear it pounding down on the pavement outside. She pushed the chair she was sitting on back from the writing-table, crossed the room and poured herself a brandy and soda. Taking a deep sip, she stared thoughtfully back at the notebooks. Well, she couldn't put it off any longer. Because that was what she doing, she knew. Avoiding starting the diaries. Even looking at them made her feel unpleasantly like a voyeur and, what was worse, she was betraying Alex, she was – She brought her thoughts up short. She would *not* go over all that again. She'd made the decision, for good or bad. If there was anything here that could help Alex, anything at all, however vague, she would find it. For the moment she must concentrate on that. But her hand was trembling slightly as she picked up the first notebook.

Inside the blue cloth cover was an address – *If this book should dare to roam, smack its face and send it home, to* – *Antoinette Meyer, Villa Werthenstein, Berlin-Grunewald, Deutscheland.*

And beneath the childish rhyme, a date – Sunday 10th October 1937.

Underneath the date was the first entry:

'*Twelve o'clock on a cold October day and at last they've agreed! I am to stay with Aunt Eva in Berlin!*

'*Everyone looks shocked when they are told. An English girl in Germany? A Jewish girl? Are you crazy? You prefer Hitler to Mussolini? But I only smile enigmatically at their questions and don't answer as I'd like to – that it can't be any worse there than it is here, living in Italy with my mother and stepfather at – oh, that grim word! – home . . . *'

Angel skimmed through the next dozen pages, looking for Alex's name. It didn't turn up until page thirteen when there it was in girlish black and white – *Alexander Sorel.* Alex in 1938, her Alex, the same. For a second, her stomach turned to water. She forced herself to read through the paragraph through several times.

'. . . *Zarah Hoffman is engaged to a young Englishman called Alexander Sorel. She will live with him in England once she is married. She attends the same school as Marta and I . . .* '

Angel frowned. Was *this* the reason Antoinette had sent her the diaries? Because once she'd known Zara Hoffman in Berlin? Known her in the days before she'd married the young Alex Sorel and moved with him to England? It didn't make much sense. But then, according to her old nurse, a lot of things Antoinette had said and done didn't have much rhyme or reason.

Angel sat there, feeling there was something right in front of her nose that she wasn't seeing. It was so close, she could sense it, but she couldn't bring the idea into focus. After a minute, she shook her head and let the pages fan back to the start. The first entry continued:

' . . . *Aunt Eva Klein has two children close to my age – Marta and Viktor. The arrangement is that I will attend school with my cousin Marta, under pretext of improving my German. But I know the true reason my mother has agreed to this visit – she doesn't want me around now she is expecting my stepfather's baby. The arrangement suits me perfectly, too, since I have no desire to watch her grow big and clumsy with Bruno De Finzi's child.*

'*How absurd I find him with all his* fascista *posturing, his constant, pressing desire to prove that even though he is a Jew, he is more* patrioti, *more loyal to Mussolini, more* italianita *than the Italians.*

'*I've decided that I won't write anything more for the time being – not until I reach the Kleins at the Villa Werthenstein . . . '*

The following page was a blank – presumably Antoinette had not yet reached Berlin. At the top of the next page, another date and time – Friday 12th December 1937: 3.35 p.m.

There was a strange, choked feeling in Angel's throat making it hard to swallow the brandy and soda. Some of the liquid had slopped onto the table – drips fell steadily from the bottom of the cut-glass tumbler into her lap. Swirling brandy round her teeth, Angel read: '*At last I have arrived! The Villa Werthenstein is really lovely! . . . '*

10

The First Diary

Friday 12th December, 1937: 7.35 a.m.: At last I have arrived! The Villa Werthenstein is really lovely! Not as grand as my stepfather's palazzo in Ferrara, perhaps, but very substantial and far more elegant inside. The rooms are quiet and cool, full of solid, heavy furniture carved from some sort of dark shining wood, and there are beautiful old paintings and *objets d'art* wherever you turn.

Downstairs there's a large library but the shelves are virtually bare. I was surprised but didn't like to ask why. Later my cousin Marta explained. All books which were thought un-German were burnt by the Nazis on the Opern Platz four years ago. It was quite a sight apparently because truckloads of the best literature were removed from the Berlin Library and added to the bonfire.

My bedroom is pink-and-white and luxurious with a thick carpet and a gorgeous quilt on the bed. Through the doorway, I catch a glimpse of the bathroom I share with Marta, all shining silver and fleecy pink towels.

Marta is adorable, very *simpatica*. Medium height with pretty brown hair that is rather soft and fluffy when loose, bright brown eyes and a sturdy, fluid body. Not beautiful exactly but very attractive with her pleasant, steady ways. And her brother Viktor? Thin, almost bony, and not very tall, just a few inches taller than me, with large, melting brown eyes, full sensuous lips and dark hair that is thick and wavy. He has a nervous energy about him that makes him seem very alive.

And since I'm writing this in English not German I will add that I'm a bit in love with him already. He ignores me in such a charming way that I can't help it . . .

Of course things aren't perfect in other respects. For instance, there are parks and public gardens all over the city (otherwise very flat and grey) but we aren't allowed to walk in them. On the gate of the park nearby there is a sign which says – 'Jews enter this park at your own risk!' Since two boys from the B'nai Brith group were badly beaten there last month we don't dare but just stare longingly over the wall.

'Being German' seems to be something they are awfully proud of here. Everything is German. There are German lawyers, German doctors, German teachers. They mean by this – not Jewish. There is anti-semitism in Italy, of course, but nowhere near as official or widespread.

Marta was surprised by this and questioned me closely. Are you allowed to go to the theatre or cinema with gentiles? Can you attend school with them? But Italy is fascist too, isn't it? What about Mussolini? Does he hate the *Juden* (here ducking her head and lowering her voice) as much as Herr Hitler does?

She was surprised when my answer was a definite no. I explained that many Jews, including my stepfather and my own mother by marriage, were staunch, founding members of the Fascist party in Italy. She doesn't understand how it could be different – fascist equals Nazi for her. Marta says you get used to all the anti-Jewish slogans. But I don't think I ever shall.

In the window of the womenswear store that we pass on the way to school each morning there are some more of these horrid posters. 'German *Volk*! Defend yourselves! Buy only at German shops!' And another alongside it: 'Germans, don't buy from Jews.' They are left over from a one-day boycott of all Jewish shops when no one was supposed to even *enter* a Jewish store on pain of arrest.

Just ignore the signs, don't let it spoil your mood, Marta advises, seeing my downcast face. They are years old anyway. But now, further Nazi vandalism has appeared in the clothing shop window: 'Kohn Isaak and Co . . . To Jerusalem' in thick white paint with a rather prettily drawn arrow directing them there.

Two brown shirted SA officers walked by as we were examining this elegant work of art. They stopped and made a few sneering, suggestive comments, eyeing us up and down as if to say, well, *are* you Jews? I wanted to march right over, shake my fist in their ugly faces and shout – Yes – we are! So what? But, placing a restraining hand on my arm, Marta said – Just lower your eyes and hurry on quickly. And please – *don't* tell my mother, she'll only worry. I felt a cold, repressive shiver run down my spine as we walked by.

Yet apart of this kind of Nazi unpleasantness, I *love* living with the Kleins. Onkel Walter holds a sort of salon every second Thursday of the month which tons of interesting people attend, all the artists and intellectuals that count in Berlin and the finest young painters. Also the biggest publishers and financiers who, like him, are serious collectors of art. Suddenly I feel full of life and inspired to write this diary again!

Wednesday. After school: Whenever Onkel Walter talks about a Nazi rally that was held in Nuremberg two years ago he gets very worked up and angry – we are being systematically stripped of our rights and nobody does a thing about it, he says. It is now an everyday occurrence. Jews have had to accustom themselves to living without the ground beneath their feet. Apparently Hitler said to a cheering crowd that from now on Jewish people aren't German citizens any more and so cannot vote. We are not *Reichsbürger* – we are non-persons. We cannot visit German houses nor can we marry non-Jews. It is illegal and if you do, you are guilty of the crime of *Rassenshande* and could go to jail for it. I sneaked a glance at Viktor and thought – who wants to anyway?

'Walter, Walter, calm yourself,' Eva murmured. 'You'll give yourself a heart attack if you carry on like this! Just be glad that with the passing of these laws we know the worst.' She says we girls should take no notice since anti-semitism has been a part of German life for as long as she can remember. Even after the Great War when many Jews were decorated for bravery, receiving the Cross of Honour and so forth, they still called us names.

Onkel muttered – 'yes, but it's getting worse and worse.' And Viktor seized the chance to point out that these are *laws* my uncle is talking about, not random deeds of aggression but acts coming from the Reichstag.

But this interjection had precisely the opposite effect, swiftly changing my uncle's mood so that he began agreeing with my aunt – 'Oh, things aren't so bad really.' And with the Berliner's quick sardonic wit which I'm coming to recognise – 'At least they can't stop Jews breathing the air, can they?'

Viktor pointed out that in the last few months violence towards the Jews was getting much worse, or hadn't they noticed?

At this, my aunt and uncle looked solemn. 'Oh, we've noticed,' said Onkel, nodding, 'don't worry.'

'Think of poor Leo,' my aunt sighed. 'They say his arm will never be the same again. Also Emil,' she added after a pause.

'He's emigrating. To Palestine.'

'He never had a proper job here anyway. Perhaps over there he'll do better. You never know. This is why I do not want you girls out at night,' Tante Eva explained. 'Not at the moment. But things will get better soon.'

'The German people are basically decent sorts,' Onkel Walter agreed. 'Any difficulty we experience will only be transitory.'

My aunt turned to me. 'Both Onkel Walter's grandfathers were soldiers in the Prussian army,' she announced proudly. 'Did you know that?'

'Oh no,' I said. 'I didn't.'

'And your uncle himself was a conscript, serving from the beginning to the end of the Great War. For this, he was awarded *das Eiserne Kreuz* – the Iron Cross,' she translated into English, 'So, you see, this really is his country, his *heimatland*,' she said, reverting to German, 'which he loves and fought for and where his grandparents and great-grandparents were born.'

I tried to look interested but I could see from Viktor and Marta's faces that this had all been said many, many times before. 'Oh, Hitler is a catastrophe,' Tante Eva continued. 'A madman. But it can't possibly last.'

'Perhaps England will do something about it soon,' Marta piped up.

'Oh, yes? What?' Viktor sneered.

'They could try and press Germany into getting rid of Hitler, couldn't they?'

'Ah, yes, only this morning walking down Wilhelmstrasse I passed the British Embassy and it very much looks as if they're about to do that very thing.'

'Well, they *might*.'

'So let's just sit tight and wait for them, shall we?'

I thought Viktor was being unnecessarily sarcastic to his sister but my uncle spoke firmly, ending any argument between them. 'That is enough Viktor. Marta may be right – Britain may do something soon. But whatever happens, one thing is for sure. The German people won't stand for much more of this sort of nonsense.'

'This is all going to pass over and everything will be alright again,' Tante Eva agreed firmly. 'That is what everyone says. Even the yiddish newspapers say this is just a temporary thing. There was an article in the *Jüdische Rundaschau* about it only yesterday.'

Viktor ran his fingers through the tight waves of his hair looking unconvinced but seized the opportunity to ask if Marta and I could accompany him and a friend to a café in the Kurfürstendamm on Sunday.

'Which friend?' my uncle frowned. Viktor replied it was Norbert Epstein. He's twenty and at Berlin University studying law and, perhaps most importantly, unmarried. My uncle's frown lifted instantly and he agreed we could go.

After dinner: An event is being held at the Youth Alijah to which Marta and I have been invited. Tante Eva ummed and aahed – too young or not too young? Then decided we could accept. They promise – no ideology, no religious or political controversy, no serious issues, just dancing!

Sunday. Shortly before midnight: We walked past the villas and trees of The Grunewald all the way to the Kaiser Wilhelm Church this afternoon, then turned left down Fasenenstrasse into the stretch of the Ku'damm and sat outside the Café Kranzler, drinking chocolate and eating cake with cream, enjoying the bright spring weather. All the ice cream shops are opening in the city and the *bouquinistes* offer books outside from large carts. For only one mark fifty I can take back the two books I bought today and exchange them for two more next Sunday.

Marta invited a girl called Zarah Hoffman to join us. She lives in a mansion in The Grunewald, too, so we collected her along the way. She has big cow's eyes which she rolls a lot, a well-developed chest and thick, slightly frizzy, dark reddish-brown hair, more red than brown, which she wears in great coils over her ears. She's rather elegant in the German fashion – she wore a burgundy coat buttoned up to the neck, and a dress with a fluted collar and cuffs of stiff lace. She's engaged to be married to a young Englishman called Alexander Sorel, she informed me proudly. She pronounces it oddly, stretching out each syllable – Arlixhoondah. Once married, she will live with him in England. She attends the same school as Marta and I.

Sun on the wide pavements and a light breeze ruffling the pages of the newspaper Viktor was reading. From the waiter he ordered, '*der Kaffe mit Milch*' for himself and his friend. Norbert barely glanced at Marta except to ask very politely if any of us would like another cup of chocolate but I could tell he was conscious of her all the time – his right shoulder sort of *exuded* attention. He has bright, inquisitive amber-brown eyes, receding fair hair brushed back and wore a grey flannel suit. His expression in repose is worried. But when he smiles all the anxious lines disappear. Marta confided in me later that she thinks him very handsome. I agreed, but thought to myself – not a patch on her brother.

It was very pleasant sitting outside under the striped awning with those two on one side and Marta and Zarah on the other, chatting and watching the world go by. We agreed we'd meet at the Café Kranzler every Sunday. 'For the rest of our lives?' Viktor joked, leaving some coins on the table as we rose to go. But when I replied 'yes' I was in deadly earnest.

Tuesday. Viktor is *extremely* political. He says you have no choice but to be nowadays. Tonight he is going to a meeting of the League to learn Spanish. He wants to emigrate to Palestine. He says for him finding Zionism is like finding a new world. For the first time in his life he feels proud to be Jewish. At the league they sing Yiddish and chalutzim songs. He suggested I come too but Tante Eva said firmly, no. One kibbutznik in the family is quite enough, thank you. She is less than happy about it but lets him go. He's old enough to make his own decisions, she sighs. She believes the melodies are nice for him to learn.

Thursday. After hearing a conversation about Palestine between Viktor and Uncle Walter: Onkel told us a joke about Zionism during dinner – What is Zionism? Zionism is when one Jew gives another Jew money to live in Israel.

But Viktor wasn't amused. He says it isn't a laughing matter since for many people Palestine is their only hope of getting out of this country.

My uncle's response was to ask why they should want to leave – 'We are Germans!' he declared proudly. 'Our men fought bravely for this country. We speak German and we feel German and we shouldn't let some riff-raff of a mustachekownik and some drunken rabble in uniform dispute our Germanhood!'

Viktor countered, equally heatedly – 'And where *are* your friends and fellow war veterans? If they don't want us, we don't want them! Germany is no longer our home.'

'And Eretz Israel is? Home is the land of one's childhood, the traditions of one's youth. There can be no 'new home'. This is a contradiction in terms. There is only – '

'Oh, stop, stop!' my aunt begged. 'Have some more soup both of you!'

But Onkel Walter would not be stopped. 'By religion we are Jews but politically we are Germans,' he argued, waving away the silver tureen filled with watery, white liquid my aunt was holding out. 'Are we to leave all we have worked for – all we've built over generations? Who'll take it from us? The Nazis? Oh yes, without hesitation! Shall we hand it to them gladly? And for what? A striped canvas tent and a pile of desert sand? Are we to be travelling vagabonds for the last years of our life? Do you want to learn how to milk camels and feed pigs, Viktor? Do you want your sister and cousin to grow potatoes for a living?'

'Things are different now,' his son replied sulkily. 'Don't you see how much?'

'Of course I see. But the Right won't be in power forever. We'll do what we've always done. Pay a little blood money now and then, negotiate our position, ride the storm – and wait.'

'But for how long? They've already burned all your books as un-German. What next will they burn? Is it really so sick to wonder about the meaning of life? Are the healthy ones supposed to be those who sing only *Landsknect*'s songs and march in rank and file and never question authority?' Viktor glared at us fiercely as he asked this question as if we believed, with the Nazis, that they were.

Onkel sighed and tore off a crust of challah. 'Of course not,' he replied. 'That is not what I mean.' He added: 'We passed through the Red Sea, so now we'll pass through the brown shit.' But it was an old joke and no one smiled.

Viktor threw down his napkin. 'Can I leave the table? Do I have your permission for *that* at least?'

'But you've hardly eaten anything,' my aunt protested.

'I'm not hungry,' Viktor answered curtly, standing up.

Onkel flicked a dismissive hand. 'Oh, go, go! Please don't allow *us* to detain you from your oh, so important Zionist meeting.'

'Don't worry, I won't!'

It was quiet in the room after Viktor slammed the door and left. We carried on drinking thin soup for a moment. Then Onkel Walter said with a sigh to my aunt: 'He's right, you know. Maybe we *should* think about emigrating. We carry on living this crazy existence from day to day. Our horizons grow narrower and narrower and each time we simply grow used to the difference. I must admit that sometimes it's inexplicable to me why we don't simply walk out of our homes and just go.'

'What – leave all your books and paintings? The furniture? My furs and jewellery? Our house? The business?' my aunt said, shocked.

Onkel Walter smiled sadly. 'Books? What books should I leave? As Viktor so kindly reminded us, I *have* no books any longer. The Nazis burnt most of them four years ago in another of the Third Reich's demented attempts to destroy the spirit. And sometimes I think, yes, they've done it, we *are* beaten – '

'Walter! For heaven's sake! Don't talk like that! Not in front of the – ' My aunt jerked her eyes in our direction.

'Oh, let them hear. Perhaps they agree with Viktor. Perhaps Palestine *is* the answer. They should be allowed to decide for themselves. Certainly they're old enough to have their own opinions.'

'No, they are *not*! What's got into you, Walter? You don't usually talk like this. Are you ill?' Turning to us, Tante Eva said firmly: 'Marta – Netta – you may leave the table.'

'Is there any of that bitter, grey brew that passes for coffee nowadays?' Walter asked as we rose obediently to our feet.

'A little,' his wife replied, smiling at him fondly. 'Even for you, you Zionist, you.'

'You know, Eva, sometimes I think we should just walk away from all this craziness,' my uncle was saying as we sidled from the room. 'What will become of us if we stay?'

But, of course, he's only playing at devil's advocate. He doesn't really believe we should leave his beloved Berlin. Emigrate from Germany? The thought only remains a distant and ill-defined wish that always strikes after these arguments with Viktor, nothing definite, thank G—d. Because if it were, I'd be straight on a train heading back slowly and steadily towards my mother and stepfather in Italy.

Tante Eva sighed, pouring his coffee. 'Well, Walter, one thing's for sure. Things can't get any worse.'

Monday. The branches of the chestnut tree growing past my window are now covered with leaves slowly turning red. I feel more and more at home here. Apparently my accent when I speak *Berliner deutsch* is very charming! Tante Eva has arranged for me to have two dresses made in the German fashion which is quite a feat nowadays with all the restrictions. One is bottle green velvet with a fluted collar and lace cuffs (rather like Zarah Hoffman's.) I also own a mid-brown hat with a brim that is turned up all the way round.

Sunday. The Café Kranzler. The weather is changing. This may be the last time we can sit outside this year. My new hat blew off as we rounded the corner and Viktor had to chase it up the street. When he finally caught up with it, he pretended to stamp on it again and again as if he were killing a large vicious brown rat. 'A Brown-shirt,' he explained as he handed it back to me.

We were all laughing, Zarah Hoffman the loudest and longest of us all. She wore a rather nice cherry red wool dress with its own knitted belt and flirted quite blatantly with Viktor. She kept leaning towards him, wetting her lips with a pink pointed tongue, thrusting her (over-developed) chest forwards, fiddling with a loose curl of hair – it was all extremely embarrassing. I found it especially nauseating because at school she's always boasting about 'her Alexundah' and practising writing her new name – Zarah

Sorel is scrawled in various styles at least five hundred times at the back of her school exercise book.

'Alexundah is very tall,' she says mincingly, 'and *very* handsome.' Apparently he barely speaks any German. Zarah of course has no English. She says they have no need to speak much. Seeing her in action, I can imagine exactly what she means. What's the German for pouting your mouth while fluttering your eyelashes like a perfect idiot, I wanted to ask her. She seemed to me really *strange* today with all that blinking of eyes and licking of lips and those sudden wild shrieks of laughter. Quite like a madwoman, I thought – or *meshugah*, as Viktor would say.

Luckily I don't think he fell for any of it. He agrees that she's not really good looking – that her nose is far too long, her lips too thick and that although she has pretty hair and a good figure *now*, when she is older she will almost certainly run to fat. The rumour is that Alexander Sorel is to receive a great deal of *gelt* from Zarah's Papa to make her his wife and remove her post-haste from Nazi Germany. Even so, I do admire the Englishman's guts – no amount of money could ever quite make up for that dreadful whinnying laugh.

Norbert told us over coffee that he is thinking of leaving the university. His father is a war veteran so he could continue studying if he wished but he's not convinced there will be work for a Jewish lawyer in the Third Reich. He's considering joining friends of his family who run an import-export business in metals with links to England, Sweden and France, hoping to find a way out of Germany by this means. And for his wife, too, if he married, he added, looking meaningfully at Marta who blushed bright red.

'Why does *everyone* go on about leaving *all* the time?' I burst out, almost angrily. 'I *love* it here. I've never loved anywhere else half as much.'

Viktor shot a look at me across the table. 'You're very young. You don't understand what's going on. Perhaps that's just as well.'

'Please don't patronise me, Viktor. I am not as young as all *that*.' I didn't deign to add – you didn't find me too young to dance with six times the other night at the Youth Aliyah. 'I understand all the important things – ' I said airily – 'that Berlin is the centre of

Europe for music and opera and theatre and literature . . . '

'It *was*,' Viktor admitted, looking troubled.

'It's true, Netta,' Norbert said quietly. 'There is no future for us in Germany, any more.'

Even Marta, eating cake and drinking coffee on that bright breezy afternoon seemed downcast. She looked at me and gave a tiny, sad shrug.

'So many Jews don't seem to realise what is happening,' Norbert said. 'They have a greater fondness for their bank balance than their religion. But most are just blind.'

'Well, I'm not,' I insisted. 'I agree with my aunt and uncle – this is all just a passing aberration. Lots of people who emigrated from Germany actually came *back* last year.'

'Yes?' Viktor's black eyebrows rose. 'Of whom are you thinking?'

'The Epsteins. The Flugels. The Rosenburgs.'

'Oh, *them*.'

'They still count, don't they? They're still *people*. Look at us – here we sit in this beautiful boulevard, drinking coffee, eating cake. You have to admit life is pretty good.'

Suddenly Viktor's hand reached across the table and closed over my wrist. I frowned at him in surprise. 'And those red, white and black flags we see swagged in the windows all over the city?' he asked in a fierce, low voice. 'The eagles and swastikas that decorate this, oh, so beautiful boulevard?'

'Ignore them.' I stared back into his eyes. 'Most of the flags are left over from the Olympics anyway.' Viktor shrugged and let go. 'Soon Hitler will be kicked out and everything will return to how it was before,' I said confidently, squaring up to the others sceptical look. 'Which is why we *mustn't* leave. People like us must be still living here when everything gets back to normal.'

They all smiled at my enthusiasm and soon we began talking of ordinary things again. All except Zarah who didn't say a word. She seemed very disgruntled as we walked her back. She doesn't like it when Viktor pays too much attention to me.

When we reached the Villa Werthenstein, Viktor and I hurried up the steps leaving Marta and Norbert outside for a moment alone. They've come to an 'understanding'. She's hoping he'll ask her Mama and Papa if they can become engaged. My worry is entirely selfish – I only hope it won't change our Sundays if they do.

A rather long gap has occurred since I last wrote in this diary.

We don't go to Café Kranzler any longer. A sign has gone up barring Jews from its premises – the usual kind of thing: '*Juden Unerwüncht*' – Jews are not welcome here.

Things are changing fast – though Viktor says it isn't really so fast but that only now I am noticing.

Lots of people are making frantic efforts to leave Germany but it's terribly hard because nowhere wants anyone. There are telephone books for New York and Chicago around the city and people rifle though looking for someone with the same name as them. Then they write declaring they're distant family and would they please act as sponsors for them?

Actually it's quite a palaver. First, you must get a sponsor from the country you have in mind, someone who is prepared to write this magical affidavit on your behalf promising you won't be a burden on the government when you emigrate. Then the consulate there must give you a quota number. Once accepted, you need a visa and finally an exit permit from the Nazis. And all these must be operative at once or you have to start over again! We heard there was a queue all the way around the block, up the stairs and round the room of the American consulate in Vienna after the Anschluss.

The magic word on everyone's lips these days is 'affidavit'. And 'getting out'.

Wednesday. After school: It was like a ghost ship in class this week. Half the seats were empty and no one said a word about it. Hedy, Hella, Lorre, Inge, Ditta – all absent. The teachers tried to act as if everything was the same as usual. But by the afternoon it was clear that none of the girls were going to turn up.

Friends of Onkel Walter arrived this evening looking very grave. It appears that all Eastern Jews have been rounded up by the Nazis and deported to Poland. Any families originally from Poland were taken, some of them two generations German. The Nazis call it 'being relocated'.

Monday. 2.30 in the afternoon. Today they closed the school. Not temporarily, or for the holidays or anything: it's *finito*. The German People's Party is using the catchy slogan 'Finish off the Jews'. Presumably they consider us all 'finished off', educationally speaking, for the time being.

A flag was put up outside the building – the familiar red with a white circle and, in the centre, the black swastika. Two German Youths stood outside the gate, ugly boys with acne and white eyelashes. They had red bands round their arms with the swastika on and stretched out their arms in a Hitler salute so that we had to walk under.

The teachers looked very pale as they said goodbye. Most of them have been dismissed from German schools or university already and now have no job at all. My uncle has offered two of the women a position as domestic help in our household since we're not allowed to hire non-Jews but that's hardly the same.

Veza Myer is emigrating with her family to Deventer in East Holland; Rachel Kost's family is emigrating to England. Before they were relocated, they lived in a stunning house in Dahlem – all glass and metal, very modernist, with a telephone in every room. I will miss them both terribly.

Zarah Hoffman is leaving, too, of course, but her I will miss in a rather more practical way. For the next few weeks, I'm being paid two Reichsmark an hour to help improve her English. Then, fluent or not, she will marry her Alexhundar and live in London in newly wedded bliss. I envy her a little, I must admit. If only –

But I try not to even *look* at Viktor when I'm thinking like this. Anyway, it may not be such a final farewell – there's talk of Onkel Walter getting us all visas for England.

9 November.

A shocking thing happened. My hand is trembling as I write. They attacked all the synagogues and every single Jewish shop, Jewish homes too were targeted. Drunken hordes roamed the streets throughout the night shouting and singing the horrible Nazi words about Jews and knives and blood. Early in the morning, two bullets were shot through our front window. Fortunately we were another room. But then men began banging on the heavy wrought iron and glass door and yelling, 'come out you Jewish swine!' Of course we didn't. Finally they went away.

We're familiar by now with Nazi louts smashing the windows of Jewish homes or shop fronts after they've been drinking. But this was on a scale beyond anything we'd ever seen before.

There was a strange atmosphere in the streets next morning – a sort of eerie silence. We stared in fear and trembling at the incredible devastation the Nazi thugs had wrought. Shattered glass and looted shop fronts everywhere, litter lining the streets. Glass crunched beneath our feet with every step.

There is a big Jewish café on the corner of Sächsische Strasse with outside seating where we go on Sundays nowadays. Everything was smashed, chairs, tables, the whole terrace, everything. We didn't say a word but turned round and came quickly home again. Only Viktor and my uncle carried on into the centre.

'It's like that as far as the eye can see,' they told us when they returned, very shaken. 'All the Jewish stores and warehouses have been cleared out and plundered. What's left has been flung all over the street for anyone to steal.'

But that wasn't all. We were sitting round the table trying to eat as if everything were normal when we suddenly smelled smoke.

'They've set fire to the house!' Tante cried immediately, dropping her fork and looking absolutely terrified.

Without a word Onkel Walter got up and, despite pleas from my trembling aunt, went out with Viktor determinedly following. They didn't come back for ages.

'They've set fire to the synagogue in the next street,' Onkel Walter said grimly, when they did. 'That is what you smell, Eva. People are just standing around watching the flames. There are fire engines outside – not to extinguish the fire but simply to make sure it doesn't spread to the buildings next door. Synagogues are being deliberately set on fire all over Berlin.'

'Not the one on Fasanenstrasse?' my aunt asked in a faint voice.

'No, they've just smashed that one up,' Viktor replied, white-faced. 'Wrecked the inside and dragged the torah into the street. They're trampling on it. Men and women are laughing and saying – they deserved this.'

'I'm glad you weren't there to see,' Walter said, sinking down onto an armchair and putting his head in his hands. 'They've all gone crazy. And the few who haven't are watching the ones that have, not daring to say a word to stop them.'

'Gangs of Nazi bullies are systematically moving from shop to shop,' Viktor told us. 'They're smashing windows and chucking all the wares out into the street. All the shop windows on Leipziger Street have been broken . . . '

'Please don't go out again,' my aunt begged. 'Please.' She made them both promise.

Which was just as well since we heard later that they were arresting all Jewish men. Zarah Hoffman saw hundreds of them marching four abreast being whipped along by SS men telling them to walk faster. Why they didn't come to our house we don't know.

Even the Germans seem taken aback by the scale of the destruction. Radio Strasbourg says the whole world is shocked. It wasn't just Berlin – Jewish homes and business were smashed all over the Reich.

A fine of 1 billion Reichsmark is being levied on the Jews for the damage done on what they call 'Kristallnacht'. The night of the broken glass. A fine-sounding name for all that horror. The Nazis are good at finding pretty names for things that are not.

Onkel Walter alternates between fury and despair. We will find the money somehow, he vows. He prays then they will leave us alone. Viktor doesn't think they will. 'Tonight it's wine, tomorrow it's blood,' he mutters, renewing his requests that we emigrate.

Onkel and Aunt Eva look at me grim faced. Germany is no longer safe. They tell me they have no option but to write to my mother.

Tuesday. It turns out that Norbert was definitely among the men arrested. His family say he wasn't even allowed to dress but was taken off in his pyjamas. Marta is distraught. They hadn't even announced their engagement yet.

Wednesday. The event at the Jewish League has been cancelled. We're told to expect nothing further for the time being.

Monday. Norbert is home! He returned fully dressed and wearing a hat and coat several sizes too big. When he took off the hat, his head was shaved. There's a large bruise on his cheek and apparently his body is black and blue all over. But he's alive and that's all that matters, Marta says. They've decided to get married right away. They say in times like this, why wait?

Things seem to be almost back to almost normal again. A lot of the men who were taken away have returned.

Onkel Walter told a joke about the Jew who was planning to emigrate to Uruguay. When his friends showed surprise that he wanted to move so far away he responded – far away from where?

Monday 13th January, 1939. 2 o'clock. Just back from Anhalter Bahnhof. There were hundreds of people milling round the railroad station, mostly other people like us, seeing off relatives. Some were parents saying goodbye to quite young children. Many were weeping, all seemed sad, but all very determined, too. The Laufers were there and the Waleys and the Sachs. I recognised a lot of faces. Apparently children are able to get a visa for England but the adults cannot so they are sending them ahead and plan to join them as soon as they can.

Viktor was surrounded by a group of friends, all, it seems, determined, like him, to kiss their family a fond farewell and leave Germany as quickly as possible. He was trying to persuade his parents and Marta to follow him right up till the last second but Onkel Walter wouldn't be drawn. All he would say was his usual, 'we'll see,' and, 'a few months isn't going to make much difference, is it?'

When the train came thundering into the station, his son hugged Marta tightly and said, 'Try and get them to see sense, won't you?' As he came to me, he took my hand in both of his and looked very seriously into my face. 'Don't leave it too long, Netta,' he said. 'The wolves are howling at the door.'

I thought his lip trembled as he was saying this and his eyes grew slightly damp. I forced the top button of my overcoat through its hole. 'Oh, don't worry about *me*, ' I smiled, putting a brave face on it, but feeling miserable inside. To show him how amazingly strong I felt, I quoted some words of Rosa Luxemberg's: 'I feel at home in the whole world, wherever there are clouds and birds and human tears . . . '

Except on the final words my own tears started spilling down my face, which set Marta off too, and then the sudden shriek of the train whistle over the usual station clamour, the engine beginning to move down the platform, the hiss of steam and clang of brakes, and it was time to go. Viktor and his friends heaving rucksacks and bags into the train, pushing into the carriage, shouting – '*Auf wiedersehen!*' '*Wiedersehen!*' We could barely make out Viktor's tight wavy hair amongst them, until he leant across the seat and lowered the window.

Then the train started chugging out the station with Viktor smiling out of the window till the last possible moment and waving like mad . . .

And there we all were. Standing in a railway station with only bare tracks before us and crowds all around, feeling bereft and very, very empty and alone.

Thursday. I feel the emptiness me inside like a physical pain. For hours I lie here, staring out of the window, I can't be bothered to move. I dress without enthusiasm, picking up the first things that come to hand. There seems no reason to brush or braid my hair, there seems no point to anything. I'm beginning to think, no, to *realise*, that he doesn't care for me, not in 'that way'. How I wish I'd admitted some of my true feelings to him and not appeared so brave and strong and *indifferent*.

Now I lie on my bed and go over all the things I might have said to him. Of course I knew he mattered to me but I hadn't realised quite how much. I don't know how I can bear this sharp pain inside without him. I feel as if I am locked behind glass. I am on one side and everyone else is on the other. I can see out and they can see in but they've thrown away the key . . .

Sunday February 19th, 1939. Zara Hoffman's engagement party. I didn't want to go to Zarah's engagement party but what could I say to avoid it?

Her Englishman was there, talking to Onkel Walter. I have to admit Alexander Sorel *is* as good looking as Zarah boasts – very tall, towering over most of the other men, slim, broad-shouldered and dark-haired with lids that droop over brown slightly melancholy eyes. Overall, he has a dreamy, impassive air.

He has agreed to come to one of Onkel's Thursday salons before he returns to London. He said he'd be honoured – apparently his original purpose for travelling to Berlin was to buy paintings and antiques at good prices. It seems his mother – a good friend of Reichsführer Himmler and other leading Nazis – suggested it! There are some real knock-down bargains nowadays given the climate in the Third Reich, Onkel Walter explained later. Jews have little choice but to sell their art and jewellery cheaply if it's for hard cash, especially dollars or English pounds. They are willing, even desperate to drop their price.

As for Zarah – she was very flushed and excited tonight with glittering eyes which flashed as brightly as the diamonds in her ears and wound round her neck, and looked almost pretty. Her hair was tied back in a loose bun at the nape of her neck which suited her, and she laughed often and loudly for no discernible reason and then, very suddenly and just as inexplicably, grew serious again.

In one of these quieter moments she spoke very slightingly of Viktor. She says you have to be a fool to emigrate to Palestine – on the kibbutz they live like paupers and if you *must* leave Germany it is *far* better to travel to a *civilised* country like England as *she* will once she is married to Alexunder Sorel.

It was all I could do to stop myself slapping her. People put her 'moods' down to the effects of these strange times and say marriage will settle her, but the truth is that she was always loud with wild up and down swings of emotion.

I explained very kindly but bitingly (I hope) how much Viktor despises the Jews in Germany who seem to him without ideals and given up body and soul purely to material advantage. He is not sorry to leave all *that*, I told her, staring pointedly at the watery gleam of the whopping great diamonds in her necklace.

That shut her up, if only for a moment. She recovered quickly and muttered something about Viktor's being very young and rebellious. Wait till he's older, she said, *then* he'll change his tune.

It is impossible to argue with this kind of attitude other than to say pointlessly and peevishly – well, he *won't*.

How materialistic she is. How empty inside. I do dislike Zarah.

Monday. 7.30 a.m. Zara's engagement party must have affected me more than I realised. Last night I dreamt someone had scrawled 'Don't marry the Jew,' in red letters across my forehead. Except they'd written it in German – '*Kauft nich bei juden*,' which actually means, don't buy from the Jews. In my dream the words meant – don't marry her.

I scrubbed and scrubbed but I couldn't get the paint off. When I checked next morning, of course, my brow was perfectly clear.

Tuesday. More restrictions. There's nowhere you can turn without seeing signs saying, 'No Jews', 'Jews not admited', or 'No Jews allowed'. Onkel is still waiting for our visas but it's very slow. I miss Viktor beyond all words. I will never get over our parting, never.

11

Antionette's Diary

Thursday April 16th, 1939. He told me the first time he saw me he hadn't really liked me. He could see I was beautiful but I seemed so nervous it put him off. The expression in my eyes was so open and without any sense or caution that they drew him in too deep and irritated him. He thought my hair too abundant and my mouth too full.

He didn't speak much to me at that Thursday salon – a very subdued affair. He spoke mostly to Walter Klein whom he found a man of great sensitivity, learning and also business acumen, an unusual combination which he particularly admires. They talked, amongst other things, of the changes in Germany over the past two years, the loss, both financial and other, the Jews have sustained, the greater loss that is perhaps to come, and the rise of that dangerous brand of Fascism and Nazism which is storming unchecked across Italy.

At the end of their conversation, Onkel Walter pointed to me and asked: 'What do you think of my niece? She's a beautiful girl, isn't she?'

The young man nodded politely, and looked across the room at my profile (oh so pale!)

'She's my sister-in-law's child,' Onkel told him. 'Emma longs to see her oldest daughter happily settled. And I, too, would like her to marry. Perhaps live in England?' Another quick, sly look out of the corner of his eye. 'Emma married an Italian. But even for a Fascist like my brother-in-law, Italy nowadays is no longer secure. And Germany – ' Walter shrugged eloquently.

'Is England any better?'

'Is anywhere safe for a Jew these days?'

They didn't speak for a moment while their glasses were being refilled. Then Onkel Walter said quietly: 'I understand your liaison with Joseph Hoffman's daughter is now off for good?'

The man smiled at Onkle but not with great warmth. 'Sadly, yes. Zarah's father has decided he doesn't wish her to live as far away as England in these troubled times. Our diplomatic relations with Germany may worsen at any moment – and she is too young for marriage Hoffman thinks.'

'And there were, I believe, money difficulties? Ones that, with the best will in the world, Joseph was unable to satisfactorily alter?'

'Yes, that's true. But that has nothing whatever to do with my – '

'No, no, of course not. I only mention it because – ' Walter gave a rueful little smile. 'Come, let us not be too subtle for our own good. The circumstances do not allow for it. There will be no difficulties with Antoinette's dowry, of that I can assure you. The money is sitting already in a Swiss bank account with no strings attached. I have just agreed it with her mother in writing. Nine hundred and fifty thousand pounds . . . '

'Sterling?'

'Naturally.'

While he said all this, my uncle was watching the younger man with those shrewd eyes of his. It was the first time Alexander Sorel had any notion that he'd been invited to my uncle's Thursday salon for any reason other than the acquisition and appreciation of art.

I have two memories from that evening, both incomplete. The first, the wine that I was allowed to sip. One of my uncle's dusty bottles had been uncorked and a glass poured for me – to lift my spirits, as my aunt put it. To rid me of the depression that had settled mysteriously over me like a dark, stagnant cloud, reasons unknown. My age? The dire circumstances for Jews living in all countries of the Third Reich? No one put two and two together and lighted on my cousin's departure as the source of my misery.

At any rate, the bubbles did the trick – I didn't think of Viktor once. For the first time in months, I felt the faint stirrings of happiness. The lines of apology on my uncle's face seemed to disappear, his voice grew firm again.

The second memory, blurred slightly by the effects of the first, the tall, slim, rather graceful young man in the elegant double-breasted suit with the fascinating mouth and dark, sombre gaze talking so intently to Walter Klein.

Tuesday 9th May 1939, 8.35 a.m.

I stare at myself in the dark burnished mirror.

I won't ever see this old self again.

By this time tomorrow I will no longer be Antoinette Meyer.

On the dressing table, between the silver brushes and the lamp, is a bowl and jug of boiled water. Esther brought them up with the clean linen. Tuesday is a lucky day to marry, she tells me, pouring warm, soapy water into the bowl, because in the Torah it says that on the third day of Creation, G-d saw it was good not once but twice.

I swivelled round on the embroidered stool, feeling suddenly scared. 'Do you think he will find me pretty, Esther?'

But Esther just said: 'You'd better start combing your hair or you'll be late.'

But *will* he find me desirable, I worried, beginning to brush. This tall, good looking man whom I've met with four times – once from a whole room's distance at Zarah's house – and kissed only once? This man with the passionate brown eyes that burn so intensely when they gaze at me. I watched as they rested more calmly on my uncle. Was there an admiration in them in that moment that was missing when they were turned on me? Or was it only that I mistakenly felt its absence?

But perhaps, I admitted ruefully to myself, no amount of admiration would ever be enough to slake my burning thirst. Not if it came piled sky high in bucketfuls.

'Oh, here, let me! We'll be here all night at this rate.' Esther snatched the brush out of my limp hand and began vigorously brushing.

'Ouch!'

'What?'

'That hurt!'

'Oh, don't be a baby. Not today of all days.'

Roughly, she fastened two silver combs and some sweet-smelling flowers in my hair. Then she held out the long white dress which

Marta had worn for her own wedding. Reluctantly, I slipped off my robe and stood shivering in my petticoat. When I stepped into the gown the fabric glided softly against my skin.

Esther unrolled the silk stockings. 'These are hard to get nowadays for people like us,' she grumbled. 'You're very lucky, I hope you realise.'

'Yes,' I said meekly. 'I do.'

'What it took for Frau Klein to get hold of them I can't imagine. And silk shoes? My God, she must have exchanged them for one of those emerald brooches of hers. Perhaps more. Well, for her daughter and niece I suppose she wants only the best.'

Only half listening to her grumbling, I buttoned the cream silk shoes with the delicious two inch square heels. Then, holding the skirt of the dress high, pointed one toe, then the other, and examined myself critically in the mirror, trying to imagine how he would see me, what he would think.

I uttered a little prayer before the looking-glass, on my wedding day. Please make him like me, make him love me forever, dear G—d, please, don't forget, it's the third day, a little extra luck. I didn't think of Viktor, I swear it, not once.

By this evening I'll be Mrs Alexander Sorel, I thought, staring at my reflection. I think I sighed.

'Very nice. You look very nice,' Esther said grudgingly.

She must have felt a sudden surge of sympathy for me, staring at my reflection so large-eyed and anxious. For once, on this special occasion, Esther, proud wife of the village schoolmaster, now reduced to the menial life of a servant scrubbing for other Jewish families five full days a week, placed an arm round my waist and planted a big wet kiss on either cheek. Then she stood back and considered me. What was she thinking that gave rise to that doubtful expression?

'Is something wrong?' I asked.

'No, no, you look fine. It's a pretty dress.' She nodded. 'Let's show you off to the others now, shall we?'

12

ANGEL

Regent's Park, London. April 1952

Angel sat very still, the notebook open on her knee.

I don't understand, she thought blankly, I don't *understand*. Antoinette marrying Alex? The diary must be wrong. Something had to be. Alex had been engaged to Zara. Zara Hoffman was his first wife. On that point, he'd always been quite clear. He wasn't proud of it – my first marriage failed, he'd said grimly. It wasn't exactly a happy affair being married to Zara, he'd admitted bitterly later, just how unhappy he'd only confessed when faced with no other choice.

Why should he lie? Angel thought wildly. What could he *gain* from it? Why should Alex tell everyone he'd married a girl called Zarah Hoffman when it was really her good friend Antoinette whom he'd wed?

She stared at the photographs Miss Parsons had handed her. She knew her lips were white, bloodless, she could see her hands trembling. She sat for a long time without moving, staring down blindly, the thoughts churning through her mind until, weight shifting with the slight involuntary movement of an arm, the pile of photographs toppled slightly and began to slide slowly to the floor.

She watched them land. She felt stunned.

Bending to pick them up, she set them carefully on the writing-table in front of her. At the back of her throat was the burning taste of quickly swallowed bile.

'Life's changed her beyond all recognition,' she said aloud, speaking to herself.

But that wasn't quite true. She *had* recognised her, she just hadn't known that she had.

Angel gave a choking laugh that sounded more like a sob. For she knew without any doubt (*but she'd only glimpsed her for a moment and she'd been so much older and her face so ravaged and ruined, with grey-streaked tangled hair and dulled eyes, how could she possibly be sure?*) she knew beyond question that the old spotted photographs in front of her of a hauntingly lovely young girl were also a more than twenty years younger portrait of that haggard, bloated, strange-looking creature she'd seen only once, and then fleetingly, from the window of a car: Alex's first wife – Antoinette.

*   *   *

Angel closed her eyes for a minute, trying to picture the woman she'd seen outside the isolated house in East Sussex but couldn't quite manage it. The glimpse had been many months before and, at the time, with Georgina newly found and clutched safely in her arms, she'd been in a state of numb shock and stunned relief. It was like a jigsaw with some vital piece missing – the memory fragmented, dissolved, merged and was replaced by the younger image from the photograph.

A mass of soft, dark hair . . . a shy smile revealing even, white teeth . . . a slender body . . . brown soulful eyes that held everything behind them . . .

And something else . . . Something horribly familiar, though locked within Angel's mind and thus, unlike a sepia photograph, impossible to confirm or check. Something swimming up through guilt and a burning sense of betrayal . . .

It's the eyes, Angel thought. The eyes haven't changed. Those dark eyes with the look of generations of suffering in their dark depths. A little duller, a lot older but, despite everything, exactly the same . . .

Angel looked down at the photograph in her hand and thought of the bloated, distorted, wild-haired creature she'd seen out of a car window on a dark, long ago night. Antoinette then and Antoinette now.

*   *   *

The diary lay open in her lap. Angel looked from it to the photograph and back again. There was no doubt about it. These were photographs of the woman she'd once seen outside a large, rambling, neglected house in East Sussex – a lot younger, quite a bit happier, but the same one. They showed the woman Alex later reluctantly described as his first wife.

Different name, same woman.

The photographs confirmed the diary.

And if the diary were true? Well, then – another deep breath – then Alex had jilted Zarah in 1939 and married Antoinette Meyer instead. She'd been reading the diaries of his first wife.

'*You never met her?*' Brioney Parsons had asked, puzzled. '*It's strange then – her wanting you to have her things.*'

But not so strange if Antoinette was once married to Alex, Angel thought grimly. Not so odd if he hadn't married Zara Hoffman, after all, but her equally rich young friend Antoinette instead. The ravishing girl in the photographs – the ravaged woman who'd ended her days staring out the window of a large house in Sussex, waiting for someone who never came . . .

It was Alex, Angel thought, feeling sick. *She was waiting for Alex.*

There must be some mistake, she thought desperately – It *can't* have been him. There must be something I've missed. There's no reason for Alex to lie. There isn't a *reason*.

She looked blindly at the photograph in her hand, her heart still beating far too fast. Because if she was honest with herself – which she wasn't very often, not really, not completely, not nowadays – if she were being entirely *candid*, she could think of a reason why Alex might offer a false name for his first wife, given that she was living only about thirty miles from Longlands.

She stared down at the photo and frowned.

One reason? She could think of a hundred.

*   *   *

Angel found she was in the drawing room. Putting the photograph on top of the others, she began walking slowly up the wide carpeted stairs. She felt dazed and horribly confused. There was a cold feeling in the pit of her stomach. It felt like anxiety, like foreboding, like she'd already go the measure of what she was about to read.

The image of Alex's face as she'd first seen it rose before her, fierce and tender and passionate. Was this how he'd appeared once to Antoinette? How had she looked to him? She thought of the pile of photographs on the table and the enchanting young face she'd seen captured there. The grave, searching eyes shadowed by marvellous lashes, the dark waving hair and lithe, slender body. And later, when she was mad, murderously, frighteningly mad and seen only on a dark night by moonlight – the wild tangled grey hair, the sly eyes, the yellow oily skin . . .

Angel went through the bedroom into her small sitting-room next door and sank down in the small chintz armchair. She closed her eyes tight for a second. She didn't know what to think. She didn't *want* to think. When she opened them, her eyes fell on the second notebook. The first few pages covered the entries for May '39 she'd just read. After that, it was in the form of a journal. Mostly undated, it looked like it was written in retrospect. The handwriting had a different quality – it was both smaller and shakier at the same time.

She's written this quite recently, Angel thought, just a few months before she died, then handed it to Nurse Parsons for safekeeping.

As she lifted it, the pages fell open at the start. The blood rushed to her cheeks as she saw that her own name had been scrawled drunkenly in green ink across the top two lines. Her hand fumbled, a mist rose in front of her eyes. When it cleared she read in large block letters – '*ANGEL – THIS IS FOR YOU*'.

There was a taste in her mouth like she'd eaten dust. She took a gulp of brandy but it didn't help at all. Imagining is far worse than the reality will be, she told herself. It always is. At which foolish reassurance she laughed loudly and a little hysterically later. But then? Then, still unknowing, she forced her gaze upwards.

She suddenly understood what she was feeling. She was afraid. She was afraid of what she might feel as she read on.

'*He loved me once. He really did love me. And then? Then he hated me. That's how it worked in the end. We hated each other. Except he hated better . . .*'

Angel, this is for you . . .

TWO

ANTOINETTE

This was the second time I had my dream.

    Again I have left the house in Coulibri. It is still night and I am walking through the forest. I am wearing a long dress and thin slippers, so I walk with difficulty, following the man who is with me and holding up the skirt of my dress. It is white and beautiful and I don't wish to get it soiled. I follow him, sick with fear but I make no effort to save myself; if anyone were to try to save me, I would refuse. This must happen. Now we have reached the forest. We are under the tall dark trees and there is no wind. 'Here?' He turns and looks at me, his face black with hatred, and when I see this I begin to cry. 'Not here, not yet,' he says, and I follow him, weeping. Now I do not try to hold up my dress, it trails in the dirt, my beautiful dress . . .

JEAN RHYS, *Wide Sargasso Sea*

13

Antionette's Diary

H E LOVED ME ONCE.
He really did love me.
And then?
Then he hated me.
Not much in between really. Black then white. Love, then hatred. That's how it worked in the end. We hated each other. Except he hated better. Not much once you put it into words, is it? A life?

I was married and hustled out of Nazi Germany fast, my uncle throwing in a few paintings for good luck – a Manet, a Picasso, a small Renoir seascape, two Degas and a Cezanne, each carefully removed from their frame and hidden from Nazi eyes in my new husband's suitcase, what *chutzpah*, what cheek! All Alex had to do in return was take me back to London with him, collect the money from a Swiss bank account, full number supplied, make a few telephone calls on my uncle's behalf – no real urgency, but if you wouldn't mind – and, in the meantime, as far as was humanly possible, keep me, and my Onkel's paintings, safe.

And that is what he did, in a manner of speaking. Oh, yes, I was safe, very, I'll give him that. As safe as houses. As the solid, secure houses that were disappearing around us at every moment, it seemed. Unexpectedly, unpredictably – you could never tell where the bombs would fall next until one morning you looked and – wasn't there a block of flats over there? Where that pile of rubble is now?

My pervading memory of the Blitz was the fine brick dust in the London air. And devastated houses, swallowed up by the night. Four months after we were married almost to the day Hitler invaded Poland and war was declared. No one could get out of Germany after that.

I left Berlin a child but I arrived in London a woman. I will do whatever he wishes, I promised myself from day one. Whatever keeps him happy I will do it. I have hooked him, I thought. He loves *me* – Zarah Hoffman's loss is my gain! At last I felt secure. Well, perhaps 'secure' is too strong a word. I felt I *satisfied* him. I believed he wouldn't hanker after anyone else.

And after the island, after our Italian honeymoon, I believe he was genuinely smitten. He enjoyed the way I made love, the freedom, the abandon, the way I would do anything in the world he wanted, anything. On the island I learned quickly how to please him, I even seemed to enjoy it too. All that strange stuff he craved, I satisfied as best I could. Which was rather too well I suspect, because after a few years – years mind you, not months or days – after half a decade of love he began to feel disgusted by it all, poor thing. My willing co-operation began to seem *demeaning*.

He said later that it was all my fault. That I'd started the whole thing in the first place and that he'd only joined in with me to oblige but that isn't true. Perhaps he wanted it to be. Or perhaps he really began to believe his own lies?

Very well, damn you, you can have it. Here it is – my marriage to Alexander Sorel, lock, stock and barrel. Not a pretty story, not one you *want* to hear, but it wasn't one I wanted to live either, to be honest. It certainly wasn't what I expected when we started out or we never would have. I'd have said – Marry you? A penniless, ambitious wheeler-dealer lawyer with dark, striking good looks? Not likely. Nine hundred and fifty thousand pounds sterling tax free and my heart and body yours to trample on? Oh, *no*, I'd have said – I'd rather die here, thanks very much, crammed into the gas chambers with the rest of them.

Sound bitter? Yes? No question about it. I am, very. This was my life, you see, my one and only. It drove me crazy in the end, it really did, or perhaps the seeds of madness were already there from the start as my mother-in-law suggested, the high-cheekboned, the aspiring, the promiscuous and oh so sophisticated Diane Sorel who hated me from the word go, who knows? Maybe she blamed herself for the whole fiasco. After all, she *had* sent her only son to Walter Klein's Thursday night *soirées* in the fond expectation he'd pick up a bargain, never dreaming for one crazy moment that he'd pick me up, too . . . Still, from her point of view things soon improved considerably. I mean, after the baby had died, after everyone had died, after there wasn't a soul left in the world who mattered to me – or, I might add, that I mattered *to* – there you were. Dear, sweet Angel. My curse, his future, my *invention*.

Except after the divorce it wasn't a joke any more. You weren't simply in my imagination to be taken out and dusted when required, you were *real*.

You see, I guessed what you'd be like, even before he began hating me. Even when he was still loving me, I knew. He'd chose the exact opposite of me – someone who reminded him not of *me* but of what I *wasn't*. As if he could cleanse himself of all the years and ways he'd found of loving me by finding someone entirely different: as if the future could wipe out the past. As if it could.

So if I was dark, he'd choose blonde – if now older, then sweet and young again. Wealthy didn't much matter since that was clearly sorted out – but upper class? Oh, *rather*. He became jolly keen on that kind of thing. And innocent. I mustn't forget that – as innocent and pure as the driven snow. He talked a lot about purity and my alleged innate lack of it as the years passed me by, he made me want to puke with all that stuff since he was the one who changed me – he was the one.

And I was right, wasn't I? Terrible, really, to see your own future mapped out so clearly. To see yourself no longer a beauty in the first flush of youth, but undesired and discarded, fat and wrinkled and ugly, even before you are. In the one thing you don't want to be correct about, I was. The barren, ageing first wife as seen through the eyes of the fresh and fruitful second.

Oh, for goodness sake, maybe I'm making too much of a passing reflection! Maybe, after all, it was just a big, fat coincidence? Perhaps you're so different from me simply because *he* happened to meet you and *he* just happened to fall in love. Tired of me: falls for you. Baby born, loved and adored. All quite natural.

The baby.

But that's another story.

*   *   *

I didn't take the pills today. A deliberate policy on my part. When Mary Peto pressed them on me, grinning knowingly as she does each morning, holding them out in her broad sweaty palm, three pills, one white, two blue, plus a brimming glass of clear water, I pretended to swallow them but didn't really. I tongued the lot and spat them out as soon as her back was turned, the blue ones a shade paler from my suck, then flushed them down the loo. Three after breakfast, two before lunch, three at supper and two at bedtime. Not easy to get rid of that little lot. Normally I guzzle them down quickly hoping for that sweet and desirable sense of wooziness to overtake me as fast as possible. I lose all track of the time. Hours flash past like minutes, whole weeks merge into days. But not today. Today I wanted to think more clearly. To remember. I want to tell you how it was. Which, let's face it, is hard enough to do even when judge cold sober. How the swollen, the sodden, the booze-crazed Antoinette came to *be* the swollen and sodden and boozy Antoinette.

You think I started out like this?

Well, I didn't.

I started out like anyone else – young and hopeful. I started out arrogant and in love, assuming the whole dizzy world was where it should be: at my feet. I started out – well, I started out a little like *you*.

You see, once upon a long time ago we were happy. Hard to conjure up now, veronal and other prescription drugs aside, to remember even in short-lived, smiling snapshots. But once we were a loving couple just entering married life in wartime Britain. Friends dropping by, people calling with invites to drinks, the opera, cinema, theatre, ballet – oh, the whole social whirl. Far too busy to record even a half of it in my diary, I eagerly dropped what seemed a childish habit. But now? Now there are days and days in which to drool out of the window, digesting pills, waiting for oblivion to overtake me, that pleasant sense of distance . . . Or else one of those all too infrequent visits of his . . .

So one day I decided I wouldn't wait any longer – I would *act*. I wasn't a naïve young girl, I didn't need others making my decisions for me. I was a full grown woman, drugged up to the eyeballs it's true, mostly by my own choice it's also true, but one thing's for certain, whatever he's told you, whatever he's *said*, it wasn't my fault things went so wrong. I did whatever he wanted, I swear it, I only began drinking *afterwards*. Oh, helped quite a bit by the news of my family – I mean, who wants to remain stone cold sober after hearing *that*? My mother, my sister, Rosa, Onkel, Tante Eva, Marta . . .

And Viktor? Whatever happened to poor old Viktor? Whom I didn't think of once after meeting Alex Sorel, not once, and proud of it too, poor fool.

Not my fault, no siree.

*   *   *

Looking back, it seems like another girl. A young and innocent Antoinette, a slim, dark-haired stranger. But here I am in memory, standing in an unfamiliar room and by my side, beneath my proud admiring gaze – my brand new husband.

I am dressed in a plain frock of black marocain. I wear a soft green scarf and a becoming hat. And here, too, besides me is Mr James the house agent. It is the very first house he has shown us round. And the last, as it turned out, because we bought it almost straight away, cash down, a snip at five thousand pounds, not to mention rewiring, replastering, retiling the roof, replumbing (hot and cold running water in all the bathrooms, I think, don't *you*, Mr Sorel?) The house repainted from top to bottom, the garden land-scaped and well-stocked, furniture chosen with great care – all with my money, of course.

We found out later we could have got it for less without much trouble, as much as eight hundred pounds off the asking price, perhaps more. The market was falling with alarming speed and a world war was looking distinctly possible. Although everyone *said* it was extremely unlikely, no one dared put their money where their mouth was except us and it was far and away the best offer they'd had.

With the hand holding the keys by their label, Mr James fondled his moustache. 'The garden's not much,' he said, gazing out the smeared glass. 'I haven't opened the windows yet, the catch looks a bit jammed, but I can try if you're interested.' He sounded as though he thought we wouldn't be.

I stared out at the sodden yellow-brown grass and the weeds grown knee-high. 'That's a nice tree. What is it?'

'That? No idea. I'm not really up on that kind of thing. It *is* nice though, isn't it? Apple possibly? I can find out if you like.'

He turned from the window and surveyed the empty room despondently. Dusty oblong marks where large pieces of furniture had once stood showed clearly on the red threadbare carpet. A bare electric bulb hung on a wire from the ceiling. 'Needs a bit of work but you won't recognise this place when it's done up. I can guarantee it. Good location, of course. Lovely outlook.' He gestured vaguely towards the far window. 'View's even better from upstairs. Shall we – ?' He made a sweeping movement with his arm towards the open door.

We sidled past, then let him overtake us on the stairs and followed him up to the first landing.

'Owners moved abroad,' Mr James told us as we wandered through the rooms. 'Shipped all the furniture after them. Looks a bit bare at present but all it needs is a coat of paint. Soft furnishings make all the difference.' He spoke breezily but this was clearly his sales pitch and he didn't really believe it himself.

It didn't matter. Walking slowly through the cold, echoing spaces, I was suddenly filled with confidence, I tingled down to the tips of my fingers with it. I kept my eyes on my new lizard-skin shoes and thin French silk stockings, hoping to hide the joy that had jumped into them. Almost at a glance, I knew exactly how I wanted each room to look – what colours I would put on the walls, which should be the main bedroom, which the guest rooms, where the beds, wardrobes and tables would all go. For once, my emotions were uncomplicated. I didn't remember ever feeling so certain about anything in my life before.

I have found my element, I thought with a thrill. I shall be good at this: being a wife.

Another wide flight of stairs. Bedrooms, bathrooms, long passage. Some more stairs up. On the top floor, two smallish rooms. A boxroom and an attic, converted into dingy bedrooms. 'Servants' quarters,' Mr James said briefly, opening the door.

I poked round my head. 'What's that?' I asked, pointing to where some of the faded yellow striped wallpaper was peeling off.

'That's not damp,' he replied with certainty. 'House is bone dry, I have it for a fact. Just needs a bit of plastering, that's all. Nothing serious.'

'Oh, *no*, I didn't think it was.'

'It's a choice property,' he said sternly, once we'd all trooped downstairs again. 'I should hurry and put an offer on it if I were you or you'll find it's already been snapped it up.'

'Oh, we love it, don't we, Alex?'

'Let's talk about the price first,' he said, more cautiously.

While he and Mr James discussed terms, I found an unlatched side door and slipped out into the garden. Standing with my back to the house, I drew a deep breath of excitement. It was ours. My first real home, I thought, my heart swelling with happiness. Tears of pure joy filled my eyes as I looked at the garden, seeing it not as it was, full of tall, tangled weeds with an overgrown lawn, but as it would be one day – abundant and green with canopies of flowers and well-tended bushes and myself, sitting on a graceful wicker chair in the middle of it all, under the little gnarled unnamed tree, sipping lemon tea.

This is meant for me, I thought. We'll be happy here. It's meant. I had to blink away tears to see more clearly. Guests in pale, flowing linen would take an admiring turn around the lawns and –

'Mrs Sorel?' Mr James called from the back door. He poked out his head, eyes bright. 'Oh, out here, are you? Bit parky, isn't it? You're following me to the office to sign the necessary documents. Then it's all yours.'

*   *   *

So here I am only a bit over a decade later, walking through the tall wrought-iron gates at the side of the house, dropping the catch back into place with a clank, tramping brazenly over short, springy green grass, scrunching on trembling legs over well-stocked and carefully tended flower beds. Returning to the familiar garden, a stranger.

What do I feel? I feel as if I've been dispossessed, denied, displaced, as if reality has somehow excluded me from its temporal path. I am here and not here. I am forgotten. I am lost. I feel as if I am dead already and it's my grey, wavering ghost who's returning. There are no tears in my eyes this time. My eyesight is not affected at all. No one can stop me now.

Crouched deep in the bushes I planted long ago, I watch a slim woman in an elegant black marocain dress and a pale green scarf step out from the drawing room window. She stands for a moment on the balcony, basking her face in the hot white glare and squinting her eyes to better contemplate the view. The sunlight glints on her blonde hair. She examines the garden and I examine her.

Except the sun couldn't have been shining on her fair hair, could it? For it is dark when I see her from the bushes below, it is in the dark of night, a silent and empty and enchanted night. And it is me, not her, who is wearing a plain black dress and green scarf and a rather fetching hat. Or is it?

I am suddenly confused, unsure. A fog descends on my brain. Who is it exactly? Who am I seeing at the top of the circular iron staircase? Me then, or her now? Me – or not me? *Is* it me?

*   *   *

August '39. War not even a twinkle in Chamberlain's ever optimistic eye. The upper-classes all flocking to our parties. It wasn't long before we began receiving weekend invitations in return. The Mennes Coopers had lived for generations at Alderbury surrounded by hundreds of acres of land, mostly rented off centuries ago into farms. 'Their country house is really rather splendid,' Alex said, his accent already acquiring the clipped, plummy tones of our new set. He propped their embossed card on the mantelpiece. 'We'll say yes to this one, shall we?'

We drove through parkland, past a fountain up to the domes and columns of a magnificent old house. The Mennes Coopers' had two daughters about the same age as me – tall, unmarried, blonde beauties with blue eyes surrounded by pure, shining skin, thin, shapely lips and flawless complexions. Jemmy and Dodo I think their nicknames were. My heart sunk as soon as I saw them. Faced with these dazzling blonde giants I felt myself growing smaller. As soon as I heard those confident upper class tones I could feel myself shrinking inside.

A butler took us across the great entrance hall, its ceiling painted in blue, red and gold, and showed us into one of the vast drawing rooms. The sun was shining palely outside but it was strangely chilly in the house. There was a huge fireplace but no fire in it. I sank into an exquisite Louis Quinze gilt armchair, wrapped my arms round myself and shivered.

Alex was soon frog-marched off by our hosts for an inspection of a painting in some gallery or other so I was left alone with Jemmy and Dodo. We sat in a triangle across the large room. Jemmy had one long leg crossed over the other, a slender hand flung casually across her knee. Dodo perched with a languid air on the edge of a crimson chair.

'Mr Sorel says you lived in Germany before you married?' she began.

'Yes, that's right.'

A pause. 'That must have been interesting.'

'Very in some ways. Not at all in others.'

'We went there on holiday the year before last. We crossed by car ferry to Ostend and spent the night in the Ardennes, then drove through *en route* to Austria. It was frightfully picturesque.'

'Oh, yes, rather,' Jemmy agreed. 'Do you remember that crowd on bicycles? All waving and cheering as they passed? The women with massive plaits and those funny little moustaches on the men – 'oh Fuhrer' I think they call it? The leader had that tiny bright red pennant on the front of his bike?'

'I suppose you mean the Hitler jügend?' I said doubtfully.

'I'm afraid I can't remember what they were called but they were clearly having lots of fun. They absolutely *adore* the English. They were always saying so, weren't they, Dodo? I think the papers have got it quite *wrong* about the Germans, don't you? They're really awfully friendly. Didn't you find the people so, Mrs Sorel?'

I blinked and said, 'Well, no. Not really. Actually I found Herr Hitler distinctly *un*friendly.'

'Oh, dear, did you? Of course he *is* a bit of a bully – but then foreigners are, aren't they? He's a nasty, vulgar little man but he *has* got the gift of the gab. Daddy heard him speak at a rally a few years ago and says he was wonderfully good. A bit too much heil hitlering for English taste but otherwise jolly rousing.'

'The people simply *adore* him,' Dodo said. 'They were always saying life's so much better now. And, quite honestly, you could see it in their faces. Daddy said you could actually *see* how much happier they are.'

Were they being serious? Or simply sinister? I wasn't sure. If a law were passed in England forbidding Jews to marry non-Jews or even invite them into their houses, I thought, I don't suppose these two would kick up much of a fuss. Perhaps there was a sign on those massive front gates already which I'd failed to notice on my way in – 'Jews enter at your own risk!'

Gazing into those clear untouched blue eyes, I felt such an intense longing for Marta and Viktor, for Rachel Kost and even Zarah Hoffman that I could barely speak. My throat seemed to have dried up completely. 'Your father doesn't believe they'll start a war, then?' I managed hoarsely.

'Oh, no! They wouldn't dare.' Dodo gave a small, self-assured laugh. 'Not after the last one left them so low. Daddy knows an awful lot about that sort of thing. He's terribly well informed. He simply refuses to believe Mr Hitler would be stupid enough to start another. Now, what would you like to do? I wonder whether you'd like to look round the house, by any chance? The fountain in the front garden is considered interesting. Or we could show you the pictures in the oak gallery?'

'I've got rather a headache.'

'Oh, dear. Why didn't you say?'

'It's only just started.'

'There might be some sal volatile somewhere . . . or eau-de-Cologne . . . Shall we try and find something for you?'

'Oh, don't bother. I'll just check out what Alex is up to.'

'You won't mind if we go for a ride, then?'

'Oh, no! Please feel free.'

'Well, see you at dinner.'

'Yes, see you.'

'I hope you're being friendly,' Alex said in the bedroom later. I was sitting at the massive dressing-table in a petticoat, brushing my hair. 'They seem thoroughly decent sorts.'

'They're very English, aren't they?'

'You mean gentile, I suppose. You make it sound like an insult.'

'I don't mean to.' I stared into the looking-glass and wondered what I did mean. 'You should hear them talking about their trip to Germany. I had to listen to them going on and on about how delightfully popular Hitler is with everyone these days.'

'Well, he is, isn't he? One can't really blame the German people for that. They've had rather a rotten time of it since the Great War. There's no getting round the fact that most of them are better off under National Socialism.'

'I thought I would vomit listening to them,' I said fiercely. 'I looked into their faces and felt the most intense dislike.'

'You probably made that pretty obvious.'

'They walk about as if they own the earth. They make me feel small and dirty. Like something the cat's dragged in.'

'How you feel is entirely your own affair, Antoinette. But I shouldn't blame them for it, if I were you.'

Reflected over my shoulder, his face had taken on a cold, forbidding expression. I gazed down. 'I don't suppose they mean to,' I muttered.

'I don't know why you're being so difficult,' Alex said irritably, shrugging on his waistcoat. 'You're acting like a spoilt child. These are perfectly charming people who have come to our parties in London many times.'

Oh yes, I thought, even the house of a Jewish refugee is desirable – if the champagne is flowing freely and she's wealthy enough. I could imagine them discussing it with one another afterwards – *he's married to a Jew, you know, but he's a frightfully decent sort* . . . She's *rolling in money of course* . . . 'I expect they know I'm Jewish, don't they?' I said throatily.

'I really have no idea.'

'Even *they* must have heard what Hitler's doing to the Jews in Germany.'

'I certainly haven't mentioned your religion, Antoinette. Nor do I intend to. Anyway, I don't suppose they *do* know. They certainly wouldn't have spoken so freely if they did. They'd have been more – ' He tugged the waistcoat down sharply – 'circumspect.'

Turning to the wardrobe, he pulled his jacket from a hanger. 'Really I think it best not mention it,' he said, examining it carefully. 'As far as they're concerned, you're English but were brought up in Germany. Fortunately, these days money is quite as acceptable as good birth. But being Jewish may be asking a little *too* much.' He stopped, jacket half on, and considered me. 'Just mime the response in church tomorrow if you're not sure of the words. You are in England now, Antoinette. You must try and fit in. And it doesn't much matter, does it?'

When I looked into the glass I thought I'd never seen myself looking so ugly. My eyes were ringed with blue circles and my face was very pale with a strained, anxious expression. There was none of the cool confidence I had seen in Dodo's healthy, fair face: none of the arrogance I'd found in Jemmy's dazzling blue eyes. It takes generations to reach that smug complacency, I thought – unless you marry into it.

And that's exactly what Alex would like to do, I realised suddenly. He'd far prefer being married to one of those aristocratic blonde beauties than to me any day. The thought filled me with a profound despair. All the fight left my body. I felt like giving up there and then. I said in a thin, reedy voice that quavered a little: 'I'm sure you're right. They don't give a hoot for my thoughts or feelings. The trouble is,' my chin wobbled, 'It matters to me. I feel as if I've fallen down a precipice.'

'You talk such unbelievable rot,' Alex said coldly.

I lowered my head. 'Well, I do,' I whispered, a tear rolling down my cheek.

'Oh, please don't start. Now now. Not again.'

When I looked up he was staring at me with hard, accusing eyes that hurt and confused me. 'Oh, now *you're* looking at me like I'm something the cat brought in!' I cried, putting my hands over my face to cut out his scornful eyes.

He stood for a moment, watching me crying. 'You really pick

your times, don't you?' he said bitterly. 'We're supposed to be dining in fifteen minutes.'

'I'm sorry, I'm sorry!' I sobbed. 'I will do whatever pleases you!' Tears were streaming down my face. 'Tell me what to do and I'll do it!' I sobbed wretchedly.

'What I would like you to do? My God, Antoinette. This weekend was supposed to be entertaining. But you can't enjoy it, can you? And why? Because you're hysterical over nothing as usual!' He took a step forward. 'You seem to have absolutely no conception of normal, decent behaviour. You embarrass me over and over again. You think this perfectly filthy way of acting is acceptable. You wonder what I want? What I *want* – ' another step – 'is for you to stop making such a fuss and get dressed! Stop this disgusting outburst and get *dressed*! Or we'll be late for dinner on top of everything else!'

My head was pounding, I felt suddenly dizzy. The look on his face made me cower on the stool. My cringing away from him seemed to infuriate him even more. He advanced on me threateningly. Grabbing my wrist, he pulled me roughly to my feet. The long silken skirt of my petticoat rustled.

'Stop crying!' he said in the same quiet, malevolent tone. 'Stop it!'

I half shut my eyes, choking and spluttering with the effort to calm down. I knew that he hated more than anything any display of what he called my 'masochistic self-pity'. But I felt flooded with misery. He was so cold and utterly indifferent. He didn't understand my feelings and clearly didn't want to. 'You'd prefer me dead,' I said, between choking sobs. 'Dead and in my grave.'

He laughed. 'Ah, yes' he sneered. 'A little stone cherub . . . a gentle covering of ivy . . . perhaps a tasteful inscription in Hebrew on the gravestone?'

I opened my eyes. He was smiling cruelly. 'I wasn't joking,' I said.

The smile disappeared: he let go of my arm. 'Then you should see a doctor,' he snarled. 'Or one should see *you*.'

A tear dropped onto my hand. 'Perhaps it's too late for me already.'

'Judging by this hysterical display of emotion,' he replied, turning away in disgust, 'it probably is. Oh, do whatever you wish once we're home, Antoinette. I don't give a shit, quite frankly. But please don't show me up while we're here. Just try not to embarrass me more than you have already, will you? Take that stupid, sulky look off your face and try and behave decently for once. Just bloody try.'

So I did try, I put on a bloody good show as he'd requested, a brave front, stiff upper lip and all that. I forced myself to stop weeping and splashed my face with cold water – as icy and cold as my husband's heart. I dressed very carefully and pinned up my hair. And that night I'd lain awake beside him, tormented by doubts and fears.

And his eyes behind their lids, cruel and hard, like two uncaring, beautiful, polished brown stones.

*   *   *

June 1940: I can still recall his face when I first mentioned her name that evening. The faint look of dislike that entered his eyes. I can hear my own voice, pitched a little higher than was usual, a little more defensive. I felt rather protective of her. She was, after all, the only other girl I knew who had made it from Berlin to England and relative safety before war began.

'I've invited Rachel Kost to dinner tomorrow,' I said, in this unnaturally thin, high voice.

Alex glanced up briefly from behind the city page of *The Times* and, shaking out a fold, said with cold detachment, 'Then I shall eat at my club.'

'Why are you always so unfriendly to Rachel?'

'I'm not unfriendly. Please don't exaggerate.'

'I'm not. It's true. You're *never* nice to her.'

'There's no need to raise your voice. Shouting doesn't make me listen any better. Quite the contrary.'

'Well, it's very difficult if I can't even invite my closest girlfriend to dinner.'

'You can. Only I shan't be here.'

He carried on reading, holding the paper high, but not too high for me to see the frown etched between his brows.

'What's wrong with her, anyway?' I persisted.

'I can't bear that type.'

'What *type*?'

He considered me over the top of the paper. 'She runs a flower shop, doesn't she? And, oh God, that *accent* . . . '

'She can't help having one – she *is* German. And it isn't a flower shop – it's a florist – '

'*Is* there any difference?'

'You make it sound like she's out selling violets in Covent Garden before dawn. And, actually, she's considered rather beautiful – '

'If you like that kind of thing, yes, I'm sure she is.'

'*You* obviously don't. Oh, you don't want me to have any friends but yours!'

'You're shouting again,' he hissed. 'Therese will hear you in the kitchen.'

Biting my lip, I looked down, feeling my chest growing tight.

'I haven't said you cannot see Rachel,' he said, speaking very quietly and evenly, 'despite the fact I don't much approve of her as the right sort of friend for you. I've simply said I won't be joining you, that is all. That isn't too outrageous, is it? It seems quite reasonable to me. I merely ask that you see her without my presence. Why can't you arrange a luncheon with her on a day when I am out?'

'Because I do all the time! Because she's beginning to notice you're never bloody here!'

'Please don't swear, Antoinette,' he said coldly.

'*You* always do,' I muttered.

'That's different.'

'I don't see why.'

'Don't you?'

'I don't think you're being at all fair.' I tried to keep my voice calm but it was trembling. 'I'm constantly going to *your* friend's parties. We went to the de Wittes only last night.'

'You like the de Wittes.'

'Oh, I don't, not really. I mean, they're *alright*, I don't *dis*like them, but I have absolutely nothing in common with them. I'm always wondering – what on earth shall I talk about now? My eyes have a sort of ratty desperation in them while we're discussing one thing, already searching for the next. Frankly, I find them ghastly old bores.'

'If that is how you feel about the de Wittes,' Alex said, looking furious, 'we need never meet with them again. I shall telephone Olivia de Witte tomorrow and inform her that we shan't be taking up their generous invitation of a box at the opera, after all.'

'Oh, don't be like that, Alex! It's just that Rachel is – she never gets to see you and – and she's always asking if she's going to – and it's very *awkward* because I have no other friends or – or family over – over here – and – and she's the only one who – who's – '

'Oh, don't start blubbing for Christ's sake.' Folding the paper, he put it down resignedly. 'You're so *emotional* now. Even more than before, if that's possible. Oh, come here.' Wiping away tears with my hand, I perched on the arm of the chair. He folded his arms around me with a resigned sigh. 'Whatever will you be like in a few months time? Mm?'

I sniffed. '*I* don't know.'

'Look, I'll make sure I'm back tomorrow evening.'

'By eight?'

'Yes, OK. By eight.'

I gave a tremulous smile and tried not to look too triumphant. '*Thank* you, Alex.'

The dinner was a little tense. Especially since Alex found Rachel, supposedly using a cloakroom, but actually wandering around his dressing room and study on the floor above – picking up the odd ornament, quietly opening the drawers and rummaging inside. He felt intruded upon, he told me later, coldly furious. She hadn't even bothered to put things back in the right place.

But I noticed for the first time that Rachel was attracted to Alex. It was evident in the way she agreed so eagerly with his views about music and American movies over the soup and oysters and avoided looking at him over the pigeons and main course. Complaining about her in bed that night, he hadn't noticed a thing. His manner with her was easy, always polite, but I thought his charm rather automatic and off-hand. And, yes, of course, she'd talked too much in the accent he found so appalling, an ill-judged, non-stop stream of ungrammatical chatter displaying all her weaknesses, but, still, all things considered, the evening hadn't gone off too badly, I decided.

Smiling contentedly, I placed my hands on my gently curving belly. Closing my eyes, I made a wish. For all of our happiness – for Rachel's, for my own and Alex's, and most especially, for that of our unborn child.

*   *   *

So yes, I was pregnant. Is that really so surprising? The war had started and I was with child. The two things seemed inextricably linked in my mind. War and loneliness, life and death.

I spent the first few months in the bathroom with my head in a sink, vomiting. I think of the war in terms of a white porcelain basin seen up close. Shining chrome taps, glittering chromium-plate and mirrors and the clean curve of a hand basin is what the start of World War Two brings to mind. In the afternoons I recovered on the sofa in the green sitting-room, eating chocolates and reading. It was odd to think there was a living thing growing in my belly whilst all around me a whole army had disappeared, presumed dead.

Not Alex though luckily. He'd wangled a civilian job as some-thing in the War Office – fairly easy given his legal training and large, rather flat feet – and was working on something very hush hush. I felt rather sad and lonely in a pleasantly piquant kind of way. Everything had changed. People disappeared and came back in uniform; people disappeared and never came back again. Some-times I went for a walk to meet Rachel at Buzzards for a bun and a coffee. Sometimes I just walked. Marylebone Road, Tottenham Court Road, Regent's Street, Soho. When Alex was working late I liked to carry on into Piccadilly.

The cold had set in. In the day, people stood coughing in food queues in shabby coats, stamping their feet, their gas-masks in canvas boxes slung over their shoulders. But at night you could lose yourself in the dark, unlighted streets crowded with people laughing and talking and jostling. Women loomed suddenly out of the shadows wearing square-shouldered dresses beneath unbuttoned coats, or trousers and turbans, cigarettes stuck to their brightly painted mouths, hanging onto a man friend's arm.

I moved blindly through them, occasionally bumping into someone coming from the opposite direction or stumbling over unexpected curbs. Buses appeared out of nowhere, headlights dimmed to a slit. Several times I was followed through the streets by men in khaki.

'Hello, beautiful! Can you show me around London? I'm only on leave for twenty-four hours!'

'Hello, gorgeous! Like a drink? Oh, don't be so hoity toity! Oh, go on!'

One day, someone grabbed my arm quite tightly. 'Here, what's up?' he said quite nastily when I shook him off. I looked straight into his face. He wasn't very tall. Rather good looking – a little Viktor-ish, I thought, with those full lips, curling hair and dark, soulful eyes. 'I'm expecting a baby,' I blurted out.

'Well, it's not ruddy well mine, is it?'

After that I ate at home on my own. I liked to curl up on the sofa. The air-raids had begun. The outside world seemed frightening and hostile. Official blackout was nine thirty. The West End had become full of boarded up shop fronts, plate glass windows replaced by sheets of plywood. If you walked too far in the wrong direction you might come across a bomb site – gutted buildings with wall-paper still showing on a single standing wall, a scene of devastation and destruction that ruined the day. Bad for baby, I told myself, turning quickly on my heels.

Rachel had suggested I take up smoking. 'It's chic,' she said. 'Everyone does it.'

Puffing on a cigarette, I read in front of a coal fire. I smoked and drank pale tea with milk, or ersatz coffee without, trying to while away the time until Alex came home. A glass of sherry wine made the warmth rush to my face and my heart beat faster. I found that a sherry sneaked at tea-time made the time pass quickly and every-thing feel more bearable, even death and loneliness. Even that.

*   *   *

'I bumped into Rachel Kost today,' Alex said casually over a late dinner a few weeks later.

I looked up quickly, interested, anxious. 'Did you? Where?'

'I was in Knightsbridge and dashed into a shop thinking I'd buy some flowers for you since you're feeling so poorly, and there she was. The florist is exquisite. Makes Gerard's in Regent Street look positively old hat.'

'I told you. Edouard Rocher designed it.'

'*Did* he?'

'She's having an affair with him.'

'Isn't he married?'

'With four children.' I let the disapproval I'd hidden from Rachel show in my voice.

He frowned. 'Really? Where do they meet?'

'I think, her flat. She has an apartment in that big modern block in Grosvenor Square. Like the shop, very luxurious, all glass and big mirrors and chrome. Edouard tells his wife he's working late.'

Alex grimaced. 'Sounds pretty squalid.' He wasn't at all keen on that sort of thing. He believed once married, a man should act it. He was rather old fashioned, he always told me, in that respect. 'Well, I wouldn't fancy being in her flat if a bomb was dropped on it, whatever was on offer. All that glass. I hope you don't visit there much.'

'Not often. She usually comes here. Or we meet in town.'

'Good. Frankly, it doesn't sound very safe. And in your condition I don't want you taking any chances. Well, I don't suppose her affair with Rocher will continue for much longer. These things are generally pretty brief.'

'I wouldn't be too sure of that. She seems very keen.'

'Does she? Are there any more of those delicious – thanks.'

'And the flowers?' I asked, watching as he helped himself to another peach.

'Oh, I forgot them in the end. Sorry, darling.'

'I could invite her to the dinner-party next week,' I suggested warily, and was surprised at the speed and ease of his reaction.

'Good idea,' he said approvingly. 'I felt rather sorry for her despite the grand surroundings – she seems at a loss at present. Still, at least she can start working again – she's just heard the Board has granted her exemption from Internment. Apparently, she's classed as "a victim of Nazi oppression".'

'I must say – ' I gestured to my large, pregnant belly, 'I'm feeling rather a victim of male oppression myself right now.'

He gave a small smile. 'She asked after you. I told her you're still feeling ill in the mornings. She said, poor you and she'd give you a ring when she gets the chance. Why don't you ask her to dinner when she does?'

But, unusually, Rachel didn't call all week and, when she did, Alex turned out to be right after all. 'Is Edouard well?' I asked.

'Ach, yes. I suppose so.'

'Only suppose?'

'I imagine he is aboard a Yank ship by now. We have not spoken since he left for America.'

'America! I thought he was waiting to be called up. Wasn't he a reservist?'

'Oh, yes, he *was*, very much so. But I begged and begged him not to return to occupied France. And then of course the Boche marched into Paris – did I tell you all the street names are in German now?'

'Several times.'

'My poor Edouard! I talked to him. I said – Edouard, you have your children, you must think of them.'

'Also his wife.'

'Ach, his *wife*! My God, a convinced Pétainist – a real bitch. About *her* he doesn't give one big shit, I can assure you.'

'You must be frantic, Rachel. The North Atlantic's simply full of mines.'

'Dahlink, I will be frank – not so much as you would think. It has all been fizzling out for quite a while now.'

'You never said.'

'Didn't I? I thought I had.'

'No – no, you didn't.'

'Yes, it is sad. Still, I am sure, knowing Edouard, he will be safe.'

I shivered. 'But will we? Paris is so close. I expect the Nazis will be here soon. Everyone says so.'

'Or perhaps not. They say that too.'

'Of course they will – what's to stop them? Hitler has only to cross the Channel. The American press says according to reliable sources the invasion will start in a matter of days. *Reliable sources*, Rachel. I don't know why we're even bothering with dinner-parties, I really don't.'

'I do not think about what is happening in the War,' Rachel said emphatically. 'There is nothing I am able to do about it.'

'I wish I could be as calm.'

'You? It is not in your nature. You are too excitable. Of course you must have a dinner for all of your many good friends, darlink.'

We chatted for a bit longer, then she said goodbye. 'What time is your dinner?'

'Alex said to turn up about eight.'

'Did he? Then I shall make certain I arrive on the dot.'

I wasn't sure why the telephone call bothered me so much. But it made me feel odd when I replaced the receiver somehow. Rather forlorn, as if I'd forgotten to add a remark, or something had been left unsaid. Not about the Nazi menace – as Rachel had said there was nothing we could do to change the progress of that. No, pregnancy was making me jumpy, I decided. That and, just three months later, the bombs falling nightly all around us, leaving a charred taste thickening everyone's lips and tongue, and fine brick dust lingering in the London air.

*   *   *

It was the bomb flattening the house at the end of the street that really decided it. Ambulances and fire-engines shot up and down the road, rescue workers dashed about waving the nozzles of long hoses. A thick haze of white plaster dust hung over the street. Several fires burned all day amongst the wreckage; shattered tiles, bricks and broken glass glistened on the pavements and crunched underfoot. It all gave me the shivers – it reminded me too forcibly of Kristallnacht. Long before dark, I drew the blackout curtains. But the sour stench of wet masonry and the grit between my teeth couldn't be shut out.

'You know, I was thinking, there's really no sense in your living in all this,' Alex said, when he arrived home later that evening. 'What's the point in staying in London under bombs if you don't really have to? It's madness. You'd be far better living in the countryside. These raids are bad for the nerves at the best of times. But when the bombs fall this close . . . Look at you, you're still trembling like a leaf.'

I gave a shaky little laugh. 'I thought I was amazingly calm considering that today I saw two bodies being dragged half clothed from the rubble. Do you think they had any idea that they were dead? The faintest, split second inkling? A white flash, a bang and then – what? This is it, I'm just about to be a – ' I didn't complete the sentence. I looked down at the knuckles of my gripped together hands. 'The wardens digging them out were completely covered in white dust,' I said in a low voice. 'If you were in London and I weren't, I'd always be a picturing them doing exactly that. I wouldn't be able to sleep a wink at night without imagining that it was *you* who'd been buried alive and was being pulled half dead from the debris. That it was you who – '

'There's no point in dwelling on what *might* happen,' Alex cut me short. 'We all have to carry on as near to normal as we possibly can.'

'Oh, yes,' I muttered sullenly. 'Londoners are supposed to be like the RAF, aren't they? Never discuss things like death and mutilation.'

'Anyway, there's not much choice for me, is there? I work here, you don't. Now if you were living outside London, we could send a few pieces to the country with you for safe-keeping rather than keeping everything in store. You could take a few of the miniatures and the small Carpaccio, if you like. Everything's sheeted up at the moment. It's either at the bank or packed in crates below stairs. You're always saying how much you miss it all.'

My heart began beating violently. I took a cigarette from the box behind me and lit it. 'Oh, dear. How funny. You've thought this all out already, haven't you?'

'No, of course I haven't. But I have been considering it, yes. I worry about you, Antoinette. It's hard to concentrate at work sometimes. The truth is I'd be able to relax much more if you were out of town. Listen, I don't like these bombs any more than the next man. You never know where or when they're going to drop next. It's not surprising you're so nervy. It makes the best of us feel on edge. So why stay unnecessarily?'

I frowned. 'Do you really want me to go?'

'I don't *want* you to, of course I don't. But as a matter of fact, I heard about a rather rum set up today. Remember the Brownlows? Well, they're moving to Washington and want to rent out their house. They only want six guineas a week. You're always saying how badly you want to start painting again. Well, in the country you could. Not to mention getting a full night's sleep for a change. It's quite a decent sized house apparently, there'd be plenty of space for all your stuff and no one to disturb you. You could get some domestic help – a day-woman to drop by for a few hours. Perhaps join the local Woman's Institute.'

'And sew little chintz bags for hospitals? I don't think I'm quite the type.'

'I should think it would be rather fun. You'd make a lot of new friends.'

'But I don't *want* to make any new friends. There's quite enough of those when I go down to the shelter, thanks.'

'Then live the life of a solitary painter during the week if you prefer.'

I looked at him suspiciously. 'Where *is* this house, anyway?'

'A village called Maiden Newton.'

'Where's that when it's at home?'

'It's in Sussex. The village is small but the nearest station is only five miles – Hinchley Wood? It has a good train service to London.'

'Is your journey really necessary?' I recited the words of the familiar poster. 'I mean – will it be?'

'Oh, I can usually wangle something,' he said blandly. 'Perhaps even petrol for the car.'

'Sussex is hours away,' I said moodily. 'You certainly wouldn't make it down during the week.'

'No, perhaps not . . . But Friday night like bloody clockwork.'

'Every *other* weekend.'

'Quite honestly, we don't get to see each other much more than that, anyway. By the time I get home it's so late. And there's really no point in moving out if not to somewhere safe, is there?'

My hands were shaking wildly as I put the cigarette to my mouth and sucked in smoke. 'The war has spoilt everything,' I muttered.

Wasn't there just the slightest hesitation before his – 'yes?'

'Don't you think it's a good idea?' he asked cajolingly.

'No. I don't.'

But it was true. The air-raids were getting me down. My nerves were all shot to pieces. The slightest sound made me jump about three feet into the air. And almost every night, sometimes more than once, the first wail of the evening sirens, the leap out of bed and cold hurry down the stairs. I often didn't bother with pyjamas any more – it didn't seem worth it. A few hours after the sirens droned out the All Clear they'd be off again, wailing another alert. I only ever managed to get back to sleep through sheer exhaustion, and my dreams were foggy with swirling dust and debris and choking thick black smoke.

I tried not to think about what it must be like in Berlin. How the Grunewald must look by now, or the state of the once bright shops that stretched along the Kurfürstendamm . . .

'I do *like* being near you, Alex,' I said miserably. 'Even if I can't see you much it's nice knowing that you're not so far away . . . '

'I'm afraid we all have to make sacrifices nowadays.'

'Oh, don't be such a prig!'

'There's the baby to consider now, too,' he added as a clincher. As if he needed one. 'All mothers-to-be are evacuated from the city six weeks beforehand. So why not beat them to it?'

'And scarper to the countryside first?'

'That's one way of putting it.' He leant forward and patted my hand. 'Don't make a decision right now, darling. I just want you to consider it, that's all. Will you do that for me? It really is the sensible course, you know. Apparently the house is fully furnished and quite charming. I think you'll absolutely love it. It's called Map House – grey flint, set back from road, surrounded by acres of fields. So quite safe you see – there's nothing worth bombing for miles. It isn't even *on* the flight path of the Luftwaffe. You'd have to be very unlucky to be hit down there.'

'People are,' I said darkly. 'Planes drop their loads to get rid of them on the way back from somewhere else.'

'They said they'll take less for cash,' Alex remarked.

I feel at home in the whole world, wherever there are clouds and birds and human tears . . .

*   *   *

You can probably tell what's going to happen next, can't you? You don't exactly have to be psychic to see what's around the corner. I expect you've already guessed. You've read the book, seen the film, examined the script, passed the age of consent and it all appears crystal clear. To everyone but me.

I hadn't the faintest clue, of course. Didn't see it coming for one second, even though it was so bloody obvious you'd have to be an idiot not to. Well, I *was* and I *didn't*. Not until it was right under my nose and actually happening. The train had crashed, the cars already collided, the bomb exploded ten minutes before and everything in dust and tatters around you, except for the little unexpected things, like the china teapot and your heart.

Call me stupid if you like, but I'd never imagined it for one incredible instant. I didn't think husbands *did* that kind of thing. At least, not *my* husband, and not to me. I thought marriage was forever. The fact that we were arguing more and having sex less didn't count. I was pregnant, for God's sake. And he was working so hard. How could he? Ship me off to the country and make love to my best friend? No one would *do* that. No one.

Well, they say the wife's always the last to know, don't they?

*   *   *

The telephone rang and rang till reluctantly I wiped the oil off my hands with a rag and picked it up. The painting was going well, it had suddenly fallen into place and it was a nuisance having to leave it even for a moment. A creative fever seemed to have come over me with pregnancy: suddenly there seemed so much to do and so little time to do it. An impersonal voice asked: 'What number are you, please?'

'Maiden Newton 313.'

'I have a personal call from London for Mrs Alexander Sorel.'

'Speaking.'

'Go ahead, caller. You're through now.'

A pause, a click. Thirty seconds later an imperious voice came onto the line. 'Hello. Hello. Is anyone there?' My heart sank as I recognised it. 'This is Vivienne Fox-Linton,' it said loud and clear, conjuring up a face thickly covered with orangey make-up and small, heavily mascara-ed eyes. I should have asked who it is wanted me, I thought. I should have let the phone go on ringing. I should never have picked it up. I said: 'Hullo, Vivienne.'

'Why, Antoinette, darling! How *are* you?'

'Very well. But if it's Alex you want, I'm afraid you're out of luck. He's at the Ministry most of the week.'

'But it's *you* I was specially hoping to speak with!' Vivienne squealed. 'I wanted to invite you *both* to the little drinks party we're holding. Alex has probably told you that we're leaving for America at the end of the month?'

'I think he did mention it . . . ' He had, adding, and a very good riddance, too.

'Well, before we set off, we're having a little get together for the brave folks staying behind in London.'

'I live in Sussex now, Vivienne.'

'Of *course* you do! I telephoned to *you*, remember? But you can come up to come to town for very special occasions, can't you?' I could almost hear the pout. 'It's on the fourteenth,' she persisted, 'at our little house in Belgrave Place.' Everything was always little with Vivienne. Little party, little drinks, little house – for that massive tomb? 'I know it's only next weekend,' she drawled. 'But people don't like to have too much warning nowadays, do they? They prefer not to plan too far ahead. *Quite* understandably – because one never can tell what's round the corner, can one? Shall I wait,' she said, 'while you check your appointment book?'

'There's really no need, I'm sure we're free. To be honest, we're not going out much at the moment.'

'*Aren't* you?' she inquired with interest.

'Alex is awfully busy these days and I – well, perhaps you've heard about the – he may have mentioned that I'm . . . ' I looked longingly at the unfinished painting.

'Yes, of course he did! Of *course*! He told me the happy news when we saw him the other night. How frightfully, frightfully clever of you! And when is baby Sorel due?'

'Just after Christmas. Quite close to my own birthday, actually,'

'Near your own birthday,' Vivienne Fox-Linton purred. 'Oh, how *glorious*! So you *can* come? We'd like you to so terribly.'

'That's very nice of you, Vivienne,' I replied, touched. I'd thought the Fox-Lintons didn't care a jot whether I attended their parties with Alex but they really seemed to want me to come to their farewell do. All the same, as usual with Vivienne, I was aware the conversation had a definite undertow. I didn't know exactly where the current was pulling, but that there was one I was certain. Did she want more money for one of her blasted bring-and-buy sales? An ache was beginning in my chest which should have acted as a warning sign. I should have got off the telephone straight away. But I expect if I had, Vivienne would only have hunted me down somehow. She wouldn't have let me escape that easily.

'I must say Alex looked awfully well – ' she said – 'When we saw him at the theatre on Friday.'

The hook was cast. I saw it but still I bit. 'Alex? Oh, no, it couldn't have been him you saw, Vivienne. He was working on Friday evening.'

'Oh, it definitely was. At the Ambassador.'

'The Ambassador? On Friday? Oh, no, I'm afraid you're mistaken.'

'I wasn't mistaken,' Vivienne assured me gleefully. 'Oh, the naughty boy! Didn't he mention it? He was with that charming friend of yours so I assumed he must have done. The pretty one with an accent.'

My heart stopped, then began to beat so violently I felt sick.

'You know, the one all the men are wild about,' she went on happily. 'Whatever *is* her name? The curvaceous blonde – though I expect it's from a bottle, it usually is these days, isn't it? You placed her next to Humphrey at that delightful dinner you held last year so I recognised her without *a doubt*. That wonderfully *full* figure, and one must admit – so unusual in that type – *frantically* elegant. A Charles Worth design, if I'm not mistaken? Humphrey was quite besotted with her, even though she *is* a foreigner. What on earth did she *say* to him? One asked and asked but one wasn't given even an inkling . . . '

Vivienne's laugh rang down the phone, high pitched and ugly and false

'It's sad to relate but except for your husband's friend hardly anyone seems to bother about dressing for a first night *at all*. Evening wear seems to have *completely* disappeared from the stalls and dress circle. I suppose it's because everything starts so *early* nowadays – so that we can all race home like good girls and boys in time for the blackout. You didn't miss a thing with the play, Antoinette dear – *I* thought it rather shocking. A dead first wife turning up to haunt the second? But then I never really did *like* Noel Coward . . . Did Alex?'

There was a short silence on the Belgravia end. Even a silence can seem grating down the telephone.

'Did he – did he what?'

'Enjoy *Blithe Spirit*?'

'I don't know,' I floundered. 'He didn't tell me.' Vivienne Fox-Linton's sharp, cruel ears would hear the sudden change in my tone I knew but I couldn't help it. Friday? Alex told me he was working late at the Ministry on Friday, he'd said he'd had a meeting. Who had he met at the theatre? Which friend? My heart was racing, I couldn't think clearly. Rachel Kost? But he couldn't bear Rachel, I'd only ever managed to invite her to dinner under duress. So German, so common despite her family's enormous wealth, he always said. And, implied if not actually stated, as if I weren't – so *Jewish*. Somehow I managed to say: 'I must ring off now, Vivienne . . . I can hear the pips going for the second time . . . '

'Now be sure and send Alex oodles of love from us all, won't you?' Vivienne purred, her bolt shot. 'A simply *enormous* kiss. And you won't forget, will you?'

'Forget?'

'The party, silly girl! The fourteenth?'

'Oh, no, I won't forget.'

'Well, don't. Love to Alex, mind.'

'Goodbye, Vivienne.'

Polite enough, but not waiting for a response before slamming down the phone.

Perhaps Alex and Rachel had just bumped into one other at the theatre and were standing next to one another by chance when Vivienne Fox-Linton spotted them – it happened. A purely innocent event. A coincidence. Except why was Alex even *at* the theatre that night? He'd said he was working late after all and so wouldn't be able to join me until Saturday teatime at the earliest. Jolly bad luck, he'd said. Never mind, we'll have all of Sunday together and maybe Monday too, if I can swing it. And I'd recognised the hollow, clipped tones of his senior officer in the accent he was unconsciously imitating. Awfully sorry, old bean – I had imagined him telling Alex – but the meeting's on tonight after all.

But if Alex had bumped into Rachel by chance why hadn't he said anything about it? Someone blonde and full-figured? With an accent? That bloody accent which he so despised. I tried to smile. But my hands were icy, my mind raced. I tried to work out when the Fox-Lintons had come to dinner but my brain wouldn't work properly. Like a needle stuck in a groove, it kept coming back helplessly to Rachel. In shining white, blonde hair falling in soft waves to her shoulders, full breasts almost dropping out of her Charles Worth dress as she leant towards Humphrey Fox-Linton, lips licked, innocent eyes open wide, smiling temptingly . . .

It *can't* have been Rachel at the theatre with Alex, I thought desperately. He doesn't even like her. Please God, don't let it be Rachel, I prayed – not Rachel, please.

The pain inside me was so bad it felt almost physical. I didn't know what to do with it. Clutching the hard curve of my belly I tried to retch it all out, as if in this way I could get rid of the feeling; great shuddering noises that in the end made no difference. The terrible sensation remained, the familiar, gasping, clawing emptiness that threatened to engulf me and made me feel as if I was teetering on the edge of the world. I was bloated and pregnant and living miles from London, my family were all on the other side of a war-torn world and my best, my only true friend, had just been to bed with my husband. The realisation was intolerable.

Had he enjoyed it? Had she? How could I have been so blind? Every piece fitted together perfectly now I considered it. Rachel's sudden indifference which I'd put down to the pressure of being a category 3 enemy alien in a dreadful war – the persistence of Alex's suggestion that I move somewhere a good two hours train ride from the capital – far enough but not too far, was how he'd put it. Far enough? For what? Why of course . . .

As soon as I'd heard that heartless voice intoning the words on the other end of the telephone everything had fallen into place and I knew. Rachel and Alex were in love with one another.

I thought of my life without him and my heart turned over in my side. I thought of his patronising, merciless smile, his pitying, scornful, secretive brown eyes. Empty eyes, I knew now. Dark and empty like the abyss . . .

Everything I relied on is destroyed, I thought – everything I care for is behind me. Before me, there is nothing . . .

Something hard and sharp in my throat was hurting me. I realised I'd slid down to the floor. The back of my shirt and hair were pressing against the wet paint of the canvas. My palms, when I brought them up to my face, were mauve and blue. Very deliberately I smeared the fresh paint over my cheeks and forehead. Warpaint. A kind of mask, streaks of colour to bury myself in. I cried, 'Rachel! Rachel!' and banged my blue and mauve face on the floor.

After a while I lay still, breathing loudly and quickly as if I'd been running. My face felt stiff where the paint on it was beginning to set. When I finally began moving, crawling slowly on all fours towards the still life – a chipped mirror behind scarlet dahlias and a cobalt blue cloth that I'd set up earlier, in another life – it was the face of Vivienne Fox-Linton I saw reflected there. Mrs Fox-Linton coated in a thick layer of orange pancake, her little puffy eyes surrounded by hard black lines, her thin lips a sharp blood red – not my own soft face, not Antoinette's, not mine. If I'd spoken it would be in her harsh accents with that rasping upper-class drawl.

I stared into the cracked glass. No wonder Alex didn't love me any more. It was not surprising he had sought to lose himself in those other arms, to drown himself in that other sweet embrace. Rachel, beautiful, blonde ripely voluptuous Rachel, for who all men were crazy, all men, especially Alex.

Presently the idea came to me, with the memory of the almost full pre-war bottle in the bathroom cabinet. His name was printed on the instructions underneath. '*Mr A. A. Sorel Esq., – take two tablets with a drink of water. Repeat every 4 to 6 hours as required. Do not take more than 8 tablets in 24 hours.*'

I opened the cabinet and began frantically chucking half used tubes and bottles into the sink – a squeezed out tube of Kolynos toothpaste, indigestion pills, Beechams pills, bicarbonate of soda, bottles of mouth wash, hair wash, a half empty bottle of thick pale medicine . . . Knocking them off the narrow shelves until I found it.

Then I wrenched off the cap and began spilling tablets freely into my palm. I watched from a distance as I shook them into my mouth. As I would watch them both suffer after my death, I thought.

A few bitter grains of a pill I'd bitten into stuck in my throat. I drank a glass of water to help the aspirins down. Staring at my face in the mirror as I swallowed I tried to recognise myself. Streaks of paint ran across my forehead and along both cheeks. Mauve and blue. Ah yes. It was my own face I could see reflected there, after all.

14

I thought I was back in Germany. I thought my mother was in the next bed and that she'd just lost her child, the longed-for son, a baby boy with a mass of golden curls so ravishing the nurses cooed over him even in death. I thought Viktor had come to save me from the Nazis, cunningly disguised as the doctors in charge of the sanatorium. I thought he wished to marry me and sweep me off my feet. I smiled and simpered in my sleep. For two days I believed all this, then, on the morning of the third, my dreams were shattered like glass splintering underfoot and I realised that I was the one who had lost my unborn son, that it was Alex sitting on a chair besides the scratched white iron bed and that I was in the St John's cottage hospital, just three miles down the road from our charming, rented, grey stone house, with telephone.

'Who the hell is Victor?' Alex asked coldly. 'You kept on calling his name. I found it rather embarrassing actually, since the nurses know it isn't mine.'

'*Actually* I was rather embarrassed by your behaviour, too,' I responded nastily. Not bad for someone who'd just returned to the harsh light of reality only a few moments before.

Raising his chin, he looked down his nose at me as if I was something unpleasant he'd found on the sole of his shining leather shoe. 'What on earth do you mean?'

'Can't you guess?'

'I don't know what you're talking about.'

I rolled over and turned my face to the painted pale green wall.

He denied it point blank. An affair – and with *Rachel* of all people? He was astonished. 'You must be mad.' Hardly the thing to say to someone who'd just spent the past few days recovering from a failed suicide attempt believing herself to be in a private nursing home secretly run by Hitler.

Then, as my words began to sink in fully, he turned angry.

Coldly, furiously angry. How could I believe *anything* Vivienne Fox-Linton *ever* said, the poisonous bitch? And how could I believe it of him? His meeting had been cancelled at the last minute, he'd been offered tickets to the theatre *quite* by chance, he hadn't even *seen* Rachel Kost – *had* she been there? How appalling to accuse him of something so sordid, to believe such a thing of *him*, and on such little evidence. A brief phone call from well-known muckraker? It was spite and envy and gossip. The kind of thing that went on all the time during this damn war and was only to be laughed at and ignored.

I'd felt lousy to start with, my head was splitting, my body felt like it had been pressed through a meat grinder, now I began to feel even worse. Yes, how could I? I wondered, my limbs feeling watery weak.

Was *this* the reason for my attempt to kill myself? This – this nonsense? All spat into my ear in a low, icy voice.

Defence being the best form of attack.

Why hadn't he told me that he'd been to the theatre? It didn't seem important enough. He hadn't remembered at the right moment, he supposed. By the time he'd seen me, it didn't seem to matter anymore. The play had been all right but not his cup of tea. He'd simply forgotten about it.

'Any other reason?' I asked weakly. A joke.

He didn't smile. 'If you are going to carry on like this you better come back to London and take your chances along with the rest of us,' he retorted. Then more hurtfully: 'There's no baby now to protect, anyway. You've fucked that up too.'

I began to weep. I cried and I couldn't stop. Finally, the sister put a screen round my bed. 'I'm in pain,' I moaned. 'I hurt. I'm in awful pain.' She gave me a look that seemed to say, serves you right. But a little while later she gave me a morphine injection.

When I came round the next morning I lay still with my eyes shut so no one would know I was awake. I felt tired through to my bones. I ached all over as if I'd beaten with a stick, hit hard over and over again until the wood had finally snapped. There was a strong, pervasive smell of antiseptic. Every now and then, the rattle of glass as a trolley was pushed up the corridor. Finally, I forced my eyes open and lay in a daze, watching the nurses dashing about the ward. Then one came over and said: 'You're moving today. You're in one of the private rooms now. You're lucky,' she added.

'Am I?'

'All the hospital beds in London are kept for air-raid casualties.'

She didn't say anything else, just collected up my things. I didn't want to stand ever again, I felt so tired. My legs were wobbly, they felt as if they were made of cotton wool. I shuffled after her over sage green linoleum and collapsed on the narrow metal bed like an old woman.

'Can I have a sedative?' I asked pitifully. She was younger than the other nurses and had a nice freckled face. When she said no quite coldly I turned my face to the pillow and cried like a child. I thought – even kind people enjoy being cruel to me.

All the nurses were very sharp with me. So many men were giving their lives for this country who didn't want to die, they had no time or inclination for my kind of trouble. There were real tragedies going on all the time without deliberately adding to them and giving the Jerries even more to crow about. Honestly, how could I be so selfish? There my husband was, slogging his guts out day and night doing essential war work for Great Britain. Pull yourself together, they said briskly, energetically ramming a sheet beneath the thin mattress.

When they learnt I had been living in Berlin before the war and that Alex had brought me back to London with him for love and safety's sake, that was the icing on the cake. Well, *really* Mrs Sorel. How *could* you?

Yes, how? Beneath the self-pity, my sobs took on another sound – regret. I'd had a bad reaction to the chloroform but on Friday I was allowed to go home.

Home? Well, back to the echoing, sheeted up house in London, anyway. Alex was out all day, arriving back late, dog tired. But back he did come, every single night, his very presence a rebuke. He was working extremely hard at the War Office, he told me indifferently, all stuff of the utmost urgency, the deadlines were brutal.

Left alone a lot, I carried on crying. It's amazing, really, that there's so much water in one human body. I didn't eat, drink or even sleep for more than a few hours at a time but the tears continued streaming unrelenting down my face. I lost track of why. For the waste? For the wasted life, I sobbed; for my poor, poor baby boy. I tried to pull myself together when Alex arrived home. Hearing his key in the lock, I would hurriedly sponge my face with cold water, run trembling hands through my hair and put on powder and rouge. But when he kissed me hello my eyes were still puffy, my lids and nostrils red and swollen. I look awful, I thought, catching my reflection in the mirror.

'You don't think you made a mistake, do you?' I asked one night, throwing him a wild, unhappy look.

'About what?'

'Marrying me.'

'No, of course I don't,' he said, averting his eyes.

But he made less and less attempt to please me, or even notice what I was going through. He seemed simply to have become disinterested. If I stirred any emotion in him at all it was irritation. I *annoyed* him, depressed, unhappy, childless.

And, really, who could blame him for that?

*   *   *

My Italian had been good when we married although living in Berlin, I hadn't spoken it for almost two years. On our sweet honeymoon island I had chatted like a little bird to Maddalena, the housekeeper. Her family was from Tunisia originally and the strong Genoese base to her dialect sounded strange to me at first but I soon got the hang of her accent and it amused Alex to hear me talking Italian. One day, sitting on the terrace listening to us, he suddenly grabbed my arm and pulled me into the bedroom.

'Siesta time,' he breathed into my ear, closing the shutters against the sun and pulling me roughly to him.

The love he made on that hot afternoon was savage. That was the first time love had taken him like that. Though not, of course, the last. Acquiescing, I just felt grateful that he wanted me so badly. Bruises and swollen lips are not the worst thing in the world, are they? Your husband not wanting to make love to you is far worse.

It was Maddalena who gave me the potion. 'For love,' she said knowingly, smiling with her eyes, and handing me a twist of paper.

When I unfolded it there was a small amount of white powder in the paper's crease. The grains were about as coarse as sea salt. She told me to stir half of the powder into Alex's wine one evening and see what happened. 'His loving will be good,' she assured me. She made a lewd gesture with her fist. 'You will like this man,' she smiled.

Of course it wasn't really necessary. At that time he needed no aphrodisiacs to stir him. He loved me anyway. Though it was never enough: for me it was never enough. No amount of lovemaking could ever satisfy me – immediately afterwards, lying in his arms, feeling his quickened heartbeat, the long throbs and shudders over, I would wonder – but does he still love me? Does he still? What if he'd have been happier with Zarah Hoffman had the dowry been agreed?

So I always let him do anything he wanted – I *encouraged* him to want me in all sorts of ways, he said later, purely by my passivity. It was the languorous agreement of a woman who wants to be loved so badly that she will take anything she gets.

One night I put the crystals in his wine. Maddalena had placed white flowers everywhere as if she'd known beforehand that this was the night I would choose, huge, tropical blooms that forever afterwards smell to me of love. The strong languid perfume of desire. I wore the slinky satin off-the-shoulder dress that Alex had chosen for me in Rome and the high square heeled shoes that went with it. Also, the pale pink Milanese silk chemise and drawers he'd given me on our very first night together.

Slipping his gift on me, he'd looked at me for a long time. Turned me onto my stomach, still silently gazing.

Equally silently, Maddalena served us food. Then, aware of the atmosphere between us, as heavy and hot as the night, she slipped away into the velvety darkness.

The love potion worked. Alex was crazy with love for me that night. He undressed me lingeringly, caressing and kissing every bit of my body with each tiny button he popped. But when he tied my hands together with the leather belt from his own trousers, forcing my wide satin sash over my face and knotting it at the throat, I froze with terror. I thought for one long heart-stopping moment he was going to murder me. Strangle me there and then in the savage act of love.

Had Maddalena's potion really driven him wild, filled him with cruel desire beyond all reason?

My body stiff with fear, I struggled against the taut silken bonds. But this seemed to arouse him even more and he took no notice of my resistance. Holding me in place with one hand, he thrust into me again and again till finally he came deep inside me. Collapsing on top of me, he lay, satiated, till his breathing slowed down. It was clear then that he'd never intended anything but this, this final stillness: the death only of desire.

He unravelled the cream silky scarf from round my throat and smiled almost shyly into my face.

The belt he didn't remove from my wrists. My hands still cuffed together, he led me by this leather thong naked up the wide marble stairs. I slept all night beside him with the belt cutting into my skin. The red weals on my arms next day were a token of his loving. For in the morning, seeing those bruises made him hard again and he made fierce love to me. By then, I wasn't really afraid any more but I fought and struggled as if I was to please him.

Fortunately, when we left the island, I had a little of the powder left. I determined to put it into the whisky that Alex measured out liberally each night when he returned from the ministry. Though this is damp London town not an Italian island, I warned myself, although this is a two year old marriage and not the first throes of passion – maybe it will still have the same effect.

I put a cold compress on my face and made a great effort with my clothes and hair. Outlined my eyes with kohl, painted my lashes black and rouged and powdered my face. Also, sucked a violet cachet to cover any smell of brandy on my breath.

When I looked at the finished effect in the mirror, I felt the first, faint stirrings of hope. It would surely work, I told myself. It would arouse his lost interest in me, even after everything, and I would have my husband's love back again.

*   *   *

May 8th 1945: On VE day, immediately after Churchill announced the end of the war with Germany, I switched off the radio and fired off three letters. One to my mother and younger sister Rosa in Italy, distantly referring to my stepfather in a postscript on the last page – not as Daddy as instructed but as Bruno – please send my regards to Bruno, I wrote. The other, to my beloved aunt and uncle in Berlin. I also wrote a long letter to Marta. I told her everything about my life in England, even the bad things, the failed suicide attempt, the lost baby boy. I told her how much I was dying to see her. Had they heard anything from Viktor?

From Italy I had no reply. But both the letters to Germany were returned four months later. It was an awful shock, holding them in my hand and realising they'd never been so much as opened, let alone avidly read. There seemed something ominous about their stiff, cream, sealed weight. I stood in the hall by the mat, turning them over in my hand. On the letter to my aunt and uncle it just said on the back – Deported. And a date – 22.x.42. Marta's envelope had nothing on except the same date.

Alex had already left for Whitehall. I walked upstairs, found the mauve summer dress that had just come back from the express cleaners and buttoned an angora cardigan over it. I went through the motions of fixing my hair, powdering my face and putting on lipstick. Fastened on small cabochon ruby earrings. Then I sank down on the bed. I felt quite blank.

I must think about supper, I told myself. I must get out the ration books and buy some food.

The house hadn't suffered any direct damage from bombing, just a few tiles blown off the roof by a VI in June. We had no cook or housekeeper any more. The maid had gone to be a Landgirl long ago. There was only Therese, a sullen refugee from Hungary, and the daily woman who came in grumbling twice a week. 'You Can't Black Out the Moon', 'Music While You Work' and other popular songs from the BBC blared loudly from the wireless all morning. I will make the bed, then walk to the butchers on Blandford Street, I thought. I didn't move. Just sat, head bowed, staring dazedly at my feet, thinking of all I was supposed to be doing that morning. Deported? To where?

I'll call the Red Cross, I decided. Ask them to start searching for the Klein's whereabouts. Still I didn't get up. Instead, lay down on the rumpled bed, curled my legs up to my chest and stared out the window. I could see where the tops of the tallest trees across the street had been lopped flat at the start of the war, hear the faint sound of a car circling the park.

My freshly pressed dress will get creased, I thought. I should put on shoes and stockings, my feet are chilly. Although it wasn't a cold day I started shivering. After a while, I dragged myself to the bathroom and took a cachet of veronal. Then I went and lay back on the bed, pulled the quilt up to my chin and waited for the sleeping powder to take effect.

*   *   *

It may take quite a long time before you hear anything, the woman from the Red Cross Committee warned me. How long is a long time? A week? A month? Two? I kept telling myself to be patient. But after weeks of relentless, nagging worry I suddenly snapped. I felt I *couldn't* wait any longer.

I'd tried Continental Trunks with no luck – the telephone was disconnected. Nothing, no buzz, not even a 'number unobtainable' sound. Not surprising really – Berlin had been bombed relentlessly, according to the papers, during the last two years of war. Then a chance remark from a man at a party brought an idea to my mind like a sudden illuminating flash. A detective. I'd pay a private detective to look for my family.

I didn't tell Alex. Why should a detective have any more luck than the Red Cross? But surreptitiously I took a card – The Elite Agency, Mr F. Palfrey. After all, the Red Cross had so many people to search for and he would have just a few.

The detective agency was at the undamaged end of Chancery Lane between a pub and a legal bookshop. The brass plate on the wall said *The Elite Agency* was on the second floor. Another plate read: '*Hayworth and London* Typing School.' Inside, a cardboard sign on the iron grilles said the lift was out of order. Shabby linoleum, non-existent in places, led me past an empty first floor flat and the secretarial bureau. At the top of a second flight of stairs,

I stopped and took a small Fabergé box out of my handbag. Shook a pill into my palm and swallowed it quickly. At the end of the hallway was a door marked Inquiries. I waited a second for the strength and confidence to pulse through my body. Then I pushed open the door.

There was a scarred wood desk with two empty wire trays marked 'in' and 'pending' on top, a telephone and a thin green carpet. A balding man in a creased grey suit and a striped tie was standing by a steel filing cabinet. He turned and studied me, eyebrows raised questioningly.

'Is there anything I can do for you?'

'I have an appointment with Mr Palfrey.'

'I am Mr Palfrey.'

He had a narrow face with nondescript features – fiftyish, with pale rather bloodshot blue eyes and grey hair that was thinning slightly. Parted far over on one side, a few long strands were brushed across the top so the bald patch wouldn't show. He was holding a sheet of typewritten paper and a flimsy carbon copy. He slipped both sheets inside the metal drawer and scraped it shut. 'And you are – ?'

'Mrs Sorel.'

'Ah, yes.' He gave a professional smile, revealing stained teeth. 'Please come in.'

I had dressed as I'd imagined suitable for a meeting with a private detective. In a sober but well-cut suit of fine black wool, shoulders padded, waist cinched, skirt flared just below the knee. A silver fox stole straight from the Paris fashion shows drooped glossily from the crook of my elbows. Very conscious suddenly of my staggeringly high heels and fashionable clothes, I stepped into the room.

Mr Palfrey sat down behind the desk. 'Take a seat.'

There was only one other chair, a wooden one opposite him. I draped my furs over the back.

He picked up a pencil and examined the point. 'Some details, if I may,' he said, sliding a pad towards him. 'Your present address, Mrs Sorel, and your telephone number?'

I gave them to him.

'Good area,' he said approvingly. 'You've got the tube nice and close and Madame Tussauds just round the corner. I'm a Tooting man myself. Well, I was before the war. We were bombed badly during so I had to move out for a bit. Stayed with friends in Clapham. Wasn't much better, to be honest. Still, it's all changed now. It isn't the same world. For good, or some might say, for bad.' He straightened his tie. 'Recommended, were you?'

'As a matter of fact, I was.'

He nodded. 'Recommendations count for most of our work. May I ask by whom?'

'Rupert Barnes?'

'Barnes, Barnes?' Mr Palfrey tapped the pencil thoughtfully against his discoloured front teeth. 'Ah yes, a divorce case. He wanted photographs. Am I right?'

'He didn't say. I don't know him well. He's more of a friend of a friend.' But glancing round the squalid room, I didn't feel surprised. There'd been something furtive, now I thought of it, in the way he'd pressed the card into my hand.

'I never forget a case,' Palfrey said. 'Especially one that's been brought to a satisfactory conclusion. You tend to remember the wartime ones – people don't get divorced as much, you see. Not as a general rule. They're more likely to fall in love and get married. But they aren't fooled nearly as easily in peacetime. Men start to look around and think – oho, what's *she* been up to while I've been away? They get a bit – how shall I put it? Suspicious. I've had several inquiries just this week. Nothing definite mind. But that's the way of it. People like to test the water before they jump. Now what can I do for you, Mrs, um, Sorel? Same as Mr Barnes?'

'No, no, nothing like that. It isn't a divorce or anything.'

'No?' He looked disappointed.

'I want you to find someone for me.'

'Ah!' he said, perking up. 'Missing persons. Boyfriend?' he asked, cocking his head to one side. 'Not due back from overseas quite when expected?'

'Actually my aunt and uncle.' I crossed one leg over the other, my stockings sliding together with a slight rasping sound. 'Walter and Eva Klein.'

'Kline? ' He played with the pencil, rolling it backwards and forwards a short way with one finger. 'Foreign are they?'

'Yes. They live in Berlin.'

'Berlin as in Germany?' Palfrey looked startled. He put the pencil down.

'Naturally I wasn't able to contact them once the war began. But as soon as it was over I wrote straightaway. Both my letters were returned unopened. They don't appear to be living at the same address any longer.'

'Are you certain you've got the right address, if you don't mind my asking?'

'*Quite* certain. You see, I lived with them for almost two years before I married and moved back here.'

'You're not a foreigner, too?'

'No, I'm English.' I hesitated. 'Actually Jewish.'

'Jewish? Are you now? I would never have guessed.'

'Is that intended as a compliment, Mr Palfrey?'

'Well, your hair *is* very dark,' he conceded.

'My mother's blonde. So is my sister.'

'Are they really? I never knew Jews could be.'

'They can be anything.' I gave a hollow laugh. 'We don't all have big noses.'

'Oh, that's just the men, isn't it? I understand the women are real lookers.' He smiled at me appreciatively, then, seeing my expression, added hastily: 'No offence meant, Mrs Sorel. None taken, I hope?"

I regarded him across the desk. His suit was cheap and crumpled and the collar of his not quite white shirt curled up. There was a stain amongst the stripes on his tie, a faded drip of something oily that hadn't washed out properly. What did he see? I could imagine all too well. An Englishwoman, a Jewess, dressed up to the nines, sitting before him in his squalid little office. 'That's alright,' I said caustically. 'I'm used to it by now.' And thought – Or should be.

I reached inside my handbag, extracted a carton of Turkish Royals and split the paper seal with my thumbnail. 'Smoke?' I asked, offering the pack.

He regarded it doubtfully. 'Foreign, are they?'

I was tempted to reply – 'They aren't circumcised if that's what's worrying you.' But said only: 'They do have a distinctive taste.'

'Like Pashas, I suppose? Bit of a stink those have, don't they? You don't want to be standing in a queue behind one of *them*. I suppose the Turks don't mind. No, I'm a Player's man myself. Passing Cloud when I can get them, Virginians at a push. I like my smoke nice and ordinary, if you know what I mean. But thank you, Mrs Sorel. Very civil of you. Perhaps I'll try one later.'

I lit a cigarette. He shook his head doubtfully. 'Do you know, I've been in this business thirty years and no one's asked me to search for anyone abroad before? It's not the usual run of things. And Germany of all places. This won't be a straightforward case, you see.'

Tilting my chin, I blew smoke at the ceiling. 'So you don't want it, then?'

'Now I didn't say that, did I? Just said it's not straightforward, that's all. I'll have to charge rather more than normal. But how much more I can't be certain. That's the trouble.' He chewed his pencil, looking worried. 'Have you contacted the authorities?' he asked, after a moment.

'I've spoken to the Red Cross, if that's what you mean. But that was several months ago. They're very slow. Every case is considered urgent. And there are hundreds and hundreds of them. I need you to hurry the process along, Mr Palfrey. For that, I'm prepared to pay. However much you consider necessary I will pay it,' I repeated, watching his bleary eyes brighten at the thought. 'I'm worried,' I explained. 'It wasn't very pleasant for Jews in Germany before the war. We didn't know what was going to happen to us. We feared we'd be shipped off to concentration camps at any moment.'

'All refugees seem to worry about that.'

'Believe me, it was a real possibility.'

Palfrey smiled thinly and examined frayed cuffs. 'It always seems rather exaggerated. A bit hysterical, if you don't mind my saying.'

I didn't reply, just breathed out smoke in short, irritable puffs. What would he do if I said, well, I do mind actually? Probably just shrug and say, no offence meant, Mrs Sorel. He's English, I thought contemptuously. All foreigners seem overwrought and emotional to him, especially hooky nosed Jews. To him, the war meant coupons and the blitz and fewer business opportunities. Good guys fighting bad guys, but always decently. There was always fair play.

'It's the fault of the papers,' Palfrey said reasonably. 'They sell better if they blow a story up a bit. It couldn't have been as bad as all that or surely they'd have got out when they still could.' His eyes flickered over my well-cut suit. 'The family had money, you say?'

I hadn't, but I nodded, crossing one leg over the other and putting my hand on my knee. That's one stereotype satisfied, I thought. I bit back the urge to tell him there were hordes of poor Jews all over the Reich, equal only in misery. 'It wasn't simply money,' I said, hearing my voice tremble despite my effort to keep cool. 'My uncle couldn't *get* out. He had a substantial business, a home filled with beloved antiques and paintings, friends and relations, a life. He didn't want to walk out on a whim and leave all that. Would *you?*'

I glared at him. Mr Palfrey tapped the pencil on his teeth and looked back imperturbably.

'By the time he'd realised just how bad the Nazis intended life to get for the Jews the net had tightened.' I made a single, swift wringing movement with my hands. Palfrey's eyes flickered. 'It was virtually impossible to leave however much money exchanged hands. At the very least, it was grindingly slow. Onkel Walter had his name on some list or other. But for where I have no idea. He was still waiting for a visa when I left for London.'

I rubbed my right temple with the hand holding the cigarette. It was smoke not tears that made my eyes water.

'I met Alexander when I was living with the Kleins in Berlin. He was on a short visit hoping to find certain *objets d'art*. Instead,' I gave a hopeless, humorous smile, 'he found me. The idea was to marry me quickly and get me out of Germany. It was Onkel Walter really. He persuaded a rabbi that Alex was Jewish enough. Actually he is on his father's side – his grandfather was born in Odessa to a poor Jewish family. Though he keeps pretty quiet about that nowadays. If he mentions the Russian link at all he talks of a Count Aleksandr who he says he was named after. Still – ' I grimaced – 'I don't expect you'd find many White Russians housed in the shtetl where his great-grandparents lived.'

Not looking at the detective, I blew a stream of smoke sideways. 'A *Mischling* the Nazis call it. A half Jew. The wrong half unfortunately. Since it's not on the maternal side it doesn't count in Jewish law. So he loses both ways. The Nazi's want him but the Jews do not.'

I didn't speak for a moment, just drew more smoke deep into my lungs. Mr Palfrey murmured something encouraging. I went on:

'At that time in Germany all sorts of things were possible that might not have been otherwise. It was a strange, stilted ceremony but we were married. Alexander went through it all with great exactness – sipping wine from a little silver cup, smashing the wine glass with his foot. It was only later I understood. If Onkel Walter hadn't moved so swiftly I'd still be stuck in Germany, on the wrong side of the war. I owe him a lot. More than I can say. Look, do you have an ashtray?' I asked impatiently, glancing at the ash on the tip of my cigarette.

Palfrey blinked. 'Oh yes. Of course.' He moved his knees to one side and opened a drawer. Peering inside, he found a dented green tin ashtray stamped 'Players' and set it on the desk in front of me.

'The war came faster than anyone imagined,' I said, shaking ash into it. 'Once it had begun no one could get out of Germany and of course no one could contact anyone who was left behind. I think my uncle was planning to escape with his family to England. Because before we left he gave my husband several valuable oil paintings to smuggle out in his luggage and promised to collect them as soon as he could. But he never contacted us.'

'And you haven't been in touch with any of them since thirty-nine?'

'Not since that autumn. But now the war's over and – well, I'd like you to find Walter, Eva and their daughter, Marta Klein.'

'You'd better spell that out for me. Nice and slow if you wouldn't mind. Oh, the 'e' goes first, does it? Foreign names are so funny, aren't they?'

'My aunt's maiden name was Rubens.' I spelt that too. 'She came originally from England. I'm not quite sure of the date.'

'Well, I'll certainly have a go, Mrs Sorel. But in a case like this you'll still have to pay even if I'm unsuccessful,' he warned.

'Don't worry, I'll pay.'

'Have you got those letters?'

I opened my bag and handed them to him. 'As you see, it says on the envelope they were deported in October forty-two. But it gives no indication where.'

'Deported, eh?'

I gave a small frigid smile. 'Perhaps not such a far fetched worry, after all?'

Pinching his bottom lip between his finger and thumb, Palfrey examined the envelopes carefully. 'Grunewald?' He pronounced it with an English 'w'. 'District in Berlin, is it?'

'A smart area, I assure you,' I said dryly. 'As good as Marylebone, if not better.'

'Hm. Six years, you say?'

'Almost seven.'

'Seven years is a very long time.'

I thought of the mansion on The Grunewald with its long rows of empty shelves in the library and the disconnected telephone line. 'Yes,' I said. 'It is.'

I stared down, thinking of the years that had passed since I'd left Berlin. I'd changed a lot. Though perhaps not in ways I'd expected. And my cousin, aunt and uncle? Would I find them as different too? How much would they have been altered by long years of war? Marta would be in her twenties by now. My sister Rosa would be twenty-one. It was hard to imagine her as a young woman. She'd been a child when I'd last seen her.

There was a dark crimson stain on the end of my cigarette where my lipstick had rubbed off. I stirred myself and stubbed it out in the green metal ashtray. 'Of course there's my mother and sister, too.'

'Germany?'

'No – Italy.' I frowned down at the squashed red stained tip. 'I thought that if I still hadn't received a reply to my letter by the time you've located the Kleins then perhaps you could – '

'Don't get your hopes up too high, Mrs Sorel. It may take me quite a while.' Palfrey nodded his head solemnly. 'Quite a while. This may turn into a very expensive business. Very expensive indeed. It's hard to find anyone in Germany nowadays, even with the war over.' He tried to look concerned but succeeded only in looking smug. 'Berlin was devastated by our bombers so I've heard. And a bloody good job, too, I say, pardon my French. That'll be fifty guineas for starters. I usually charge two guineas a day plus expenses but in this case I'll have to work out exactly how much as I go along. The Continental telephone calls alone could go sky high. I'll let you know if it mounts up too much.'

He watched greedily as I counted out two twenties and a ten pound note, then added four crumpled pound notes and a handful of change. 'Give me a couple of weeks, Mrs Sorel, then get in touch. Hopefully I'll have some news for you by then, even if it's that there's none. You'd better sign this contract while I'm giving you a receipt for the fifty-five pounds.'

Eyeing the butt in the ashtray, he seemed to make up his mind. 'I'll have that cigarette now, if it's no trouble.'

*　　*　　*

Just how negative the news would be Mr Palfrey hadn't in his wildest dreams imagined. Actually neither had I. Rumours had begun to filter out by the end of the war just what the Nazis had intended for the Jews, speculations about how the concentration camps had become death camps for an increasingly large number of people, homosexuals, gypsies, communists, too, amount unspecified as yet, but I hadn't taken much notice till then. Nor taken at all seriously the talk of the big round up at the beginning of forty-two after which any Jew living in Berlin was an illegal. It seemed, as Mr Palfrey had said, highly improbable. ('All those Jews in hiding? Just to avoid a deportation notice? There must be thousands in Berlin alone. Where would they go? Probably greatly exaggerated, Mrs Sorel. I shouldn't take much notice, if I were you.')

The trunk lines into Germany were reserved for the military and civilian calls often took days but Palfrey managed it eventually. He looked awkward as he explained that when the letters said deported they meant to Auschwitz-Birkenau. He'd even written it down in capitals, painstakingly checking each letter so he wouldn't get it wrong. I stared down at the name he handed me.

'It's in Poland,' he told me gruffly. 'One of their concentration camps. They took a lot of them there by train.' He told me that

Onkel Walter, Tante Eva and Marta had arrived at Auschwitz on October the twenty-sixth 1942: they'd all been murdered by the Nazis the next day. Looking pale and uncomfortable, Palfrey actually used the word himself – murdered.

A train-load of Jews? How? He couldn't say. Lists would be posted in Bloomsbury House very soon if I cared to go and see them myself. A great many names and numbers.

Numbers?

He cleared his throat as if there were something stuck in it. Then unwillingly he replied that all arrivals had been tattooed with a number. The numbers were put besides names on the Red Cross lists for ease of reference, he supposed.

I went so white, he offered me a drink. Hastily, he took a bottle out of a drawer of the filing cabinet and poured some Irish whiskey into a chipped mug. 'Here, drink this. You're all to pieces. You don't mind a cup, do you? The glasses all need washing up. I haven't any soda, I'm afraid.'

He watched me expertly down the whiskey in one go. I felt a little better once I'd drunk it. Not quite so icy cold and the room stopped spinning. I could feel the blood returning to my lips.

His attitude towards me had changed. There was no talk of hysterical foreigners or over-emotional refugees, Jewish or other-wise, now. He seemed quite shaken. He wiped his forehead with a handkerchief before stuffing it back in his trouser pocket.

'Frankly, I wouldn't mind one myself,' he said, taking the mug from me and refilling it. 'Krauts,' he muttered. 'It's bloody unbelievable. Funny lot, foreigners. Incredible really. Worse than savages. There seems no end to the cruelty they're prepared to wreak on each other.'

'Do you think it hurt?' I asked after a moment.

He stared at me, puzzled.

'I mean the tattoos.'

'Shouldn't think so,' he replied, looking embarrassed. He stood by the grimy window, watching me with a strange, uneasy expression, passing a hand backwards and forwards across the mug.

'Do you ever open that?' I asked.

'Open what?'

I gave a jerk of my head. 'The window.'

He half turned and considered it. 'Can't say I do. There isn't the need. And then there's the traffic fumes . . . '

'Yes, I see. It doesn't look like it's ever been.'

He stared at me. 'No?'

'The glass is so dirty,' I explained. 'You should give it a clean.'

'I dare say I should. But with the bombs and all – it didn't really seem worth it. You never knew where one of them might fall next . . . ' He gave a short, uncomfortable laugh. He was still staring at me oddly.

I got to my feet. 'Thanks for the whiskey,' I said. I put the chipped mug down on the desk, counted out the rest of the money and caught a bus home.

*　　*　　*

In England, we'd been cooking meals, hailing taxis, attending cock-tail parties, chatting with friends. And in Germany they'd been herding Jews into cattle trucks and shipping them off to Death Camps. I'd been sipping sweet South African sherry and they'd been busy tattooing numbers on the outside of Jewish wrists.

A nice cup of tea, Mrs Sorel? Oh yes, I'd said, I'd love one, I'm parched, a dash of milk but no sugar, thank you, for me. And gulped it down, perhaps at the very moment some Nazi guard had been assembling my friends and relations on the tracks at Berlin-Grunewald railway station, ripping off my uncle's tortoiseshell spectacles, wrenching out his gold teeth and murdering him. How as yet I didn't inquire. That particular horror came later. Onkel Walter, Tante Eva and Marta?

And, as the lists later showed, Bruno De Finzi, Emma De Finzi and, four neat rows down, Rosa Meyer De Finzi from Italy, too. Send my regards to Bruno, won't you?

*　　*　　*

I was given pills. Pills to send me off to sleep and then to wake me up again. Sleeping pills, pep pills, tranquillisers, hypnotics, narcotics, all the barbituates you could think of. You name it, I got it. All mixed with alcohol, my own sweet, secret weapon. Threatened with a pressure I couldn't bear, trying not to imagine the un-imaginable, over solitary lunches I'd drink foul Australian port or Algerian wine left over from the war as well as the good stuff when I could get my hands on it. A glass or two, a bottle. Then, if that didn't work, I'd pop another pill 'for my nerves'. I hid the evidence – what the eye didn't see the heart couldn't grieve. Well, perhaps it could. How did other people do it, I asked myself. How did they carry on?

I took to calling Alex at work on any pretext. To check he was really where he said he was, to confirm he was still alive, that he actually existed and wasn't just a figment of my, by now, hopefully sodden, imagination. Or perhaps, irrationally, to ensure he hadn't been carted off by the Nazis to the horror camps, too. ('Six months isn't going to make much difference, is it?' says Walter Klein. Another glass of wine, a mug or two, a gallon.) I must have sounded pretty pissed when I did because it became an open secret between us that I was bottled for most of the day.

If I thought about it at all, which I didn't really since I was trying very hard not to think about anything much, I suppose I believed I was still in control. Of him, of myself. Maybe at that time, I was. Maybe.

And also, about this time, I began telephoning Rachel more frequently, too. When stoned, I felt strangely compelled to keep her within my sights, despite Alex's bold declarations of innocence. Not checking on her exactly, but keeping her covered, you know. When I fell pregnant again, she was the first person I told. I believed she was the only person who understood how I felt – most of her family had disappeared into the Death Camps too.

Or perhaps somewhere in my heart, somewhere deep down inside me, I guessed what my best friend was really up to. Well, we all handle pain differently, don't we? Perhaps betrayal was her way.

*   *   *

Belligerence was mine, so Alex claimed. When we weren't making love – his way – we argued. Ugly, drunken rows in which we both said things we'd never thought before, didn't even know that we did until we said them aloud, and afterwards regretted bitterly. Or hopefully did.

'Not the bloody Jews *again!*' Alex groaned. 'You're just guilty because you're not dead too!'

I screamed and threw the glass I was holding at him. He ducked. The glass splintered against the wall.

'Oh, great!' he said, looking at the mess I'd made on the Persian rug. 'Yeah, jolly good idea. Let's create another Kristallnacht, shall we?'

'You *bastard!*'

'I saved you! I got you *out!*'

'For a great deal of money,' I yelled back between deep, choking sobs. 'You were penniless before I came along! Unsuccessful and ambitious and penniless! You only did it *for the money!*'

'It wasn't worth it!' he shot back furiously. 'If it had been a hundred times as much, it wouldn't have been! Do you blame me for rescuing you? Is that it? Should I have left you in Nazi Germany, Antoinette? To die with the others?'

'I wish that you had,' I sobbed. 'I wish I were dead!'

'Well, what are you waiting for? Kill yourself! *Do* it! And this time do it properly, will you? Don't screw it up again!'

Yet he was always so jealous of me, incredibly jealous, almost crazed with it at times. I couldn't even *speak* to another man without it bringing out a stream of savage abuse and all that inevitably followed. He thought my skirts too short, my dress too tight, my neckline too low, I looked like a *tart*, he said. Oh, yes, any fun I might have he'd really make me pay for later. Yet I'd never even *looked* at another man, I swear it. Not seriously. Or only for fun if I did – only to wind him up. Because the truth was, I'd become as openly jealous and untrusting of him as he was of me and continually, persistently questioning him about other women.

'Yes, I had an affair with Rachel!' he shouted wildly one day at the end of a particularly blazing quarrel. 'You're right – I *fucked* her! And not just her! There's been others since and I fucked them all! And, yes, I enjoyed it! Do you hear me, Antoinette? I enjoyed every single second away from you – you crazy, depressed bitch! Of *course* I only married you for your money – what other reason could there be? You should be in a bin! You've gone off your rocker – you're mad, Antoinette! Really you are.'

I flung myself on him, crying and sobbing, hitting him with my fists. I hated it when he called me crazy, his continual, ultimate taunt. I wanted to hurt him badly, wanted to scratch his face with my nails and make him bleed. I felt a white hot rage. Hatred was all I felt for him in those moments. If I'd had a knife I'd have plunged it into his stomach, I would have stuck it in and twisted it and laughed loudly when his blood began to flow. And then, afterwards, out of the kind of self-pitying, masochistic pleasure he so hated in me, just to spite him, I'd turn the blade on myself . . .

'You're like a painting by Schiele – ,' he mocked me as I stood there, sobbing in fury ' – *that's* how you look to me. All orange lips and wailing mouth, with jagged edges and dark, puffed up, druggy, shadowed eyes.'

He was holding me tightly, one arm outstretched, the heel of his hand on my brow, keeping me just out of reach, and I remember trying to bite his wrist in frustration. He snatched his arm away from me and swore. I remember smashing a bottle against the wall and threatening him wildly with the broken shards. The bottle was empty – I'd made damn sure I'd poured a good glug of cognac into my tumbler first.

It was like a nightmare, all of it, holding that broken glass up to his face and screaming at him. His frightened, murderous face. Screaming and screaming. The whole scene coloured bright red. Blood red, the colour of murder, the pure distilled tones of hatred. All of it red – except for the undiluted amber-gold fire in my glass.

'You'd like that wouldn't you?' I was raging, swigging the spirit down in one go. No soda – I'd forgone soda a long while before. Much better, I'd found, without. 'Rather mad than dead!' I was screaming. 'Because people think of what the dead say later – they remember it! But no one ever listens to a mad woman! No one! Ever!'

I was still weeping as I drained the glass. Dropping the broken bottle from my hand, I collapsed to the floor. Alexander had to carry me upstairs, mix a bromide for me and wait with me patiently until I fell asleep. Two powders from the box beside the bed he gave me. The grains fizzed gently in the bottom of the glass.

I searched for his eyes through the fog of bromide. 'Alex – '

'Yes?'

'Are you sleeping with her?' I was crying quietly again. 'Are you and Rachel having an – '

'No, no – ' he responded quickly. 'I just said that to hurt you. You get me so riled. I can't think straight. Of *course* we're not.'

'Really and truly?' I asked pitifully, tears silently streaming.

'Really and truly.' He smiled back soothingly. He must be telling the truth, I decided. No one could look as tranquil as that if they weren't. My arm flopped back onto the quilt. 'It was an awful thing to say,' I said in a small voice.

'You're all I want, Antoinette. I love you,' he said, smoothing the tangled blankets. He sounded so persuasive. I believed him. (You fool, you fool.) 'You know that really, don't you?'

'I'm sorry I hit you. I shouldn't have drunk so much with dinner.'

'No.' He rubbed his jaw ruefully.

'But the Tilneys kept on topping up my glass.'

'Yes.'

'Or else I wouldn't have.' The sedative was beginning to work. My eyelids closed without warning. I forced them open again.

'You're a nasty drunk,' he said gently. 'Some people get nicer when they've been drinking but not you. You get mean.'

'Do you hate me for it?' I asked drowsily, my voice half way to sleep.

'Well, sometimes feel as if I'm of no importance to you and that you'd be happier making love to a bottle. You're a little undiscriminating when you're inebriated, Antoinette. Any man will do.'

I waved my hand. 'I mean for the way it is between us in bed. For bringing out that side of you. For making you feel that way. You said that you did.'

'Did I?'

'Yes. You did.' I flung out my arm as I said this and knocked over the bromide glass. Falling back on the pillows, I stared at it helplessly.

He set the glass upright again. 'I don't hate you, Antoinette.

Sometimes I – ' He hesitated, looking down at me. His eyes grew distant. 'Sometimes it's the only way to treat your kind,' he finished softly.

'What kind am I?' I murmured with an effort. My voice drifting. He didn't reply. Perhaps I didn't voice this question, or he make the comment. Perhaps I only thought he did. I whispered, allowing my eyelids to droop: 'So if you've . . . never been to bed with . . . anyone else . . . then we won't have to get . . . divorced . . . '

'What did you say?'

'I said – if you haven't been unfaithful . . . then we won't need a . . . ' I forced my eyes open. Was he frowning that deeply or was I simply imagining it? Blurred with bromide, it was difficult to focus. ' . . . A divorce,' I finished. It took too much effort to keep my eyes open. I allowed them to drop heavily shut again. Eyes closed, I mumbled, attempting a laugh: 'I've sunk my claws in far too deeply, Alexander Sorel, to let go now . . . '

'Try and go to sleep,' he murmured.

My lips curved into a dopey smile. I was almost four months pregnant by then, already swollen and uncomfortable with a big belly and an even bigger investment in believing him to be a loving, faithful husband. From somewhere far away I could hear a faint snoring as, still smiling gently, I fell into a deep, dreamless slumber.

*   *   *

But his words rankled. I just couldn't forget them. 'I only said that to upset you . . . ' A slip made to jolt me? But Alexander never *made* slips. *In vino veritas*, they said. Did it work in the same way with anger? Under pressure, pushed to his limit, had he become careless and dropped his guard? Had he, for once, been telling the truth?

I looked at him from under my lashes and wondered till it nearly drove me mad.

Yet he was always at his desk when I rang unexpectedly – or almost always. Today? At three o'clock? Oh, I was on the second floor seeing Peter Chalfont. At twelve? At lunch with old Joshua Matthews at Trumptons, he had steak, I had lobster. Or, more impatiently, I'd just popped out for a breath of fresh air, Antoinette, is that allowed?

I should have listened to my heart. I should have known. I shouldn't have wasted my breath asking for excuses from my husband. My darling liar, my dark, handsome, adulterous man.

He could no more have remained faithful to me than he could fly.

*　　*　　*

Mr Palfrey. Same greyish shirt, same crumpled suit and striped tie, same faded grease spot. I hid my bulging belly under a pale mink coat the colour of weak English tea. I was surprised how glad I was to see him. We chatted across the desk like old friends about the general state of Central Europe for a while. Then he cleared his throat. 'Now what can I do for you, Mrs Sorel?' he asked a little warily. 'Another missing persons case?'

'No. It's not that.' I took a cigarette out of my handbag and took a moment lighting it. 'Do you recall the friend who recommended me in the first place? A Mr Barnes? You took some photographs on his behalf? Well, I'd like you to do the same for me. It's my husband. I think he's involved with another woman.'

'Adultery? I see.'

I smoked for a moment in silence. This was harder than I'd imagined. Adultery – my God, what a word, I thought distastefully. Spoken aloud in this little office it sounded so nasty, so formal. It conjured up pictures of countless men discovered in cheap set-ups in the act of being unfaithful to their wives. Trousers around their ankles, surprised expression on their face. Told of secrets long harboured and cold, blatant lies. You don't see, Mr Palfrey, I thought. You don't see at all. I nearly stood up right there and then and left. But I didn't. I inhaled a lungful of smoke and tried to gather my unravelling thoughts.

Seeing me hesitate, Mr Palfrey smiled reassuringly. Moving his legs aside so that he could open a drawer, he took out the same dented green tin ashtray and placed it on the desk in front of me. 'There's no need to feel embarrassed, Mrs Sorel. Not with me. I've heard it all before. I've been in this business for thirty years. There's nothing you can tell me that will surprise me.'

So I began. 'I believe I told you Alex and I were married in Berlin shortly before the war?' Remembering the occasion on which I

235

had, neither of us looked at each other. 'Seeing the dangers in Nazi Germany – ' we both kept our eyes fixed firmly down – 'Onkel Walter told Alex he would be entitled to a lot of money if he'd marry me and take me back to England as his wife. My uncle had the foresight to open a bank account in Switzerland. Not that it did him much good . . . ' I took a tense drag of the cigarette. 'Anyway. He arranged for my mother to open an account for me, too. A dowry, she intended it. To be given to the man who married me. And Alex did. Less than three weeks after we met we were married – I was only seventeen.' I glanced at him. 'I think I told you all this?'

'Most of it, yes,' Palfrey murmured dutifully.

'After the marriage, the greater part of the money remained tied to me. Still does. That was part of the deal. If you can call it that. Only madness or death make any difference to the terms of the arrangement. Under those circumstances, all the money goes to Alex. Otherwise, should we divorce, he gets a fifth. My uncle was a clever man but he had little choice – we'd only known each other a matter of weeks and it needed to be arranged quickly. So it was agreed. If we split up Alex loses his share in any property we jointly own but gets one fifth of a substantial fortune. Which means he'd still be pretty well off. Though not of course as well off as our present day standards.' I blew out a stream of smoke. 'Nowhere near as well off as *that*. So clearly divorce changes everything – ' I paused to allow this to sink in fully – 'From my husband's point of view.'

Palfrey nodded understandingly. 'You think he only married you for your money?'

'Oh, no! Financial gain was incidental. I mean, it may have played a part at *first*. But afterwards – well, he fell in love with me.'

'And so he should,' Palfrey said quickly. 'You're a good looking woman, Mrs Sorel, if you don't mind me saying.' But he hesitated, noting the black circles beneath my eyes, the general puffiness and broadening of my face and figure. Well, she *was*, he was clearly thinking. These foreigners go off very young, don't they? 'Oh, yes, very good looking,' he repeated heartily. 'That is, when you're not – ' He cleared his throat, averting his eyes from my obviously pregnant stomach.

I shifted my fur coat to cover it. 'Our marriage wasn't simply a financial arrangement,' I said a touch peevishly. 'Alex could never have loved me in all the ways he did if money was his main motivation. Or perhaps it was more than I realised? Perhaps youthful confidence blinded me to the truth?' My confidence suddenly evaporating, I stared across the desk with haunted eyes. 'I don't know, I don't *know*. Money really is the root of all evil, Mr Palfrey.'

'It certainly is,' he agreed, sounding unconvinced.

'I've been plagued by suspicions about Alex for so long. Reasons I haven't dared admit even to myself – possibly all quite unfounded . . . ' I gazed haggardly at the detective. 'Yet I simply can't seem to get them out of my head.'

'When did you first notice anything wrong?' Palfrey said hastily, hearing the tearful note entering my voice. 'That's always a good place to start in these matters. Did he become cold? Or indifferent? Perhaps he took to buying you lavish gifts? Some do, you know. They feel guilty, you see. Especially when the wife is, um, when she's – ' He averted his eyes deliberately again from my large, rounded belly.

'I tried to kill myself,' I said abruptly, tapping ash from my cigarette into the ashtray. 'Unsuccessfully, as you see. I was informed – wrongly it turned out, the woman who told me was a real *bitch* – she kindly informed me that Alex was having an affair. Apparently with Rachel Kost, my best friend. If true, it would have been unbearable. I mean, *really* unbearable.' I shuddered, genuinely if theatrically. 'Believing them to be, I took an entire bottle of aspirins. The daily woman found me in a heap on the bathroom floor. I was rushed to the nearest hospital. I was expecting a baby at the time and it died.'

I looked at him defiantly. 'We said it was a miscarriage though the nurses knew differently. Well, it could have been. Only – ' I bit my lip. Only it wasn't, I thought. My hand shook wildly as I put the cigarette to my mouth.

'Oh, dear,' Mr Palfrey said weakly. 'Is suicide even legal?'

'Legal? This all happened during the Blitz. No one was much interested in what was happening to me, whatever the status in law.

My worries seemed trite by wartime standards. There were other far more important matters of concern.'

I gave a brave, bitter smile. Palfrey smiled back nervously. I went on.

'At my husband's instigation I was living outside London. He *said* it was to get me away from the bombs and give me space to paint. But I always wondered – what really were his motives in arranging that I move to Sussex?'

'Safer there?' Palfrey suggested hopefully.

'Of course that is what I believed at the time. That is what he *told* me. But when I heard he was engaged in a – oh, I don't know! I don't *know*! I have such regrets, Mr Palfrey! You simply cannot imagine!'

'No, probably not,' he said nervously.

'After the failed, possibly illegal, suicide attempt, it was decided I should return to London.'

'Agreement on behalf of both parties?' he asked more briskly, back on familiar ground again. 'Your return to the city,' he supplied, when I looked blank. 'Did you both agree it was for the best?'

'Oh, yes, we agreed. But looking back, I don't think Alex ever forgave me. The baby was a boy I was told. I'd been carrying a boy. So in a way – 'I stared at Palfrey – 'I murdered his son.'

Palfrey looked back at me helplessly.

'After the baby's loss I was depressed, very depressed. I never painted again. Not a stroke. I didn't even finish the picture I'd started. I felt as if my whole life and all myself were floating away from me. There was nothing to get hold of, nothing . . . ' I stared at him. 'It's a beastly feeling, Mr Palfrey.'

'I'm sure it must have been.'

'It made me feel sick to my stomach.'

'Sounds very unpleasant.'

'Alex was indifferent, cold, oh, all the things you mentioned just now, and more. There was real hatred in his eyes. Quite often. Oh, I saw how he looked at me when he thought I wouldn't notice! And, yes, if you really want to know, I did get gifts, lots of them – '

'Believe me, I have no wish to be intrusive. No wish at all. To be frank, I'd prefer it if you didn't give me too many of the – '

'He always liked to give me a present afterwards,' I cut across him. 'Especially when he'd been particularly rough. Especially then. The more bruises, the more expensive the present. A gold bangle, ruby earrings. Once I got an exquisite brooch in the shape of a crescent moon.' I gave a twisted smile. 'He likes to hurt me, you see.'

'You mean, your feelings?'

'No. I mean my body. He likes to humiliate and hurt me sexually. He always has. *That* hasn't changed.'

'My dear Mrs Sorel . . . ' Palfrey looked shocked, despite the thirty years experience.

'About a month ago we argued rather bitterly,' I continued inexorably, ignoring the appeal in Palfrey's eyes. 'It was the usual sort of thing we go in for nowadays, bickering, throwing objects we rather like about. Except in the middle of it he sort of snapped and admitted he'd often been unfaithful to me – with several women he said. Not just one but several. Can you imagine how I shaken I was? I was shattered. He said he wished I were dead. He wished I'd succeeded that last time – I should try again, he sneered, but this time do the job properly. Oh, the things he says! All sorts of horrible things, you can't imagine!'

Palfrey said weakly: 'Are you implying – '

'Oh, the actual words aren't important! I'm just using it as an *example* of the sort of thing he says to me. He has a kind of magnetism, you see, a dark, brooding, sadistic quality that makes him extremely attractive to certain woman. They sense what he's really like underneath and *fling* themselves at him, like foolish moths to the flame. One day after we'd quarrelled he leant towards me and said very quietly, it was almost in my ear, he said quite coolly but *fiercely* you know, dreadfully fierce, he said – I don't like you. I just don't.

'Oh, he took it back later of course! I love you and only you Antoinette, surely you know that by now? But I can't forget it. He says he still cares but does he *really*? Is it me that he loves – or my money? Oh, I try not to think it but I'm convinced that everything he said that night was true.'

'Perhaps simply a lover's tiff?' Palfrey suggested hollowly. 'People say all kinds of things when they're annoyed with someone, even expressing feelings as unpleasant as these. I'm sure he doesn't really dislike you enough to wish you were *dead*, Mrs Sorel.'

'That's what he said. His exact words.'

'Oh, it may not amount to anything much. These things rarely do. In fact, I'm quite sure it doesn't. You're probably reading far more into it than he ever intended.'

I gave a short bitter laugh. 'You have no idea, Mr Palfrey. Really you haven't.'

'No?' he said, looking like he didn't want to have.

'You see, I believe him. I believe there *is* someone else. Knowing him, that's what I think. He *enjoys* lies and secrets. Keeping one thing apart from another. The more hidden the better. I've found *that* out over the years. The man is ruthless and cold and – oh, yes, I'm sure he saves all his savagery for me. He's telling the truth when he says I'm *special* to him,' I said with emphasis. 'Aren't I the lucky one?'

Palfrey looked appalled. I didn't care. 'Oh, God, God,' I moaned, putting my head into my hands. 'Am I maligning him horribly? I feel so muddled nowadays. They give me all this medication, you see. Pills to put me to sleep, then pills to wake me up again . . . and mixed with the alcohol . . . Sometimes I can't remember anything and half the day has gone. It isn't like I just dozed off or anything. I'm in a different *place*, I'm wearing different *clothes*. And Alex tells me – he tells me something I've promised him, apparently sworn quite *emphatically* and in great detail and I don't remember a word of it. Because he's been *out*, you see, I'm sure he's been with one of his damned *women* and he's simply trying to cover up his absence by telling me that I've said – '

I stopped and looked up through my fingers. 'Of course these suspicions may all be groundless . . . there's no *evidence* . . . no reason to believe any of it. Only this recurrent sense of . . . this sense of total emptiness . . . ' Raising my face, I stared despairingly across the desk. 'Oh, it's so black, Mr Palfrey. All so very, very black . . . '

'It's always darkest before dawn,' he responded, eyes evasive but attempting cheeriness.

'I do love him so terribly. Without him, I'm nothing. My family's all gone . . . I have nothing and no one . . . '

'Here, steady on,' Palfrey said nervously. 'I wouldn't say *nothing*, Mrs Sorel . . . '

'Sometimes I think I must be going mad,' I said, staring blankly at the detective. 'This goes round and round in my head till I sure I'm going to. Around and around. Around and – '

'Be careful, Mrs Sorel. You'll catch yourself alight in a minute.'

I looked at him uncomprehendingly, my eyes full of tears, only realising after a second that he was warning me about the cigarette in my hand which was threatening to burn my hair. I chucked the half-smoked cigarette into the ashtray and fell back carelessly in the chair, my stomach thrusting upwards.

Mr Palfrey picked up a pencil. He didn't look at me. He kept his bright, bloodshot eyes firmly down on his notepad. Now he hates and despises me too, I thought miserably. He cleared his throat. 'I'll need the address of your husband's workplace. He has one, I gather?'

I gave him an address. 'He also owns a picture gallery on Old Bond Street. There's no real need but he likes to get out of the house. Away from me most probably. He acquires paintings. Then sells them. About one every couple of years if he's lucky. He loses far more money than he ever makes.'

My tone was growing bitter again. Palfrey kept his eyes fixed on his pad. 'Any clubs or bars he frequents – which are his usual haunts, that sort of thing,' he asked hastily.

'He seems to eat lunch at a place called Trumptons quite a lot,' I said in a subdued voice.

'On the Strand?'

'Yes.'

'Good, good.' Frowning, he noted this down. 'And he's known as Alexander?' He looked up, still not meeting my eyes. 'Alexander Sorel?'

'Just Alex.'

'That could be important.' He jotted down the name. 'Now have you a good photograph you could let me have? Nice and clear?'

'I suppose I have one somewhere.'

'Well, I'll get cracking, Mrs Sorel. I'll contact Mr Brent with these details straight away. He takes care of that side of things. Do you want a report weekly? Or would you prefer a fuller one at the end?'

'Oh, I don't know . . . Just a final one, I think. How long will this take?'

'One month. Two. Hard to predict, really. It depends on the man in question. Oh, I should add that there's an additional charge per photograph if any are taken.' Adjusting his tie, he attempted to smile reassuringly. 'Of course you may find no photos are needed and there's nothing extra to pay. You needn't worry, Mrs Sorel. We don't just snap away for the sake of it.'

'It's driving me out of my mind. I just need to know.'

'They say suspicion's like hope. People prefer to hear the worst rather than bear the uncertainty.'

I heaved myself to my feet. Across the desk, I stared at him. In all of our meetings it was the only really intelligent thing I'd ever known him say.

*　　*　　*

There were thirty-five photographs in all. Thirty-five glossy A4 prints showing Alex in a variety of poses. Helping a fair-haired woman in an off-the-shoulder dress with a full flowery skirt out of a long shiny Daimler, not his own, perhaps rented for the occasion? Kissing the same woman on the cheek, before dinner, after dinner, and one showing them, hands tightly linked across a table, during. A visit to the park. The zoo. Lunching outside on a terrace somewhere in the London sun, both wearing sunglasses, toasting each other, the rims of their wine glasses touching provocatively.

Another woman, dark and slim, in an enchanting little hat, going through all the usual hoops. Sliding out of the long dark car, dinner, park, zoo, luncheon. The pair of them emerging from a hotel lobby one afternoon, arms linked, blinking in the sun's glare before sliding on dark glasses. Even through the blur of horror that has risen in front of my eyes, I recognise the heavy doors of Claridge's Hotel swinging to and fro behind them. Three weeks later, judging by the dates in royal blue ink on the photograph's back. Did Alex get bored that fast, exchanging them one for the other? Did he hope for no entanglements? A quick turn over with no regrets on either side?

There was one taken from outside the building, two shadowy figures locked in a passionate embrace on a balcony, two floors up.

Breaking free of the clinch, they turn and walk into the interior brightness. Even in the single flashlight of the night I couldn't fail to recognise the broad, unforgettable shoulders of my husband. There seemed no need for the neatly printed 'Mr A. A. Sorel. 10 p.m. The Ritz Hotel, London' on the reverse side.

Staring at it blankly, I wondered how long Mr Brent had to wait to get his shot. Had he sat patiently in his car below for hours and hours, while his dinner grew cold and his wife irritable?

But it was the last five pics that really got me where it hurt, the ones that sent me spinning to uncork the Cointreau bottle the second I reached home. Alex is kissing a woman on the cheek in the marbled lobby of some fashionable restaurant. Her face is for the moment hidden. His hand is resting low down her back, lower than would normally be considered seemly for a married man meeting a stranger by chance even in post-war Britain. She is blonde, though a quite different kind of blonde to the woman in the earlier pictures, and far more voluptuous, I see. The others are skinny by comparison with this luscious peach.

In the next shot he has pulled back, smiling, to acknowledge the head waiter come to lead them across the smoke-filled room to their table. The woman, too, has turned a touch, she, too, is smiling and – this is where I vomit all my breakfast down the loo, where I race to empty the whole bottle, where one bottle does not seem quite enough, in fact, will never be enough – for I am looking at a full face portrait, a perfect black and white print of Rachel. Rachel Kost who is having dinner with my husband, old friends unwittingly posing for all posterity as they meet for an uproarious champagne supper. I'm looking at *proof* in glossy black and white that they really are, despite all denials, in spite of all protests to the contrary (oh, for God's sake, Antoinette, give it a rest. Lighten up, will you, darling?) that they really are fucking one another, Alexander spoke true.

And it doesn't need the last photograph to show them at a table on a terrace outside, clinking delicate fluted glasses and smiling, smiling fit to burst, their eyes locked over the bubbles and filled right up to the brim with soon to be satiated desire.

*   *   *

I am wearing my red dress. A little tight admittedly, especially from the rear view, but I have managed to zip myself into it somehow and even tie a matching ribbon around my hair. My hands, fumbling not only with misery now but also excessive alcohol, drop the delicate brooch I'm trying to pin to the dress onto the floor. For a second I stare at the half moon in twinkling diamonds by my feet. Reaching to pick it up, I lose my balance, stumble slightly and find I'm slowly but remorselessly falling forwards.

My cheek on the rough rug, I lie there for a moment, staring on eye-level at the diamond pin.

Have I hurt myself? Harmed the baby swimming so happily inside my big fat tum? Who knows. Who cares. Not me, that's for sure. But up I heave myself anyway, brooch clasped loosely between nerveless fingers, and stagger to my feet. With some difficulty, I get the delicate thing pinned onto the shoulder of the dress and, spinning the tiny gold catch, close it. It's hard to focus my eyes from this angle – let's face it, from any angle – but I get it in the correct place eventually. I like the dress, I like the brooch, I like it pinned just there.

Satisfied by this little victory, I topple sideways onto the bed and close my eyes. I drift into a sort of alcoholic trance. At any rate, I'm snoring faintly when Therese peers round the door and softly asks if I am all right.

I rub my eyes, sit up straight and drawl, 'Alright? I'm fine – I'm *fabulous*, dahlink.'

'Shall I pull to the curtains?' she inquires warily.

I tell her not to bother and yawn widely. I think craftily of the sealed full bottle of cognac waiting for me on the sideboard shelf one floor below. 'You can take the day off, Therese,' I say, waving my hand in the air magnanimously. 'Take the rest of the day off.'

'But Madame,' she protests, 'what about tomorrow? Today is not my day out. Tomorrow is.'

'Take that too. Take 'em both.'

'You are sure?' she says uncertainly.

'Yes, yes.'

'Yet the other staff are not now in attendance,' she persists worriedly. 'Whatever will the master say? The house without me, it will be empty. It is me that he blames, I think.'

'For God's sake – do you want it in writing? It's *OK*!' We both ignore the decided slur in my pronunciation. 'It's OK,' I say more crisply. 'And it isn't 'not now in attendance'. That sounds stupid. You say – the rest of the staff have left for the evening.'

'Yes, Madame.'

'Or something of that nature.' I tip my head to one side with more of a jerk than I intend. 'You think I'm pissed, don't you? You think that I'm plastered.'

'I don't think *anything*,' she replies with spirit. 'I try not to think.'

Squinting my eyes for better focus, I consider her. 'You're quite ugly, Therese, aren't you? No offence meant, of course. But you're an ugly little thing, aren't you?'

'Will that be all, Madame?' she asks wearily.

There is something rather nasty, a little spiteful in the way that she says this particular 'madame', if I'm not mistaken. Of course I may be. But just in case I'm not, I keep her standing there while I examine her sallow little refugee monkey face. Perhaps I've told her she's ugly before. Perhaps I'm always telling her. I don't know and, right now, I don't care. There's enough to worry about without that. Enough to bloody well worry about, I think. I find I can't even be bothered to mention the moustache on her top lip. Alex is right about one thing – I'm a nasty drunk. Tears fill my eyes at this thought. Poor drunken me: poor plain Therese: what can life hold in store for either of us?

I ask penitently: 'Whaz the time, Teresah?'

Therese looks at her wristwatch. 'It is ten minutes of five o'clock.'

'Then Mr Sorel will be home quite soon.'

'Yes,' she agrees, backing hurriedly from the room before I can change my mind and ask her to stay. Or perhaps discuss the spread of mannish dark hair growing above her mouth.

When she's gone, I kneel on the carved bedstead with my bottom stuck high and, in this ungainly position, slide a green silk cushion up to the headrest. Turning so I can place the cushion comfortably against my back, I draw up one knee. Both is quite an effort. The other seems to flop back down again as soon as one seems stable. I feel I'm sobering up. The room has stopped whirling. Horrible reality is about to move in for another bite.

'I will go down to the drawing room and get the bottle of cognac,' I say aloud, before it can. 'I will scavenge – ' I have a bit of trouble with this word. It comes out more like 'scervinch'. I try again. 'I will scavenge the things I need,' I say to myself more successfully. 'And return to the safety of my lair before dear dalink Alixundah arrives home.'

Smiling crookedly, I consider this plan. Then, suddenly, I recall the photographs. I remember why I'm quite so astoundingly drunk in the middle of the day, I remember the glossy black and white image of Alex grinning leerily into my best friend's face. The image hits me like an iron bar in the gut. The lopsided smile is wiped immediately off my face. My head lolls back on the pillow. I stare sadly up at the ceiling.

I always knew it was true. In my heart I always knew it. He was making love to her all along. All these years of acquiescence, and for what? To be discarded like trash? I give a little hiccupping sob. He always was a beyond belief bastard. Always.

Tears roll unheeded down my cheeks. I begin weeping. I hear my own harsh, lonely, noisy sobs coming from a long way off.

* * *

I'm not sure what I intended to do with the knife. I didn't really have a fully formed plan to begin with. The only thing I remember clearly now is that the murderous rage which had begun boiling within me at the first sight of the glossy photographs of Alex and his women, courtesy of Mr Brent – the attentive gestures beforehand, the all too familiar smug, self-satisfied, basically disinterested fare-well smile afterwards – I didn't intend to vent on myself. Not this time, boyo. Oh, no, suicide no longer figured chief amongst my plans. The Nazis had had all the members of my family they were getting for the time being, as far as I was concerned.

The knife was for him. That much I remember. It was him and the searing memory of his hateful smile that I wanted to cut out of my heart. How best to do it, my only question.

But – you inquire, trés politely – it was the baby who acted as the final straw, was it not? *Certainement*, I answer, equally mannered. Non dubito. It was indeed the babe that finally broke this particular humped and foolish back. My sweet baby. Unborn as yet, but soon to be dragged kicking and screaming out of my belly into this vale of tears. Very soon to be. Oh, have no fear about that. Oh no. Oh no no no.

I hid the photographs on the top shelf of the wardrobe beneath carefully folded tissue paper, on my side not his, and sank back down on the bed, heavy cut-glass decanter of liquid gold clutched by the neck, glass stopper out, long, sharp, shining blade of kitchen knife thrust into the lap of my cherry red wool dress and, with the aid of a small top-up now and again, patiently waited.

It wasn't long before I heard the front door unlocking. By then, I was sprawled flat out on the quilt, one arm out-flung, hand relaxed and dangling near the decanter on the floor. My tears had stopped flowing long before, only the odd hiccup remaining, the odd shuddering sob, but even they were fading by the time I heard him shout:

'Darling! Are you home?'

I didn't answer. I breathed through my nose.

Below, in the entrance hall, I could hear him moving around unconcernedly. Footsteps stomping across the stone floor. Tramping slowly up the stairs. Halting briefly on the wide first landing. He always was a heavy walker for such a graceful man.

When I judged he was not coming any further but heard his steps ringing out in the direction of the drawing-room, I swung my legs off the bed and silently opened the door. Softly, slowly, with only the occasional lurch, I tiptoed downwards. The house was quiet around me. So quiet that I halted two steps from the bottom wondering if I'd somehow missed him and he'd gone straight out again.

Peering over the stone banister, I focused on his hat and raincoat on the hall peg. At the same moment there was a clatter, a sort of slapping of leather soles on the parquet nearby. I looked slyly to my right. The drawing room door was ajar. Got ya! I thought triumphantly.

Holding the knife, I crept quietly in my stockinged feet towards the open door. There he was straight ahead of me. His back to me, walking nonchalantly towards the window. Alex the shit.

I raised the knife and, before I'd given myself quite enough time to take careful aim, threw it wildly at the back of that unfaithful, hateful, adulterous, lying, bastard head.

15

ANGEL

Regent's Park, London. April 1952

Angel stared ahead of her.

She found she'd been gazing into space for some time.

Her heart was beating. The blood tingled in her fingertips. A swirl of yellow, white and crimson formed a shape before her eyes. It's a flower, she thought, slightly dazed. I'm in my sitting-room. Staring down at the floral pattern of the rug.

She rubbed her eyes, trying to get her mind clear. She'd been reading for hours – for a moment she couldn't recall why she'd risen to her feet in the first place. Why exactly had she got up?

Oh yes. The baby.

Antoinette had been pregnant, she had written. One reason she hated Alex for his betrayal quite so much – her unborn baby. Meaning what? That Alex had another child somewhere? A son or daughter he'd somehow neglected to mention? Not yet born in 1946?

The only light switched on was the lamp on the small pedestal table by the armchair. Its pale, marbled shade tilted, it threw a brilliant white glare over the pages of the notebook at its base. Beyond this, the room fell away into darkness. Turning towards the pool of light, Angel caught sight of her image in the dull, silvery glass of the mirror over the fireplace, fierce-eyed and angry and desperate.

How strange, she thought, staring at the darkness of her own eyes – the second wife finding out about her husband through the eyes of the first.

She took a deep, steadying breath.

If she was learning about him.

Because she mustn't jump to false conclusions. Alex had always unswervingly warned her not to believe a word his first wife ever said. Told her about the dramas, the drinking, the murderous thoughts and perverse sexual fantasies in a voice filled with despair. About what had really fuelled Antoinette's belief in him as adulterer: her own drunken affairs. About the kinks in her mind that turned her into an heiress and he into a poor man who'd married for her money – who'd stop at nothing to get it . . . *Was* she discovering the truth about Alex – or simply about the workings of a crazed and jealous mind? A clever mind – the distorted psychology of a woman who could calculate quite coldly how to steal another woman's child . . .

This could all be a ghastly mistake, she reminded herself – the whole thing – the betrayal – the baby – the diary – just another of Antoinette's romantic fictions. One more calculated twist from an already damaged, devious mind . . .

What if Alex hadn't want her to see the diaries because he was trying his best to shield her from Antoinette and all her tricks – from *her* false version of his first marriage? Was *that* was the reason he'd told her he'd once been married to a woman called Zara? So she wouldn't discover exactly where his first wife was – discover her, or be damaged by her. By throwing up a smokescreen, so thick, so high, so blinding, he must have reasoned, he'd be making doubly sure Angel wouldn't, either by accident or design, find her way through. If it hadn't been for a chance letter, she probably never would have.

Another deep breath.

Yes, she thought – Yes. He knew what she was like. He was trying to protect me from Antoinette in the only way he knew how. And I nearly fell for it, she realised, feeling slightly sick at the thought. I was almost tricked by her into hating him.

Angel shook her head, confused, afraid. The flash of anger was gone, replaced by the crush of confusion and fear. What had Antoinette said at the start of her journal? '*We hated each other. Except he hated better . . .* '

Who hated better in the end? Antoinette? Betrayed wife, alcoholic, child-stealer, liar? '*If I had a knife I would have plunged it into his stomach and laughed loudly when his blood began to flow . . .* '

Angel felt such a fierce, sharp ache of worry and longing for Alex that for a moment all she could see in front of her eyes were black spots.

The curtains were open. The headlights of a passing car flashed across the ceiling and shot back from the mirror. Also, the sound of a soft click from below. A click?

Re-playing the sound in her mind, Angel drew in her breath sharply, suddenly recognising it. A key turning softly in the lock? Someone stepped in the front door – she heard the shuffle of the mat. The door closed quietly.

A light sweat broke out along her hairline. She kept very still, head cocked, listening. Footsteps crossing the hall. A downstairs door opening. A quiet click as it shut again.

Apart from the slight stiffening of her body she didn't move. Just clutched the blue quilted collar of her dressing-gown more tightly to her neck. Her mind was empty yet horribly clear. Only her body registered any reaction – the quickened beating of her heart, the cold sweat on her palms and under her eyes, the chill feeling round her forehead.

She tugged a tissue out of the box of Kleenex on the table and slowly wiped her face and hands. Then pushed the shreds to the bottom of her dressing-gown pocket. Automatically, checked her wristwatch. Seven o'clock. *Seven?*

It's stopped, she thought blankly. The watch-hand has stopped on the hour. Unsurprising really since she couldn't remember winding it for days. She slid the strap over her cupped hand and set the watch down on the table. The silver clock ticking on the bedside table said twenty past three. That was more like it.

A slight scuffling sound came from downstairs before the house relapsed into silence.

Angel suddenly came to life. Moving swiftly, she scooped up the notebooks. Then, looking round wildly, ran across the room and thrust them into a drawer of the tall escritoire against the wall. The photographs were downstairs where she'd left them hours before, spread out on the writing-table. If Alex went into the drawing room he would see them straightaway. Well, there was nothing she could do about that.

And if it wasn't Alex? If someone else had his key? She felt suddenly afraid.

There wasn't time to dress. She pushed her feet into the blue mules she kept under the bed. Knotting the belt of her dressing-gown into a half bow, she inched the bedroom door open and stood for a moment listening, hearing nothing but the deep tick of the clock in the hall below and the pounding of her own heart.

She crept out into the passage and ran lightly down the thickly carpeted stairs. On the last step she kicked off the slippers and stuffed them into her dressing-gown pocket. They were making too much noise. Cold from the stone floor travelled up her bare legs. The single lamp on the table cast long shadows as she silently crossed the hall.

She laid her ear to the closed study door. No sound came from inside. Then a chair scraped across the floor. Angel felt her heart stop. Someone sitting down? Silence again. Her neck and forehead were clammy with sweat.

As she hesitated, gathering her courage, she saw a poker in the brass bucket by the fireplace. She moved softly across and carefully lifted it out, holding the brush and bellows to one side with her other hand for greater silence, then crossed quietly back again. She stood for a second, listening, her eyes wide, her hearts missing beats, trying to focus, to centre herself – then took a deep breath.

Raising the poker high in the air, slowly, very slowly, she opened the door.

Dark panelled oak. A strange, dishevelled figure hunched at the table at the far end. A face turning towards her. The door creaked loudly as she pushed it wider and stumbled into the room.

'Oh – ' she said. Then, stating the obvious: 'It's you.'

*　　*　　*

She didn't switch on the light. The curtains were open wide. A sort of unearthly bluish glow from the street bathed everything. Her legs felt weak. She sat down suddenly on the chair near the door.

Alex was sitting at the massive pale oak table he used as a desk. Out of date correspondence and torn open envelopes littered the top. Usually he was so organised. He was smoking. His body was slumped forwards across the table, one elbow resting on it, his hand cradling his forehead. The other arm was stretched straight out in front of him over the strewn out papers, a cigarette burning between two fingers.

He looked different. Angel had never seen him like this before. His hair was greasy and flattened unattractively to his scalp, his face grimed with dust as if he'd been rubbing it with dirty hands. His cheeks were dark with stubble and his suit creased and rumpled as if he hadn't taken it off for days. Even his features looked pinched and drawn.

She said, 'You're alive.'

'You sound disappointed.'

'Relieved, that's all.'

'Yes?'

'Very. I was dreadfully worried. Your note – I wasn't sure what to do . . .'

'Well, here I am. Safe and sound. No need for any more worry. Not on my behalf anyway.'

'I thought – I thought something must happened to you.'

'Yeah, well, I suppose you could say something did.' Without otherwise shifting his body, he moved his hand towards the ashtray to stub out the cigarette and said in a flat voice: 'You see – I've killed someone.'

She'd only fainted once before but she wondered if she was about to now. The room seemed to darken and recede and she had the giddying sensation that she was in another wood panelled, book-lined room – in the library at Longlands – before marriage, before childbirth, on the night they'd first met. And it was as if he'd said, in those first few moments, away from the heat and noise of the party, a cigarette smouldering between his fingers like now, hadn't asked her name or age or inquired why she was living with her cousins, but instead, to the blonde girl in the pale ball-gown before him, had begun – *I killed someone.*

'Killed – ' she heard herself say – 'Who?'

The dark eyes didn't flicker. 'My first wife,' he said.

No attempt to soften the blow. Just the harsh, cold fact – I killed her.

For one, long confused moment she sat there unmoving. And then the room came back again and she felt as if she had been waiting for this moment for a very long time.

'It was self-defence,' he said, more forcefully, looking up at her challengingly, as if she were judge and jury, to believe him or not. 'She came at me with a knife.'

He met her eyes, then looked away again.

The air felt hot in her throat. Scalding. She was finding it difficult to breathe. There was a lump in her throat she couldn't quite swallow. She pressed her feet down on the floor hard enough to feel the grain of the boards and sat rigidly, fighting for control. That felt important somehow. To stay cool, keep calm. Keep her wits about her. But it was hard not to let the feeling of horror show on her face.

Leaning so that her hair fell forward covering it, she took the slippers out of her dressing-gown pocket and pushed her feet into the mules. Sat for a second, studying her foot in the slipper. Her mouth was dry, her throat tight. But she was surprised at how normal her voice sounded when she asked: 'What happened?'

'To be honest, I don't remember much about it.' He stared down broodingly at his mashed out cigarette. 'I suppose I wrenched the knife out of her hand. Well, I must have, because when I looked down she was lying on the floor with it in her up to the hilt and I was covered in her blood. I called her a bitch. I said, I could kill you. And I did.' He said dully: 'I killed her with her own knife.'

'Did you check her pulse? Her heartbeat? I mean, maybe you only *thought* that you – '

'I'm afraid there's no doubt about it,' he said, his mouth white and set. 'One moment she was standing screaming at me, the next she was down. You see, she often tried to attack me. Often. It wasn't unusual. I was used to defending myself against her. Only this time – ' He frowned down at his hands. 'This time I went a little too far.'

Angel felt any life left in her face drain away. Her heart was throbbing so violently she thought he must hear. 'I thought she must have killed *you*. And then herself. You once told me that she tried to. I thought – this time she's succeeded.' She felt a sudden flash of rage – at her own stupidity, at her own guilt and grief.

'You're talking about Antoinette, aren't you?' she said, trying not to show any of this. '*She* was your first wife. Not Zara Hoffman.' But her voice wobbled, betraying her.

He didn't speak for a moment. Nothing altered in his face. Not a muscle twitched. Only in his forehead a small pulse began to beat. 'Yes,' he said at last. 'Yes, that's who I'm talking about.' His mouth twisted. 'Antoinette.'

He didn't ask her how she knew the name. It was as if he was too tired to care. His voice was very cool and formal as he carried on: 'I'm going to give myself up to the police. I've had a few days to think it over.' He sounded almost indifferent as he said: 'I believe it's for the best.'

Her first reaction was anger, blind, unreasoning fury. After all her confusion, her struggle, her fears . . . Then something else. Something harder to bear. Because she'd suspected it from the start of the diaries, hadn't she? If she were honest, somewhere deep down inside, she'd always known. It had been growing in her all day but it had taken the realisation of her own deliberate blindness to the truth staring her in the face to arouse in her this full sense of self-loathing.

Angel found she wanted to scream. She wanted to let go for once in her life and start screaming. Who *are* you? she wanted to yell at him. What aren't you still *saying*? For one moment, she contemplated hitting him as she knew Antoinette would have done. Her hand in her lap twitched as she imagined raising it and beating him with her fists and crying – you bastard, you *bastard*! She'd have liked to put her arms on the wide oak table and her head on her arms and sob wildly, regardless of what he thought or felt. One terrible frenzy of abandoned rage and tears. She wanted to scream into his face – go to Hell! Go to Hell! But she did not. She wasn't Antoinette, she wasn't even like her. She couldn't begin acting her way even if she wanted to.

It isn't so easy to drop the protective role of a lifetime, she thought despairingly. Even now, a part of her wanted to guard Alex from harm.

I'm still trying to make him happy, she thought incredulously. I still believe I can.

She suddenly wanted not to only sob but to laugh loudly at herself; wanted to laugh out loud and cry – you fool! The question Antoinette had written on her wedding day drummed loudly in her brain: *Will he love me forever?* Then his – *I killed her* . . . She felt sick.

When he got to his feet, she still didn't move. She felt hopeless beyond all belief. *This is it*, she thought. *It's all over. You bloody idiot.*

'I'm going to shower, shave and change my clothes,' he said in the same terse, matter of fact tone. 'After I've done that, I'll telephone my solicitor. I'll follow his instructions on how to turn myself in. I believe that's the expression one uses. One turns oneself in.' The smile that he gave was almost humorous but he was extremely pale and she saw that his hands were trembling and moist.

He got up stiffly, his joints not working smoothly, and walked round to her side of the table. She watched him stop at the door and turn back.

'Oh, and I'll make myself a sandwich.' A puzzled expression crossed his face. 'I'm very hungry. I haven't eaten for days.'

Angel turned a white, despairing face on him. 'Alex, what have you done?' she whispered.

He didn't answer for a moment. He stared down at her blue mules as if there were something very interesting on the inside of them that he couldn't quite fathom. Then, 'I've ruined my life, that's what,' he replied steadily.

And Nina's, she thought. And mine. And, oh, God, Antoinette's . . .

'I've fucked it all up. Haven't I?' He looked at her and said: 'I do love you.'

'Do you?' she said faintly.

'My White Girl.'

Just words, she thought, sickened. He's just mouthing the same old, tarnished words. Who is he really, this man I've married?

'It was just – ' He didn't finish the sentence. When he tried to smile his lips caught on dry teeth. He looked at her stiff white face and reached out his arm to the door handle. 'I had to protect myself against her,' he said flatly as he twisted it. 'I had no choice.'

'Alex,' she said. 'Alex – ' Her voice faltered.

He turned slowly back to her. She shook her head, staring at him, unable to speak. She made a gesture with her hand in slow motion. She felt a physical emptiness in the pit of her stomach. 'Nothing – ' she brought out at last.

She remained sitting in the chair, staring down at the floor as he let himself out. I will be all right, she told herself. I will be *all right*. But the thudding of her heart made her feel weak and sick as if that swollen pumping muscle was all she had left in her body.

She hadn't asked about the baby. His and Antoinette's child. Or even mentioned the diaries. Her head jerked up, then lowered again. Did a broken promise even matter now? But she knew that the coldness in her belly wasn't really a physical thing at all but the feeling of complete and inconsolable loss.

When she got to her feet some time later and walked towards the door, opening it wide, she heard a loud squeak. The hinges badly need oiling, she thought, passing through.

*   *   *

Early next morning, the telephone started ringing. Startled, Angel shot out of the armchair she'd been sitting in all night, staring into a dead fire, and went to answer it. Someone said, 'Hold on a moment, please, I have a call for you.' A click, then Laura's voice.

'I found it!' she said excitedly. 'By pure chance! I motored around for a while feeling *completely* useless – the looking for a needle in a haystack feeling growing stronger all the time. So I decided to stop and have a bite to eat in the Plough and Harrow – the only pub in Maiden Newton, as it turns out – thus killing two birds with one stone – attempt to cheer myself up and, at the same time, perform a subtle inquisition of the locals. And very disgusting the food was there, too. However, lunch was not a *total* waste of time because, when closely questioned, the barmaid disclosed that she knew Mary Peto. Apparently, she goes there all the time, good old Mary – it being her nearest public house and her being a bit of a boozer, by all accounts. Oh, yes – and this was the *really* clever bit, you'll like this – it isn't Zarah Hoffman who Mary is housekeeper for – it's someone called Antoinette . . .

'Well, that threw me a bit, as you can imagine. But, awfully pluckily I thought, I went and checked the house out, anyway – tall iron gates, high porch, all a bit decrepit, *just* as you described, right down to the blistered green paint. I was home by five feeling pretty bloody pleased with myself. A jolly good day's work, I thought. You can congratulate me later. Shall I give you the address?'

At last Angel spoke and she barely recognised her own voice. 'There's no need,' she said.

'What do you mean?'

'I don't need it any more.'

'What's the matter, what's happened?' Laura said sharply. 'Is it Alex? Is he – '

'Alex is home,' Angel said, tears catching in her throat. 'I don't need the address any more. He's home.'

And then suddenly she broke down, the stifled rage and despair and sheer horror hitting her fully for the first time in all that long, sleepless night. Sobs came up in her throat and choked the words. Great rending sobs without tears.

'It was her – always her. He never loved me – not really. I was always just a reaction to her. In his mind, the mirror opposite. Even his hatred was the stronger force. And no regret . . . no remorse for what he's done . . . only for himself . . . for *his* broken life . . . And now he's – oh, it's terrible. Poor, poor Antoinette.' The tears came at last. 'Can I stay with you for a bit, Laura? I need to talk . . . You were right . . . ' Angel managed to smile through her tears. 'That handkerchief you once mentioned? Oh God, I really need it now . . . '

16

Entry in Antoinette's Journal. December 1946

It was a girl.

A little wizened scrawny girl, with scraggy arms and puny legs, slightly undersized the nurse admitted sternly, under six pounds at birth. Like it was my *fault* that this mewling, crying, ugly little thing I was supposed to love and cradle adoringly in my arms, who wanted feeding all the time and came with such difficulty eventually out of my body, was too small.

Well, it's got to *come* out, the doctor commented, when the pains started pulsing regularly and I was staring up at him, sweaty and bog-eyed with desperation. In some form or other it has to emerge and quite honestly, Mrs Sorel, the best thing would be to start pushing *now*, he said, staring at my fat, widely stretched out thighs. Yes, I'm afraid, right now!

And so I pushed and pushed and, almost eighteen hours later, to the doctor's satisfaction and my relief, out the tiny thing popped.

What hair she gained over the first few months looked blonde. Unmistakably, horribly blonde. What I'd least wanted seemed to have come to pass. What I prayed wouldn't happen, had. I'd given birth to my own mother! Emma De Finzi lived on in this hideous puking infant. In despair, I couldn't help thinking as I held the flailing baby aloft, with as much distance between me and her as is possible yet still count as nursing, as I looked with disgust at the thin struggling legs and pale flaking scalp, I thought coldly – this one should have died, too.

And this was my main emotion towards her – coldness. The only strong feeling I can recall was the unremitting, pressing urge to smack the cry out of her. At moments – quite frequent if I'm honest – I badly wanted to fling that frail body across the room and watch it thump broken to the floor. Or perhaps chuck it out of the first floor window and see it smash forcibly on the pavement below.

So intense an urge, so unnatural, that sometimes I just had to throw her roughly down in her cot, uttering a furious, 'Oh, shut *up!*' and go and sit on the bed, cross-legged, some distance away from her.

From there, fingers stuffed in my ears, I listened in desperate, furious silence to my baby's blind choking wail, to the angry cry that never seemed to stop, day or night.

Perhaps Alex was right. Perhaps deep down I felt too much guilt, the forceful, irrational blame of the survivor pressing too weightily on me, growing heavier and harder to bear as each year passed. The burning question facing me every time I picked up, looked at even, my sweet infant girl – why? Why her? Why me? Why was I the only one out of all my family to survive? So I could give birth to *this*?

*   *   *

Alex has forgiven me. Darling, sweet Alex. He's forgiven me for the god-awful fight we had the day I saw Mr Purvis' photographs. The day I discovered he was an adulterous bastard and that all his incredibly credible protestations of innocence were worth nothing, all just lies and falsehoods, the whole thing, our life together, just a sham.

He has even forgiven me for my attempt to throw a knife straight between his unprotected shoulder blades which I never, ever believed he would. I thought he would take it out on me in some indirect way or another but he has sworn on the Bible – or the Torah if preferred, he suggested straight-faced – that he would never again be unfaithful to me.

'You are my family,' he insisted. 'I must have been crazy to risk any of it – and for what?'

In my turn, I have pushed all thoughts of divorce out of my mind, any suspicion that he only remains married to me for the money, that he's grown accustomed to the lifestyle that comes so easily with it – the houses, the string of brand new cars and holidays in hot expensive locations – and doesn't really love me any more, not really. Because that sort of love doesn't last forever, does it? That's marriage for you and, anyway, that's the sort of man he is –

faithful in his fashion. You have to work at relationships, Antoinette, and I'm certainly going to from now on, I swear it. We will start afresh. And perhaps – now this is just a gentle request so please don't take offence – lose a little weight, could you? Cut down on the drinking, at least, which would help greatly. Reduce the consumption of brandy daily from two bottles to one. That lovely girl I married? That slim, young thing? Where is she now, I wonder?

That slim, young, *rich* thing, I couldn't help thinking furiously. I agreed, pleasantly but rather futilely, as it turned out. Yes, yes, I'll tell the vintners to lessen the supply of cognac, darling. But I still could not bring myself to willingly touch the baby.

'We'll call her Sarah, after Antoinette's best friend in Germany but with the English spelling,' Alex announced proudly to the world, puffing on a big, fat celebratory cigar when the midwife went to find him to break the good news. 'Middle name Diane, to please my mother.'

Which of course it didn't in the least. Wrinkling her nose when told she exclaimed in disgust, 'Sarah Diana Sorel? Oh, my dear boy. Oh *no*. You can't be serious. Sarah? Isn't it a bit *Jewy*?'

*   *   *

Even before I opened my eyes my head felt heavy. It felt worse once my lids were unglued. My tongue seemed to be stuck to the roof of my mouth. I blinked twice and tried to wet my lips. The hammering behind my temples really started then, thundering for all it was worth.

Alex was up already. The sheets on his side pulled back, the door to the bathroom ajar. Through it, I could hear him singing to himself, deliberately loudly, as he showered.

Another day, I thought, listening to the hiss of running water on tiles. Another bloody day, I groaned to myself, wondering if a painkiller would help. Maybe several.

I heaved myself out of bed. I didn't even recognise my bleary face when I first caught sight of it in the mirror. A fat woman with long matted black hair was sitting on the end of the bed in my flouncy white nightdress.

For a moment I felt too depressed to move. I contemplated swinging those thick ankles straight back under the quilt and pulling the covers high.

Little Sarah Diana, fifteen weeks old, was in the next room. The nanny wasn't due to leave for her afternoon off until two o'clock prompt. I didn't have to do anything in that department yet. No pretence of motherly feeling necessary for another six glorious hours. It was only the thought of the pills on the bathroom shelf that decided me. I placed the tender pink soles of my feet on the floor and shuffled towards the sound of splashing water.

'And how are we this fine morning?' Alex asked warily, emerging, stomach flat, biceps bulging, feet large and ungainly, wet from the shower.

I stared at him, my cupped hand halting midway to my mouth and croaked: 'We wish we were dead.'

He smiled humourlessly. 'You drank a hell of a lot last night. You must have a terrible hangover.'

At least he hadn't added – even for you. He must be in a good mood, I thought darkly.

'You'll feel better after you've taken a painkiller,' he commented disinterestedly.

I continued raising my hand and swallowed the pill cupped within it. 'That's just what I intend doing.' Gulping a couple, I stared at myself in the steamy bathroom mirror and contemplated another. 'Do not exceed the stated dose' it said on the packet. Ignoring this advice – well, they didn't have my head, did they? – I shook out two more. Then I added one of the small purple tablets I took every morning.

'Nanny came snuffling in at seven while you were still snoring loudly,' Alex said, towelling himself dry, 'to inform us she has a cold. She's feeling dreadful, she says. Actually she does look it. She's taken a hot water bottle and a glass of hot lemon and honey back to bed with her. I told her you'd look after baby until reinforcements arrive in the shape of the daily woman. Alright with you?'

I stared at him, my head still thumping. No, it is not all right, I thought. It most definitely is not. I said nothing.

'I said you'd look into the nursery as soon as you were up.'

'Baby's still quiet,' I grunted. 'Presumably sleeping.'

'Leave it ten minutes then.'

I nodded and swigged back the painkillers.

And that was it.

Leave it ten minutes.

In those few words, our life together came to an end. A definite, final closure to all pretence of happiness on our part. A nod of agreement and – woomph, all over. The door swings open and Cold Revenge enters the calculation. If Nanny hadn't had a runny nose; if it hadn't been me who'd gone straight into the nursery, bar ten short minutes, to check on presumably sleeping Sarah; if I hadn't confided in Alex in a fit of honesty only the day before how violently inclined I felt towards her, how very much I would like to belt the living daylights out of her – If I hadn't admitted quite how much I'd enjoy doing that . . .

If, if, if.

I can't help wondering. I mean, if things had worked out differently, I wonder – where would we all be now?

*   *   *

The nursery was very still when I finally shuffled in. Nanny hadn't opened the blue chintz curtains. 'Too ill even for that?' I frowned crossly, swishing them back. 'It's only a cold, after all.'

Light streamed in showing blue carpet and cream rugs with pink and blue borders.

The baby was quiet for once. She'll make up for it later, I thought cynically. She'll bawl and bawl the second she realises it's me and not Nanny holding her. I walked across the room and bent over the cot, sliding the catch so I could open the barred side. Luckily, I didn't reach out my arms to pick her up.

She was lying without moving, her face turned towards the door. Eyes closed, mouth open, nose pointing misleadingly outwards and upwards. A pale pink crocheted blanket was drawn up so that only one thin shoulder was revealed. At least Nanny's covered her, I thought, looking down at the baby's unmoving body.

She didn't stir a whisker as I regarded her. Very peaceful she looks for once, I thought in that second. Not a sound from her. Not a peep. She isn't even breathing.

Fear started to creep through me, chilling the arms I hadn't yet raised, seeping across my chest and into my mouth. Asleep, Sarah looked so pallid. Well, she always does, I told myself quickly. She's always been that sickly jaundiced shade, her hair that dirty blonde. But why wasn't she moving?

I touched her skin, a hurried, darting movement of hand to cheek. Stone cold.

I knew then, of course I knew. Actually the moment I'd entered the nursery I'd understood I was in the presence of something other than life, something that was not quite of this world –

'Alex?' I called calmly up the wide corridor. 'Oh, Alex? Would you come in here, please? Just for a minute?'

*   *   *

'Oh!' Alex said. Standing by the cot, he looked down at Sarah (blue lips, clouded eyes and cold, very cold) and gasped through lips as stiff as hers: 'Oh, my God . . . What have you – '

He didn't say another word after that. Just turned right around and stared at me, and in his eyes such a look! I laughed out loud in amazement.

I laughed and laughed loudly till the doctor arrived and gave me a shot to make me sleep.

*   *   *

How can I put into words the feeling of dislocation that shook me after my baby was born? How can I tell with any vehemence what I felt when she died? Can anybody hear me? Is there anyone out there at all? There was a crevasse I plunged into, an alarmingly deep and wide split in my mind out of which, from that time onwards, memory blasted off, rocketing into the back of beyond.

Looking up at the world from the depths of my grown-up life, I wondered dully – how did I get here? I made no wrong choices, took no false turns. Everyone did what they thought best for me. Everyone tried. How? Was it bad luck or was it inevitable? It certainly feels like it most of the time. It has a kind of certainty about it, thinking back. All the signs of a bloody great plot to destroy me and all mine, derived directly from above. If we can't get her one way, we'll get her another.

I didn't choose this, I yell into the silence. Not any of it. In the blackness I fall sobbing to my knees.

Perhaps the mistake was calling the baby after my jilted girlfriend, Zarah, even with the English spelling? Did some of the Jewish ill-luck stick to her? A kind of killing glue? Perhaps, in her own way, Diane Sorel intuitively understood that you don't call a child after a slaughtered people. Not ever.

Blonde, my baby was, like gentile babies, like poor dead Rosa. Golden curls like my mother, she had. Perhaps they will look after her, up there, high above the clouds? I ask them, though without any true passion. I don't have much hope any more. But still I pray to everyone in my family – please look after her. Cradle her in your arms as I never did, rock her and sing her your favourite tunes as I couldn't. Because who else will care for her if you don't?

There's enough of them up there to manage it, I think quite angrily, when I can be bothered.

*   *   *

Alex thinks I did it. He thinks I throttled my own baby, or the equivalent. Held a pillow over her sleeping face. Pressed the smooth sheet into her damp mouth. With a thick pink blanket held her wriggling tongue still. Oh, has she stopped breathing? How odd. How very, very odd.

My tears of sorrow count for nothing with him. Nor does my wretched silence. He doesn't listen to my denials. There's nothing more I can say. Well, I suppose he has his own reasons for allowing doubt to grow into certainty. He's seizing his chance, isn't he? – If he can convince himself I'm mad enough for *that*, he can convince himself of anything. His eyes hold no horror in their depths any more.

Looking at me over the small pit that constitutes our daughter's grave, they are – as usual nowadays – quite, quite blank.

17

Entry in Antoinette's Journal. September 1951

Midnight.

The house hadn't changed. I had. But it hadn't. Perhaps houses don't as much. Same glass globe lighting the porch and chipped, cream stucco columns by the front door. Same pillar box on the corner of the street and tall trees swaying gently across the road. The beautiful spear-headed railings round the park gates hadn't been put back in place, I noted. Still only chain fencing. So one change then.

The good always end up as scrap, I thought bitterly.

I skirted round to the back of the house and made for the high gates at the side. As I'd reckoned, not locked. I knew they'd make a bit of a racket as I opened them but hoped it would be put down to general street noise. Luckily, a car swept past, headlights full on, as I pushed them to again. A good omen, I decided. For once the gods were on my side.

I only wanted a quick look at the garden by night to get some sense of how the land lay. I hadn't counted on the sweat my skin would break into or the trembling of my limbs at the sight of the familiar place. I still loved it, I realised. Shit.

How strange life is, I thought. Here I am, standing in my own garden – a stranger. 23 Portman Terrace: mine no longer, in all except name.

A feeling of foreboding filled me as I stood there. Some emotions never die, or not for long anyway. To calm myself, I glanced at my watch. Ten past twelve. By now, Mary Peto would be lying flat on her back snoring like a pig. For the last two nights I hadn't taken my sleeping pills. I'd ground them up and stirred them kindly into the hot chocolate I offered her. How pleased she'd been as she glugged it down before dropping off into a deep, dreamless slumber. You're improving, she said in surprise taking the proffered drink – thanks very much, Antoinette, don't mind if I do. It was worth the long, sleepless nights spent vacuously staring into the darkness. Well worth them.

I'd nicked the car keys from her fake lizard skin handbag and started up the old Morris 12 with surprising ease considering how long it had been since I'd done anything like it. It's like riding a bicycle, I thought happily, zooming off, the skill, once gained, never leaves. Speeding towards the main road I thought of that great fat bulk, mouth open by now, a silver thread of drool glinting on her chin, the smile of almost forgotten pleasures creasing her plain, pudgy face. She has no idea, I thought with a grin. The petrol gauge will be down a bit if she checks in the morning but I'll be back long before she wakes for her porridge.

Still smiling at this thought, I trod softly across the dark, well-tended lawn. The gardeners had been busy. No leaves covered the grass, not one, though it was early autumn. It hadn't changed. I recognised every bush, every flower, each tree, all chosen by yours truly with the greatest care. I was just pressing my body to the gnarled trunk of the *Morus nigra* in hello when I heard a sound from the window above. Hastily, I darted into the thick bushes at the side.

From the long drawing room window a woman stepped. Blonde, slim, attractive. I could see her clearly by the electric light that spilt onto the balcony from inside the house.

She's *smiling*, I thought accusingly. At nothing. Can you beat that? And they like to call *me* nuts.

She stood for a moment, one elegant hip thrust against the ironwork, this small, idiotic smile on her lips, before pulling herself upright and spinning down the stairwell. Her feet made a loud clonking sound on the metal so I was able to squeeze further into the bushes unnoticed. She was humming a tune under her breath. A Viennese waltz? Bloody hell.

I crouched there, hidden, forced to listen to this quiet, tuneful rendering, watching her as she wandered around the garden, stooping occasionally to acknowledge ownership of a bush, or claim a whiff of a late flowering rose. Madame Carriére *actually*, I thought, recalling planting it. Very English-looking, I saw as she paused for a second, turning slightly towards the lighted house, the fragrant rose still clutched in her lily-white hand. Very ladylike. Oh, yes, a fair English face, not like Alex and I, dark semites that we are. This happy little lark was obviously Angel, the new wife.

I ground my teeth. I had to resist shouting out her name there and then – *Angel, Angel!* It wasn't too hard to control myself knowing what I planned to do next. That will wipe the smug smile off her pretty face, I thought nastily.

The feeling of foreboding in my bones turned suddenly to exultation. It was a brief but very sweet moment before dread returned to claim me. I breathed hard through my nose and moved deeper into the undergrowth.

Back she stole across the lawn in the general direction of the house, me watching intently all the time. As she reached the spiral iron steps, I allowed my lips to curl briefly into a triumphant little smile. She has no idea, I thought, as she ascended. None whatever.

(Oh but I did, Angel reflected, reading these words. I did. I heard you.)

Like Peto, they're all deaf, dumb and blind in regards to anything that really matters, I thought bitterly, watching her climbing higher and higher above me. One thing I knew – she'd soon regret with all her heart this blithe innocence. There was more than a touch of malice in this idea, despite my lowly position. Or perhaps it was this very difference in height which made me feel so vindictive?

I shifted slightly, clamping a hand over my mouth, shaking with suppressed mirth, wanting to laugh out loud for sheer joy. A twig snapped beneath my foot. It sounded incredibly violent in the stillness of the night.

Shit, I thought, the smile wiped instantly from my face. She'll hear that. Everything will be ruined. She'll find me. She'll know. But she didn't pause. Even so, I waited a minute or two after hearing the sound of bolts being shot across from inside before silently leaving.

I don't owe no one nothing, I crooned as the gate clanged shut behind me, not nothing to no one. No more nut house for me, I sang softly.

Not wanting to be caught hanging about, I decided to check

inside for Onkel Walter's paintings another day. I wasn't entirely sure what the position was on ownership – could I be done for breaking and entering if the house deeds were in my name? Not worth the risk, I decided, pocketing the house keys and scooting up the street.

Round the corner, I stopped. No car. I stared hard at the kerb as if one was going to suddenly materialise out of nowhere. It isn't here, I thought disbelievingly. Definitely, it isn't here. There was the public call box on the corner from where I'd called on arrival. But not the brown Morris next to it, as should be.

Peto won't like this, I thought nervously. She won't like it at all.

I began to tremble. Where the hell was it? I couldn't remember. That frightened me badly. My head felt a big blank. Where had I put the damn car? Had it been stolen? Or was it parked by some other telephone box, on some other street corner, patiently waiting for me to reclaim it?

I badly needed another drink, I thought, rattled. Everything will be better when I have one. Or a tablet. Perhaps a trimethadoine or phenytoin or one of those large pink ones that energise you so bloody well. How I wished I had a big pink pill.

Then it came to me in a flash. Round the next corner and on the left. Of course. Glee rose in my breast as I hurried round and saw the familiar brown chassis, the bent fender and discoloured wind-screen, the long lines of the running board and the sweet little plastic dice swaying from the rear view mirror.

Don't you worry little Sarah, I promised, as I shuffled up to the car, I'll soon be back to claim you.

But a part of my brain was asking – why? Why was I going to do this? I frowned. Frankly I was puzzled myself.

It will show him, I reasoned, inserting the key in the lock – it will show him what he's really up against. Underestimate me? I could plant things deep in the soil and watch them unfurl for years. Years and years. It would be easy. Nanny Hubbard, or Hilliard, or whatever her name, was off for her fortnight's hols in a few days, as Alex had unwittingly told me via Mary Peto. And new wifey ain't gonna miss her one bit. I smiled. Easy peasey. Oh yes, I'd nurse baby Sarah so amazingly well, I'd be so bloody sweet and kind to her that

Alex would be forced to acknowledge how good a mother I really was – or would have been given half the chance.

But I was moving stiffly, jerkily as if my mechanism was already winding down. A part of my brain told me I was about to do something very foolish indeed and it would all end badly for me. Don't do it, it told me.

Opening the car door and stuffing myself inside, I ignored my own wise advice, as usual.

Undated entry in Antoinette's journal: Map House. East Sussex.

There's a yiddish word *beschert* meaning 'meant to be'. I escaped the Nazis, I came to England, I was married, I was safe. I have no children, no grandchildren. Was this meant to be?

Now *he's* divorced me. *He's* put me in this house in Sussex, bought with my money, and taken his share of the rest. Also acquiring along the way the large house in north London, the income, the antiques and diamonds, the fast cars. It's like a game of Monopoly, isn't it? Winner takes all? Park Lane? *That's* mine too, I fancy, thank you *very* much. You can have Map House, Antoinette, *and* a nurse to look after you *and* – what else? Oh, my dear girl, you don't really need anything more, do you? In *your* state? I mean, down there, in the country, far away from anywhere?

And what of the paintings? My Onkel Walter's paintings? The Cezanne, the Manet, the Picasso and two Degas, the charming little Renoir?

He's sold them, I suppose. Or worse, given them to Mother. That's why he's put me here, isn't it? So I can't complain. Or even notice. *I'm* no fool, *I'm* not mad – he wants to get me certified insane but he can't. You can't divorce someone who's in a lunatic asylum, can you? Not for five long years – that's the law, for once on my side.

But now he has his divorce, the money and houses – all the things he wanted so badly he was prepared to marry to acquire – he wants me put in a loony bin. Then he gets them, fair and square. Such are the terms of the nuptial agreement – bit of a mistake on Uncle Walter's part, really, but how was he to know? Oh, I take the pills the nurse offers gladly enough but they'll be a bloody long wait for that. I'm frightened though. Because he'll do it, I'm sure. He's biding his time. He's waiting his chance. I can see it in his eyes. Yes, he wants me mad, that's the conclusion I've come to. Then he can keep me here, a prisoner. He can pretend – *it's for my own good*. He may even come to believe it himself. I may be a lunatic, but I'm *his* lunatic. I'm his, all his and no one else shall have me, ever. That's how he reasons deep down.

And in the end, I will be mad. If that's what he intends, knowing him, I will be. I won't get out of here, not in one piece.

So I keep quiet. In my charming brick and grey flint prison in the countryside. Glorious, bolted shut Map House. I haven't given up hope. Well not entirely. I wanted his love and what did I get? His disgust, his denial, his hatred and stone cold contempt. Did I once gaze into those dark eyes adoringly? How long ago it seems. A lifetime – another Antoinette. Staring into those eyes now, I see only greed. Black eyes, I see, depthless and cruel. He's used me up, squeezed me dry, then spat me out into the rolling, lush green and lonely English countryside.

So I take the pills that are offered and wash them down with a teensy drink. Just an insy-winsy one, nurse, just one, oh, go *on*. What else is there to do? Down here, far away from everything? He visits rarely. Less and less often. These days, hardly ever. He can forget about me. And what he needs me for. At least, for most of the time. That side of him – for my consumption only.

But the grand house in Portman Terrace, the cars, the paintings, the things they both enjoy, really they all belong to me.

And the baby? *His* baby girl. Is it mine, too? I mean, if he can take what's mine, can't I take what's his? It seems only fair.

* * *

No. That wasn't meant to be either. As it turns out. Taking their baby was wrong. I see that now. Very wrong. She's *her* child, not mine. Because my baby is long dead. Little Sarah Diana, with the golden curls and the forceful wail and the pale pressing, pouting mouth. Quite dead. Just four months old, may she rest in peace. I may have been a little confused. I don't have a child any more.

It wasn't – it wasn't *beschert*.

* * *

The old dreams have come back again. Someone scrawled across my forehead – '*kauft nich bei juden*', which of course means in English, 'don't buy from the Jews.' Except in my dream it always means – *don't marry her*.

And a truer word was never spoken, I snickered, checking my brow next morning for warnings of a defamatory nature. There was nothing to be found on my face of course, nothing at all, except for a terrible emptiness and a bitter, lingering sense of shame.

My name is Antoinette. I've lived in England and Italy and Germany. My dream is proof of that. Because I dreamed that dream in the other life. And if I did, then I must have lived it once – you see?

On the worst days I doubt it. The Nazis, Kristallnacht, the sunlit café on the Ku'damm enjoyed in the company of Norbert, Marta and Viktor?

And the trains which left promptly from Berlin-Grunewald station, in their packed chilly carriages, the Kleins, the Hoffmans and Kosts, all the old friends and relations? Deliberately snatched from the earth like they'd never existed. All gone, like glass from a shattered window pane, like cool water running through the fingers of a cupped hand, like a puff of stale cigarette smoke lingering for a few brief seconds on the midnight air . . .

My name is Antoinette. I lived first in England, then Italy and Berlin, then returned to England again. I've come full circle. I know my present and my future. But the past? It seems unbelievable, even to me.

Perhaps I am mistaken. My memory must be faulty. Please – take no notice. Tear up these pages, Angel – tear them up, and forget all you've read. It couldn't have happened like that. It just couldn't. It just

18

ANTIONETTE

Maiden Newton, England. 21 September 1951. 10.38 p.m.

When the first blow struck she was asleep. She was aware of a violent streak of white light, then another blinding flash, then of being dragged to her feet. The pain hit fully as she struggled out of blackness. It took her breath clean away.

Gasping, she opened her eyes and saw a contorted face glaring at her, eyes up close. Before she could recover her balance, her head was yanked backwards. A hand twisted in her hair. Instinctively, she raised her hands to her head, trying to catch hold. The pain in her scalp was so bad she thought her hair was going to be pulled straight out by the roots, then realised it already had been – a long black strand threaded with silver was curled on the pillow.

With the little breath she had in her, she gave a strangled sob.

Another blow. She crashed to her knees, her neck and shoulder on fire, gazing up through a red mist of pain. She recognised him now. She'd have recognised him even if she'd never opened her eyes again – if he'd killed her outright while she slept, she'd have known.

'Bitch!' he spat at her. 'Did you imagine you'd get away with this? Did you really think you could? You must have been planning it for some time. All those tricky little details.' He was thumping her shoulder with each word. 'Well – now – you're – going – to be sorry. You're going to wish – you – never – had!'

She was lying face down on the floor. Her arm and shoulder felt numb where the blows landed. The other arm was curled up around her head, trying vainly to protect it. 'I am,' she managed to mumble into the weave of the carpet. 'I'm really sorry!'

'Not as much as you're going to be.' An extra big thump with the last word. 'Not by a long chalk.'

He dragged her onto her haunches and began roughly winding a piece of rope around her wrists. Before she fully realised what he intended, he'd clamped her hands together, palms in, knotting the rope so tightly they couldn't move. Her head slumped forward. A mistake. He brought his fist down on her nape, choking out: 'You've humiliated me – you've made me look a complete fool – you've made me very, very angry. You aren't going to even *think* of doing anything like this again. Not in your wildest dreams.'

She was lying helplessly at his feet. She could hear her own ragged panting. Her lips formed words but no sound came out of them. She'd never seen him this furious before. He was usually so controlled. Scarily disciplined even in anger.

'Do you understand what I'm saying?' he hissed into her face, jerking the rope. 'Or are you too far gone as usual?

'I – I understand,' she forced out. 'I *understand*,' she said again more vehemently, seeing his expression.

'Good. Because we're going for a little walkies, you and I.'

She stared at him in fear. 'A walk? Now? Where?'

He hit her just hard enough on the chin that she couldn't hear his reply. Bare planks against her cheek. From the floor she whimpered: 'I'm sorry. I really am. I won't do anything like it again. It was a *mistake!*'

Actually, now she'd sobered up, now the pills had worn off fully and clarity returned, it really did seem like one. For once, she could understand why he was so angry. It had been an awful thing to do, that she freely admitted. A terrible thing – a complete and utter misjudgement. To be honest, her whole life – one huge misjudgement. But he took no notice in any case. He had another long piece of rope that he was winding round her neck. Jerking the loop he hauled her to her feet.

Hastily, she slid a hand inside the noose to make room to breathe. The other hand, tied tightly to it, dangled helplessly in mid-air. She was really frightened now. And in pain. Her lip was cut. Warm blood trickled down her chin. She could feel a loose tooth with her tongue. 'Look, I said I'm sorry.' Her voice sounded strangled, fearful. 'Where are you taking me? What are you going to do?'

'You'll see. It isn't very nice, not knowing, is it?' A sharp tug. 'Well, now –' he said mincingly – 'now you can have a taste of your *own* medicine.'

He dragged her by the rope down the stairs and out the front door. Desperately holding the coarse knot a fraction of an inch from her throat, she had to run to keep up with him. The chill night air hit her though she didn't really feel the cold through her fear. She was glad she'd taken two sulphonal tablets earlier in order to sleep – they were dulling the pain. Though not a lot. Only slowing her reaction to it.

She stumbled, scraping both heels and the soft skin of one sole along the stoney ground.

By the gates, he halted, fumbling with the catch. She took advantage of the lull to inch the rough hemp a little further from her throat and gasp: 'This is crazy! They'll find out!'

'Yeah? Who exactly? Nobody's interested.'

Which was probably true, she had to admit. Nobody was. Seeing the expression on his face she couldn't help flinching. She took a step backwards, even though she knew it was pointless since the other end of the rope was gripped tightly in his hand. Instinct, really. Desire over-riding logic. If only she had the chance to run. She'd jump the wall, hide in the trees, he'd never catch her. *Then* she'd make him sorry. Oh, it would be her turn then. *He'd* be the one apologising. Profusely.

'Look, this is all crazy –' she choked out again, desperately playing for time – 'You know it is.'

'Crazy you think? *You* think? That's a good one.'

But the cold night air seemed to have sobered him up a bit. He considered her thoughtfully for a moment. 'OK. You have a point. For once, you're sounding almost rational. Enough chat.' He jerked the rope viciously. 'Let's go inside.'

She felt relieved. Inside was better than out, wasn't it? She desperately hoped so. Prayed this was all he intended – drag her about for a bit, loop a rope round her neck, frighten the shit out of her. If so, he's succeeded, she thought, as he led her by the rope back up the path and through the front door which he hadn't even bothered to shut so confident was he that no one would come looking for them, that vast stretching space, miles and miles of it, fields of darkness, and hauled her back up the stairs like a dog.

The pressure of the noose round her throat made her want to vomit. By the time she'd reached the top step, she'd barked her shins several times. Which was the least of her worries, she told herself, staring into his hard face, the very least of them.

She bent over and retched. A stream of thin yellowish liquid shot out of her mouth and dangled from her lips, mixing with the bloody snot from her nose. She took longer than was strictly necessary to straighten up again.

He looked at the mess down her front in disgust. 'Christ.'

Her long white bloodstained nightgown was splattered with blood from her mouth. She could feel her chin beginning to swell. She couldn't see properly out of her swollen left eye. Her legs were beginning to go. She could feel her knees collapsing, they buckled out from under her, it was amazing really that they'd held out for so long. Quite hefty, she thought, but strong. She grabbed the small table next to her for support. Too delicate, it toppled over, the porcelain commemorative plate and ornate silver-framed photograph on top sliding off with a crash.

She sank slowly, almost gracefully, with them, to the floor.

'Christ – ' he said again, looking at her, sitting there on the hall landing – 'What a mess.' He sounded for a moment almost tender. 'What a bloody mess you've made of everything, Antoinette.'

'Look – ' she said, talking fast. 'I can explain. There are reasons – things that I had to – '

'It's too late for explanations now. We're past all that.'

'It's never too late for – '

'It is for us.'

'I just wanted to tell you how I felt compelled to – '

'And I said it's too late. I don't care. I don't give a shit about you or your damn motivations any more. They bore the hell out of me. Actually always did. I – don't – care.'

He didn't even raise his voice, he was so relaxed. Too relaxed, she thought slyly. Beneath the folds of her nightgown the sharp edge of something was digging into her crotch. The scalloped edge of the plate? The silver frame? Smiling lopsidedly, wobbling her loose tooth with her tongue, she watched out of the corner of her eye as he moved towards her. Saw him let go of the rope. Watched it slowly slither to the ground. Now's my chance, she thought, calculating distances. Now's – my one and only –

It was the porcelain commemorative plate she could feel pressing against her thigh. Elizabeth and George VI's coronation. Two gently smiling faces in a circle of royal colours. He'd always disliked that plate. She saw his eyes briefly. Just a flash as fear transformed them from confident to terrified. Watched the contempt drain out of them and be replaced by something else. To completely shit scared in one fell swoop. Hearing her own cry, she almost scared herself.

Launching herself into the air with a blood-curdling scream, she smashed the plate down hard on top of his head. Before he'd had a chance to recover, she'd picked up a large broken shard and brought it down again. And again. It shattered into small pieces. He didn't move. Just staggered slightly, then straightened up. It was as if he was waiting for her to do it again. As if he was stuck in front of her, feet clamped to the floor, while she picked up the ever-dwindling pieces of porcelain, simply waiting for her to crash them down repeatedly on his scalp.

She was breathing heavily. She looked down, considering whether to pick up the last shattered fragment of Royal Winton at her feet.

He lifted a hand to his brow. Blinked, faintly puzzled.

No, she had to get away. He wouldn't stand there forever. She turned, stumbling towards the stairs. Hitching up her nightdress, took the first step. Her foot slipped. She felt it go. The end of the rope was still tied round her wrist and a length of it caught beneath her heel. Grabbing for the banister, she steadied herself. Got her balance. She felt the heat of relief shoot through her whole body. Teetering there for that single split second she looked down. She was safe. She was –

Falling.

She didn't have much time to think. With a sickening plunge she moved downwards, groping for a hold, head first, arms flailing, running, sliding almost. Hands scrabbling desperately in the air, she heard his voice behind her – or perhaps not. Perhaps she was simply imagining it? Another voice found only in her own mind?

But just before she hit the bottom step, she heard him laugh quite clearly – 'Yeah, fly, girl, fly.'

Thought she caught him saying: 'That's it – go, Antoinette – go! Don't hold back now, don't stop – you stupid crazy bitch . . . '

THREE
ALEX

. . . she smiled, no doubt,
Whene'er I passed her; but who passed without
Much the same smile?

Robert Browning, *My Last Duchess*

19

Pentonville Prison

2.ix.52

DEAR ANGEL – This is a hard letter to write, impossibly hard, but I shall try. Here it is, a veritable hodge-podge of shame and failure and regret: my life.

I realise I should have told you about Antoinette from the start. Perhaps it would not have seemed such a shameful thing if it had been out in the open from the first. But I think I explained why I felt I could not? And oh, what a web we weave, for once I'd started down that road it was impossible to retract. Once I'd said I hadn't seen Antoinette for years and didn't know what she was doing or if she had ever remarried or gone back to Germany – everything, in fact, that I *wished* were true – it was already too late to turn back. You fixed those innocent, trusting grey eyes of yours on me and I thought – if I can convince you of this, then I will be allowed to be happy again. I was a fool to think that because of course I couldn't. *She* would have never let me be.

My first wife was a witch who would not let go of me. She was hating and murderous right from the start, attempting to poison me twice by slipping powder into my food when she believed I was not looking, attacking me by throwing a knife at my retreating back, and so forth. Most of this you've heard already at the trial: her drunken behaviour, her insane rages, her fantasy that she was being watched and that everyone had turned against her.

In order to prove my plea of self-defence, I had no alternative but expose all this to the world and reveal just how crazy she had become as she descended into a world of drugs and alcohol addiction. For all this showed at what cost I had remained quiet over the years, the Judge even commending me in his summing up for my forbearance in paying for a house in Sussex and for staff to watch over her.

Just how much watching it needed you know only too well given what happened to our child. It was yet another thing that showed Antoinette in her true light. It also showed why I was forced to see her so frequently. I had to keep a constant eye on her because I could never be really sure what sly ideas would enter her head to taunt me with next and so could not easily guard against them from afar. In that respect, Nurse Peto, otherwise a good woman, was of no help to me at all.

This brings me to the main purpose of this letter.

Whatever the jury decide tomorrow, I want *you* to know the truth – I did not intend to kill Antoinette. It really was self-defence as I claimed in Court: it was her or me and there was not much choice in the end. They must be right about what I did to her beforehand since the evidence is clear but I do not remember *any of it*, I swear. If I hurt her more than I should have done I am sorry but it truly was only to protect myself. That is the same for all the other times, too, whatever the prosecution say. I'm not a violent man, as you know best. I only recall thinking that I could not let a mad woman destroy us as she wielded a knife in my face. The rest is a blur.

My counsel said that what happened between us was mutually destructive. Our hatred of one another spiralled into something over which we had no control. He also said that we brought out the worst in each other. Some relationships are deeply destructive: ours was, he said. We *created* each other. Finally we tipped each other over the edge.

Since Sir Charles was asking for leniency I understand why he made this point so powerfully but I agree with him only to a certain extent. I think Antoinette was a truly wicked woman but I do not believe I am an evil man. I have my flaws it is true – I admit that I was unfaithful to her more than once (as the prosecuting counsel went to such pains to point out) but, in my favour, I was very young when we met and, soon realising what kind of woman I'd been tricked into marrying, stopped loving her early on. Too honourable to press for divorce, here lies my deepest regrets.

I certainly did not marry Antoinette, stay married to her or try

282

to get her certified insane after our divorce for her money, as was suggested by the prosecution. I find the idea deeply offensive. She had a dowry, it is true (though a paltry one, nothing like as large as claimed) and for close on nine deeply unhappy years we lived together. During this time we argued bitterly without ceasing and most of which I spent trying to help my wife to stay sober and in touch with reality. Would I have done that if money was my main object?

This was always *her* suspicion; a part of her illness, I was told at the time; an idea that grew stronger and stronger till it became certainty – that she was an heiress possessing a huge fortune and that I was her enemy trying to steal it.

Can you imagine the inferno that was my first marriage? Have you gained a glimpse? If my KC, Sir Charles, is right and Antoinette and I brought out the worst in each other, all I can say is that you, without question, bring out the best. What I like to think of as the ninety-nine point nine per cent that would have been all there was of me if a black witch called Antoinette had not come into my life.

You were terrific during the trial, so strong and calm and downright sensible. The adoration in your steady gaze did not waver for a moment. I am sure you will not be easily swayed by all the lies that have been told about me and will find it in your heart to forgive me now the court case is almost over and my actions fully vindicated.

Remind yourself that even the Judge said that I had little choice but to protect myself from a woman who had become a 'crazed and bitter fiend'.

Remind yourself that it was really only one mistake, however terrible that one was – a single moment of insane, impulsive rage, and a marriage that should never have taken place; the former now seeming the almost inevitable result of the latter.

You must, of course, judge for yourself. Surely, my darling, you can overlook that one foolish, early mistake?

Your loving husband,   ALEX.

Maisie came into the room with the tea tray at that moment but at the sight of Angel's face, backed hurriedly out again. Angel didn't notice through her tears. It was almost half an hour before she rose from the writing table, stuck the letter in her belt and took the circular stairway down to the garden. Sitting on one of the painted iron chairs at the foot of the steps, she stuck her hand inside her belt and drew out the letter. Unfolding it, read it through once more.

Stupid, reading it again and again as though the words might change their meaning. The meaning was clear enough – though not the one Alex had intended. Not what he'd intended at all.

She shivered. The sun must have moved across slightly. She found she was sitting in shadow. She wrapped her cardigan more tightly around herself and stared fixedly into space, scanning the rockery, the sheltering beeches, the crooked little mulberry tree, without seeing very much at all.

*   *   *

From the moment Alex had been arrested, the diaries lay on Angel's conscience like a crushing ten ton weight. What should she do with them? If she showed them to the prosecution she could be signing Alex's death warrant – if she gave them to the defence, she was throwing Antoinette to the wolves. Or she could simply pervert justice and tell no one.

She was barely sleeping. The horror of Antoinette's killing, the memory of Alex admitting he was implicated, the words and images from the diaries – who could sleep with those rattling around in their brain?

Eventually, she'd put the dilemma to Laura in as abstract a way as possible, without losing all meaning. 'If someone had something which, if she showed it to someone else, might harm another person, possibly irreparably, yet was vital to a third person's good name – ' she'd begun haltingly – 'what should the first person do? Should she tell the truth and endanger the second person, or let sleeping dogs lie?'

Despite the vagueness of the question, Laura had no doubts. 'If it's a choice between love and justice – ' she said firmly, shrugging off the ins and outs and getting straight to the point – 'the choice has to be justice.'

284

Always?

Always.

But the answer still didn't solve Angel's problem. Because in what did justice consist? *That* was the dilemma in a nutshell.

Strangely, the only person she could be completely open with was Alex. Even then, when she'd visited him in jail and admitted reading the diaries, his shock threw her off balance. He couldn't talk for a moment. 'You have her *diary*?' he said, looking appalled. 'How on earth did you – '

'Brioney Parsons gave them to me.'

'The old nurse? I didn't know she was still in contact with Antoinette.'

'Yes, well, she was.' She hoped she didn't look quite as guilty as she felt. 'Surely you realised something was up, Alex? I mean, how else would I have known who your first wife really was?'

'I didn't think. That you had the diaries? It didn't occur to me. So much was happening and I never imagined for a moment – ' He recovered quickly. 'They're a pack of lunacy and lies, you know that, don't you?'

'So you knew they existed?'

'Of course I *knew*. Oh, I never read them. But Antoinette delighted in telling me about them. Often. One day I'm going to tell my side of the story, she'd say. You can imagine what she meant by *that*. Her side? Well, she always enjoyed making things up. Reality was never of much interest to her. God.' He clenched his hand into a fist. 'This is *exactly* why I didn't ever speak about her to you. I always knew that if I opened that door just a crack she'd somehow find a way of squeezing through. I *knew* it. And she has. In the worst way imaginable. I wanted to protect you from her and I failed miserably. Even from beyond the grave she's somehow managed to – '

He stopped, took a deep breath and glanced sideways at Angel. 'Yes, yes, I know – never speak ill of the dead, especially if you're the one accused of murdering them.'

He gave a wan smile and rubbed his chin. He hadn't shaved very well that morning. There was a slight cut on his cheekbone. At the advice of his barrister he'd shaved off his moustache. Wrong kind of impression on the jury, Sir Charles had said. Too suave.

Naked, his top lip looked bare and somehow vulnerable. 'She was insane,' he said, the smile disappearing. 'You do realise that, don't you?'

Angel said carefully: 'The diaries didn't *seem* like the writings of a madwoman.'

'Oh, she's very devious,' he said miserably. 'You have no idea. Oh, God,' he groaned, looking hunted, 'this will finish me. The diaries contain lies, but damning lies. They'll get me hanged.'

He looked around the visiting room, at the brick walls, the barred door, the bare comfortless floor, then his eyes returned to her face. 'Have you told anyone else?'

'No.'

'Not Brioney Parsons?'

She shook her head. 'She just handed me a package. She had no idea what was inside.'

He sat for a moment, not moving. Only a muscle ticked in his temple. 'Well, it may not be such a bad thing that you've got them,' he said at last. 'At least you can hide them. Get rid of the bloody things somehow. Burn them, shred them. Anything.'

She hesitated. 'And if Miss Parsons tells the judge?'

'We'll face that hurdle when we come to it,' he said grimly.

'I can't *destroy* them, Alex.'

'Why can't you? They're false from start to finish, I assure you.'

'It would be perjury,' Angel said uneasily. 'Or something equally illegal.'

'You'd be quite safe. A wife can't testify against her husband.'

'No – but I'd be destroying evidence. I could go to jail. That would be interesting – you get off and I end up inside.'

She laughed but it was a strained and humourless sound. Because she knew that wasn't the real reason she didn't want to destroy the diaries. It would be like killing Antoinette all over again, she thought.

'Then keep quiet about them,' Alex urged. 'And I'll warn Sir Charles.' He frowned moodily. 'Or perhaps I shouldn't. If he knows we have her diaries he may have no alternative but submit them into evidence.' He thought for a moment. 'Well, I'll hint at the possibility of their existence, not say that they're actually in

286

our possession. But they're false, Angel. And if there *is* anything at all accurate in them, Antoinette will have put a slant on the truth that distorts it so that it isn't any more. Believe me, you won't be hiding anything that really matters. The diaries will make me look guilty when I'm not. They'll only prevent justice from being done.'

That word again – justice . . . Angel looked down at her fists clenched on her knee and said rather distantly, 'Yes, I thought so.'

But, really, she'd known then, hadn't she, whatever she said or allowed herself to fully admit, known that she'd touched on something more powerful than some madwomen's garbled, bitter nonsense. She could feel it in her body like the strong beat of a pulse. Recognise it in the shadow of guilt that crossed his eyes and was as quickly gone – in the almost imperceptible hesitation before he responded. In the ache in her bowels that was always her physical reaction to bad news however hard she tried to thrust it from her conscious mind.

Perhaps sensing this, he took her hand, as if he were glad the whole thing had been aired at last and now, explained and understood, could safely be forgotten. 'We were destined to be together, Angel,' he said, with that curiously pleading expression his face took on nowadays when he looked at her. 'Otherwise I wouldn't have gone to Longlands with St Clare that evening. I was waiting for you in the library, even though I didn't realise it. I was pulled into that room. Something drew me in – it was intended.'

'But you told me you didn't believe in that kind of thing,' she replied uncomfortably, sliding away her hand.

'Did I?'

And Alex who had always been so certain of everything and was never torn apart by private doubts like her, or ever admitted he was mistaken, said: 'Well, I was wrong. Give me your assurance that you won't tell the prosecution about the diaries,' he said, as she was getting ready to leave.

He looked at her, his eyes dark with that look of sombre sincerity.

'Think of what the Law will do if it finds me guilty,' he said urgently. 'They'll hang me.'

She felt an intense cold invading her. So a perverter of justice it is, Angel thought unhappily, listening to the prosecution outlining the case for the Crown.

But the decision had been taken out of her hands only three days into the trial, anyway, when Brioney Parsons had climbed into the witness-box and taken the oath. Angel felt her palms grow clammy as she watched her in her black coat and shapeless felt hat take the stand.

Unlike Mary Peto who had told of violent rages and wild, deluded fantasies centred round Alex, the old nurse only described Antoinette as a poor, troubled soul. In her opinion the main cause of her problems was her drinking which, she admitted, was something that needed constant watching, but said quite firmly that she didn't think there was much more to it than that.

No, she couldn't say she'd ever seen Antoinette behave violently. Moody, yes, and she could certainly be very difficult but she'd certainly never seen her *hit* anyone. She was emotional and she drank far too much. Nothing more.

Sir Charles, Alex's KC, knew better than to press any harder, merely getting her to agree that Antoinette's condition might have deteriorated considerably since she'd left her employ.

And then, without his even asking, Miss Parsons brought up the letter she'd posted to the present Mrs Sorel – yes, to Mrs *Angel* Sorel, that was correct – she could certainly point her out, if he wished, she sitting at the front row just *there* – no, she hadn't realised *quite* what their relationship was at the time since she'd only known her patient under the name of Meyer – Antoinette Meyer, she'd always been called – but she recognised Mrs Sorel perfectly well because it wasn't so *very* long since she'd enjoyed four o'clock tea with her, at the end of which she'd handed over a brown paper parcel on Antoinette's behalf, contents unknown.

Guessing what was inside, the KC called an abrupt halt to the proceedings and addressed the Judge. He wished to argue a point of law, if His Lordship would be so kind.

Alex had told her what his counsel would do if the question arose – Sir Charles would contend that the diaries were not admissible as evidence and should be excluded from the trial. The Crown sought to prove that Alex Sorel had committed an act of murder. But a diary, by its very nature, could only throw light on a state of mind, he'd argue, and one person's emotional state made no difference whatever to what kind of act had been committed by another. Hence, Antoinette's diaries were irrelevant and ought not to be admitted into evidence.

After a short deliberation – *very* short, Angel noted – the jury were led back into the courtroom. The Judge had accepted Sir Charles' submission. The diaries were out.

Angel glanced at Laura. Laura gave a quick smile and looked away. Angel was glad of it. She wasn't entirely sure what Laura would see in her eyes if she looked into them right now.

Turning the whole thing over in her mind now almost two weeks later, recalling the bewildering array of emotions she'd felt at the time, relief, dismay and guilt all cobbled into one solid lump in her chest, Angel stared at the letter on her knee. It had started to drizzle lightly but steadily. A few spots of rain had fallen onto the page blurring the 'Your loving' at the bottom. The signature was clear enough though. *Alex. Your loving husband.*

Were the diaries a very clever confidence trick aimed at turning her against him? Had she simply fallen for a pack of malicious lies? Lies that, if disclosed, would sway a jury in entirely the wrong direction? The fantasies of a poor woman that she was rich, an heiress whose husband would stop at nothing to get hold of her wealth? Perhaps stories Antoinette even half believed true herself – her writing some sort of mad vindication? It certainly looked that way – at least, according to everything Alex told her. And she wanted to believe him, God knows, she wanted to. But as she'd shifted about on a hard wood bench waiting for the Judge's ruling, Angel had known that the coldness in the pit of her belly wasn't the fear that she *did*, but the growing sense she did *not*.

Unwittingly, Sir Charles had provided hard proof the very next day. Ironic really, she thought. That an argument to get Alex off a charge for murder should prove him guilty of quite another sort of crime.

Arguing persuasively that his client could have no possible financial motive for wishing Antoinette dead, Sir Charles handed round evidence to show that number 23 Portman Terrace had been bought with her money and was, in fact, owned by her right up till her death.

Waving the title deeds before the jury, Sir Charles had declared that murder was a laughable idea since his client gained nothing – precisely *nothing* – by his ex-wife's death. On the contrary, the barrister pointed out, he stood to lose everything by it. The large income he received during Antoinette's lifetime ceased when she died and, under the terms of her will, even the house in London – his home for many years – would no longer be his.

For Antoinette had in a fit of momentous pique – 'one might be inclined to say *spite*' – bequeathed 23 Portman Terrace to Georgina Sorel. The house and a rather large sum of money, amount undisclosed as yet, to be held in trust for Georgina, Alexander Sorel's rightful child, and no relation to Antoinette *whatsoever*.

Sir Charles looked disgusted at the hypocrisy.

An act of pique? Of petty spite? No, Angel didn't think so. She was *glad* Antoinette had left the house to Georgina. It didn't seem to her threatening or malicious. On the contrary – it seemed as if Antoinette was trying to heal some deep wound.

She meant it as an act of reparation, Angel thought, I'm sure she did. It was her way of saying sorry.

And for Alex to have lived with *her* in the house he'd once shared with *Antoinette*? For them to have lived together in – what the diary had claimed and the trial shown beyond doubt – was still Antoinette's house?

Angel slid up straight in the little painted iron seat, suddenly furious. An audacious act of contempt and sexual spite on Alex's part – *if* one wanted to attribute that particular motive to anyone.

'Can you imagine the inferno that was my first marriage?' he'd asked in his letter. 'If Sir Charles is right and Antoinette and I brought out the worst in each other, all I can say is that you, without question, bring out the best. What I like to think of as the ninety-nine per cent that would have been all of me if a black witch called Antoinette Meyer had not come into my life . . . '

Which she'd done in '39 Berlin aged seventeen, as recorded in her diary, date and place undisputed by the defence. Quickly and eagerly embraced by the Jewish community there, Alex had been offered a large dowry if he'd slip his new young wife out of Germany with him. Seeing the climate under Hitler, he'd been more than willing to help.

'To save one poor woman of the Levant from the Nazi threat,' Sir Charles had proudly declaimed. 'To help at least one Jewess stuck behind enemy lines get to safety. And thus it was that he married this young woman – ' he'd summed up in his ringing baritone – 'giving her the love and protection of his name.'

But why – Angel found herself wondering now – why had Alex travelled into the Reich in the first place? Sir Charles did not ask *that*.

According to the diary, it was to acquire from their Jewish owners a few oil paintings on the cheap – to try and make a fortune from a Picasso, a Manet, a charming little Renoir. And if, along they way, he'd found himself a wealthy young wife and brought her back to London, too? A heroic act of rescue performed in good faith, as Sir Charles had claimed. (*Because love doesn't last forever, does it? Not that sort, anyway.*) Or one that seemed increasingly tainted by something that smacked unpleasantly of exploitation? It could never be described as a pleasant way to make a killing on the backs of vulnerable and desperate men. But put the two together – the reason Alex had travelled into Nazi Germany in the first place with his marrying a Jewish heiress whilst there?

Then the venture began to radically alter shape – the entire set of circumstances took on a dark, chillier aspect. Of course, no one could have dreamt just how badly things would turn out for Jews in the Reich. But even in ignorance of these later events – even without any idea of the Nazis' future crimes – to take advantage of Antoinette's situation at such a time . . .

But no one raised this question because it wasn't *relevant*. For the same reason they'd thrown out the diaries – it had no legal bearing on a case for murder. Angel swallowed, her mouth dry as dust.

Could he really have been so calculating? So arrogant and cold? Why had she never felt it? But she had, hadn't she? Oh, she'd put it down to lots of other things, but, at this moment, alone in the garden – in *Antoinette's* garden, she told herself starkly – she couldn't fool herself any longer. Because none of it *felt* right – it was as simple as that. None of it had felt right for a long time now.

She'd invented Alex – she'd created him in the image of her own father. Evelyn Merlowe, a lost and decent man, a man who needed saving. But you can't save someone from themselves. She'd loved a man who didn't exist. Did that mean her love didn't exist either?

But the pain in her chest was suddenly so intense that she had to grip the arms of the iron seat tightly till her knuckles showed white.

There was a lump in her throat. She wanted to cry but she couldn't. She didn't think she could ever cry over Alex again. It was as if something had dried up in her along with her belief in his basic goodness.

Raindrops glittered on the blades of grass by her feet. The shower had stopped but it was still cold. She picked up the letter from her lap and folded it in half, then half again. Getting up stiffly, she began climbing the circular iron staircase. She took the steps slowly as though her legs were made of some heavy metal too. The drawing room windows at the top were ajar. Shifting the letter from one hand to the other so she could push them wider, she saw against white wood that the pages were folded unevenly. The signature still showed. *Alex. Your loving husband.*

She shut her eyes briefly but she knew it was stupid. The words stood out clearly before her. Like an accusation, like a broken promise, like a claim that ignorance is no excuse. Thrusting the letter into her cardigan pocket was pointless but she did it anyway. Swaying slightly, took a deep, deep breath.

'I have never ever loved a man as I have you – ' she remembered saying to Alex, lying beside him in bed on the first night of their honeymoon – 'and I never will again . . . '

She let out her breath. As she stepped into the house she could taste salt on her lips. She must have cried after all.

20

Court 1, The Old Bailey. September 1952

The Judge's summing up seemed to go on forever. After the first fifty minutes, Angel had to force herself to concentrate. She could see his lips moving but she wasn't properly taking in his words. She felt so wrung out and empty that it was an effort to lift her hand and put it over the other in her lap.

' . . . *If you are satisfied on the evidence as a whole that it is proved that Alexander Sorel did intentionally push the knife into the body of his ex-wife and so cause the wound from which she died . . . '*

She examined the faces of the twelve men and women sitting on the bench. Every one of them looked engrossed but it was hard to tell what they were thinking.

' . . . *Then he is guilty of the crime of murder and no feeling of pity or sympathy should deter you from the duty you are called upon to do . . . '*

Chafing together the icy palms of her hands, Angel frowned down at them as if she were listening very hard. Admitting to herself yesterday what she really felt seemed more of a betrayal than anything she'd ever imagined before, though a betrayal of exactly what she wasn't quite sure.

Looking up, she felt a quick, involuntary contraction of the throat – the Judge had almost concluded. A few more words, then he'd risen to his feet and was leaving the courtroom; Alex was being led down below. No more long speeches, no more evidence – only the verdict now. Her legs felt shaky as they all shuffled out the courtroom to wait.

'Could be hours,' Laura muttered. 'Do you want something to eat? No? Not even a cup of tea? Well, we can get something later.'

But it wasn't very long at all – whatever decision the jury had come to, they had done so very quickly. Angel had chain smoked only six or seven cigarettes before everyone trooped back in to the courtroom again. Her heart was beating wildly, stomach clenched tight, as she took her place next to Laura on the hard wooden bench. Alex was back in the dock already, gazing straight ahead as if unaware of her presence only a few feet away. He looked a bit pale, otherwise surprisingly normal considering that in the next ten minutes his life hung in the balance. Her eyes met Laura's. They both looked away, neither able to hold the other's gaze for very long.

The foreman stood and cleared his throat. Laura was gripping her hand very hard. The air seemed to have suddenly gone out of Angel's lungs, her heart stopped beating. In a self-conscious voice, he gave the jury's verdict to the hushed, expectant courtroom. Angel couldn't quite take in what he said at first. It took a long, slow second for the words to sink in fully. To hear – Not guilty.

Around her, the room erupted.

They aren't going to hang him, she thought numbly. Thank God.

Because she didn't think he was guilty. Not of murder, anyway.

She had to get away. She couldn't face Alex. Not yet. Couldn't congratulate him along with all the others who surged forwards, hands outstretched, slapping each other on the back, smiling broadly at the result. She needed some breathing space.

She touched Laura's shoulder lightly, mouthing – 'Later – I'll see you later . . . ' Before she could respond, Angel stumbled out the row. Moving in precisely the opposite direction to Alex, surrounded by well-wishers, she slipped from the room. She caught a glance of him grinning and shaking hands as she pushed through the door, saw by his side Diane Sorel's glittering, triumphant smile as he began looking around over heads, searching for her, his loyal, loving wife, but she was already off, heels clattering across the wide tiled hall. Almost running down the great stone steps at the front of the building. Already hailing a cab and climbing in.

Not guilty.

She threw her handbag onto the seat and collapsed on top of it.

The window opposite was open a crack. The metal surround rattled noisily as a draught whistled through. She couldn't be bothered to lean over and close it. A splitting headache was tightening her brow. Elbow propped on the leather bolster, she massaged her temple with her hand and breathed.

She thought of a girl with long, wavy black hair dressing for her wedding day. A lovely young girl with grave, long-lashed eyes staring at her own reflection and wondering – will he love me forever?

She thought of Alex, grey-faced, just before the trial, saying to her – 'The man you fell in love with – the man you married – it was me . . . '

And it was him, standing before her in the dock taking an oath – 'I swear by Almighty God that I shall tell the truth, the whole truth, and nothing but the truth – '

The truth?

She let out her bottled up breath.

If it's a question of whether Alex deliberately murdered Antoinette, Angel thought, her head still throbbing, then Sir Charles is right – Alex isn't guilty. He wouldn't hang. What did he have to gain from Antoinette's death? Horribly little. Yes, he had killed her, no, it wasn't premeditated.

But he's still guilty, she thought, though not of anything the Law can punish him for. He'll never be charged with his real crime – destroying a life.

For whatever the Law decided, murder or manslaughter or innocent, the fact was that Antoinette was no longer alive and Alex had killed her. Killed her, in fact, many years before the act for which he'd been tried. He'd used her, exploited her circumstance, her body, her money, and, finally, destroyed her.

I could forgive him the murder, Angel thought, I'd have stuck by him through all of that. But how he treated Antoinette in life I can't forgive.

She leant over and slammed the window shut.

Staring out at street after street slipping by, she tried to remember her life before him, but everything had him in it. It's only been two years, she thought dully. Instinctively, she lowered her head so that her hat shaded her face. Which was just as well, because as the taxi lumbered up to the house in Portman Terrace, she saw three men hanging around on the pavement outside. Trilbies tilted to the back of their heads, cigarettes stuck in their mouths, a camera slung around one neck – unmistakably newspaper men.

Deciding quickly, she kept the brim obscuring her face as she leant forwards and rapped on the glass panel.

'Can you go straight to Victoria station without stopping?' she asked the driver.

'What – back again?'

'Please.'

'Rightio, lady. Makes no difference to me. I can drive backwards and forwards all day, if you like.'

'Just the once will be fine.' She glanced at her wristwatch. There was still time – just. 'As fast as you can. I've got to catch a train.'

As they pulled away, Angel felt a sudden surge of energy. Stay or go. London or Sussex. Simple choice. She slid back in the seat, not feeling anxious any more but suddenly full of purpose. Yes, she'd go directly to Victoria and travel down to Haywards Heath with Laura. Georgina had been at Longlands for the last few days, anyway, being looked after by Francis and Aunt Margaret. After she'd collected Nina, she'd decide what to do next.

Not much of a decision, she thought. More to the point – I'll have to tell *him* what I've decided.

I don't even want to see him again. There's nothing left to say. What – that he fooled me and that I was a fool? Not once but again and again? I can hardly bear to look into his face. No, I'll write and tell him I want a divorce.

Who would have thought it? she asked herself wonderingly. That one day *I* would ask *him* for a divorce?

And she had a strong suspicion that as soon as he realised that the adoring look had disappeared from her eyes – when he noticed that the light of love had gone entirely and forever to be replaced by something quite different – a kind of horror – well, he wouldn't want to remain married to her, either.

The strain that Angel had been feeling for months began to lift ever so slightly as the taxi swung round the corner. She'd buy everything she needed when she arrived at Hayward's Heath, she decided. Anything else she'd collect from home later. Home . . . The word had a new significance. It was Georgina's home now and, though she knew she would never live there with Alex again, the link between her and Antoinette would never be broken because the house that had once been Antoinette's was now Georgina's.

Antoinette didn't send me the diaries to prove Alex guilty, Angel realised suddenly – she did it to affirm her own life. To try and make sure it meant something in the end. She wanted to be remembered.

As a matter of justice . . .

Angel knew precisely what she thought *that* consisted in now. She'd told Laura only the night before. How betrayed she felt, how *fooled*.

'You'll look back on all this one day,' Laura had replied consolingly, 'years and years from now and see this as just one episode in what looks like being – ' she'd smiled ruefully – 'a really rather active life.'

'He only ever confessed what I knew already or was certain to find out. And I believed him. Every time.'

'He was very believable. You can't blame yourself for that.'

'It *suited* me to believe him.'

'You can't blame yourself for that either.'

'Can't I?'

'Of course you can't.'

'I was a fool. Worse than a fool.'

'A lucky fool. Actually very lucky, I should say.'

'What do you mean?'

'Next year you're twenty-one. You get your money then. And now Antoinette's dead – well, who knows what he might do next?'

'That's a *bit* far-fetched, Laura.'

'Is it? Are you sure?'

'I'm not sure of anything any more.' Angel smiled a little grimly.

Laura considered her thoughtfully for a moment. 'You won't hate him forever, you know. Whatever you think now.'

'Yes, I will.'

'No.' Laura gave a sly smile. 'You won't. He *is* Georgina's father. He's given you that. Rather a lot, really.'

Yes . . . Georgina . . .

Here was her only cure, stamp out all else. Forget Alex, Angel told herself, puzzle over him, despise him, if you must. But life goes on . . .

There was a jam at the corner of the Edgware Road, cars hooting, traffic slowed to a crawl. She almost missed the train. And as she dashed up the platform, it was not the rows of first-class carriages she was leaving behind that she saw before her but Laura waving wildly to her from the train window – not the trolleys piled high with baggage that she was cutting quickly passed but the future right ahead of her. For only by hating can you get rid of love, only by remembering can you truly honour the dead.